THE ONE YOU FEED

JAMES DRUMMOND

This book is a work of fiction. Names, characters, businesses, organizations, places, events, and incidents either are the product of the author's imagination or are used fictitiously. Any resemblance to actual persons, living or dead, events, or locales is entirely coincidental.

Cover design by Wojtek Batko

ISBN: 1500724475
ISBN 13: 9781500724474
Library of Congress Control Number: 2014914386
CreateSpace Independent Publishing Platform
North Charleston, South Carolina

We all have two wolves living inside us.
One is the wolf of fear and doubt,
the other brings us courage and strength,
and these two wolves quarrel time and again
to determine what we are capable of doing—
to determine who we are capable of becoming.
Umatilla Fable

Contents

CHAPTER 1

A PREDATOR

The high-pitched squeals intruded on his dreams right before waking him.

It wasn't the first time his swine's cries had slipped into Henry Jennings' subconscious while he slumbered. After seventeen years as a pig farmer, he often found himself working the paddocks, even after falling asleep. Sometimes his high school sweetheart, a Sasquatch, or a renowned historical figure might join him to lend a hand—his dreams weren't *entirely* void of imaginative elements— but hogs were frequently the focal point.

However, this time the ruckus in the stables wasn't merely part of some unpleasant dream. As the stout farmer blinked away the cobwebs and progressed further into consciousness, the frantic oinks and squeals from outside intensified, overpowering the strong patter of rain against his bedroom window.

What the hell was going on out there?

Turning on the bedside lamp, Henry dragged himself out from underneath the covers and surveyed the floor for a suitable pair of jeans to pull on. Kicking a few options aside, he uncovered a pair speckled with dry mud. He looked again at the downpour outside, then donned the muddy jeans along with a worn flannel shirt.

The clock above the kitchen stove read 4:35 a.m. Trying to fall back asleep after investigating whatever was going on outside would be pointless. By the time he settled into a good slumber, his radio alarm would wake him with the day's weather and the latest country hits. He might as well check the farrowing huts as long as he was up. Maybe Betty had finally had her new litter.

Betty, of course, was an exceedingly pregnant pig.

Most folks were surprised when they found out Henry named his swine. They seemed to think that by doing so he was just increasing his chances of growing attached to them, making it harder to slaughter the animals when the time came.

Henry figured that people assumed this because that's how they would feel, and because at fifty-two years of age, he hadn't developed many relationships outside of the ones he had with his pigs.

But Henry didn't name them out of a need for companionship. That wasn't it at all. He named them simply because they deserved names.

They were intelligent animals that would provide for humanity in innumerable ways. Pork was obvious, but most people didn't realize that weed killers, rubber, makeup, and antifreeze all came from hog fatty acids. Their glands and organs sometimes supplied insulin for diabetics and ventricles for certain heart surgeries, while the skin of a pig could be used for gloves, shoes, and various types of clothing.

These were just a few instances of how Henry's hogs might one day benefit society, and already *far* more than he could come up with for most of the people he knew. That being said, for the moment his precious animals were just being a raucous pain in the ass.

Snaring his jacket and a flashlight from the hall closet, Henry headed outside. A blaze of lightning and the boom of thunder greeted the gruff farmer as he stepped out into a torrential rain. He flipped on the flashlight and sloshed over to the stable.

The door was securely locked, just as he'd left it.

Cursing the downpour and his livestock, Henry dug out a set of keys from his front pocket and, shining the light on them, thumbed his way to the one he needed. He then slid the key into the padlock and opened up the stable.

Once inside, he became instantly aware of how the stable's usually close, pungent odors were diminished, almost replaced, by the fresh smell of rain.

That was when the gaping hole in the structure's side wall became apparent. Henry shone his flashlight through the splintered opening. The rainfall outside sparkled as it passed through the beam.

Stunned, he moved the light to the ground, expecting to find tire tracks. It would have taken one drunk or reckless driver to veer this far off the road, but Henry couldn't think of another explanation for the damage he was seeing.

There were no tracks in the mud.

One of his hogs, Milton, went toddling for the breach. It occurred to Henry that the exterior fence might be damaged as well, and he couldn't afford to lose half his stock out in the surrounding forest. He moved toward the makeshift exit to keep the pig from escaping, but only made it a couple of steps before a low, muffled growl stopped him dead in his tracks.

A predator.

And just like that, Henry's main concern was no longer preventing his hogs from getting out of the stable, but determining what had gotten in. Spinning around, he shone his flashlight into a nearby stall, then another. All he found were squealing pigs.

He caught only a glimpse of the intruder, out of the corner of his eye, just before the animal struck.

It was powerful, whatever it was. The creature knocked the hog farmer off his feet and sent him sailing across the stable.

As Henry tumbled to the ground, he felt a sharp pain shoot up his left side. At first, he thought it was strictly the result of a hard landing, but when he brought his hand to his ribs, he discovered his jacket and shirt had been torn open by the animal's strike. Although he couldn't make out anything in the darkness, his fingers came away covered in a sticky wetness Henry could only assume was his own blood.

He spotted his flashlight laying several feet away and considered scrambling for it. Then, from the shadows just beyond where the flashlight lay, two glowing yellow eyes appeared. They were all Henry could see of the creature that had attacked him. They were all he *wanted* to see.

No longer caring about the flashlight, he rolled onto his hands and knees and began crawling for the door, adrenaline overtaking any pain. After a yard or two, he lurched onto his feet. The ache in his side returned with the effort. His hand instinctively went back to the wound.

Henry's clothes were now soaked with blood.

And the animal responsible for the damage was on the move again. He heard the heavy patter of its footfalls loping across the dirt floor, just prior to feeling its teeth gliding through his calf. The beast's jaw clamped down like a bench vise. It then yanked him back, and before he'd even really registered the attack, Henry found himself soaring though the air again.

He hit the ground hard, skidding across hay and manure. When he finally came to rest, he was lying beside the hole the massive beast had created in the stable wall.

He had to get through that opening.

Maybe this thing had decided to claim Henry's stable as its own and was simply defending it. If he could just pull himself out into the pen, then maybe he'd be safe.

He reached out and grabbed at the splintered wood with his bloody hands, his muscles straining as he pulled himself through the breach. The welcome sensation of the rain pelting his face lasted only a second. Then Henry felt the beast's razor-sharp fangs chomp down once more. He cried out as the creature jerked him back inside the stable.

There would be no escape.

The squealing of his hogs grew louder, but their commotion was no competition for Henry's own terrified screams. He felt the sensation of claws cutting through him, but no pain. Henry could no longer feel pain. In the next few moments, he'd stop feeling altogether.

CHAPTER 2

The Hero with a Thousand Faces

Its title was what had drawn Toby to the book: *The Hero with a Thousand Faces*. According to the blurb on the back cover, it delved into the structure of popular myths, specifically analyzing the ordeals, and sometimes tragedies, heroes endured in order to ultimately achieve victory—in their quests and in life.

Toby had checked the book out from the library hoping that it would contain just one relatable tale that illustrated exactly *how* to find meaning in misfortune, and how to use that meaning to overcome anguish. He needed to know how to start getting over his own tragedy. He needed to know how to get on with his life.

Sadly, none of the deconstructed stories Toby read offered such guidance. And this wasn't the first place he'd gone looking. He'd spent the past two weeks searching for inspiration within the Bible, some self-help books, even a couple of paperbacks on depression.

None had given him the healing allegory he desired, and he was starting to think it'd be the same with his latest selection.

While the characteristics of their different champions were distinct, each story basically followed the same narrative. The hero-to-be would start out in the ordinary world, but then always ended up in some supernatural land full of strange powers and events. That was the world in which his angst and doubt gave way to a newfound courage and conviction. And that was the problem.

Reading about how some lost soul found his true self by slaying fairy-tale beasts in a mythical realm wasn't helpful. Toby needed to know how to conquer his guilt and grief in the world he actually lived in. *That* was the world in which he'd failed to save his mother's life; in a dark, cold river where he'd been overcome by panic and dread, unable to see or think—unable to act.

And ever since, inaction had pretty much become the norm. Deep down, Toby knew that reading alone in his room had as much to do with avoiding everyone and everything that reminded him of his mother as it did with trying to find a way to move past her death. It was just a heck of a lot easier than facing an outside world that continually forced him to acknowledge her everlasting absence.

Most days the painful reminders started with breakfast.

His mom had always been the morning person, the family invigorator, who readied her bleary-eyed husband and son for the day ahead with cheddar cheese scrambled eggs, cinnamon French toast, or pancakes bursting with blueberries. She'd had other breakfast specialties, always serving them with heaping sides of cheer and encouragement, but those had been Toby's favorites.

Now he had to settle for cold cereal. Sometimes there'd be bananas he could slice on top. And because his dad regularly left for work before he left for school, Toby often ended up eating alone.

More than anything else, that was what triggered the tragic events of forty-three nights ago to replay themselves inside his head—the bridge, the charging pickup, and his losing control of his parents' Chevy Equinox.

As a result, he'd started skipping breakfast altogether, preferring to go to school hungry rather than suffering through another miserably lonely bowl of cornflakes.

His flashbacks weren't limited to the kitchen though, and now, having allowed his attention to stray from his book, Toby felt another one coming on. Thankfully, a knock on the bedroom door derailed his mind from taking him back to the Chetco River.

Toby put down *The Hero with a Thousand Faces* and rolled over on his bed to find his father standing in the doorway. Here was someone who knew how to play the role of hero in the real world. He also knew how to look the part. His sheriff's uniform was freshly pressed, his hair sharply parted, and his shoes sported a polished shine—all a stark contrast to Toby's less than refined appearance, punctuated by his disheveled hair and grubby t-shirt.

Walter's Sunday shift started in less than an hour, but after seeing the all-too-familiar empty haze in Toby's eyes the sheriff decided it might be a good day to call in late. He needed to spend some long overdue quality time with his teenaged son.

"Think you might venture out of your room this afternoon?" he asked.

Toby responded with a noncommittal shrug, his eyes returning to his book.

Walter tried again. "It's a beauty of a day out there."

Again he received no meaningful response. Maybe Toby just needed some more time. The sheriff's eyes moved to the posters of soccer stars Wayne Rooney and Didier Drogba on the opposite wall, the fishing pole propped in the corner, and then to the handful of sports trophies scattered among his son's bookshelves—all symbols of the active, enthusiastic boy he'd been prior to the accident.

The room's musty scent and random piles of dirty laundry served to signify what his son was now—disengaged and detached. There was no evidence here that giving Toby more time to work through what had happened would be of any benefit. It simply wasn't healthy for him to spend so much time in his room alone.

"Okay, get up. Time for some fresh air."

"I've got the window open," Toby half mumbled. Barely distinguishable utterances had become customary for him since his mother's death.

Walter clapped his hands together. "I said up. Now."

Toby reluctantly put down the book and rolled off his bed. He shoved his feet into already tied sneakers and pulled on his black, faux-leather jacket. Keeping his gaze lowered to avoid eye contact, the boy skulked out of his room.

It had indeed turned out to be a nice Sunday, with the sun helping to lessen the slight chill of the mid-April afternoon. The calf-high grass of Miller's Pass brushed lazily against Walter's pant legs as he watched his son take aim at one of three Mr. Pibb cans perched atop the rotted out posts of an old barbed-wire fence.

Toby's sullen mood had lasted the entire twenty-minute drive out to the open field and into the start of their competition, but Walter remained convinced that this short excursion was a good idea.

The boy squeezed off a shot, sending a resounding crack rolling across the flat, open meadow.

Walter watched one of the soda cans zip into the air like a hummingbird, as the lush evergreen forest surrounding them swallowed up the blast's echo. "You're getting almost as good as your old man."

"Almost?" Toby responded quietly with the raise of an eyebrow.

Walter had first let Toby fire one of his pistols a little over two years ago. It was a decision that had led to quite a bit of debate between him and the boy's mother, who had disapproved of introducing a thirteen-year-old to guns.

Walter had always been compulsive about locking up his weapons, but he knew that when children became teenagers, getting their hands on things they shouldn't stopped being an impulse and started becoming a skill. So to him, thirteen had seemed like the perfect age to educate Toby on gun safety. Once he took the time to explain this to his wife, she agreed. Although, he'd still been thoroughly chastised for not making his argument *before* he put a loaded firearm in the boy's hands.

Letting the memory of his wife's cross expression fade away, Walter lifted his pistol and fired without taking more than a second to aim. The bullet nearly sawed a Coors Light can in half.

Toby wrinkled his nose, discouraged by the ease with which his father had hit his mark. Their little contest consisted of who could shoot the most empties of their favorite beverages. So far the score was two to two.

Toby promptly swung his gun over to the next can and pulled the trigger. Another hit. The kid had indeed become a heck of a shot.

Which, given Walter's profession and skilled tutelage, wasn't a surprise. The sheriff knew this was now his son's favorite pastime, yet he'd only convinced Toby to come out here one other time since the accident. Walter had even let him win in hopes that the victory would brighten the kid's mood.

For about an hour or so afterward, it seemed as though it had. But Toby's overriding grief soon washed away any fleeting joy he'd experienced from the unexpected triumph.

Walter considered letting him win again today, but quickly ruled out the idea. The kid was certain to question the legitimacy of back-to-back victories. Ending this contest in a tie was the wiser option. After all, the point of this trip was not just to cheer Toby up but also to lower his defenses.

"So I ran into Ms. Parker yesterday," Walter said as he fired at his next target. The beer can whirled into the air. "She said you haven't been to see her in a while."

Toby's shoulders slumped, and his answer came out as little more than a mumble. "I thought how much I talked to the school counselor was up to me."

"It is," Walter responded, trying to keep an indifferent tone. "I just thought, as she does, that she might be able to help you make a little more progress."

Ms. Parker was the lone student counselor at the high school, and the closest thing Silver Falls had to a professional shrink. A couple days after the accident, she'd called and graciously offered to conduct some pseudo-therapy sessions with Toby. Not knowing how else to help his son, Walter had accepted her offer. Another example of when he'd decided on something without first talking it over with all interested parties. Not surprisingly, the decision hadn't gone over well.

Toby fired and knocked the final Mr. Pibb can into the air. "I don't need someone to tell me how I should feel about what happened."

"I think the idea is more that she's there to help you work through your feelings," Walter replied as he aimed at his sole remaining target.

Just as he pulled the trigger, the police radio inside the SUV parked behind them crackled to life. The sudden disruption distracted him just enough.

He lowered his weapon and stared scornfully at an unscathed Coors Light can. The bullet couldn't have missed by more than an inch.

The anxious voice of his deputy, Billy Rogers, called out over the radio. "Walter. Walter, you there?"

Toby turned to his father, showing not even a hint of excitement. "I win."

The boy's indifference was really starting to trouble the sheriff. Ms. Parker had once mentioned to him how the victims of trauma sometimes lost interest in activities they once enjoyed, but if winning at target practice wasn't enough to lift Toby's spirits, even just temporarily, Walter was at a loss for what else might.

Hearing his deputy's voice call out again, he jogged over to the SUV and reached in over the door, which was adorned with the golden emblem of the Silver Falls Sheriff's Department.

He pulled out the radio's receiver. "Yeah, I'm here. What's up, Billy?"

"We've got another domestic dispute call over at the Schultzes'," Billy's voice came back, book-ended by static pops.

Walter sighed. This was the second domestic dispute for the Schultzes in as many weeks, to go along with half a dozen others at different residences around town.

A little over eight years ago, he had taken the job as sheriff of Silver Falls to free up more time for his family. They'd moved to the quiet little town to enjoy all the benefits of a quiet little life. And for the majority of those eight years, everything had gone according to plan.

But now, when he most needed some free time to cope with the loss of his wife, Walter found he was fielding more calls than he ever had as a detective in Portland.

"Okay. Be there in fifteen."

Apparently a rematch, or any kind of heart-to-heart, would have to wait. He waved Toby over and climbed into the truck.

Toby let his mind wander as he sat slouched in the SUV's worn leather passenger seat. It wasn't that he necessarily had anything against Ms. Parker. He believed she meant well, but her sessions had made him extremely uncomfortable.

The second one had included her asking him to visualize, and consequently relive, the accident. It was a tactic that, if repeated over time, was supposed to neutralize the memory and help him become better at coping. At least that was what she'd told him.

Instead, the practice had laid the groundwork for his excruciatingly vivid flashbacks.

Ms. Parker had explained to him that in cases like his things often got worse before they got better, but Toby didn't feel like letting things get any worse. He felt miserable enough as it was. After seeing her once more, he'd decided to take a break. That had been a little over three weeks ago.

He blinked away the memory of his ill-fated therapy sessions and gazed at the green, metal roadside sign that marked his municipality's eastern border: WELCOME TO SILVER FALLS, EST. 1853.

Not long after the sign whizzed by, Toby spotted the oversized mansard roof of Mr. and Mrs. Currie's grocery. The middle-aged married couple was out front placing apples and pears into crate displays, a routine they spent about an hour on every day, carefully rotating each fruit so that even the most minuscule bruise faced to the back.

A block later Toby and his father passed Carrie Cantwell's five-bay, two-story bed-and-breakfast. She gave a wave and, for just a moment, Toby considered asking his dad to let him out.

He'd been hooked on Mrs. Cantwell's homemade ice cream ever since trying one of her waffle cones when he was nine. Or had he been ten? The question floated around in his head as he watched the strawberry-blond proprietor grow smaller in the SUV's side rearview mirror.

An antique shop, two unassuming office buildings, a Laundromat, and several ranch and raised ranch homes sailed past until Walter turned onto Leland Street.

The first thing Toby noticed as they pulled up to the Schultzes' split level home was how the lawn was in dire need of a mow. Deputy Rogers's cruiser was already parked in the driveway, and just as

Walter threw the SUV into park, the wiry deputy came stumbling out of the house, grappling with fifty-five-year-old Hank Schultz.

"You stay put," Walter ordered as he bolted out the driver's side door.

Toby watched as his father rushed over to help restrain Mr. Schultz and wrestle the barrel-chested man toward the cruiser. As he observed the struggle, Toby felt a million miles away. Or maybe that was just how he wanted to feel—far removed from these people and their problems.

Lifting his jacket's inset cotton hood up over his head, he slouched a little deeper into the passenger seat and longed to be back in his room.

Blocking out the world like this helped...slightly. His faux-leather jacket had become a safety blanket of sorts since the accident. Toby often hid beneath its hood to avoid all the sympathetic eyes that greeted him seemingly everywhere he went.

"Stop," shouted Hank's wife, Sally, as she darted from the home with mascara-streaked cheeks. "Please! Everything's okay now."

She raced over to the three men and grabbed at Walter, trying to pull him away from her husband. The disruption was just enough for Hank to get an arm free, and he caught the sheriff square in the chest with an elbow.

As Toby witnessed his dad stumbling backward, his left hand slid down to the seat belt release, but he didn't press it. Instead, he sat still, staring at the scene playing out on the Schultzes' unkempt front lawn. He glanced down at his fingers, which remained frozen around the seat belt's plastic latch cover.

Why had his dad made him leave the house? Why hadn't he gotten out at Mrs. Cantwell's? Why wasn't he getting out *now* to help restrain Mr. Schultz?

By the time Toby looked back at the scuffle, his father had regained control of the situation. Hank had been cuffed and Silver Falls' only two lawmen were pulling the aggressively angry man toward the deputy's cruiser.

Toby shifted his gaze off his father and toward the Schultzes' home.

His breath caught in his throat when he spotted Ashley, seventeen and super-hot, standing on the front porch. Her face, framed by shoulder-length blond hair, showed no signs of shock or sorrow as she watched the out-in-the-open spectacle. She looked resolute. Or maybe just resigned. It was hard to tell.

She glanced over at the SUV, as if she'd sensed Toby watching her. The moment Ashley saw him, her resolve faltered and Toby noticed her face go flush. Her family's troubles playing out in public *did* affect her. Or, more specifically, his being there to witness them did.

It wasn't any secret that Ashley's mom and dad had been fighting a lot lately, but Toby figured it had to be pretty humiliating to have one of your classmates actually witness your parents screaming and wrestling with law enforcement on the front lawn. Before he could offer even a sympathetic wave, she rushed back inside.

"So we can go home now, right?" Toby mumbled as his father got back into the SUV.

Walter started the vehicle, watching the cruiser drive past with Mr. Schultz cuffed inside. "I'm gonna have to help get Hank settled in and sobered up first."

Toby slumped even further into his seat. Before he could whine about the way the day was progressing, he felt his father pat him on the shoulder and heard the sheriff let out an empathetic sigh.

"I realize that all these mini-crises haven't come at a real good time for us."

Toby shrugged off his dad's attempt at consolation. He appreciated the efforts his father had made to keep things as normal as possible, but there were just too many things that *weren't* normal. Not just with them, but among the entire town.

"A lot of folks are struggling after the changes at the plant," Walter continued. "But it'll all get sorted out soon enough, and then you and I can...well, not have to keep doing stuff like this."

"Stuff like this" wasn't going to stop happening anytime soon. It seemed like half the residents of Silver Falls were out of work, now that Mr. Bennett had decided to automate production at his metals manufacturing plant, and very few of them were handling it well.

Toby felt he'd seen enough fallout from the layoffs for one day. "I think I'll just walk home."

"That's a pretty decent hike."

"You said you wanted me to get outside and enjoy the weather."

Walter chuckled. "Okay. This shouldn't take long. I'll be home in time for dinner."

Toby undid his seatbelt and hopped out. Giving his dad a wave over his shoulder, he started down the sidewalk. He couldn't wait to get back to his room.

Walter pulled out from the curb and followed after Billy's cruiser, glancing at Toby in the rearview mirror. Hopefully the walk home would do his son some good. Something had to, since Walter's duties as sheriff had once again disrupted his efforts at cheering up the boy.

Many in town were surprised when he'd returned to work so soon after the accident. He'd wanted to take more time off to focus on his son, and to search for the driver who'd caused his wife's death, but it just hadn't been feasible, not with everything else that was going on.

Today it had been Hank Schultz getting drunk and roughing up Sally. Tomorrow it could be Dave Clark threatening to jump off Rockfish Bridge again, or Janie Harris sunbathing nude after one too many early morning cosmopolitans. Not something a lot of people would have complained about twenty years ago, but Janie's best days were quite a few days behind her.

More idle time among the town's recently unemployed meant more work for Walter—whether he wanted it or not. He still tried to investigate the accident when he could, but too often there were too many calls about too many heated situations for Billy to handle on his own. As a result, the sheriff struggled to find even a couple hours per week to dedicate to finding the other driver.

There was one man in particular he could thank for that.

"Speak of the devil," Walter muttered as he pulled up to the sheriff station. Out front waiting for him was the balding, pudgy bane of his existence: Bruce Bennett. The fifty-five-year-old plant owner wore a bomber jacket and a sternly set jaw; he was in the sheriff's face before Walter could even fully step out of his SUV.

"You want to tell me how many more times my plant is gonna have to get vandalized before you decide to do something about it?" Bruce shouted, jabbing his plump finger in Walter's direction.

"What happened?" the sheriff asked halfheartedly, wiping a droplet of the man's spittle from his cheek.

"Spray paint," Bruce grumbled. "All across the southern wall. And someone threw rocks through three more windows."

"Your plant isn't exactly in my jurisdiction, Bruce."

"The people in this town are, damn it!"

Walter tensed, not appreciating Bennett's tone. "And I've had my hands full since you put half of them out of work. Got Hank Schultz inside right now."

Bruce scoffed, unaffected. "Times are tough these days, Sheriff, for everybody. But that doesn't give people the right to start defacing my property. It's not my fault that folks like Hank can't manage a little duress in their lives."

"It's kind of what you were hoping for though, isn't it?"

Walter regretted the question the moment he'd asked it. As the town's sheriff, he needed to stay above the fray, stay professional. Even toward the man who'd made his daily life exceedingly more difficult.

"I automated my plant to make it more profitable," Bruce growled. "And there's nothing you can do or say to make me feel guilty about that. If a few missed paychecks get folks around here to support my plan to bring their jobs back, well then, that sounds like an everybody-wins scenario to me."

"For some a lot more than others."

By automating and restructuring his metals manufacturing plant, the wealthiest man in Silver Falls was well on his way to landing a huge contract to produce steel pipe for oil processing and transmission. The next steps on his agenda were to secure the support of the Oregon Metal Industries Council, expand the size and production capacity of his plant, and to construct a new road that would allow him to haul his pipes to their destinations throughout the Pacific Northwest.

His initial plan had been to build that road through the neighboring Indian reservation, but the Umatilla had turned him down flat. They were also protesting his plant's expansion and could probably be blamed for at least some of the vandalism Bruce was shouting about.

The next best option for the road was to build it alongside the outskirts of Silver Falls. And while the support of the townspeople wasn't necessarily required for Bruce to add onto his existing facility or lay down pavement, given his level of wealth and influence, it was still desired.

With so many folks unemployed, that support was also very probable. If Bruce got the contract, he would need to rehire many of his ex-employees to serve as supervisors, inventory managers, and drivers.

Many of those workers had moved to Silver Falls to enjoy the pristine beauty of the Pacific Northwest, but even the staunchest of environmentalists were likely to come around and support the new contract, as well as the new construction, if it meant they could afford to feed their families again.

Knowing Bruce was using hunger and affordable health coverage as leverage was just one more thing that pissed Walter off about the man.

"Hopefully I'll be able to help a few folks out," Bruce replied indignantly. "*If* things go my way. If they don't…well, there just won't be much I can do."

"We'll have to keep our fingers crossed, I guess."

"Bottom line is I don't count on others to solve life's challenges, Sheriff. I handle 'em myself."

"Is that right? So, then, why are you here bothering me?"

Bruce's nostrils flared as he gave the sheriff an angry stare. Walter held his look, unwavering. It was a short standoff. The plant owner threw up his hands and stomped off, cursing under his breath. Walter let a few choice words slip as well as he turned toward the station.

He entered the building's beige main room to find Hank sitting on the cuff bench and his deputy on the phone, a stunned expression across the kid's face. Walter shot him a quizzical look.

Billy covered the phone's mouthpiece before answering the sheriff's unasked question. "I've got Harriet Taylor on the line. She's pretty hysterical and kind of hard to understand, but I think someone, or something, killed her brother in his hog pen last night."

Walter immediately motioned for his deputy to hand over the phone.

CHAPTER 3

RACHEL

Turning the corner onto his block, Toby popped the final bite of a butter brickle waffle cone into his mouth and let the flavors of toffee and almonds melt over his tongue.

As anxious as he was to get back to his room, he'd allowed himself a quick detour by Mrs. Cantwell's bed and breakfast, hoping that a treat from her ice cream parlor might lift his spirits. While Mrs. Cantwell truly was a maven when it came to creating masterpieces out of milk and heavy cream, the double-scoop cone she'd presented him with had done little to dent Toby's dour mood.

He was starting to wonder if anything ever would.

Toby reached into the front left pocket of his jacket as his smartphone started to ring. He pulled out the device to see Nate's name on the display.

Nate Schaffer was the first friend he'd made after moving to Silver Falls, and while their interests had diverged a bit midway through middle school, Toby still considered Nate to be his best buddy.

He swallowed the final bite of his ice cream cone and answered the call. "Hey, what's up?"

"Dude, I just beat the Leviathan!" Nate shouted back through the phone.

"Um, that's…Awesome?"

"Super awesome! You know what this means, right?"

"Not really," Toby responded, as he passed underneath an expansive lattice of peeling bark branches belonging to the Kellys' ageless sycamore tree. It was the most popular landmark on his block.

"It means I'm a total bad ass," Nate semi-clarified.

Once he was past the sycamore, Toby glimpsed a moving truck parked in his neighbor's driveway. It was an unexpected sight. He hadn't heard anything about Mr. Franks moving out, or about anyone else moving in.

As if on cue, Alan Franks emerged from the rear of the vehicle lugging a hefty cardboard box. As the paunchy fifty-seven-year-old stepped warily down the loading ramp in his wingtip oxfords, the front door to his house swung open and a Native American woman, Devi Chochopi, hurried out to give him a hand.

Devi and Alan had been seeing each other for a little over a year, and their relationship was the source of quite a bit of neighborhood gossip. For one thing, Devi was fifteen years younger than Alan. However, most of the scuttlebutt Toby overheard while at the general store or at Mrs. Cantwell's had more to do with where Devi was from than her age.

Mr. Franks's apparent new housemate was a member of the Umatilla tribe.

The Umatilla Indian Reservation neighbored Silver Falls, with the main village being only a twenty-minute drive away. Despite the short distance between them, residents from the two towns rarely socialized. In fact, Toby didn't know of another couple like Mr. Franks and Ms. Chochopi.

As he watched his neighbor hand the large cardboard box down to the much spryer Devi, who then carried it to the house, Toby realized that he'd tuned out most of Nate's excited retelling of that day's online conquest.

"Peter and his rogues almost blew it after this Burning Adrenaline attack," his friend continued between anxious breaths. "I thought for sure it was gonna be a guaranteed wipe."

"Uh huh," was the best response Toby could muster.

"You're not even listening to me, are you?"

"Sorry. I got distracted by something, but the little bit I heard sounded totally…" Toby slowed his pace and trailed off as he once again became distracted—this time by a slender Native American girl with raven hair and lean legs wrapped in skin-tight jeans who was exiting the truck. "…amazing."

Nate kept going with the details of his online battle. "You have no idea—the stuff my hunter can do now, the powers I've got. Nobody messes with—"

Transfixed by the stunning mystery girl, Toby absentmindedly ended the call. He continued watching her as she carefully maneuvered her way down the truck's ramp with short, shuffling steps, carrying her own large cardboard box.

Halfway down the ramp, her left foot slipped.

She promptly crouched back on her right leg, trying to maintain her balance, but it was too late. The box pitched to the side, following her momentum, and slipped out of her arms. She frantically snatched at it, trying to regain her grip, but the container tumbled away.

Already on the move since seeing her first lose her footing, Toby swooped in. He grabbed the box, saving it just before it hit the driveway. The girl watched frozen, still in her half crouch, as he hoisted the box up into his arms. He secured his grip and then glanced over at her, getting immediately lost in her burnt acorn eyes.

Everything about her was that much more striking up close.

The girl exhaled a sigh of relief. "My hero."

"Me?" Toby replied, his mesmerized mind providing no additional words. He felt a flutter in his chest. His stomach contracted into a tight ball. Fumbling to regain his composure, he vainly attempted to articulate a better reply. "Uh, it wasn't…it was no big deal. I was just walking by, and I…I, um…uh…Is Mr. Franks moving?"

"Nope." The girl straightened up and hopped off the ramp. "My mom and I are moving in. She and he are…" She hesitated, unsure of how to finish her thought. "Actually, I don't really know what they are. Can you be newlyweds if you're both on your second marriage?"

Toby's eyes widened with surprise. "Ms. Chochopi's your mom?"

"She is."

"I didn't even know she had a kid. I've never seen you around."

The girl looked over toward the house. "That's because I never really was around. I mostly stayed back home. Or, back around my old home."

"Where was that?"

"The reservation."

"*You* lived on the Indian reservation?" Toby asked, unable to hold back his surprise.

Of course she did. She was Native American. Her mom was a known Umatilla. Toby's surprise had more to do with the fact that someone so attractive could live so close and yet be so unknown. Having never actually set foot in the reservation village, he'd only met a few of its residents and knew very little about the town.

He'd never imagined anyone there looking like this girl.

"Yep." She nodded toward the box he was holding. "And try to be careful. That has all my tomahawks and headdress in it."

Toby glanced down at the flimsy cardboard container wrapped in duct tape. He hadn't thought Native Americans still wore stuff like headdresses. "Really?"

The girl smirked and shook her head. "No. Not really. Sorry. I don't know why I said that."

Toby rolled his eyes, embarrassed. However, the way he figured it, his lack of knowledge about, or interaction with, the residents of the reservation wasn't *entirely* his fault.

Most of the ghost stories he'd been told when he was younger had been set out in the reservation's woods. As a result, he'd grown up associating anything or anyone from the area as "spooky." On top of that, friends and neighbors often grumbled about Indians stealing items from their garages or vegetables from their gardens. Even though his father had usually found the true culprits to be forgetfulness and misplacement, or rabbits in the case of the garden thefts, the recurring complaints had still managed to shape Toby's opinions over time.

He'd also heard how some Indians still held a pretty serious grudge against white folks for being stuck on the reservation to begin with. Yet another reason to avoid them altogether.

Bottom line, there were plenty of experiences and influencers Toby could blame for his opinions of the Umatilla. But any biased beliefs he had about his Native American neighbors weren't intentional, or even something he'd been all that conscious of, until this very moment.

"It's okay, I just, I wasn't really sure since, um…" Toby mentally groped for a way to save the conversation, his words becoming less enunciated as his voice grew quieter. "It's just that people from our two towns, they don't…"

"Intermingle all that much?" she offered.

Realizing that he was near mumbling, Toby cleared his throat. "That would be one way to put it."

"I know. I'm moving barely fifteen miles, but I feel like I'm entering a foreign land or something. Like this is a whole different part of the world."

She started to subconsciously twirl a strand of her raven hair as she spoke, which went a quarter of the way down her back. "My mom would always bug me about spending more time here and getting to know Alan better, but I've lived my whole life in the village. All my friends were there."

"*Were?*"

"Yeah, well," she caught him gazing at her twirling finger and promptly dropped her hand to her side. "A lot of them weren't real supportive when they found out I was moving here with my mom and becoming an intermingler."

"That sucks," Toby offered.

"They showed their true colors is all." She managed a weak smile that didn't quite succeed in covering up her sadness. "But like my mom keeps telling me, I'm only sixteen. I've still got plenty of time to make new friends."

Blinking away the moment, she forced her smile wider and raised a hand toward him. "I'm Rachel, by the way."

Toby made a futile attempt to shake her outstretched hand, almost dropping the box. "Um, Toby."

Rachel Chochopi extended her arms out to accept her belongings. "Well, thanks for the help, Toby," she said sweetly. "You're a real lifesaver."

He handed over the box. After getting a firm hold, she gave him a slight nod and, with a twist of her hips, headed up the driveway. Toby watched her for a moment, still a bit discombobulated.

"Yeah. Sure. Anytime."

He hadn't masked his nerves well at all, but he also hadn't vomited, which, for a moment there, he'd felt pretty close to doing. In fact, Toby couldn't remember the last time his insides had felt this stirred up.

He'd grown accustomed to the numb stillness that had resulted from the accident. It hadn't seemed possible that he could be this strongly affected by something—or in this case, someone—after his mother's death.

But here he was…seriously affected.

His smartphone rang again. Nate was calling him back.

Henry Jennings's place was about fifteen minutes outside of town, and Walter Hoffman had thought that the drive would provide him with the time he'd need to prepare for what was coming. Mentally, maybe it had, but his emotions struck harder than he'd anticipated as he entered the man's rustic farmhouse.

Harriet had called the station about an hour earlier to report how she'd discovered her brother brutally murdered in his hogs' stable. Henry was the first death due to unnatural causes since Mary, and there hadn't been one before her in years.

Due to a serious shortage of private time, Walter had never really allowed himself to mourn his wife's death. Now repressed feelings of suffering and loss were bubbling up, a dull pain spreading from his chest to his throat.

Nothing like seeing others grieve the death of a loved one to bring a person's own unresolved grief rushing to the surface.

Not here though. He had to shut off his sorrow and conceal it. Swallowing his angst, Walter gave Harriet's daughter, Beverly, a solemn nod as he stepped into the living room. When he entered the kitchen and addressed the people sitting around the table, he was going to need to be the sheriff of Silver Falls, not some grief-stricken widower. Henry's family and friends were going to expect him to be their rock. That's what he was going to be.

Outside, Deputy Billy Rogers followed Albert Taylor, Henry's brother-in-law, along the side of the victim's whitewashed cottage home. They rounded the rear of the residence to see the hog pen and damaged stable encircled in a weak early-evening fog.

A raven's caw caused the deputy to look up. His eyes followed the black bird as it coasted downward onto a well-trodden patch of dirt where it joined the rest of its murder, pecking away at one of Henry's massacred pigs.

Billy shifted his gaze away from the bloody bird buffet and peered through the chilly evening mist at the massive hole in the side of the stable. It looked as though the structure had been hit by a Buick. The wood panels were all bowed inward around the opening, ultimately snapping off into jagged peaks.

Albert stopped once they got within about thirty feet of the entrance and nodded toward the door. "He's right inside."

"Would you mind showing me?" Billy asked.

"As a matter of fact, I would." Albert's sagging face was grim. "I'm sorry, Deputy, but that's not a sight I want to see again."

Walter had relayed the remainder of Harriet's call to Billy before they'd left the station, including the few gruesome details she'd provided. The deputy could understand how a victim's kin, or in this case the victim's kin-in-law, wouldn't want to see such a grotesque scene more than once.

"So…just right inside?"

"Yeah," Albert said, looking out toward the surrounding trees. "You won't miss him."

Deputy Rogers continued toward the stable, approaching cautiously, as if whoever or whatever had killed Henry might still be inside. Of course, his apprehension was really due to what he was about to see and how he would react to seeing it. He'd never worked a murder case before. Never laid eyes on a murder victim.

Realizing his behavior wasn't very deputy-like; Billy furrowed his brow and picked up his pace. This presentation of professionalism was short-lived. Once he stepped into the stable, the grisly sight inside caused him to stumble back. Almost immediately, his cheeks bloated around his tightly drawn lips. He spun around, leaned out the doorway, grabbed his knees, and retched.

The scents of a freshly baked apple pie, a tray of lasagna, and several other homemade goods brought to help comfort Henry's grieving sister filled the dead farmer's kitchen. Walter sat with Harriet at a reclaimed pinewood table in the center of the room, listening patiently as she talked through her tears.

"He was supposed to come over this morning for breakfast," she sobbed into two or three shredded tissues that were gripped tightly in her fleshy fingers. "When he didn't return my calls, I drove over here and…"

She broke down, unable to retell the details of her horrible discovery. The sheriff put a consoling arm around her shoulder, glancing up at her family and friends who stood around them heartbroken and unsettled.

"I'm so sorry, Harriet," Walter said, trying to offer her some comfort. "Your brother was a good man."

She leaned further into him, bellowing guttural hollers into his armpit. Walter looked past a few weeping relatives to see Billy slowly entering the kitchen. He held up a finger as his deputy opened his mouth to speak.

Harriet was understandably beside herself with grief, and Walter wanted to give her a moment. This was not the time to bring up the situation in the stable or to try to figure out if she had any suspicions about who might have wanted to murder her brother. Billy nodded his acknowledgment, but still wore a very anxious expression. Clearly rattled by whatever he'd seen outside, he waited only a few seconds before taking another step forward.

"Uh, Sheriff," he broke in. "You're going to want to come take a look at this."

Walter gave a nod and passed Harriet off to one of her cousins. He excused himself with a slight bow and followed Billy out of the room.

Outside, the sheriff trailed his deputy around to the hog pen and immediately noticed the hole in the stable wall. What could the killer have used to cause that kind of damage? And what was the point?

"We know anybody who had a beef with old Henry?" Walter asked as they approached the door.

"Not sure this was the work of a 'who,'" Billy responded, a slight wavering in his voice. The kid was clearly shaken.

"What then? Cougar?"

"Would have had to have been a big one."

A hog dashed out of the stable and into the pen, causing both men to take a step back.

"Around here they don't get much bigger than three or four feet," Walter replied.

He entered the stable, blinking rapidly as his eyes adjusted to the dim interior. The sheriff then made out Henry's body. Caught off guard by the atrociousness of the sight, he glanced away from it. His eyes fell on a coiled rope that hung above one of the stall doors. He kept his gaze fixed on the thickly braided twine until he'd steeled his nerves enough to look back at the victim.

Henry's torso had been completely ripped from his legs. Mangled guts covered the disemboweled body and the ground around it. With his eyes now fully adjusted, Walter noticed that he'd almost stepped on something that possibly might have been the man's liver. He followed a trail of blood, smeared over stamped hay, to find one of Henry's legs in a corner stall, dragged there by either the thing that had killed him or one of his hogs.

A few of the man's pigs also lay butchered, killed right alongside their owner. Their blood was splattered across the walls and several of the stall doors. It was a total massacre.

Billy was right. This wasn't the work of a "who."

CHAPTER 4

Capability and Transcendence

With Mr. Wright's honors philosophy in English class nearing its conclusion, focused students sat at their desks writing feverishly in little blue books. Some fidgeted restlessly, cracking knuckles and tapping their feet—briefly interrupting the soft scratching of pens scribbling away on paper. Others wrote calmly and confidently, as if they could fill up two or three more booklets.

Nate Schaffer was one of the confident ones. He slapped his booklet shut and glanced at the clock above the door. Finished with ten minutes to spare. His narrow chest swelled with pride. He didn't even need Mr. Wright to grade the exam to know he'd aced it. His confidence came from the fact that he'd aced all the teacher's tests so far and, of course, from his good-luck charm.

He picked up Duncan Balfour with his thumb and index finger. The two-inch tall, hand-painted, battle-axe wielding, pewter dwarf had seen him through not just countless role-playing missions, but many important tests as well. They'd never failed one another.

Of course, the constant studying and additional effort Nate put in didn't hurt either. He'd accumulated so much extra credit in Mr. Wright's class that he could blow off the final and still receive no less than an A-minus for the semester. Not that he'd actually consider skipping the exam, or even adjusting the fourteen-hour study schedule he already had planned for it.

His eyes moved to Toby, who appeared to still be hard at work writing out his essay answer. Nate smiled, pleased to see him so focused. He hoped this was a sign that his down-and-detached friend was starting to bounce back.

Although he knew Toby would never rank in the top ten, or even top twenty, percent of their class, his best buddy was certainly a better student than he'd shown himself to be over the past few weeks.

While it appeared to Nate that Toby was working hard on his essay, his booklet's pages contained only 3-D shapes and other doodles, along with Rachel's name written in several different styles and sizes. He couldn't stop thinking about her. What had she thought of him? What was she doing right now?

Could she be the key to him getting on with his life?

He wanted to get to know her better, before anyone else had a chance to. He wanted her to get to know him—get to like him. In a way, he'd been granted first dibs with her moving in right next door, but how long would that advantage last? Gossip traveled faster than light in Silver Falls, and news of the town's most recent resident was bound to be all over school by tomorrow morning, if not sooner.

The bell rang. Toby flipped his booklet shut, dropped it on Mr. Wright's desk, and quickly exited the classroom. Maneuvering around a herd of freshmen migrating toward the east wing, he strode down the hall at a brisk pace, hoping to avoid a recap discussion of the essay test he'd just blown off.

No such luck.

Mr. Majer's German class spilled out into the hallway directly in front of him, creating just enough of a bottleneck for Nate to catch up. The obvious spring in his friend's step let Toby know that Nate was very pleased with himself—yet again. However, as confident as he often was about his test-taking performances, Nate was the type who liked reassurance.

"So did you put camel, lion, and child for the three metamorphoses?"

"Sure, that sounds right," Toby lied. He actually had no clue if it sounded right.

"But is that what you put?"

"Um, yeah. Camel, lion, and um…"

"Child."

"Right," Toby confirmed with a nod. "Child."

"And what did Nietzsche say happens after a person goes through the three metamorphoses?"

The answer came from behind them. "He overcomes himself fully, reaching new levels of capability and transcendence. He becomes something beyond man."

Toby and Nate glanced over their shoulders to see Willard Kraus, who had provided the answer, and fellow classmate Peter Fox following right behind them.

A fitting poster boy for the obesity epidemic among American youth, Willard had developed a bit of a waddle in his step. His Izod shirt and Diesel jeans stretched tightly over his ample frame. Peter was on the opposite end of the body-type spectrum, sporting a loose fleece jacket, baggy jeans, and spiked blond hair. All served to divert attention away from his wiry torso and limbs.

"Speaking of reaching new levels of capability and transcendence," Nate said with a grin. "Who wants to watch me kick more butt at Demon Destroyer tonight?"

The boys strolled up to their lockers, spun the combination locks, and popped open the doors. Toby glanced over to see Nate carefully placing Duncan on his locker's top shelf.

The pewter dwarf's appearance was to be expected. It was a test day, after all. While Toby knew his friend fought mostly online battles these days, he also knew the tiny figure covered in chipped paint would always hold significance for Nate. The thing had been a third wheel in their friendship since seventh grade.

Actually, if Toby were to be totally honest with himself, there'd been more than one occasion where *he'd* felt like the third wheel.

"Did you tell Toby about our latest mission?" Willard asked excitedly.

"Yeah, but he was too cool to come over and check out the digital recording I made of it," Nate responded, using an overly despondent tone that Toby suspected was meant to conceal a certain level of true disappointment.

Peter reached over and slapped Toby on the shoulder. "Dude, you gotta join our guild."

Toby shook his head as he dug through an enormous pile of crumpled and torn papers that had accumulated throughout the school year, hunting for his biology notebook. "I need to try to find new levels of capability and, um…what was it?"

"Transcendence," Willard offered.

"Right," Toby said. "I need to try to find that stuff in real life before I start looking for it online."

"You can't hunt demons in real life," Willard scoffed.

"Yeah, I know that I can't hunt…" Toby paused as he spotted a tattered green notebook. Snagging it, he quickly realized it was a leftover from first-semester English and tossed it back into the pile.

He heard Nate speak up, his voice sounding hesitant and unsure. "We're all just a little concerned about how you haven't really tried at much of anything since the acci–"

Toby shot him an angry look that quieted his friend immediately.

"I know you don't like talking about it," Nate mumbled. "It's just that…we just thought…never mind."

Toby crouched down to resume his hunt. He suddenly felt anxious and frustrated by the mess in his locker and turned to look for a trashcan. No luck. As he went back to digging, he realized it wasn't really the mess that had him upset.

The anxiety and apathy that had plagued him since the accident weren't Nate's fault. He shouldn't have glared at him like that.

It also wasn't fair for Toby to dismiss his friends' efforts at cheering him up without first giving them a chance. Playing a fantasy online game probably wouldn't prove to be any more of a waste of time than continuing to read the fantastical stories in *The Hero with a Thousand Faces*. Why not give it a try?

Toby had only played Demon Destroyer once and done so using one of Peter's characters. What had they called it? A rogue? Maybe a mage? Whatever it was, Nate hadn't approved. He'd said a player couldn't really get into the game until he created a character of his own. Toby figured it was the least he could do.

After all, why should he expect anyone to help him feel normal again, or at least slightly less fucked up, if he wasn't willing to accept the help of his three closest pals?

"Say I did decide to play." The words came reluctantly, but he managed to spit them out. "How would I create a character?"

No response. Toby glanced up to see his three friends looking past him, transfixed by something down the hall.

"Um, guys?"

He looked over his shoulder to see the source of their fascination. Rachel.

Heading their way, she maneuvered down the hallway studying a slip of paper in her left hand. Apparently she wasn't going to just be changing residences. She was changing schools as well.

And just like that, her existence in the Silver Falls' universe was no longer something only Toby knew about. She was publicizing it to the entire student body by wearing the hell out of a pair of skinny gray jeans and layered tees—neon pink and sky blue.

She spotted Toby, and her face seemed to brighten. "Hey."

"Hey," he echoed back, trying not to sound too surprised or disappointed by her sudden appearance. "How's it going?"

She swerved toward them. "Pretty good. Or, you know, as good as can be expected for being the new kid. There haven't been *too many* furtive whispers or odd stares."

Toby glanced over to see Nate, Peter, and Willard gawking at Rachel like a pack of hungry zombies, Nate's mouth slightly agape.

"Yeah, well, that's good," Toby said, nudging his transfixed friend to snap him out of his slack-jawed state. "I mean, I've only heard maybe two *really* vicious rumors about you so far."

His little joke received an approving smirk. Yes! She found him funny. At least a little bit. He was thrilled to have demonstrated the ability to be witty after he'd barely demonstrating the ability to string together a sentence during their first encounter.

Still smiling, Rachel glanced down again at the slip of paper in her hand, then up at the classroom doors on either side of the hall. "I've got calculus next period with Mrs. Carlson. Is this the right way?"

"Me too!" Nate blurted out loudly. "Sorry. I meant, yeah, you're going... It's just right over...Me, I mean, I...I'm in the same class. I'm Nate."

The awkward introduction reminded Toby of his own cringe worthy performance from the day before. He was more than happy to let one of his friends take over as the stammering shy kid of the group, especially if it helped cast him as more of the cool and collected type in Rachel's eyes. Of course, when it came to vying for her attention, Toby wasn't too worried about competing with the Demon Destroyer crew.

Nate took a moment to gather his thoughts. "I could show you where to go if you want."

"That'd be great," she said cheerfully. "I'm Rachel, by the way."

Nate flashed a beaming smile, but it only lasted a moment. Then his expression swiftly shifted to one of concern.

Toby followed his distressed gaze to see Mike Mulligan approaching from down the hall. The muscle-bound junior was flanked by his football buddies, Jerry Ituha and Andrew Staley. They all sported their varsity football jackets and an unassailable swagger.

These three epitomized the kind of competition Toby would have to worry about.

Jerry was even Native American, although, he'd been born and raised on his family's ranch just outside of town and didn't really seem to associate with anyone from the reservation. Toby figured that was probably a calculated decision on Jerry's part, to preserve the popularity he'd achieved by becoming a varsity athlete.

Not any more thrilled to see the jocks than Nate was, Toby glanced down, hoping that if he avoided eye contact, they would just continue past. Unfortunately, Nate wasn't as quick to look away. Mike met his stare and immediately veered over.

"Hey, Schaffer." The strapping junior stepped right into the center of the group, flashing a superior grin, and gave Nate an over-zealous slap on the back. "You finish that calculus assignment?"

Nate slouched away from the bully like an abused pet. "Yeah. You know, it was pretty easy. You could probably do it yourself if you worked on it during class."

Mike gave the suggestion a dismissive wave. "How about you just give it to me?"

"Yeah," Jerry chimed in. "Don't be a dick, Schaffer."

Filled with the long-established frustration of not being able to do anything about these unwanted interactions, Toby glowered at Jerry. It was a reflexive glare, and one that he tried to flatten out immediately. But Andrew had been watching him, and Toby's scowl prompted the smug lackey to shove him hard into the lockers.

"Got something to say, Hoffman?" the overzealous bully challenged, pressing his forearm into Toby's chest.

Toby had been granted a short reprieve from these daily exchanges after the accident, but it now appeared as though recess was over. He stayed silent, slowly becoming aware of the dull pain spreading through his shoulder, which had taken the brunt of his collision with the lockers.

Even if he had the nerve to act, his chances of winning a one-on-one fight with Andrew were slim. Any kind of valiant stance taken against all three jocks would only result in his being stomped into a fine paste.

All the boys knew this, which was why this scene would play out exactly as all the others before it had. Mike wanted something from them, and so they would give it to him. Nobody would put up a fight. It would be the same deal tomorrow.

"Why would he just give you his homework?" Rachel challenged, her forehead creased in a look of annoyance and confusion.

Toby's eyes widened. He shook his head slightly, trying to discourage her from saying anything more. It was too late. Mike had registered her presence.

"Because that's the way it works around here, new girl," the jock replied, turning toward her. He looked her up and down, then gave her a playful wink.

Rachel seemed unimpressed. "Something in your eye?"

THE ONE YOU FEED

Mike just laughed the question away as he grabbed Nate by the back of his collar and pulled him from the group. "C'mon, Schaffer. We don't want to be late for class."

Andrew withdrew his forearm from Toby's chest, curling his lips into an arrogant sneer. Another thing Toby would just have to let go. Mike's minions then fell in line behind him, and they all headed off down the hallway.

Rachel started after them, her eyes narrowing into slits of contempt.

"Where are you going?" Toby called after her, rubbing his sore shoulder.

She responded without looking back. "To class."

Nate stumbled over his own feet as Mike pulled him into Mrs. Carlson's classroom. The bully hauled him down the second row of seats, still dragging him along by his collar, and planted him in the third desk down. Pain reverberated through Nate's forearm as his funny bone banged against the chair's laminate.

The quivering sting was the latest of innumerable reminders that reaching the same levels of capability and transcendence he enjoyed in online gaming wasn't an option for him at Silver Falls High. Not with Mike around.

His tormentor slid into the desk to his left. "Okay, let's have it."

Nate heaved a sigh and opened his binder. This routine had been going on since he was a freshman, about two weeks into his first semester. He'd never understood how his teachers hadn't caught on over the past year and a half, especially with a class like calculus. Mike wasn't even capable of handling long division.

Mrs. Carlson should have figured out this fraud long ago.

Maybe she had. Everyone was well aware that Mike had several football scholarship offers. This wasn't a kid who was ever going to care about calculus. Maybe when teachers encountered a student this unreachable, they decided to save their energy for those they could reach.

Nate could see such an approach making it easier to endure the profession, but it was making his existence as a student insufferable.

Glancing over to see Mike's impatient stare, he quickly swallowed his bitterness and withdrew the homework from his binder's inside pocket.

Before he could hand it over, Rachel slipped into the desk to his right. "Don't you dare give that to him."

Nate paused, unsure. He appreciated what she was trying to do, but she didn't appreciate the repercussions of standing up to Mike Mulligan.

Mike slapped his palm down on Nate's desk, fixing Rachel with a cold stare. "This don't concern you, new girl."

"Good morning, everyone." Mrs. Carlson entered the classroom with a few late arriving students. She dropped her oversized suede bag onto her desk and looked to the class. "Can everyone pass their assignments forward please?"

Mike shifted his gaze to Nate, staring right though him. Nate diverted his eyes over to Rachel, who was locked in with an equally unyielding look. There was no winning scenario here. Whatever he did, one of them would end up disappointed. He focused on the sheet of paper quivering in his hands. Light crinkles had formed where he pinched it tightly between his fingers and thumbs.

Just as Mike reached over to snatch the sheet away, Nate passed it to the student in front of him.

"You little bitch," the bully snarled.

Mike's cold stare continued as he turned to collect the assignments from the students sitting behind him. He finally looked away as he set the papers down on his desk and began hurriedly copying the top one in the pile.

The typically reticent Melanie Anderson, who sat behind him, took notice and spoke up. "What are you doing?"

Mrs. Carlson walked over to Mike's row. "Is there a problem, Mr. Mulligan?"

"Uh, no," he said, giving up his attempt to copy Melanie's homework. He passed the sheets forward with a frown. "No problem."

Mrs. Carlson collected the row's papers and leafed through them. "I don't see your assignment here."

Mike lowered his head and spoke into his chest. "I don't have it."

"What was that?"

"I don't have it," he said a little more loudly.

Mrs. Carlson gave a disapproving look. "Please see me after class."

A few giggles bubbled up from different corners of the classroom. With each snicker, Nate felt a slight sting, knowing that his classmates' reactions were only serving to infuriate Mike that much more. There was no question that punishment was coming. The only questions were what would it be and when?

CHAPTER 5

BAD MOVE, HOFFMAN

Fifty minutes later, the bell rang to signal the end of the class period, and students emptied into the hallways. A mass withdrawal of smartphones from purses and pockets produced a brief symphony of catchy chimes as the latest texts, tweets, and status updates were quickly, yet carefully inspected.

Nate Schaffer darted out of calculus like a frightened squirrel, not wanting to give Mike even the slightest opportunity to exact any sort of revenge. As she watched him scuttle down the hall, Rachel found Nate's behavior to be a little melodramatic. Could the jock's bullying really be all that bad?

Walking among her bustling classmates, she once again checked her schedule to determine where she was headed next. The task of navigating her new surroundings left her too preoccupied to notice the domineering junior striding up behind her. Within moments, Mike was on her heels.

"Your ass is lookin' fine in those jeans, new girl," he squawked.

Crap. Maybe Nate's strategy had been the right one after all. Rachel quickened her pace hoping Mike would back off. Instead, he hustled up alongside her, giving her butt a firm spank.

She spun to face him. "Don't touch me, asshole."

"Whoa." Mike smirked and raised his arms in mock apology. "You gotta learn how to take a compliment better."

Rachel felt her face go flush. A face-off in the hallway with the school's star linebacker had not been part of the plan for her first day. She'd wanted to draw as little attention to herself as possible, but now that she was stuck in this situation she wasn't about to run off and hide. Determined not to waver even a little, she stood her ground—and realized that she had no one to blame for this predicament but herself.

Well, she could possibly blame her Uncle Bimi. At least that's what her mom would tell her. After her dad had abandoned the family when she was six, her uncle had taken over as the father figure in her life and, in doing so, apparently passed along his stubborn nature and scrappiness.

Those exact traits had prompted her to persuade Nate not to give up his homework, and hence led her straight into this confrontation.

Mike took another step toward her, crowding in close. "You also need to learn not to stick that ass where it don't belong."

Just as he'd done by the lockers earlier, the hefty jock ran his eyes up and down her body, taking time to assess each and every curve. "So you're an Injun, huh? How come Jerry never told me about you?"

"We don't really know each other."

"His loss." Mike pursed his lips approvingly. "I might just have to try me some of this Native American flavor sometime."

He placed a hand on her waist, like she was already his, and Rachel went rigid. The tough girl act hadn't been a total bluff, but considering she was the new kid without any real friends, it hadn't been a very well-backed play either. Now Mike was calling her on it.

Rachel felt a slight sense of nausea as he touched her, repulsed by him and with herself for letting him harass her this way. She took a deep breath and shifted her eyes away from his, glancing down at his hand.

Then she slapped it away.

Ready to give the bully a piece of her mind, Rachel glanced back up to look him straight in the eyes. But before she could utter a word, he was promptly knocked out of her field of vision by a swift right cross. It happened in a flash, and she had to take a step back to assess what was going on.

To her surprise, Toby had just popped Mike in the jaw. The clumsy punch had landed solidly enough to daze the jock, sending him stumbling back. And now Toby stood at Rachel's side, gritting his teeth in agony and cradling the hand he'd used in the assault.

Having been completely caught off guard, Mike leaned against the wall to recover his balance. Rubbing his chin, he looked around until he located his assailant. "Fucking bad move, Hoffman."

Rachel watched, still a little stunned, as Mike pushed himself off the wall and slugged Toby hard, sending him reeling backward. Toby reached out and tried to grab at the jock as he moved in to follow his overhand left with a concrete right. Mike shoved him back effortlessly, knocked aside Toby's arms, and began pummeling him.

Rachel shook off her shock and sprang into action. She grabbed at Mike, but the bully was far too strong and driven for her to deter. She was about to give him a swift kick when two hands suddenly grabbed her firmly by each forearm and yanked her from the fray. Rachel glanced back just as a young male teacher released her and moved in to separate the two combatants.

"Hey! Knock it off! That's enough!"

And just like that, the fight was over. Rachel looked over at the now battered and bloodied Toby with the realization that she had made at least one friend during her short time in Silver Falls.

She'd also created quite a scene. Every student in the hall was now staring at her, wondering who this girl was who had just gotten Mike and Toby to brawl. This was *so* not a part of her plan to gradually fit in at her new school.

As much as she wanted to thank Toby for helping her, she was far too flustered and embarrassed to do so right then and there. After seeing that he was okay, she ducked her head and hurried off down the hallway.

Not surprisingly, Toby soon found himself in Principal Carter's cramped office with an ice pack pressed firmly against his upper right cheek. Despite his sore jaw, aching hand, and a likely black eye, he actually felt pretty good.

He'd stood up to Mike and gotten to help out Rachel in the process. And he was as surprised as anyone that he'd actually had the nerve to do so. When he'd seen Rachel was in trouble, he'd been filled with indecision about what needed to be done or if he was the guy to do it. Then Mike had touched her.

At that point, some inner instinct had taken over and Toby had sprung into action.

He'd even managed to land a pretty solid punch, although things proceeded to go downhill very quickly after that. He seriously doubted that his good mood was going to last through his visit with Anthony Carter, the school's chinless, middle-aged principal.

Carter sat at his desk, flipping through the pages of a file that Toby had seen grow in size significantly over the past month, due mainly to abandoned therapy sessions, a couple unexplained truancies, and several blown-off exams.

Eventually finding what he was looking for, the principal nudged his horn-rimmed glasses up the bridge of his nose and studied the contents of the file quietly. He then glanced to his left, where the prim Ms. Parker sat on a small sofa against the wall, and simply shrugged, as if to question why they were even bothering with this meeting.

Toby wondered the same thing. He didn't like the fact that Ms. Parker was there. She undoubtedly had a theory on why he'd acted to help Rachel, but he didn't want to hear it. He just wanted his punishment.

"Once again, I have to suggest that perhaps you returned too soon," Principal Carter said as he flipped through a few more pages.

"Mike was being an asshole," Toby muttered back.

"You've failed two exams this week," replied the principal without any real concern in his voice. "Let's focus on that first, shall we?

Then we can discuss your altercation with Mike Mulligan. Given the circumstances, I can talk to your teachers about letting you retake the exams once you've finally processed everything you've been through. Until then—"

"No thanks," Toby said abruptly.

Principal Carter set down the file with a heavy sigh. "Tell me, what are your plans for the future, Toby?"

His future? He was having enough trouble coping with the events of his recent past. He wasn't interested in considering or discussing what came next. Not with his jaded principal and definitely not with Ms. Parker. He just wanted out of the room. He felt trapped.

"Well, I've got a chem test Thursday," he responded, doing his best to stifle his mounting frustration. "Mr. Weaver gave Mike and me detention on Saturday, but I'm sure you already knew that."

"I was talking more long term," Principal Carter said after another exasperated sigh. "Like what are your plans for after high school? Have you started researching any colleges yet?"

"I don't really care about college anymore."

"You'd be closing a lot of doors by foregoing a higher education."

Toby peered past Principal Carter to look at the man's diploma hanging on the wall. What had that framed, yellowing piece of paper gotten him? Had *his* plans for the future been to sit in a windowless office with lifeless, pea green paint and deal with smartass teenagers all day?

Ending up like this disinterested authority figure was a door Toby was more than happy to slam shut. "Some of them probably weren't worth opening anyway."

Principal Carter furrowed his eyebrows, seeming to have picked up on the subtle dig. "Don't you think it's time you move on, son?"

Ms. Parker leaned into the conversation and attempted to get it back on track. "Toby, losing your mother at your age, I know how it can make things like exams and college seem trivial. But like Principal Carter, I also believe that your mother's wish would be for you to move past her death and start thinking more about your future."

Toby felt his belly heating up with anger. How the hell did Ms. Parker know what his mom would want? More important, what made her think it was okay to even bring her into this discussion?

"Have you ever thought about her wishes?" Ms. Parker pressed.

"She's pretty much *all* I think about," Toby snapped back.

Principal Carter decided to chime in again. "So, then, have you thought about how disappointed she'd be if she could see you now?"

The anger inside Toby's belly inflated. He straightened in his chair, his hands clenching the armrests.

Ms. Parker again tried to soothe the situation. "What Principal Carter means to say is that, while it was nice of you to help our new student—"

"You told me in our sessions that I needed to stop avoiding the things that make me afraid," Toby vented, turning toward his school counselor. "I would think you'd be happy that I stood up to Mike."

"There's a difference between taking action and acting out, but we can discuss that another time. Right now you need to worry less about others and focus more on helping yourself."

That's exactly what he'd done. After popping Mike in the jaw, Toby had felt better than he had in weeks. And that was *because* he'd helped another person. It was because he'd helped Rachel. There was something about her...

"If not a brighter future, then what is it you want, Toby?" Mr. Carter asked in an unmistakably condescending tone.

"For you to go to hell."

"And you just earned yourself a second Saturday detention."

Toby stood and knocked over his chair. He was too angry to speak, furious that he was not only being punished for standing up to a bully, but apparently also for making his own decisions about how to live his life. He stormed out of the office without another word.

Stomping off down the hall, he heard the principal call out after him. "You just made it a third!"

CHAPTER 6

NATE'S PUNISHMENT

Nate walked home from school filled with a reinvigorating sense of pride that the reality of a cool and misty April afternoon couldn't dampen. He still had some serious concerns about what the repercussions would be for his earlier display of bravery, but it had felt *really* good to finally tell Mike no. It had also felt good to have Rachel care enough to encourage him to take a stand.

Nate wondered how well Toby knew the new girl. How close were they? Would she become a member of their little group? Had she been impressed when he'd refused to give up his homework that morning? What else could he do to impress her? What were her interests?

He figured he should probably hold off on introducing her to Duncan Balfour or talking up his latest virtual monster-hunting accomplishments until he knew more about *her* hobbies. But how would he access such information? The question kept him so preoccupied that he didn't notice the pickup truck slowly rolling up alongside him.

"Hey there, Schaffer."

Nate glanced over his shoulder to see Jerry behind the wheel of the vehicle and Mike and Andrew perched in the truck bed. They all looked like predatory cats poised to strike. This was going to be trouble.

Immediately darting away from them, Nate didn't look back again until he was halfway down the block. Mike and Andrew were already out of the truck and in pursuit, both sporting ear-to-ear grins. They chased him down effortlessly, before he even reached the corner, and pulled him back toward the pickup.

As his feet dragged along the sidewalk, Nate became singularly focused on another question: Why had he done such a stupid thing as to tell Mike Mulligan no?

Wrapped in a snug headlock, he sat helplessly as Jerry drove the group away from town. The jocks apparently had a punishment planned that they didn't want anyone else to witness. Soon they were cruising down Highway 70 with nothing but trees on either side. The farther away they got from Silver Falls, the more panic-stricken Nate became.

With the exception of the reservation village, there wasn't another town within forty-five miles. The surrounding area, much of which was the Umatilla Indian Reservation, consisted only of dense forest. It was easy to hide in these woods, and kids often did just that to escape the watchful eyes of their parents. They came out here to drink, smoke, hook up, or on this particular occasion, torment and abuse one of their classmates.

Jerry's pickup turned off the main highway and onto a narrow dirt road. The rough terrain made the ride considerably rockier, causing Nate to shift his weight with each jolting bump. Another turn and the vehicle headed deeper into the forest, rumbling through the woods for what seemed like a mile or so before coming to a stop.

Andrew finally released his headlock.

"Look. I'm sorry," Nate pleaded, uneasily surveying the trees and darkening dusk sky. "Really, truly, very sorry."

Ignoring Nate's appeal, Mike opened a duffel bag and pulled out three sleek, charcoal gray, military-style paintball guns.

"The Spyder MR4," he said as he handed one of the weapons to Jerry. "Semi-auto with an accuracy range of up to a hundred and fifty feet."

The second gun went to Andrew. Next, Mike pulled out the paintball tanks and passed them around. He affixed his tank to the top of his weapon. "I ordered these babies off Amazon a couple weeks ago. Twenty-ounce CO_2 tanks, each with eighteen hundred shots in it."

"I'll do your homework for the rest of the week," Nate bargained anxiously. "*The rest of the month.*"

The jocks all started laughing, and Nate attempted to laugh along with them. Just as he did, Mike abruptly stopped.

The lead bully fixed on him with a cold-blooded stare. "Better start running."

There would be no negotiating his way out of this. Letting that grim realization set in, Nate knew he'd be better off saving his breath for the unwanted exercise he was about to get. There were more laughs as he hurriedly stumbled out of the truck bed and fell to the forest floor.

Scrambling to his feet, he scampered into the trees, managing to make it only about fifty yards before he was gasping for air.

Mike hollered out from somewhere behind him. "We're coming for you, Shaffer!"

Andrew followed with a gleeful howl, the sound of his baying echoing through the trees. The joy they were taking in this was flat-out sadistic. They weren't going to rush things or grow bored quickly. As paint balls began to whiz by, Nate envisioned himself feeling the sharp sting of the pellets well into the night. The thought brought tears of frustration to his eyes.

He weaved through upland oaks and Lodgepole pines as quickly as his tiring legs allowed. His lungs were already burning and sweat dripped from his forehead. Cutting to his right, he darted between two more trees, brushed off a spider web, and then came to a sudden stop as a putrid smell invaded his nostrils.

The source of the stench lay several yards ahead in a clump of weeds and grass. It was a dead deer carcass, but the animal wasn't just dead. It was butchered—its stomach ripped open, guts spilling out onto the forest floor. Nate knew he should keep running, but he couldn't bring himself to look away from the gory remains.

As the bullies closed in, he remained frozen in a wide-eyed stupor.

A paintball splattered a tree less than a foot away, snapping him back. Before he could start running again, another paintball exploded on his thigh. The sucker stung and Nate yelped in pain.

"Yes!" Jerry hooted excitedly. "That's a hit!"

Carefully circling his way around the dead deer, Nate took off again. He looked back into the gloomy nighttime woods to see the jocks gaining ground, clearly undeterred by the rotting animal.

His eyes stayed on his pursuers a little too long.

Not watching where he was going, Nate clipped his shoulder against a pine tree. The glancing blow spun him around, and he stumbled into a small clearing. As he brought his eyes forward and tried to regain his footing, he spotted a large opening in the ground directly ahead.

Nate shouted out in surprise and dug his heels into the dirt, trying to stop, but it was too late. His momentum carried him over the edge.

He fell nearly twenty feet before his left foot hit the cavern floor. An intense pain exploded through his ankle as he rolled over on it, and he hit the ground with a bone-reverberating thud. Dirt and dust clouded up around him and then settled as he lay still for what seemed like several minutes. Eventually, Nate opened his eyes with a groan to see the three jocks carefully leaning over the cavern opening.

Andrew shouted down to him. "Shit, Schaffer, what'd you do?"

"Nothing." Nate took in a shallow breath. He rolled onto his hand and knees and then hobbled to his feet, wincing. "I just…fell."

A paintball splattered his chest, causing him to stumble. As he shifted his weight onto his left ankle, he felt a sharp pain shoot through it again. The ankle buckled and he collapsed, landing flat on his ass. The three jocks howled with laughter.

"I'll expect my calculus homework before first period tomorrow, Schaffer," Mike called down. "Make sure it's ready."

Apparently satisfied with the results of their retribution, the jocks turned and strolled off, still enjoying a good laugh at Nate's expense.

"Hey!" he shouted out after them. "Hey, wait! Don't leave me!"

Nate frantically began looking around for a way out, unable to distinguish much in the darkness and shadows. What the hell was this thing? A sinkhole?

He reached into his back pocket and took out his smartphone, praying that it hadn't been broken in the fall. He swiped on the display and used the dim light to survey his surroundings. There were several small animal bones on the cavern floor around him.

What the hell had he fallen into?

Fighting off more tears, he called out again. "Hey! Come back! Please! Mike!"

His cries went unanswered. The bullies' laughter was barely distinguishable at this point, and within a couple more seconds, it was completely drowned out by the chirping and squeaking of the forest's nocturnal creatures.

Those assholes weren't coming back.

Nate once again staggered to his feet and limped over to the cavern wall, hoping it would be jagged enough for him to climb his way out—if his ankle would let him. He shone the display light over the subterranean stone to see it was covered in Native American cave drawings. Steadying his shaking hand as best he could, he hovered the light over one particularly unpleasant image of people being attacked by what appeared to be some sort of furry monster.

Seriously. What the hell had he fallen into?

Just then, out of the corner of his eye, he thought he saw a hulking figure dart through the darkness behind him.

Nate turned quickly, uncertain if he'd really seen something or only imagined movement in the shadows. He held out his phone, using its dim glow to frantically search for any sign that he had company. Again he thought he saw something move.

Any doubt about whether or not he was alone vanished when a low growl emanated from the opposite end of the enclosed space. Some sort of animal was in here with him, and whatever it was, it wasn't happy that he'd trespassed into its home.

Nate's heart pounded in his chest as he remembered the bones on the cavern floor, likely leftovers of this creature's past meals. A lightheaded sensation followed as he contemplated meeting the same fate.

Two luminous, yellow eyes emerged from the shadows. Nate stared back at them and stayed perfectly still. The phone's display was too dim for him to make out what sort of animal the eyes belonged to. He considered shouting at it, thinking that if he made enough of a commotion, he might scare it deeper into the cavern. But he'd read somewhere that animals could sense fear, and if that was true, this thing already knew that he was scared shitless.

The eyes charged toward him.

Nate yelled out in terror and heard his cry echo through the cavern. Then everything went black.

Toby trudged home with shoulders slouched, hood up, and his hands shoved deep into his jacket pockets. He was still stewing over getting slapped with three Saturday detentions. This was all Mike's fault, and Toby would bet anything that the oppressive jerk wasn't getting three Saturdays.

As he turned onto Wilson Street, he heard someone shout his name. "Toby!"

Ashley Schultz hustled up the sidewalk behind him, flashing her bright, hallmark smile. She was wearing her cheerleader uniform, which Toby couldn't help but notice hugged her snugly in all the right places.

"Hey there, slugger." She threw a playful punch into his left shoulder.

"Yeah, more like slugee," he responded self-consciously, eyes peering out from beneath his jacket's hood.

"I heard you got him pretty good. And that he was being a real ass."

"Nothing new there," Toby said without thinking. He quickly realized how Ashley might take the comment and tried to back peddle a bit. "No offense."

It was the best halfhearted retraction he was going to be able to muster. Toby knew how committed Ashley was to her relationship with Mike, but even she had to realize that his being an ass was more the rule than the exception.

"I know he can be…difficult sometimes," she conceded.

To her credit, Ashley didn't use her status to torment kids at school the way her boyfriend did, although she didn't exactly go out of her way to associate with the less popular crowd either. This was already the longest conversation Toby had had with her since they were in middle school, and he had to wonder what was prompting it.

There were times when he felt like being a sheriff's son made him more skeptical of people's intentions than he ought to be. This wasn't one of those times. There had to be some sort of ulterior motive here. What the heck did she want?

"What exactly happened?" she asked. "What did he say to that new girl?"

There it was. They'd arrived at the real conversation Ashley wanted to have. The conversation that would help her begin to determine whether the new girl was going to present a threat.

Of course she was. With Mike, any girl within a thirty-mile radius posed a threat. But after the incident at school, Toby seriously doubted Rachel would have anything to do with the cocky jock. He wasn't sure how much of that doubt he wanted to share with Ashley though. He certainly wasn't in the mood to make Mike's life any easier.

Let her be suspicious and give the bastard some grief. He deserved it. As Toby considered how to best phrase his response, he spotted headlights approaching from down the street. He quickly recognized the advancing vehicle as Mike's pickup.

"I don't want to say anything that might affect your guys' relationship," he replied, nodding his hooded head toward the truck. "You should ask *him* what happened."

Mike slowed his pickup and pulled up alongside them, immediately challenging Ashley. "What are you doing with this prick?"

"He's walking me home," she fired back. "My boyfriend apparently had better things to do than pick me up after cheer practice."

Mike looked to Toby and flashed a superior grin. "I was taking care of a little unfinished business with Schaffer."

"What's that supposed to mean?" Toby asked, taking a step toward the vehicle. As soon as he took the step, he wondered what he expected his posturing to accomplish. If he were to actually provoke Mike to get out of the pickup, the results would likely be the same as they'd been earlier—beat down.

"Oh, you'll see," Mike replied, showing no immediate interest in giving Toby another pounding. He'd apparently met his quota of ass kickings for the day. "You'll be getting the same treatment soon enough."

He turned his attention to Ashley. "C'mon, babe. Get in."

Ashley shot Toby an apologetic look. Maybe she really did appreciate what a jerk her boyfriend was. She began walking backward toward the truck, staying turned away from Mike as she quietly revealed the other reason she'd tracked Toby down.

"By the way, thanks for not saying anything around school about my fucked-up family," she murmured softly, so that only Toby could hear. "I'll get Mike to tell me what he did to Nate. Make sure he's okay."

Toby had completely forgotten about the previous day's confrontation between his dad and Mr. Schultz, which had resulted in Mr. Shultz spending the night in jail. Meeting Rachel afterward had knocked the event from his memory.

He was happy to let his unintentional thoughtfulness score him some points though, especially if it meant Ashley would find out what had happened to Nate.

"No problem," he whispered back. "And thanks."

As Mike pulled out onto the road, Ashley noticed the shit-eating grin still plastered across his face. She pursed her lips, irritated. He could be such a child sometimes. Most of the time, actually. A selfish, narcissistic, obnoxiously cocky child.

But he was also an All-State linebacker who was receiving full-ride offers from Oregon and Washington State. Mike was well on his way to escaping this nowhere town and becoming someone special, and Ashley was determined to escape with him—and maybe help him start acting more like an adult somewhere along the way.

She quirked her mouth in annoyance. "Just tell me he's all right."

"He looked all right when we left him," Mike replied with a nonchalant shrug.

Ashley already had a bone to pick with her boyfriend concerning his possibly hitting on the new Indian girl at school, and his self-satisfaction over what was sure to be just another childish prank was only adding fuel to her fire.

She'd never understood why he enjoyed picking on the unpopular kids so much. It wasn't like she'd ever want to spend a Saturday night with the math team, but she'd also never seen the point in tearing down those who were socially beneath her.

As head cheerleader and class vice president, she would have no shortage of targets if she ever changed her mind, but Ashley had other plans. She was setting her sights on those above her. Those who had tormented her during a very traumatic middle school experience that had included several bad cases of acne in sixth grade, braces with headgear in seventh, and breasts that had waited until the very end of her eighth grade year to finally develop.

Those like Deanna Schuster, the previous captain of the cheer squad. Deanna was the type who demanded adoration that she'd done nothing to deserve. She'd kept two of the squad's most talented members off the team first semester just because they hadn't tweeted enough glowing compliments about her during tryouts.

The quota had been twelve, and each had been more painful for Ashley to write than the one before, but she'd been driven. She composed twenty-five flattering tweets, made the squad, and started her insurgence before the first week of practice was over.

Ashley found allies within the squad quickly, and three weeks later, Deanna was no longer captain. She no longer required adulation. She was no longer special.

Ashley was, and, unlike Deanna, she'd earned the adoration she received. With junior year almost over, she had climbed to the top of the social ladder and was already formulating her strategy for doing the same once she started college. She was never going to be that awkward, picked-on, fourteen-year-old outcast ever again.

And that's where Mike came in. As a scholarship athlete, he'd have major social status the moment he stepped onto a college campus. Status she, as his girlfriend, could take advantage of to get in with the elite crowd. Once in, she'd find every diva-wannabe who'd never struggled a day in her life for anything, yet felt she was owed everything, and take her down—while of course making her own way to the top.

She'd first need to get her foot in the door though, and simple Twitter posts wouldn't accomplish that. As exasperating as he could be, Ashley knew she needed Mike's help to become special among the college crowd.

Right now, however, she just needed him to tell her what he'd done to Nate.

"Left him where?" she asked.

CHAPTER 7

RESERVATION HORROR STORY

Crisscrossing his flashlight beam with Ashley's, Mike scanned the cavernous pit in the forest floor. He saw no movement inside the underground enclosure. Not a single sign that the skinny geek was still down there. Just a small pile of bones and a lot of dark and quiet.

Ashley called out, breaking the silence. "Nate?"

Mike joined in. "Shaffer! Come on out and show yourself if you're down there."

Nothing. The only sounds Mike heard in response to their shouting were the chirps and hoots of the woods' nighttime creatures. He darted his flashlight beam out of the cavern and landed it on Ashley. She held a hand up to block the light from her eyes and shot him a look to let him know she was still plenty miffed.

"See?" He lowered the flashlight and clicked it off. "I told you the little shit would find a way out."

Ashley shook her head and turned back toward the pickup. Mike watched her as she strode through the shafts of lunar light that shone down through the trees, her ponytail swaying from side to side. He threw his hands up, not understanding what she was making such a big deal about, and followed after her.

Somewhere off in the distance there was a faint howl.

Climbing into his truck, Mike glanced over to see Ashley sitting in the passenger seat, arms crossed.

"So what's up?" he asked. "Are you seriously like pissed at me now?"

She stared straight ahead, refusing to respond or even look at him. What the hell was she so angry about? Nate had clearly found a way out. As far as Mike was concerned, it was time for her to stop worrying about the scrawny dweeb and start rewarding him for coming back out here in the first place. After all, now that they'd made the drive, they might as well take advantage of being alone in the woods.

He leaned in on Ashley, attempting to change the mood. "Nice night, huh?"

She let out a disgusted sigh and instantly leaned away. "I just want to go home."

Now *he* was getting pissed. "What's your problem?"

She finally looked over at him, regarding him with a cold speculation. "Did you hit on the new girl today?"

"What?" Mike's eyes widened. What had she heard? What had Hoffman told her? He should have dragged that punk out here today too.

"No." Mike dismissed the idea with an uncomfortable scoff. "Did Hoffman say I did?"

Ashley shook her head, too angry to answer. He couldn't really blame her for being pissed, even though he hadn't actually done anything with the new girl...yet.

His loyal girlfriend had already looked past the stories about him and Vanessa Trent in the closet at Jerry Boudreau's party and forgiven him for when he broke up with her for a week so he could bang Debbie Grant. He knew Ashley would forgive him for pretty much anything he did, but not until after she'd given him plenty of grief for it. Fact was, she'd always have a reason to rip him a new one, but tonight he just wasn't in the mood.

And it didn't look like he was going to get any of what he *was* in the mood for. Mike opened the door to get out of the truck.

"Where are you going?" Ashley asked impatiently.

"I gotta take a piss." He hopped out and walked toward a small embankment.

Ashley flipped on the radio, turning the knob hard, and music blasted from the speakers. Startled, Mike glanced back to see his vexed girlfriend pulling her smartphone from her bag. He groaned as she began typing out a text.

Great. Time for another Facebook post about how he was being an asshole again. Walking over a nearby ridge and trotting down the other side, he wondered just how many dirty looks he'd be receiving from her friends at school in the morning.

"Drive all the way out here and not even a piece of tit," Mike muttered as he unzipped and relieved himself on some brush.

Another howl cut through the night air, closer this time. Mike jumped, slightly pissing himself. "Dammit."

Just like all the other kids in town, he'd been told plenty of reservation-based horror stories growing up. He started to recollect a few of them as he looked around at the dark forest, growing uneasy.

He turned toward the truck, calling to Ashley. "Hey, did you hear that?"

Of course she hadn't. She couldn't hear anything over the blaring radio, including him. It was probably that damn music that had the animal so worked up. He assumed it had to be a coyote, although the howl had sounded deeper than any cry he'd ever heard a coyote make.

Moments later, a low, guttural growl came from behind a crop of trees to his right. It was definitely not the whiny snarl of some scraggly coyote. Whatever this thing was, it was big.

And it was close.

Mike's mind conjured up more images of the ghouls and monsters he'd been told about in those scary childhood bedtime stories. He zipped up and started scrambling toward his truck, making it only a couple steps before stumbling over a tree stump. From somewhere in the shadows behind him, he could hear footfalls approaching. Another growl.

His hands twisted over dirt and shrubs as he worked to regain his balance, trying to pick up the pace. Just about a half dozen more steps and he'd be to the top of the ridge. The panicked athlete took three more strides before tripping on an exposed root. He hit the ground hard, knocking the air from his lungs.

His heart now felt as though it was pounding in his throat. Hearing the animal's muffled footfalls trotting up the embankment, Mike guessed it couldn't be more than a few feet behind him. He jerked his head around to see what it was, but all he could make out in the moment prior to the attack were giant white fangs and two glowing yellow eyes.

The bully's screams were barely distinguishable over the latest chart-topping hit from that new pop tart with the electric blue hair. Ashley was blanking on her name. She turned down the radio and looked in the direction in which her boyfriend had walked off, uncertain if she'd actually heard anything.

She listened intently for a moment and detected a faint crunching sound coming from the other side of the embankment.

"Mike?"

Silence.

"Mike," she called out again. "Quit messing around."

Again she got no response. Her agitation growing, Ashley sent the text she'd been typing and shoved her phone back into her bag. She then slid across the pickup's bench seat, positioning herself behind the wheel. Putting the pickup into drive, she slowly turned it toward the ridge, leaning forward to peer into the forest. Her face dimly lit by the dashboard lights, she let a deep sigh escape past her lips.

Why did Mike have to be such an ass? Was this his idea of teaching her a lesson?

Not long ago, she began considering the possibility of finding a new prospective boyfriend once she'd arrived at whichever college she and Mike decided on attending—just as a backup plan in case he were to suffer a career-ending injury or something. Situations like this made her think she'd want to start that search on the first day of orientation. It would be nice to have the option to drop him quickly if his childish behavior didn't improve.

The thought of finding someone new made her smile as she drove the pickup over the ridge. Maybe she'd even be able to find someone she shared some common interests with. These were pleasant thoughts, but the moment she clicked on the truck's high beams, all those dulcet dreams vanished. The color left her face and her mouth burst open to let loose a horrified scream.

Toby lay on his bed trying to focus on *The Hero with a Thousand Faces,* but it was no use. He'd get through a paragraph, maybe two, and then his mind would return to his confrontation with Mike—both confrontations actually—and the equally poor results of the face-off he'd had with Principal Carter. He tried shifting positions, but it wasn't as if lying on his left side instead of his right was going to help him stop obsessing over all the things he could have said or done differently.

His cell beeped to alert him of a text message. Thankful to have something else to think about, even for just a few seconds, Toby eagerly snatched the phone off his bedside table. The text was from Ashley. He stared at her name on the phone's display, a little stunned that she'd actually followed through on her promise.

Toby had, of course, also been trying to find out what happened to Nate. He'd called his friend several times, but only gotten Nate's voice mail.

He opened the text message and read it, furrowing his brow. He quickly closed the text and tried calling Nate one more time. After several rings, his friend's voice mail picked up yet again.

"You've reached the slayer of the Leviathan. Guess I'm too busy dominating to take your call."

Toby hung up, bothered. The slayer of Leviawhoever had been too busy to take his calls or answer his texts for almost three hours now. He'd never known Nate to be that unavailable.

Ashley's message had mentioned where she and Mike had gone looking for Nate, and Toby decided he needed to go have a look there too. He jumped off his bed and headed downstairs, hustling through the living room. His pace slowed as he neared the kitchen. Stopping in the doorway, he looked past an ornate, cherry wood kitchen table to a key ring that hung by the back door.

His belly stirred as he stood at the edge of the room listening to the hum of the refrigerator. After a deep breath to quell his queasy stomach, Toby stepped forward. His feet whisked across the hardwood floor until he was standing in front of the plastic ring, staring at the keys that dangled from it.

Toby hadn't driven since the night of his mother's death, and the thought of getting back behind the wheel brought with it recollections of the accident. First there was the thunderous splashing down of the Equinox into the lazily flowing river, then the vivid fear of drowning. Finally there was the panic. He remembered the way it had seized him when he couldn't find his mom in the dark, murky waters.

He had to get past this. Nate could be in trouble. There wasn't time for indecision. Just grab the keys and let's go.

CHAPTER 8

NOT MY BLOOD

Cruising down an empty two-lane highway, Toby formulated his search plan. Ashley's text had said she and Mike had driven out to the reservation to look for Nate, but unfortunately it hadn't said specifically where. Different kids hung out at different spots, but there were a handful of locations that were pretty commonly shared among everyone at school. Toby would start with those.

"Thanks for driving me out here," he said, glancing toward the driver's seat. "It's just that I don't actually have a driver's license yet, so…"

Not that *that* was the reason he wasn't driving.

Rachel sat next to him, behind the wheel of her canary yellow Jeep. It was apparently a gift from her new stepfather.

"It's no problem, although I'm not sure how much help I'll be," Rachel said, as she glanced at Ashley's text. "I've never seen an 'underground cave thingy' in these woods before."

Toby managed a slight grin in response as she handed him back his phone. In a way, her presence made this nighttime excursion kind of fun. He was actually happy to be out of his room for once, despite the unfortunate reason.

He was happy to be with her.

The forest on either side of the road grew deeper and darker as they approached the land designated for the Umatilla Indian Reservation. Toby tried to ignore the elation he felt from being in Rachel's company and instead focus on the task at hand—finding Nate.

"I could call my uncle," she offered. "But he's never mentioned anything to me about there being a cave or cavern out here."

It really wasn't much to go on. Toby had texted Ashley back asking for a few more specifics, but she hadn't responded. It looked like "underground cave thingy" was as good a lead as they were going to get.

Rachel began to nervously twirl a lock of her raven hair around her index finger as she briefly changed the subject. "So listen, I, um…I wanted to say thanks for what you did at school today."

Toby shrugged off her gratitude uncomfortably. "It was no big deal."

"It was no big deal to get beat up?"

"Well, no, I mean…I guess I didn't really think too much about the consequences. It just felt like I should do something."

"How come?"

"I don't know." Toby shifted uncomfortably again. "Mike has a way of making kids feel kind of…powerless. It's not a fun feeling, and I should know because I've been feeling it a lot lately. To be honest, I think it might have been because of you that I finally decided to stop feeling, and acting, that way all the time."

"Well, yeah." Rachel smirked and rolled her eyes. "Because I was dumb enough to get the school's biggest asshole pissed at me on my first day."

Toby shook his head. "No. Not because of that. It's, like, your whole attitude. The way you're not afraid to take on stuff. Like, with you and your mom moving to Silver Falls and everything, and how you just deal with it. I guess you kind of inspired me or something."

Rachel's smirk turned into a sincere smile, but her appreciative response to Toby's words went unnoticed. Something up ahead, off to the side of the road, had caught his attention.

"I didn't mean to just take off like that," she said. "The whole thing kind of caught me off guard, and I didn't really know *how* to react. Once I saw you were okay, I just kind of got out of there. I hope you didn't get in too much trouble."

Rachel might as well have been talking to the floor mats. Toby was locked in on a large white object over in the brush, visible just ahead of the tree line.

"Could you click on your high beams?" he asked.

Noticing the object, Rachel did just that, and the extra light revealed it to be the back of a pickup. The vehicle apparently had veered off the road and come to rest in a ditch.

"Is that a truck?" Rachel asked.

Not just any truck. As they got closer, Toby realized it was Mike's pickup.

Rachel jerked the steering wheel and pulled over, parking directly behind the vehicle. The two of them sat and watched the truck for at least a minute or two, looking for any sign of movement. There was none.

"I've got a flashlight in the glove compartment," Rachel offered quietly.

Toby opened the compartment and grabbed it. "I'm gonna take a closer look."

Glancing at the night sky, he swallowed the lump in his throat, and got out of the Jeep. He stepped cautiously across the highway pavement, darting the flashlight over the tall grass and brush that partially enveloped the pickup. It occurred to him that Mike and Ashley might be rolling around in the bushes somewhere nearby. Except that wouldn't explain why Mike had parked like such a jackass.

The truck seemed to be pretty well wedged into the ditch it'd been driven into. The front bumper was buried deep in the dirt on the far side, preventing the front right tire from touching the bottom of the trench.

Toby stepped down into the ditch, sliding right alongside the truck until he was able to check the passenger side door handle. It was unlocked. He gave it a pull, and the door swung open with a moaning creak. He aimed the flashlight onto the front seats— empty. He then placed a knee on the passenger seat, leaning in to check the back of the cab.

As he moved the beam onto the rear seats, Ashley sprung up into the light, her eyes wild with panic.

Caught by surprise, Toby jerked back, bumping his head against the doorframe. "Ah, damn!"

Ashley cowered back, shivering and panting anxiously. She turned away and stared out the window with terrified eyes. Bothered by her panicked state, Toby glanced around at their surroundings and tried to discern what she was looking at. If other people were out there, he wasn't seeing them.

"Ashley?" He said her name tentatively, more than a little unsettled. "Are you okay?"

She gave no response, just continued to rock back and forth. Toby was now seriously freaked out. Ashley had seen something out here that scared her witless and he had to wonder how close whatever she saw still was. And where the hell was Mike?

"Is she all right?"

Toby glanced back to see Rachel standing a few feet from the pickup, looking equally concerned.

"I don't know." He motioned for her to come closer. "Can you help me get her out of here?"

They each took an arm and helped the catatonic Ashley out of the truck and into the passenger seat of Rachel's Jeep. After his high school's head cheerleader was settled in, Toby stepped back from the vehicle and surveyed the area again with the flashlight. Should he call out? Nate could be close, but then so could whoever, or whatever, had Ashley so spooked. He glanced over to the opposite side of the highway and went rigid.

Two luminous yellow eyes stared out at him from the forest.

The dim outline of the animal behind the glowing eyes was barely distinguishable. However, Toby could still tell it was massive. He instinctively swung his flashlight over to get a better look, but the animal turned and abruptly loped off. He caught just a glimpse of fur as it disappeared deeper into the trees.

Toby was amazed by how fast the thing had moved, given how large he'd thought it had been. Maybe the trees' shadows had made the creature appear bigger than it actually was. Everything had happened so fast, Toby was only half sure he'd spotted any-thing at all.

No, he definitely had. He'd definitely seen those yellow eyes.

"Do you see something?" Rachel's voice came from directly behind him.

Toby jumped, startled. He gathered his wits and looked back at the spot where he'd glimpsed the pair of lucent eyeballs. "Um…I'm not sure. But I think we should get back in the Jeep."

Toby backpedaled to the rear seats and hopped in. Rachel slid in behind the wheel, giving the panic-stricken Ashley a sympathetic glance.

"So now what?" she asked, her concerned eyes looking at Toby in the rearview mirror.

"We know we're close to…something," he answered. "Let's go a little further."

"You sure that's a good idea?"

"No," Toby answered matter-of-factly. "But Nate could be just around the next bend. I want to keep looking for a little bit longer before we turn back."

Rachel nodded in agreement. Toby figured she probably felt at least a tinge of guilt for setting this all in motion. It was a pretty safe bet that they wouldn't be out here if Nate had just given Mike his calculus homework.

She pulled out onto the road, barely getting the speedometer over fifteen miles per hour as they scoured what little of the for-est they could see before the trees dissolved into an impenetrable blackness.

"What could she have seen to get like this?" Rachel asked.

THE ONE YOU FEED

Obviously it was a rhetorical question. Nobody in the car, except for Ashley, could say what she'd seen, and what she'd seen had put her in a state where she couldn't say anything at all. However, if Toby had to guess, he would guess death.

When he was ten years old, he'd seen the same stricken, saucer-eyed look that Ashley bore now. His family had just moved to Silver Falls, maybe a week or two before that Sunday morning when he'd answered the door to find Troy Harris standing on the front steps with a similar traumatized expression.

Troy had been out hunting bucks with his cousin and accidentally had shot the man with a Remington Bolt Action Rifle. His cousin had died from the injury by the time Troy got him back to their truck. After securing the body inside the trailer bed, he came straight over to report the fatal incident to Toby's dad.

It was a morning—and a look—Toby would never forget. And it was how he knew that death made someone look the way Ashley did now. Maybe she'd seen something happen or had just stumbled across the gruesome aftermath, but Toby felt it was the only explanation for why she seemed so rattled.

Rachel slammed on the brakes, snapping Toby back into the moment.

Several yards ahead, Nate stepped out from behind some bushes and wandered into the road. His shirt was torn at the shoulder and covered in blood. His head swiveled about, as if he was lost or just really confused about something. It seemed as though he didn't even notice that he was standing in the middle of the highway, or that he was only a few yards away from Rachel's Jeep, despite being bathed in its headlights.

After several seconds, he finally turned and seemed to register the vehicle.

Then he ran over to it, not appearing to be in any sort of pain. Nate jumped into the rear seats next to Toby, but instead of saying anything, he kept his eyes focused on the trees and shadows around them. There was no acknowledgment, no explanation. Nate was still seemingly unsure of where he was or what was happening.

Toby stared in stunned disbelief at his disoriented friend. "Are you okay?"

Nate nodded blankly, offering no additional reply.

"What the hell happened?" Toby grabbed his friend's forearm and jostled him slightly. "Hey. What happened to you?"

Nate just stared out at the road and then back at the forest.

Toby tried again. "Nate?"

"Nothing," he responded quietly, looking down at the red splotches on his arms and clothes. "Nothing happened to me. It's not my blood."

"Your shirt is all torn up," Toby said urgently. "I can see the blood on your shoulder."

Nate took the flashlight from Toby's hand and clicked it on. He then flashed the beam onto his shoulder and leaned over to give Toby a closer look at the skin underneath his tattered shirt. Sure enough, there wasn't a single scrape.

Toby stared at Nate's shoulder, astonished. "Whose blood is this then?"

"I don't know."

"What do you mean you don't know?"

"I mean I don't know!" Nate shouted, finally seeming engaged in the conversation. "I don't know whose blood it is or where it came from! I just woke up and..." He trailed off and looked back out at the surrounding forest. "Are we on the reservation?"

Toby and Rachel exchanged a concerned glance. Nate noticed the look and glanced toward the front seats, only then seeming to realize that Rachel and Ashley were sitting there. His eyes stayed on Ashley as she stared back at him. His presence seemed to ratchet up her anxiety another notch, and she began to shake even more severely.

"Why is Ashley Schultz here?" he asked. "And what's wrong with her?"

"She's in like...shock or something," Rachel responded.

"In shock from what?"

"From what?" Toby repeated incredulously, his voice cracking a bit. "You're covered in blood! *Something happened out here.* Do you seriously not remember anything?"

Once again Nate gave no response. He just looked back out at the forest.

Toby noticed Rachel absentmindedly twirling her hair again and looking very uncomfortable. Who could blame her? They were sitting in the middle of the road with a terrified mute and a bloody mess, neither of whom could offer any details about what they'd been through. Never mind that they were all sitting ducks, stopped near a location where something *clearly* horrible had just happened.

Toby decided he was going to figure out what that something was. The decision was as impromptu as the one he'd made to slug Mike in the hallway at school that day, and it felt just as right.

Ever since the night of his accident, he'd lived with a debilitating grief and draining guilt that he couldn't do anything about. Or, at least he hadn't thought he could do anything about them. He now realized he'd only been partially right. The grief was as permanent as his mother's death, but he could do something about the guilt. That stemmed from his failure to rescue her, from his failure to act, from his always feeling too afraid to be the hero.

He could counter that failure and guilt by succeeding in helping others, starting with Nate and Ashley. He was going to get to the bottom of whatever had happened to them on the reservation. It was simply something he had to do.

"Can we go home now?" Rachel asked anxiously.

Yes. That was a good idea. The start of Toby's investigation could wait until morning. It would be much safer and more productive in the light of day. Maybe he'd even feel more comfortable driving.

Toby had done his best to explain the few facts he knew about why Ashley had been out on the reservation and how he'd come to find her. He'd tried to make it sound as innocuous as possible, but despite knowing her daughter was safe, Mrs. Schultz seemed more concerned *after* she'd heard his story than she was before he'd started it. Ashley had remained in traumatized silence throughout.

With nothing more to add, Toby nodded goodbye and headed for Rachel's Jeep. As he walked across the Schultzes' front lawn, he looked up to see Nate and Rachel leaning against the vehicle, anxiously waiting for him.

"Did she say anything when she saw her mom?" Nate asked as Toby approached. His behavior had returned to somewhat closer to normal once they'd gotten back into town.

Toby shook his head, unsettled. "Not a word."

His mind raced as he tried to make sense of the night's events. If Ashley wasn't able to provide any answers, Toby wasn't sure where they would come from. There just wasn't enough information to even try to speculate on what might have happened to her and Nate.

He said the only thing he could think of to say. "We need to go back out there."

Rachel and Nate both gaped at him.

"Like right now?" Rachel asked.

"No, not now. In the morning."

She considered the idea for a moment and shook her head. "I don't think it's a good idea for me to be playing hooky on my second day."

Toby nodded, appreciating her unique position. He turned to Nate. "You up for it?"

"I don't want to go back out there."

"But we *have* to go back out there."

"No, we don't," Nate squawked. "I've got a ton of homework I still have to get done, and I'm pretty sure you've got a first period U.S. history test to worry about."

"You're covered in blood," Toby shot back. "*That's* what I'm worried about."

Seeing as how the blood wasn't Nate's, Toby could understand how his friend might not want to remember where it came from. The argument could definitely be made that the best thing for them all to do was to pretend like this night had never happened. Everyone had at least come back from the reservation safe, if not one hundred percent sound.

And it was true that he had a U.S. history test first thing in the morning.

The thing was, he didn't care about the test, just like he hadn't cared about much of anything since the accident. But *this* he cared about. As tempting as it might be to do so, they couldn't just act like the past few hours hadn't happened. Not after everything they'd been through.

"Come on," Toby urged. "My dad won't be home from working the night shift until maybe nine or ten. I could pick you up around seven, and we could go have a look around. Just for an hour."

Rachel shot him a perplexed look. "I thought you didn't have a license."

"I don't," Toby responded. "But it'll be a quick trip."

It would also be in the light of day and wouldn't require that they cross any bridges. It was a drive he felt fairly certain he'd be able to make.

Nate tried again to talk his way out of a return trip to the reservation. "I told you, I have a ton of homework."

"Forget about your homework," Toby said assertively. "Today at school you told me you were worried about how I haven't really tried at much of anything lately. Well, this is something I want to try at. Let me help you figure out what happened out there—figure out where all that blood came from."

"I didn't hurt anyone," Nate said defensively. But immediately after spitting out the words, he looked uncertain. "I mean, I'm sure I'd remember if I…"

"Let's go find out for sure." Toby gave him an encouraging pat on his unbloodied shoulder. "The best thing for us to do is to try to figure out what happened and how to deal with it before Ashley starts telling everyone what she saw."

Toby could almost see the gears working inside his friend's head as Nate mulled over his options. The slayer of Leviathan clearly had his concerns about whether he'd slain someone in real life.

"So how about seven o'clock?" Toby prodded.

Nate nodded reluctantly. "Yeah, okay. Seven o'clock."

CHAPTER 9

THE THING UNDER THE GROUND

Toby barely slept a wink that night. Visions of Ashley's saucer-eyed stare, Nate's bloody, but uninjured shoulder, and those menacing yellow eyes flickered like an old home movie on the inside of his eyelids every time he tried to close them.

As he stood weary in the reservation woods the following morning, he figured there had to be a tale behind each of those images, perhaps even an explanation that tied them all together. But he was running out of time to find his first clue as to what that explanation might be.

The morning's investigation of the reservation's dew-covered forest had only consisted of Nate mutely scanning the trees, looking discouraged and unsure.

Their silent search was interrupted by the sound of a car whizzing down the highway asphalt, somewhere beyond the tree line behind them. Toby had stayed quietly optimistic for as long as he could. His dad wouldn't approve of him driving without a license, or without an adult in the car, so he needed to get the hatchback home before the sheriff of Silver Falls returned from working the night shift.

The day of the accident in the Chetco River was supposed to have been Toby's last as an unlicensed driver. He and his mom had planned to go to the DMV in Oakridge the next morning so he could take the driver's exam. A trip they'd never take together, and one he still hadn't.

"This is pretty much right where I picked you up last night," Toby said with a hint of desperation in his voice. "Nothing looks familiar?"

"It all looks the same," Nate responded. "Trees."

"What's the last thing you remember?"

"Running," Nate replied. "They were chasing me with paintball guns. Jerry had just shot me. I tried to duck behind some trees and then…"

Nate trailed off, as though he'd recollected something, then started to walk with purpose, striding through the woods. Toby hustled after him, growing hopeful.

As they weaved through blue spruces and Ponderosa pines, Toby was surprised by how gracefully his friend traversed the uneven terrain. Nate moved like he was striding down a sidewalk, while Toby's feet seemed to find every exposed root and divot in the forest floor.

He tripped and almost fell as he ducked under the extended branch of an Oregon ash. Nate cut to the right and Toby followed him, yet again stumbling over an uncovered root. Gritting his teeth, he kept hobbling, trying to walk off the throbbing in his big toe. Eventually, he came to a clearing to find Nate staring down into what appeared to be an underground cave.

"I remember this," Nate said. "Or, at least I think I do."

Toby stepped up alongside him and looked down into the cavern. The gleaming, early morning sun penetrated the shadows just enough for him to see how far the drop was.

"Ashley's text said that she and Mike came to a cave like this to look for you," Toby replied. "Do you remember falling down there?"

"I remember *being* down there," Nate said softly. "Or, not really being down there, but, looking up."

"How the hell did you get out?"

Instead of responding, Nate suddenly twisted his head around to look at the forest behind them. His eyes studied the trees, like a deer that had sensed a predator. "Did you hear that?"

"Hear what?"

"Footsteps."

Toby hadn't heard a sound.

Nate's eyes locked onto something. Toby followed his gaze and spotted an elderly, disheveled Indian with a wild rat's nest of black hair standing among the trees. The gaunt-looking man wore shabby clothes that appeared to be made from animal skin and stood perfectly still, just staring at them.

Although Toby knew they were well within their rights to be where they were, the Indian's scrutinizing, deep-set eyes made him feel as though he and Nate were trespassing.

"Good morning, sir." Toby attempted to greet the man. "Um, sorry if we disturbed you. We're just looking for something my friend forgot out here."

The Indian turned and stalked off, apparently uninterested in what Toby had to say. He moved in a nimble, fluid motion, seeming to glide across the forest floor. In a matter of moments, he was no longer in view.

"Well, that was weird," Toby said, pulling out his smartphone to check the time.

Nate returned his focus to the black abyss below ground, studying it with a strange fascination that Toby was also starting to find a bit bizarre.

Staring at a hole in the ground wasn't providing them with any answers. Unfortunately, they didn't have time to look for anything else that might. Even if they left right now, Toby would be lucky to get the car back before his dad got home from the station.

This was truly disappointing. He had thought they'd for sure find something that would help him make sense of the previous night's surreal events. Then, as Toby took one last look inside the cavern, he had another thought altogether. What if none of the previous night's events were in fact *real*?

His friends had been trying for weeks to find a way to snap him out of his funk. What if everything that had happened was just one big distraction cooked up by Nate to help Toby take his mind off the accident and his mother's death?

He eyed his friend for a moment. Doubtful. And it was even more doubtful that Ashley would have gone along with it. However, as the sheriff's son, Toby had been taught to look at every angle when trying to make sense of a situation he didn't understand. Ashley *had* been really grateful about him not telling the kids at school about her parents fighting and Mr. Schultz getting taken down to the station.

Toby looked past his potentially scheming friend and spotted a set of tire tracks that went up over a nearby ridge. He momentarily shook away his thoughts of a grand conspiracy and followed the tracks. But within a couple of steps, he was already starting to feel suspicious again, even a bit foolish.

Was all this being a cleverly planned hoax really harder to believe than the alternative? Was it more plausible to think that Nate had been involved in some super-bloody fiasco that had left Ashley stupefied and mute?

He wondered what his friend's end game could possibly be if this was indeed an elaborate diversion. What had Nate used for the fake blood?

The hardest thing to rationalize was Mike's involvement. There was no way he'd go along with something like this. Unless... Maybe Ashley had somehow made it worth his while. Maybe his resuming his bullying yesterday wasn't just a coincidence but actually a part of the show, a clever misdirection.

Toby felt like he was on to something, and he was also starting to feel really stupid for not seeing it all sooner. Then he reached the top of the ridge.

And then he felt sick.

Every inch of his skin prickled as his insides went numb. This wasn't a hoax. It was something much, much worse than anything his friends could have dreamt up. Nauseating spurts of adrenaline coursed through his veins. He stumbled back a few steps, then turned and retched.

The first thought that popped into his head was that Mike had been stabbed, but he quickly discounted that notion. The jock's body hadn't just been cut. It had been ripped apart—shredded and strewn about the forest.

Toby glanced over to see Nate staring at him with wide, worried eyes.

"What is it?" his friend asked fearfully.

Both the boys were too distracted by the bushy-haired one's discovery to notice Bimisi Chochopi watching them from just beyond the tree line. He studied them with pinched eyes. This wasn't something he'd accounted for. While his sharp facial features showed no signs of concern, he was in reality quite bothered by their discovery of the cavern.

He turned to the Indian standing beside him, Dyami Askuwheteau, who was a good twenty years his elder. "What should we do?"

"We needn't do anything," Dyami answered evenly.

It was Dyami who had first told Bimisi about the cavern and the stories of what had been buried inside. For a long time, that's all Bimisi had thought they were—stories. Then about two months ago, on the day his sister-in-law had told him about her plans to move to Silver Falls and one day after he'd lost his job at Bruce Bennett's factory, Dyami had brought him here.

The location of this clearing was known by only a select few members of their tribe—the ones who knew just how real the stories were. The ones who had been selected to watch over the cavern. By bringing Bimisi here, Dyami had officially recruited him into an exclusive club of guardians.

"Many in our *own tribe* do not even know of this place's existence," Bimisi protested. "Or about what lives here under the ground."

"It lives above ground now," Dyami corrected.

The elder turned and sauntered back into the woods. Bimisi stayed put, watching the boys for another moment. As the scrawny one went to join the one with the bushy hair at the top of the ridge, Bimisi noticed how he moved much more gracefully than his awkward frame suggested he should. It was a bit unsettling. Then, just as his friend had, the scrawny boy buckled over and retched when he reached the top of the embankment.

It lives above ground now.

Dyami was right. Whoever these kids shared their discovery with would soon die right along with them. No action was needed. Bimisi slipped back into the forest, going unnoticed by the two white intruders.

Walter Hoffman stepped out of his police SUV and onto the gray asphalt of Highway 70. He surveyed the forest around him, his eyes coming to rest on Mary's hatchback parked a little farther up the road. How long had this been going on?

Toby knew better than to drive around without a license. If he'd gotten comfortable behind the wheel again, why hadn't he just asked Walter to schedule another road test?

Billy got out of the passenger side of the SUV and noticed the car as well. "Hey, isn't that—"

"Yep," Walter replied before Billy could finish the question. He furrowed his brow and walked toward the trees, calling out for his son. "Toby!"

"Over here," Toby's voice called back from somewhere within the woods.

Walter and his deputy continued straight through the forest for several yards until they walked out into a clearing to find Toby and Nate standing near the opening to an underground cave.

"Where is he?" Walter asked brusquely.

His son glanced uncomfortably at a nearby ridge. "What's left of him is just over that hill."

Walter looked at the embankment while asking a question he already knew the answer to. "Was that our car I saw parked back on the side of the highway?"

Toby's head and shoulders dropped. "I know I'm not supposed to be driving, but…" Unsure of how to explain his actions, or more accurately, of what sort of explanation he wanted to make up, Toby trailed off.

Walter gave him another moment to think, then pressed him. "But what?"

"But Nate forgot something out here last night," he answered in a barely audible mumble. "And he needed a ride so he could come back and find it. Then when we saw Mike, well, obviously I knew I had to call you."

"What was Nate doing out here last night?"

"Mike and a few kids from school were messing with him, chasing him around…"

Walter pointed toward the ridge. "That Mike?"

"Yeah, but they got separated before whatever happened to him happened," Toby replied quickly.

Walter moved his eyes to Nate, who remained by the cavern. His son's friend stared at the ground, shifting his weight from side to side while apprehensively kicking at a patch of dirt.

"What did he forget?" Walter asked.

"That's…kind of hard to explain."

Walter studied the boys for a long moment. He would need a lot more answers from these two, but for the time being Walter was far more concerned about *what* his son had found than how he'd come to find it.

What had happened to Henry Jennings was no longer an isolated incident.

He snapped his fingers and beckoned Nate over. The boy plodded toward him, dragging his feet, until he stood alongside Toby.

"You're both okay?" the sheriff asked.

Toby and Nate answered with nods. Walter extended his palm toward his son. "Give me the keys. Billy will drive you and Nate back into town."

"Then what?" Toby asked anxiously. "I don't know what attacked Mike, but whatever it was, it's—"

"For me to worry about," Walter interrupted. "You get your butt to school. And you come straight home after. We're going to talk some more about what the heck you were doing out here."

Toby sheepishly handed over the keys.

Billy stepped behind them, putting a hand to each boy's back, and began guiding them in the general direction of the SUV. Walter watched them walk into the woods until they disappeared from sight. He then started up the embankment.

About halfway up the short hill he stopped with a sudden thought and turned to shout some final orders. "And not a word about this to anyone until I've talked to Mike's family."

"Got it, boss," he heard Billy call back, his words muffled by the forest's lush evergreens.

Stories of Henry's death, and the manner it came in, had already started to spread around town. Walter had no intentions of trying to hide Mike Mulligan's demise, but he wanted to have some control over how the details were released. The way people were informed would make all the difference in how they reacted. The sheriff's hope was to steer the residents toward justified concern and away from frenzied panic.

Then he reached the top of the embankment and laid eyes on the ravaged remains—a gruesome mess of blood and guts strewn across the forest floor.

Walter spun away from the sight, turning his back on the carnage to try to settle his nerves. It didn't help. The images of detached limbs, guts, and blood were stuck in his eyes like the remnants of a bright light he couldn't blink away. He stared at a small cluster of blue spruces for a long moment before turning back to what was left of Mike's body.

Maybe frenzied panic was the more rational response.

The boy's torso was still reasonably intact, but it had been separated from the lower half of his body just below the ribs. One leg lay nearby. His arms were each ten or fifteen feet away. Intestines and other internal organs had been shredded and now dusted the area like bright pink confetti. Walter wondered if that was a result of the attack or the scavenging raccoons and possums that likely showed up afterward.

He'd call the coroner prior to contacting the mayor. Maybe a closer examination of the second victim would provide some clues as to just what they were dealing with. He'd also want to get a hold of Oregon Wildlife Control and figure out what the steps were for dealing with what appeared to be a bloodthirsty animal. He had no idea what the protocol was for something like this, or if one even existed.

CHAPTER 10

Astonishing Abilities

Nate hustled into honors biology about halfway through the class period. Scurrying past Mr. Sanders, he pretended not to notice how the stoop-shouldered teacher was awarding his tardiness with a disapproving frown.

He surveyed the disinterested faces sitting behind slate-topped tables, looking for an opening. Spotting an available seat in the second row, Nate quickly planted himself in it and opened his notebook.

Not surprisingly, he found it extremely difficult to take his usual copious notes. All he could think about during Mr. Sanders's explanation of protein synthesis were Mike's ravaged remains. What the hell had happened to his former tormentor? Had Ashley seen it happen? Had he? Was it Mike's blood that had ended up all over his shirt and shoulder? If it was, why couldn't he remember? How could he forget?

Just then an image flashed through his head. It lasted only a split second, but was extremely lucid—and mostly teeth. His entire body flinched in reaction to the short clip of a memory, causing him to almost fall off his stool.

Nate repositioned himself on the seat and took a deep breath.

It was the thing he'd seen in the cavern.

It had attacked him, or at least that's what Nate thought he'd just remembered. But he was alive and all in one piece. How was that possible? How had he survived while Mike had ended up in shreds?

And why was Mr. Sanders talking so loudly?

Nate looked up from his notebook and focused on his teacher. While Mr. Sanders didn't appear to be straining to speak, his voice was raised to where it sounded like he was on the verge of shouting. Nate found this super-strange, until he started becoming aware of all the other noises his teacher was competing with.

The first he picked up on was a loud tapping. It almost sounded as if someone were trying to drive a nail into their lab table. Nate glanced over his shoulder at a dark-haired boy, Matt Singer, who was simply rapping his pen absentmindedly against the tabletop.

Then he turned his attention to a girl sitting behind him, Heidi Moser. She was merely chewing gum, but the typically unobtrusive sound smacked and resonated against Nate's eardrums. He covered and uncovered his ears, hoping to make the amplified sounds return to normal.

Another classmate noticed and shot him an odd look.

Nate promptly rested his hands on the table and tried to sit still. Eying the clock above the door, he apprehensively counted down the remainder of the class period with each distinct click of the second hand.

What the heck was happening to him?

Twenty minutes later, the volume of the class bell nearly caused him to fall out of his seat again. He quickly gathered his books, and his wits, and hurried out into the hallway. He had no reason to believe that whatever he was experiencing might change once he got out of the classroom, but he still hoped like hell it would.

It didn't.

Nate started focusing on different conversations and quickly realized he was able to hear each and every student, regardless of how far away they were or how softly they were speaking. He stood overwhelmed, unable to process it all. His pulse quickened, and he felt a trickle of sweat roll down from his armpit. He was freaking out, and for good reason.

"How are you feeling?" Rachel's question was swallowed up by the sounds of laughter, lockers slamming, text messages ringing, and all the other noises clamoring for Nate's attention.

"Nate?" She moved into his line of sight. "Hello?"

His eyes went to hers, locking in on them.

"You okay?" she asked, looking more than a little concerned.

Nate had to take a moment to consider how to answer that. He definitely wasn't okay, but he had no idea how to explain what he was experiencing. A simple nod seemed like the best way to reply.

"Listen, I um...I wanted to apologize for yesterday," Rachel continued. "If I hadn't gotten involved with that homework thing—"

"It wasn't your fault," Nate mumbled.

"Well, I feel like it kind of was. At least a little. And so to make up for it I'm inviting you over for pizza tonight."

"You are?" Nate was genuinely caught off guard by the offer, and he assumed the sudden rise in his voice had likely given that away.

"Yeah. And, well, full disclosure...I was hoping maybe you could help me get caught up in calculus too."

For a brief moment, Nate forgot all about the disturbing boost in his sense of hearing. His anxiety was supplanted by a sudden exuberance. Rachel was coming to him for help.

He'd wanted a reason to see her more often and now he had it. Becoming her study partner was the perfect excuse. In fact, helping her get to a point where she was on pace with the rest of the class would probably require they get together at least two nights a week.

Rachel's lips curled into a sheepish grin. "I figured that if you're the one whose homework everybody wants to copy, then you'd probably make a pretty good tutor."

"Sure," he replied excitedly. "I mean, yeah. I can totally help."

"Terrific," she said before quickly changing topics. "So I haven't had a chance to ask Toby yet—did you guys find anything this morning?"

And with that, the horrors of the day came flooding back. Nate opened his mouth to respond, but had no words. He realized he couldn't tell her about what they'd seen. Sheriff Hoffman had ordered them not to say anything to anyone.

Before he could make something up, he detected Jerry's voice among those babbling in the hallway behind him. "Hey, look who got out of the woods."

Nate spun around to see Jerry and Andrew approaching. They made a beeline for him, backing him against the lockers.

"You got my history homework?" Andrew asked.

Jerry ripped Nate's backpack off his shoulder and opened it. "Bet it's in here somewhere." He turned the backpack upside down and dumped its contents onto the hallway floor.

"I ain't looking through that shit," Andrew responded. "And we'll need Mike's assignments too."

"Actually," Nate said hesitantly, "I don't think you will."

He felt the corners of his mouth curl upward, and his inappropriate glee caught him by surprise. Did he really just make a joke about Mike being dead?

Unaware and not amused, Jerry shoved him against the lockers. "You tryin' to be a smart ass?"

What *was* he trying to do? Talking back was only going to make them think he'd forgotten his place, and they'd be all too happy to help him remember it. Jerry gave him another shove, and again Nate banged against the lockers.

The jock got right in his face, crowding him so that Nate had no escape. Feeling completely cornered, something inside him snapped. He impulsively thrust both his palms into the Jerry's chest and pushed him back.

Jerry's feet left the floor as he flew backward. Coming down awkwardly on his heels, the bully stumbled into the wall on the opposite side of the hallway, slamming against it. Everyone standing nearby stopped what they were doing and stared.

It had all happened in an instant and surprised Nate as much as anyone. For the nearly two years he'd suffered through this routine, he'd never considered fight over flight. It was as if he'd acted on impulses that weren't his own.

He'd also just shoved a boy nearly twice his size clear across the hallway.

An especially astounded and rather embarrassed Jerry pushed himself away from the wall and straightened up. "You little prick."

He started toward Nate, his eyes smoldering. The look typically would have sent Nate running, but this time Jerry's actions sparked a swelling rage. Nate swung his arm out, slamming his fist into a nearby locker.

"Back off!" he shouted.

Jerry froze, his expression promptly going from vengeful to stupefied. Seeing the stunned look on the bully's face, Nate glanced over at the locker he'd struck. The door was caved in, looking as though it had been hit with a sledgehammer.

Nate stared down with disbelief at his tightened fist. It didn't even hurt.

Equally flabbergasted students started to gather around and gaze at the dented locker. Someone snapped a picture with their smartphone. Jerry tried to stay tough, given the growing audience, but his voice shook as he delivered his final warning.

"G-g-get me that f-f-fucking homework by lunch," he stammered. "Or we're g-g-going out to the woods again."

As Jerry and Andrew hustled off, looking back with baffled expressions, the hint of a smile returned to Nate's lips. However, it vanished swiftly when he realized that everyone was still watching him. There was another flash as someone else snapped a picture. Then the pointing and whispering started.

Uncomfortable with all the attention, Nate hastily picked up his papers and books and attempted to make a quick getaway.

Rachel stood directly in his path. "How did you do that?"

Nate paused for a moment, but he didn't have the first clue how to explain his astonishing new abilities. "I'm going to be late for class," he mumbled, scooting around her and hustling off down the hall.

"Nate did this?" Toby asked, as he stared skeptically at the smashed locker.

"That's what I heard," Willard answered. "And I heard he did it with just one punch."

Toby pushed his fingers against the narrow, crumpled door, expecting it to be defective in some way. He'd seen kids dent their lockers before, but this wasn't just a dent. The painted metal was caved in, and the middle hinge had completely snapped off. Nobody could do this kind of damage with just a punch, especially not Nate. A feat of strength for him was carrying more than one textbook at a time.

Willard continued relating the gossip about Nate's run-in with the jocks. "I also heard he shoved Jerry clear across the hall."

Toby glanced over toward the other side of the hallway. It wasn't a particularly wide distance, but still... "C'mon. There's no way."

"Something's up with him today," said Willard. "He's not himself."

"Well, he's also not the Hulk," Toby fired back.

"The facts seem to say otherwise."

"Shut up," warned Peter from behind them. "Here he comes."

Toby turned to see Nate walking toward them. His friend stared down the hallway with a limp, unfocused gaze, looking as if he didn't even see Toby or the others standing in front of him. Without so much as a nod to acknowledge them, Nate simply stopped once he was alongside the group.

"So, who am I then?" he asked quietly.

Toby shot him a quizzical look. "What?"

"If I'm not myself, or the Hulk, then who am I?" he asked again, not addressing anyone in particular.

Toby glanced back in the direction Nate had approached from. He'd been halfway down the hall when Peter noticed him.

"You could hear us?" Peter asked, apparently just as surprised by Nate's sharp-eared exhibition.

Flustered, Nate continued down the hall without responding. Toby shot Willard and Peter a dubious look as he followed after his friend.

He certainly couldn't blame Nate for seeming off, not after everything they'd been through. It had been a stressful day, having to keep Mike's death a secret while also trying to figure out how many of their own secrets they were going to share. That decision needed to be made quickly, as Toby's father was certainly going to want to know more about why they'd driven to the reservation.

It wasn't so much that Toby felt they had something to hide. He didn't think for a second that Nate, or anyone else for that matter, could have physically ripped a person apart the way Mike had been so thoroughly shredded. But his friend had stumbled out of the woods with somebody's blood all over him. It was pretty safe to assume that blood was Mike's.

But why had he been covered in it? How had he ended up that way?

These questions ricocheted around Toby's mind as the group headed home. He was so distracted by them that he was only half able to pay attention to a conversation Peter was trying to initiate.

"Think about all you'll be missing out on," his friend argued. "The parties, the new crowd…the new girls."

"I'm just not sure college is the right thing for me anymore," Toby replied. "I feel like I need to be doing something else. Something greater."

"Like what?"

"I don't know, but whatever it is, I don't think it includes four more years of school, followed by an office job and crushing student loan debt."

"I think you're focusing on the wrong things here."

"Right, because with all the dates we've been on so far in high school, we're bound to slay in college," Toby responded sarcastically.

"Well *I* am," Peter fired back. "The girls in college are bound to be more appreciative of my incomparable wit and charm."

"You mean they'll be more drunk?"

"Or just drunk more often."

"Better hope for both."

And what about Nate's shirt? The way it had been all torn up as if he'd been attacked. That's why Toby had assumed the blood had been Nate's, but he'd checked his friend's shoulder and arms. There hadn't been a single scrape.

"I just don't see how you can be so negative about what will probably be the best years of our lives," Peter said as he peeled away from the group and headed down his block. "Anyway, I'll see you losers tomorrow."

Toby gave a slight wave and considered his friend's words. It wasn't that he'd become negative about college, more like indifferent. It just didn't seem all that important anymore. Not much did after the accident. Not until last night.

They were halfway home now. Nate had stayed a couple steps ahead of them the entire time, not interacting in any way. No new tales of his Demon Destroyer conquests or recaps of the latest exam he'd aced. He was apparently content with whatever conversation he was having inside his own head.

As they came to Jackson Avenue, Willard gave a slight wave and headed toward his house. Toby nodded goodbye and then sped up to walk alongside his uncharacteristically silent friend. He could understand why Nate might have not wanted to say much around Peter and Willard, but now Toby needed some answers.

"So what's going on with you?" he asked.

"What do you mean?"

"Well, for starters, did you really cave in that locker?"

Nate picked up his pace, growing uneasy. "I don't know how that happened," he confessed. "The only thing I've been able to come up with is that maybe it was like an adrenaline rush."

"An adrenaline rush? Are you serious?"

"Yeah, you know, like that story you always hear about the mom who lifted a car to save her kid?" Nate spat out the explanation unconvincingly, keeping his eyes straight ahead. "It all just sort of happened before I realized what I was doing."

THE ONE YOU FEED

"It *all* just sort of happened?" Toby asked while putting a hand to Nate's shoulder to bring him to a stop. "So does that mean the thing about you pushing Jerry across the hall was true too?"

Nate stopped walking but still couldn't bring himself to make eye contact. "Don't ask me how, but yeah."

The thing was, that's exactly what Toby wanted to ask. How the heck had Nate been able to do those things? And how were they related to whatever had happened out on the Umatilla Indian Reservation? Until Toby figured out the answers to these questions, he wouldn't be able to help his friend.

"Well, I need something to tell my dad," he started. "He's going to put me through a serious interrogation when I get home, asking about why we—"

Nate's demeanor rapidly shifted from reticent to frantically direct. "You can't tell him what happened."

"I don't know what happened," Toby replied. "What I *do* know is that it would have taken a lot more than an adrenaline rush to rip Mike apart like that."

"Yeah, but please, just don't say anything. Not until…"

Nate trailed off as he spotted something down the street behind Toby. His eyes locked in on whatever it was, and he seemed unable to look away. Toby turned slowly to see the same elderly, disheveled Indian they'd spotted on the reservation that morning. The guy's hair still looked like a mangled shrub and his clothes were torn and tattered. It seemed reasonable to assume that he might be homeless.

The Indian stood perfectly still, about a block down the street, watching them. His face showed no emotion, and Toby would have assumed he was completely uninterested in them, if not for the intense stare of his dark, gunmetal eyes.

"What's the deal with this guy?" he asked uneasily.

Nate stayed silent, continuing to stare.

Just as he had on the reservation, the Indian started to walk away. But he kept his eyes trained on the boys as he moved toward an alley across the street.

Without warning, Nate darted after him. Without really thinking about it, Toby joined him in the pursuit. The Indian picked up his pace, rushing into the alley.

The chase was on, and Toby managed to keep up with Nate for about twenty yards. Churning his legs at top speed, he watched stunned as his friend raced ahead with world-class acceleration, like a cheetah chasing down its prey.

As Toby slowed his pace, he took a moment to actually think about what he was doing. What *was* he doing? Who was this crazy Indian, and why were they chasing him? And how the hell was Nate moving so fast?

By the time Toby rounded the corner into the alley, Nate was already walking back toward the street wearing a bewildered expression.

"Where did he go?" Toby asked, between gasps for breath.

"I don't know."

Looking past his friend, Toby took a peek down the alley to find it quickly turned into a dead-end. The Indian was gone. "You didn't see how he…?"

"How he what?" Nate replied, flabbergasted. "There's no way out of here."

Which was exactly why Toby hadn't finished asking the question. There literally was nowhere for the Indian to go, nowhere for him to escape to.

"Why did you run after him like that?" Toby asked.

"I don't know. I just...I got this feeling. Like I knew him somehow."

Toby turned toward Nate, completely befuddled. "What does *that* mean?"

As Nate opened his mouth to respond, his smartphone beeped to alert him of a text. He pulled out the phone and checked it.

"Okay, look, we need to start trying to make sense of all this," Toby continued. "I want you to tell me everything you remember about being chased by Mike. Right up to where you forget the rest of the night."

"I can't," Nate said, holding up his phone. "I've got to go meet Rachel."

"Rachel?"

"Yeah. She just texted to ask what I like on my pizza." He typed out a reply and slid the phone back into his pocket. "And I swear I don't remember anything else. I *really* wish I did."

Toby mostly believed him, but he wanted to shelve that discussion for a moment. "Why are you going to Rachel's for pizza?"

"She felt bad about Mike taking me out to the reservation. I told her it wasn't her fault, but she invited me over anyway, to, like, make up for it."

Make up for it how?

Toby was speechless. Any concern or curiosity he had about the haggard-looking Indian vanished, just as the unkempt man himself had. They were replaced by feelings of exclusion and something else—jealousy.

"Seriously though, about your dad," Nate continued. "Please don't tell him how you found me last night. Definitely don't mention the blood."

"So you're going over to her house?"

"Please promise me you won't say anything to him," Nate pleaded.

"Yeah. Okay. I promise."

"Thanks." His friend gave a wave as he hustled off. "Sorry, I gotta go."

Toby took a step to go after him, his brain spinning, overloaded by the growing number of questions he had no answers for. Before he could shout one of them out, his phone began to ring.

He anxiously pulled it from his pocket, thinking the call might be a late invitation to join the pizza party. After checking the display, his chest sank. It was just Willard.

Toby answered the call with a sigh. "What's up, Willard?"

"Dude, I think I know what's going on with Nate. I need to show you and Peter something."

"What is it?" Toby asked skeptically, unaware of the Indian watching him from a nearby rooftop.

"It'll sound stupid over the phone."

"I've got to get home," Toby replied, pulling up his hood. And he really did. His dad had given him very specific orders: get his butt to school and come straight home after.

"Just stop by here for like fifteen minutes," Willard begged. "I called Peter too, and he's on his way over. If I'm right, this is pretty huge."

CHAPTER 11

THE THERIANTHROPE

A gainst his better judgment, Toby soon found himself in the Krauses' musty, wood-paneled basement, playing pool on the family's well-used billiards table. Hood still up, he fired the cue ball toward a cluster of solids and stripes. A few of the balls clacked together, with the six ball eventually rolling away from the rest and dropping into one of the table's tattered side pockets.

"Um, you know I'm solids, right?" Peter asked.

Toby surveyed the table. Registering his mistake, he shook his head and stepped aside. It's not like he could be expected to concentrate on pool at a time like this anyway.

"Did you know anything about Nate and Rachel hanging out tonight?" he asked as casually as he could.

Peter shook his head no as he lined up his shot.

Toby knew there were more important things to worry about, given everything else that was going on, but he couldn't help dwelling on this unforeseen development. He'd been the one to first meet Rachel and introduce her to the rest of the group. It wasn't right for her to now be making plans with *his* friends without his knowing about it.

He continued to brood, his hands twisting tightly around the Krauses' nicked-up cue. Dinner between Rachel and Nate should have been planned *through* him.

Just as Toby's knuckles went white, he loosened his grip and exhaled a deep sigh of resignation. Who was he kidding? Rachel could make plans with whomever she wanted. She didn't need his approval, and that wasn't really what was bothering him anyway. He was upset because her plans hadn't included him.

"She invited him over for pizza," Toby continued. "Felt bad about getting him in trouble with Mike."

"Is that right?" Peter responded, more interested in his next shot than their conversation.

"No pizza for me though. I mean, I only *fought* the guy."

Peter hammered the four ball into a corner pocket, then straightened up and shot Toby a sideways grin. "Wasn't much of a fight from what I heard."

Toby pulled his hood down and opened his mouth to respond, but was cut off as Willard shouted out from upstairs. "Found it!"

Their portly friend came trotting down the steps. He held a large board game box decorated with knights and different fantasy creatures that he set down on the pool table, knocking aside the balls that remained on the frayed felt surface.

"You called us over to play D&D?" Toby asked with a scowl.

"Um, no, unless…Do you guys want to?"

Toby sighed and rolled his eyes, answering the question definitively without saying a word. How much crummier could this day get?

"Right, well, first of all, this isn't D&D," Willard corrected in a slightly hurt tone. He opened the box to retrieve the game cards, snapping off the rubber band that held them together. "It's Middle Earth Conquests."

He began rifling through the cards one by one. "Second, what did you guys think when Nate suggested we all go out for lunch today?"

"That it was a good idea," Toby answered brusquely. "The best the cafeteria had to offer was meat loaf."

Willard continued to glance at card after card. "Yeah, but remember when I asked him how he knew we were having meat loaf, and he said he could smell it?"

"That garbage always stinks up the cafeteria," Peter chimed in.

"But we weren't in the cafeteria," Willard noted. "We were at the opposite end of the building."

"So Nate's got super strength *and* super smelling now, is that it?" Toby snapped. Nate and Rachel's unexpected get together already had him upset, but now he was fuming. He'd been due home over an hour ago, and the time he'd wasted here had likely added *days* to whatever punishment his dad already had in store for him.

"And super hearing," Peter added.

"Don't encourage this!" Toby barked.

Willard inhaled a short, excited breath as he drew a card from the rest and proudly held it up. "Here it is! Faster reflexes, enhanced senses, superior strength." He held the card to each of his friends' faces so they could get a good look. "Sound like anyone we know?"

On the card was the image of a ferocious beast covered in clumps of uneven, mangy fur. The creature stood on its hind legs and had blood running down its front paws. Although, they weren't really paws. More like clawed fingers. Across the top of the card was the beast's name: The Therianthrope.

Willard's beaming smile evaporated as Peter burst into laughter.

"What the hell is that?" Toby asked, far less amused.

Willard pointed to the name on the card. "It's a therianthrope."

"What the hell's a therianthrope?!"

"A werewolf," Peter gasped out between guffaws.

"Only complete newbs call it that," Willard responded.

Toby wanted to punch his chubby friend in the gut. With his own search for answers turning up frustratingly few leads, he'd actually allowed himself to believe Willard might have something worthwhile to share. Now he was going to catch major hell for not coming straight home, and *this* was going to be the reason? He reached out to slap the card from Willard's hand but paused when he got a second look at the creature drawn on it.

The beast had glowing, yellow eyes—eerily reminiscent of the ones he'd seen staring out from the reservation woods the night before. The memory of them triggered an anxious sensation that supplanted his irritation.

Settling into plush sofa cushions, Nate glanced around at the framed nature scenes hanging on the dark blue walls of the Frankses' living room. The tutoring session had been going pretty well so far, but he was finding it increasingly difficult to concentrate. He was still having a hard time believing he was even there—hanging out with Rachel, alone, in her house. It was a miraculous turn of events.

A cool evening breeze came in through the den window, rustling the leaves of a four-foot houseplant and turning over some papers on the coffee table. Nate snatched up the papers and slid them under his laptop.

His inability to focus was also due to the fact he was getting hungry, like ravenously hungry. The pizza had just arrived, and he could smell the gloriously greasy aroma of cheese and pepperoni wafting in from the kitchen. He couldn't remember the last time he'd felt this famished.

Could his intense hunger have anything to do with all the strange changes he'd experienced throughout the day? His friends were right. He wasn't himself. Nate didn't have the first notion of how to explain what he'd been going through, so he'd decided to handle the situation with denial.

He'd just finish out the day and see how things felt in the morning. Hope that the changes were temporary.

Rachel appeared in the hallway between the rooms, carrying two plates. Saliva pooled in Nate's mouth. His stomach rumbled. The moment she set the plates down, he grabbed a pizza slice and voraciously took a bite.

"How is it?" Rachel asked, sitting next to him on the sofa.

Nate barely managed to answer her between mouthfuls. "Delicious."

She smirked and then glanced down at the books and papers on the table. "So what's next?"

Nate put down the pizza and started flipping through his calculus textbook. He found the page on derivatives he was looking for and scooted the book closer to her, nudging the other textbooks and laptops on the coffee table out of the way.

He sat on the edge of the sofa and pointed to one of the formulas on the page. "Okay, we can figure out the derivative by using the concept of an arbitrary change, or increment, in the value of x."

Rachel slid a little closer to him, leaning in to get a better look. Nate hesitated for a moment, feeling a quiver of excitement as her arm brushed against his. He took a short breath and refocused.

"Now if x was simply ten months, we could easily determine the rate of change in the function," he continued. "But the question is asking for the rate of change at a particular point x, not a span of ten months. So the derivative is the limit approached by the rate of change in the function, when x becomes arbitrarily small."

He glanced over to make sure she was following along. Rachel gave him a look that said she definitely wasn't getting it.

"Sorry," Nate said with a self-conscious smile. "I went through that kind of quick. Let me start over."

"Thanks," she said. "I guess I'm a bit further behind the curve than I thought."

She leaned a little closer and returned her eyes to the book. Nate's eyes stayed on her. He could feel her thigh pressed against his, smell the fragrance of the raspberry shampoo she used to wash her hair. His heart started to pound in his chest. It was so loud he felt certain she could hear it.

He took another breath to try to calm down and then started his explanation again. "Okay, a derivative of a function depicts how the function is changing at point x. So it's necessary for the function to—"

A sharp pain suddenly shot through his left ribs. The sensation was like being stabbed by a blood elf's blade. Or, at least comparable to what Nate imagined such a stabbing would feel like. He grimaced and grabbed his side. Within seconds, another piercing pain surged through the right side of his rib cage, causing him to buckle over further.

A low groan escaped through his clenched teeth.

Rachel placed a hand on his shoulder. "Are you okay?"

He fought off the urge to moan through the pain again and stood up. It was getting harder for him to breathe, and he wondered if he was experiencing some sort of Rachel-induced panic attack. Any chance he had to impress her would be greatly diminished if he passed out cold on her living room floor. He had to pull it together.

"Yeah," Nate answered, forcing a smile. "I just need some water. Your kitchen is back here, right?"

There was another sharp stab as he headed into the hallway.

"I can get it," Rachel said with concern in her voice, standing to follow him.

He waved her off. "It's okay. I got it."

Nate had no idea if water would actually help. He just felt like he needed to get up and move around. His thighs seized as he staggered into the kitchen, sending him stumbling into the kitchen island. Grasping at the granite top, he leaned against it to keep from going to the floor. His entire body started to shake. Beads of sweat formed on his forehead and dripped onto the polished stone. It was becoming even more difficult to breathe.

Forget the water. He needed fresh air. A few deep breaths would hopefully calm him down and mitigate whatever breakdown was taking place inside his body. Nate spotted a sliding glass door that led to the backyard and made a break for it. Every step required deep concentration and monumental effort. It was if he'd been coated in concrete that was starting to dry.

Finally, he reached the door. Grabbing the handle and pulling it open, he wobbled his way outside. He was sweating profusely now. The pain had spread to his shoulders and arms and had become too powerful for him to remain standing any longer. Was this a heart attack? At sixteen?

He fell into a wicker chair and then collapsed onto the porphyry stone patio.

His face twisted in anguish as he rolled onto his side. Gnashing his teeth together, he did his best to hold in a scream as an excruciating pain shot through every fiber of his muscles and tendons.

Nate eyed a cluster of evergreens that ran alongside the neighbor's lawn and felt a sudden impulse to crawl toward them. He needed to get out from under the patio lights and find some cover.

As he pulled himself toward the tress, the muscles in his arms and legs began to bulge. His bones appeared to grow as well, and shift, jutting out in new directions. His skin stretched like Silly Putty to accommodate the restructuring of his insides.

No longer able to stand it, Nate let loose a howling cry.

His clothes ripped away. Then came the hair, bursting forth in clumps all the way down his body. Right then Nate realized what he was becoming, just before he blacked out.

Completely disheartened, Willard returned the therianthrope play-ing card to the stack and wrapped the rubber band back around the deck.

Peter was still struggling to hold back laughter. "You seriously think Nate is a werewolf?"

"Therianthrope," Willard retorted, refusing to give up on his theory. "You saw what he did to that locker. The hearing. The strength. He's got all the characteristics."

"You just pulled that card out of a *fantasy* role playing game," Peter snickered.

Toby remained silent as he contemplated Willard's hypothesis. It was, in fact, completely ridiculous. It was also the most reason-able explanation for everything he'd seen since picking Nate up on the reservation the night before. The increased speed, the increased strength—how the hell do those things happen, seemingly overnight?

Peter noticed Toby lost in thought and quickly gave him grief for it. "You're awfully quiet over there. I thought you didn't want to encourage any of this."

Toby stopped pondering. "I'm not."

Truly he wasn't. Although Willard's theory would explain a lot, this was real life, not Middle Earth Conquests. Werewolves didn't exist in real life.

"*I'm not*," he repeated a bit more vehemently when he noticed Willard looking at him with hopeful eyes. "But other things have happened that…Hell, the whole town will be talking about it to-morrow. I might as well just tell you."

Peter and Willard exchanged a curious look.

"Tell us what?" Willard asked, getting excited again.

CHAPTER 12

BIMISI'S WARNING

Rachel glanced at the clock that hung above the television, then down at the congealing pizza slices and scattered papers on the table. Nate had been in the kitchen for almost fifteen minutes. Had she done something to upset him? Was he offended by her inability to wrap her head around calculating the derivative of a function?

This was silly. She had to find out what was going on.

Twirling her hair, Rachel got up off the couch and headed for the kitchen. As she entered the room, she felt a cool breeze pass over her forearms. The sliding glass door to the patio was wide open.

Had he ditched her? Decided she was too hopeless a case and slipped out to avoid wasting any more time? Maybe that was why he'd scarfed down the pizza so fast.

For the past several weeks, Rachel had lost plenty of sleep worrying about how her new classmates would accept her. Worrying *if* they'd accept her. While she'd been sitting in the front office on her first day, waiting for her class schedule, she'd played out all sorts of scenarios in her head.

One, of course, was how they would all assume she was an uneducated simpleton. She imagined that they probably equated being raised on the reservation to being reared by wolves. However, Rachel had determined after her first day that she was ahead of the curve in her English literature and world history classes.

Physics and calculus were different stories. She had some catching up to do in those subjects, and she'd considered herself lucky to have made friends with the kid who the other kids bullied for his homework. Now she wasn't so sure Nate was a friend. It looked like she was going to have to get caught up on her own.

Rachel trudged over to the sliding door to close it. She grabbed the handle and started to pull, then paused when she noticed two of the patio chairs had been knocked over.

"Wow," she muttered to herself. "He really couldn't get away fast enough."

Rachel stepped onto the patio and surveyed the backyard. Empty. She walked over to the wicker chairs and placed them upright, fixing the floral-patterned polyester cushions.

As she slid the first chair back underneath the table, she suddenly felt a prickling sensation spread throughout her entire body. It was like goose bumps, but on the inside. She'd felt something similar the night before on the reservation, but had attributed it to having been totally freaked out.

A twig snapped behind the evergreen trees bordering the lawn next door. Rachel looked in the direction of the sound, but all she saw through the branches and pine needles were the lights of the neighbor's house. There was no movement.

The prickling feeling subsided, but the fact that she'd felt it put her on edge. She took a deep breath and returned her attention to the chairs, sliding the second one back into place. A sudden rustling caused her to jump, and she spun around again. Again there was nothing. The trees all appeared still.

Rachel stepped cautiously toward a particular section of the evergreens, peering at the spot where she thought she'd heard the noise. That area of the yard was blanketed in shadows, so much so that she wasn't able to tell if the pines were still swaying.

"Nate?" she called out uncertainly.

No answer. Rachel listened intently, standing perfectly still. There was only the chirping of crickets. She finally turned back toward the house, exhaling the breath she'd been holding in for the past several seconds.

She barely managed to swallow a scream when she found Bimisi Chochopi standing directly behind her.

"Jesus, Uncle Bimi! What are you doing here?"

"I have come to take you to the reservation," he answered brusquely.

Rachel gave him a confused look as she tried to settle her nerves. It was the only immediate response she could muster.

It had been over a month since she'd last seen her uncle. When her mom had informed him of their plans for a permanent move to Silver Falls, he'd not taken the news well. First came several weeks of the silent treatment, which had annoyed her, and then he just disappeared. At that point, her annoyance turned to anger. She felt like he'd disowned her, which made him the second father figure in her life to have done so. And she was still plenty pissed at him for that.

Rachel shook her head as she started back inside. "Um, I've got school tomorrow," she replied with more than a hint of ire in her voice. "Besides, I didn't think decorating for the Mother Earth Ceremony started for a couple more weeks."

"I have not come about the ceremony."

She glanced back at him as she stepped into the kitchen. "Then why are you here?"

"Your mother has chosen to live among these people," Bimisi responded, his expression going from earnest to grave. "But that does not mean that you must."

"I'm here because I *want* to be here."

"Only because you have let your mother manipulate you. Deep down you know that this is not where you belong. My home has more than enough room for two people, and you can stay for as long as is—"

"Hold on," Rachel interrupted, struggling to make sense of her uncle's random appearance and stated mission. "Don't tell me what I'm supposed to know or feel. I haven't seen or heard from you in over a month! How could you possibly think you could just show up here and convince me to come back to the reservation...to live...with you?"

He gave no reply, instead casting his eyes upward. Rachel did the same. Her uncle seemed to be observing the pale, nearly full moon.

"Well?" she pressed, turning her eyes back to him. "Why would you think that?"

He continued to regard the bright lunar satellite above them. "Because if you stay here, you will be in very serious danger."

The annual camping trip to the Umatilla woods had become a family tradition, starting back when Chris Ritter's daughter was five and his son was three. They were now ten and eight. Still plenty cute in their junior-sized flannels and hiking boots, but right on the cusp of an age when they would no longer be excited by the prospect of camping out with mom and dad.

Chris figured he had maybe two years left, tops, before his daughter stopped valuing this weekend away. His wife, Megan, was already becoming a passive participant in the event, electing to stay in the family's Dodge Caravan and read Us Weekly instead of joining them by the campfire for ghost stories.

"And then," Chris said in his extra spooky voice, crouching closer to the crackling fire. "When the little boy peered under his bed...he saw what was making the sound."

"What was it?" the children asked excitedly. Thankfully, they still provided him with a captivated audience. "What was it?"

"It was..." Chris paused a moment for dramatic effect, shifting his gaze back and forth between his daughter and son. "The boogeyman!!"

Chris sprang to his feet, motivating his children to do the same. He started to groan, slowly stepping around the fire toward his riled-up kids. They shrieked and scurried away, running for the Caravan. Chris lumbered after them with a Frankenstein-like stagger, waving his arms wildly.

None of the family members noticed the disheveled Shaman standing in the shadows of the pine trees that encircled their campsite.

The nearly two-century-old Indian's eyes flashed yellow as he watched the children and their father race past.

Megan's daughter was the first to reach the Caravan. She opened the rear driver's side door and jumped into the vehicle, followed immediately by her brother. They hurriedly shut and locked the door behind them, giggling with excitement.

Staggering along after them, Chris continued to growl and groan while banging on the windows. The children responded with laughs and screams of delight.

"We'll never get them to sleep now, you know," Megan said in a none-too-pleased tone.

Chris smiled and ducked down, disappearing from view. The children scampered from one side of the Caravan to the other, trying to spot him, full of energy.

"I knew letting them have those extra s'mores was a mistake," Megan muttered, returning to her magazine.

All of a sudden Chris sprang up next to the passenger seat window, startling her half to death. She fumbled her Us Weekly onto the floor and shot her moaning husband an irritated glance. He continued to sway and groan, more goofball than ghoul, until her lips fluttered into the hint of a smile.

Megan shook her head as Chris once again ducked out of sight. The children shrieked with delight, fully amused by their father's antics.

Attempting to suppress her smile, Megan reached down to pick up the magazine. "Okay, I think we've had just about enough of the boogeyman."

The Caravan suddenly rocked violently, knocking her forward. Her shoulder slammed against the glove compartment as she fell halfway onto the floor.

Planting her hands against the dashboard, she lifted herself back into the seat. More than a little shaken, she scanned the area for her husband and for whatever had just struck them.

The sound of her son crying got her attention, and she turned around to see him down on the floor. Her daughter sat frozen in the seat behind her, hands clasped tightly around the armrests.

"What was that?" Megan asked nobody in particular as she helped her son back into his seat. Her daughter stayed silent, staring out the windshield with terrified eyes.

"Are you okay, sweetie?" Megan asked. "Did you see something?"

The girl gave no response. Her face stricken, Megan glanced around at the surrounding forest and called out for her husband. "Chris?"

Silence.

She craned her neck to look along the side of the vehicle, not wanting to open her window any more than the five inches she already had it cracked. "Chris? What was that?"

There was no sign of her husband. What she did see, she only saw for a second—the swift glimpse of a large, hairy animal in the side rearview mirror.

She recoiled into her seat instinctively.

"Chris!" she called out again, her voice strangled and shrill.

Her husband's hand flopped onto the hood of the Caravan, covered in blood. Megan looked on in horror as he pulled himself up using just his left arm. Most of his right arm was gone, severed just below the shoulder.

She locked eyes with her husband for a brief moment, before there was another flash of fur and Chris was yanked out of sight. Megan heard his final agonizing yelp, and then his voice was silenced with a loud crunch. The terrified family members inside the vehicle all screamed in unison.

A triumphant howl drowned out their cries.

Willard and Peter stood in stunned silence. Their gawking expressions were the direct result of Toby telling them everything that had happened in the past twenty-four hours. He'd told them about finding Ashley too scared to speak in the back of Mike's pickup, about Nate appearing from out of the forest covered in somebody's blood, and about why Mike Mulligan hadn't been at school that day.

Recapping all of the events out loud had left Toby a little stunned as well. They sounded like a collection of scenes from some B-movie horror flick, and even though he'd witnessed them all, he still struggled to accept that each of the incidents had really taken place.

"Whoa," Willard gasped.

Peter shook his head, struggling to comprehend the story he'd just been told. "Wait. What do you mean Mike was all ripped up?"

Toby's smartphone started to ring. He pulled it from his pocket to check the display and saw three letters that made him cringe: D-A-D. He quickly pressed the ignore call button and shoved the phone back into his pocket.

"It looked like he'd been attacked by an animal," he said quietly.

"Whoa," was again the only response Willard could muster.

"What kind of animal?" Peter asked.

"Something big."

"How could you tell?"

"Because…" Toby sighed, uncertain about whether he should mention this next part. "I think I might have seen the thing that did it, right before I found Nate."

"Whoa," Willard gasped again.

"I didn't get much of a look, but it had these yellow eyes and was pretty big. Like big enough to be a bear or something."

"Whoa." Willard had become a broken record.

Peter took out his phone. "I'm calling Nate."

He dialed quickly, and the room went silent. Toby could hear the faint buzz of his friend's smartphone ringing—and continuing to ring. He began to chew on his lip as Peter let the call ring several more times.

"He's not answering."

"Wh—" Willard started again.

"Cut it out," Toby snapped at him. "Okay, that doesn't mean anything."

But what if it did? What if Nate was too busy to answer his cell? Too busy with Rachel.

Toby felt the pit of his stomach heat up as he contemplated her being the reason Nate was ignoring the call. Were they just too deep into studying to be bothered, or were they too deep into something else? He thought of the two of them lip-locked, and the heat in his belly intensified.

Then another thought occurred to him. What if Nate *was* some sort of threat? Not a werewolf, obviously, but what if the characteristics they'd all noticed actually did make him unsafe to be around? What if Rachel was now in imminent danger?

The fire in his belly turned to ice.

"I gotta go," he said as he rushed for the stairs.

"What should we do?" Willard asked as Toby hit the steps.

He spun around, taking a moment to look both his friends in the eye. "Don't do anything."

Toby knew how the story he'd just told them must have sounded, which was one of the reasons he hadn't wanted to say anything at all. Another being that if his dad knew he'd spilled about Mike, he'd be grounded for another year on top of whatever punishment was already coming his way for not going straight home.

"So, you don't think Nate's a..." Peter trailed off, not even able to bring himself to ask the question aloud.

"No," Toby answered in a far less convincing tone than he'd meant to. "Keep trying to get hold of him. I'm going to go see if he's still over at Rachel's."

Andrew Staley gunned his ATV around an elm tree, bouncing over the small mounds and divots in the forest floor. He was already a good twenty yards behind Jerry and losing ground fast.

These races through the woods outside the Ituha family ranch always tended to be an exercise in frustration for him. He'd come out here countless times since becoming friends with Jerry freshman year, but he could tally on a single hand the number of races he'd won.

To be fair, Jerry did have the advantage of racing on his home turf, but still, this was embarrassing. Andrew swerved around a pine, twisting the throttle to try to make up the distance between them. The growl of the ATV's exhaust echoed through the forest as the vehicle lurched ahead.

Jerry glanced back with a smug grin, which only added fuel to Andrew's fire. Leaning forward to try to lessen wind resistance, he veered to avoid another pine tree. As he zipped past the conifer, he thought he saw something race by him off to his right. He glanced over to take a better look, but there was nothing.

He figured it was probably just the shadows playing tricks on him, but then he saw it again, farther ahead and still a good distance to the right. It was hard to make out much in the dark, especially when he had to stay focused on where he was steering, but Andrew estimated it had to be about the size of another ATV, maybe even a little bigger.

Whatever it was, it had cruised right past him and was heading toward Jerry.

It was Mike. Had to be. Trying to catch them off guard. The guy had some serious balls, driving an ATV through these trees at night without headlights.

Andrew chuckled to himself, then called out to Jerry. "Hey, hold up a second."

Jerry didn't hear him over the roar of the ATVs and continued to race ahead. Andrew waited for him to glance back again with another of his self-satisfied grins, then waved for him to slow down.

Jerry slowed his ATV and spun it around.

"What's the matter?" he chirped. "Can't keep up?"

The headlights of Jerry's four-wheeler shone right in Andrew's face. He took his left hand off the throttle and used it to shield his eyes as he coasted toward his friend.

"I think I saw another ATV out here," Andrew answered.

"Where?"

"Over there." Andrew pointed with the hand he wasn't using to shade his eyes. "I thought maybe it was Mike."

"I don't see anything."

"His lights were off."

"Well, we'd still be able to hear him, jackass," Jerry snorted. "I think you're just making excuses."

"I'm not," Andrew fired back. "I'm telling you, I saw something. Right over there by the—"

A dark, hulking figure suddenly launched from the trees and snatched Jerry off the seat of his ATV, stunning Andrew into silence.

With the headlights still in his eyes, he couldn't tell what kind of animal had just attacked his friend, but the thing was enormous. It had taken Jerry down behind a cluster of pines and brush, which further obstructed Andrew's view. He could only glimpse flashes of the massive creature thrashing about as it savagely mauled his friend, but he had no problem hearing the brutal attack.

Jerry's screams pierced the night air, as did the beast's snarls and the sounds of claws ripping through clothing and flesh.

The horrific noises snapped Andrew out of his stupor. Twisting the throttle on his ATV, he spun the vehicle around and zipped away from the scene, still hearing Jerry's cries above the roar of the engine. Then the cries stopped.

He took a moment to glance back. His eyes widened with fear.

It was coming for him now.

Unable to turn away, Andrew stared with fascinated horror at the hulking silhouette running him down. The creature howled with glee, seeming to enjoy the chase.

Stupefied and distracted by the beast's menacing yellow eyes, Andrew steered his ATV straight into a ditch, flipping it. He flew through the air, clipping an oak tree and then slamming down onto the dirt. He rolled several times, finally coming to rest near his upturned four-wheeler. Thoroughly battered, he slowly turned onto his side, feeling the stings of several fresh bumps and scrapes.

His eyes darted about maniacally, searching the surrounding darkness. There was a low growl, then footfalls. The hulking shadow of a massive creature slowly cast over him. The animal let out a loud snarl.

"No!" Andrew cried.

His cry ended suddenly as his blood and guts splattered across the wrecked ATV.

After listening to her uncle state his case, Rachel moved to the opposite end of the kitchen to put some space between them. When he'd disappeared after her mom's announcement about moving to Silver Falls, she had assumed it was strictly because he was too upset to be around them. Now she wondered if maybe their decision had broken more inside him than just his spirit.

She leaned against the fridge, eying him incredulously. "You're making this up."

"I am not," Bimisi answered matter-of-factly. "All of this land was ours to live off of once, and it should be ours again. What is about to happen will allow us to reclaim what was wrongfully taken from our ancestors."

With her uncle, it always came back to what had been taken from them. She wished he would just let it go.

In her short lifetime, Rachel had seen positive changes within her small village in this respect. Many of its residents had decided to stop playing the victim and refocus their efforts on turning the reservation into something they could all be proud of. It was, in its own way, still a defiant movement, but one driven by the tribe's desire to make the most of their current situation, instead of dwelling on what their circumstances used to be.

Rachel looked forward to one day doing her part to further the tribe's progress.

While her uncle saw her and her mother's move as just more thievery by the white man, Rachel knew that relocating to Silver Falls would allow her to attend a better school, possibly even pursue a higher education, an education she could one day use to help her people.

She wanted to argue this point with her uncle now, but she was honestly questioning his mental status. He'd told her some pretty unbelievable stories growing up and had never been shy about expressing his disdain for Silver Falls, but the tale she'd just heard topped any from the past—both in creativity and bias.

Bimisi stepped across the room, getting within inches of her. He leaned in and spoke in a near whisper, his lips directly next to Rachel's ear. "This was our home once, to treasure, respect, and protect. The people of this town are destroying it."

Rachel pushed herself off the refrigerator, moving away from him again. "Well, I doubt you'll be able to stop them with spooky campfire stories, but best of luck."

"The Shaman is real," Bimisi insisted. "As is the threat of which I speak. He hunted the white intruders many years ago, and now he has returned to hunt them again."

Rachel's look switched from concerned back to irritated. "The white intruders? Seriously?"

Bimisi gave no response, but shot her a look that left no question about his sincerity.

"Okay, so ignoring the fact that even mystics die when they get old, why don't you tell me where this Shaman has been hiding for the past hundred and sixty or so years?" Rachel couldn't believe she was actually humoring her uncle. "Why'd he wait until now to come back?"

"Because now is our last chance. Soon Bennett will desecrate even more of our land with his factory's expansion. And there is no telling how much of the forest will be stripped if he is successful and decides to expand even more."

Rachel walked over to the sliding glass door and opened it. "I'd like you to leave."

"You need to come with me," he persisted.

"No," she responded forcefully. "Look, I'm trying to fit in with the *white intruders*. Okay? Make some new friends, which is going to be hard enough without having to deal with whatever this silliness is."

"You do not appreciate how much danger you are in."

"I appreciate plenty. I more than appreciate how you feel about mom and me being here, and how obsessed you are with trying to get us to come back to the reservation. But by now *you* should appreciate my feelings about your prejudice against this town and its people. I'm staying."

Bimisi stepped over to the door. "Staying is a mistake."

"Good night, Uncle."

He lowered his head and continued into the backyard. Rachel slid the door shut behind him. She shook off the strange and vexing encounter as she walked over to the kitchen island to put away the leftover pizza. Just as she closed the box, the front doorbell rang.

It rang three more times before she could reach it.

"Where's the inferno?" she muttered, opening the front door to find Toby standing outside, just about to press the bell again.

"Hey," he said, greeting her with a relieved smile. "Are you okay?"

Rachel gave him an odd look, confused by the question. "Um, yeah. Why would you ask if—?"

"Is Nate here?"

"No," Rachel responded. "But his books are if you want to take them."

"His books?"

"Yep, and don't ask me why he left them here because I don't know. I mean, obviously you know him better than I do, and maybe he's always just been a little off, but I think something is definitely wrong with that kid."

"What happened?" Toby asked, pulling down the hood of his jacket.

"He got all weird and left," she answered. "No goodbye, nothing. Just disappeared."

"He disappeared?"

"Well, not like poof into thin air," she replied with a roll of her eyes. "But yeah. Just took off for no reason."

"That is…weird."

Rachel leaned her shoulder against the doorway. "Yeah, well, weird has kind of been a theme again for me tonight."

"Why? What else happened?"

"Oh, my uncle was just here, and he…"

Rachel hesitated for a moment, unsure if she really wanted to retell Bimisi's story. She'd already apparently lost one potential friend today; did she really want to lose another by telling him about her irrational uncle who despised all white people? No, she did not.

"He was just in a strange mood," she said finally. "But he's always been a little odd. Hey, you're not going to turn into a weirdo on me too, are you?"

"I'm not going to turn into anything," Toby said with an uneasy smile. "And listen, Nate's been acting strange all day, around me and the other guys too. So don't take it personally. I'm sure he had a good reason for leaving the way he did."

Rachel wasn't so sure that was true, but she appreciated him saying it all the same.

Toby's smartphone began to ring. He pulled it out, checked the display, then glanced over at his house with a heavy sigh. "I need to get home."

"Talk tomorrow?" she asked.

"Absolutely," he replied sincerely with the hint of a reassuring smile. "We need to figure out a way to break this streak of strange nights. I don't know about you, but two in a row is more than enough for me."

Rachel smiled and nodded. "Me too."

She was beginning to really like Toby Hoffman and was considering herself very fortunate to have him as her new neighbor, and as a new friend. Perhaps when things settled down a bit they could maybe even try becoming *more* than just friends.

CHAPTER 13

THE PAW PRINT

The moment Toby set foot inside his house, he felt distraught. There would be no more speculating with his friends about what might have happened on the reservation or talking to his new neighbor about the oddities they'd experienced. All that remained on tonight's schedule was his reprimanding.

He stood in the front entryway, not wanting to take another step, and stared blankly into the living room. Leaning back against the front hall dresser that stored the family's collection of board games, old photo albums, and just about every size battery ever invented, he waited for his dad to call out his name.

Silence. Maybe his dad hadn't heard him come in. Toby considered sneaking back out and heading over to Nate's, just to confirm his friend wasn't a made-up monster. There was no way to escape the punishment that was coming, but he could put it off for a little longer.

The thought was tempting, but before he was able to muster the nerve to leave, his father came trotting down from upstairs dressed in his sheriff's uniform.

Walter furrowed his brow when he saw his son. "Where have you been?"

"I'm sorry," Toby said. "Willard called and he—"

"I told you to come straight home after school."

"I know. Dad, something is going on and—"

"And I know all about it," said Walter.

"You do?"

"I talked to Principal Carter today. He told me about your fight with Mike Mulligan."

The call about the fight. Toby knew there would be one. He'd had every intention of telling his dad about what had happened, but that was before he'd found his friend covered in blood, rescued a catatonic cheerleader from the woods, and been semi-stalked by an insane-looking Indian. During the course of all those developments, he'd actually forgotten about the fight—until they'd found Mike's body this morning. And that had definitely not seemed like the right time to bring it up.

Given what had happened to his clawed-up classmate, bringing up their scuffle now also seemed inappropriate. Toby wondered what exactly his dad's point was in doing so. Feeling as though some sort of implication was being made, he turned defensive.

"You can't think that I did that to him."

"What I think is that I have enough going on right now without having to worry about getting calls from your principal!" Walter's voice seemed to rise with every word. "What I *think* is that the

THE ONE YOU FEED

sheriff's son shouldn't be driving out to the reservation, without a license, to look at a dead body nobody else knows is there! And that when I tell you to come straight home from school, you better damn well obey me!"

Okay, so no implication, just a lot of good points. Toby dropped his eyes, unable to meet his father's heated gaze. The two shared an awkward moment of silence. He then heard his father take a deep breath and exhale a lengthy sigh.

"You don't go anywhere, except school and back, until I get some answers about what you were doing out there." Walter stepped by Toby and opened the front door.

Not wanting the conversation to end just yet, Toby reluctantly blurted out what he could before his dad got outside. "He doesn't remember what happened to him."

Walter paused in the doorway. "What?"

"When I said I drove Nate out to the reservation because he forgot something," Toby spoke barely above a murmur. "The thing he forgot was what happened to him while he was out there last night."

Walter stepped back into the entryway. "What does that mean? Nate doesn't remember what *happened to him*?"

Putting it like that had been a mistake, and such an easy one for his dad to pick up on. Toby knew better than to be so careless with words around his ex-detective father, but he had too many things on his mind to be cautious about his phrasing.

If his dad hadn't already heard about Ashley, he would soon. Then he'd hear from her mom about how Toby had been the one to drop her off. Eventually he'd hear from Ashley herself—about

Nate, about the blood. None of which Toby was any closer to being able to explain than he was the night before—not without bringing a mythical monster into the mix.

He'd promised Nate he wouldn't say anything, but it was time the sheriff of Silver Falls knew the whole truth, or at least as much of it as Toby knew himself.

"When I picked him up, he had blood on his shirt and some on his arms. It wasn't his, and he doesn't know how it got there. The last thing he remembers is being chased through the woods by Mike, Jerry, and Andrew."

"How do you know the blood wasn't his?"

"Because he didn't have any cuts or scrapes."

Walter's voice rose again. "Why didn't you tell me about any of this before?"

"*Because he's my best friend,*" Toby exclaimed, finally raising his voice to match his father's. "And it's not like he could have done that to Mike. Trust me, he was just as messed up by the body as I was when he saw it."

"Okay, just hold on," Walter said, raising a palm toward his son. "I can't do this right now, but you're going to tell me every last detail about what happened out on that reservation when I get back."

"Where are you going?"

"Some hunters just found more bodies out at a campsite in the woods. Sounds like this thing might have attacked a whole family this time."

Walter exited the house, leaving Toby with his head spinning. More attacks? And Nate was once again MIA. No way. Another odd coincidence for sure, but two plus two did not equal Nate was a werewolf. There had to be another explanation.

So what was it? As the sheriff's son, he'd been taught to look at every angle before eliminating any. Werewolf seemed like an easy lead to rule out, but what the heck kind of animal would, or could, kill a person the way Mike had been so thoroughly filleted?

Maybe there was a way for him to figure that out. What if there were reports of attacks like this someplace else? What if other bodies had been found in the same condition as Mike's? If any had, what sort of information might be available about what had done the killing?

Toby rushed upstairs to his room and sat down at a small desk, not even bothering to flip on the lights. He turned on his laptop and sat in the pale blue glow of the screen as he waited for the system to boot up.

This was what he needed to do. He was still determined to figure out what had happened to Nate, but he was also going to figure out what was attacking the people of Silver Falls—and establish if the two things were in any way related.

So what kind of creature was capable of doing the sort of damage that had been done to Mike? Certainly nothing that was indigenous to the area. Toby brought his fingers to the keyboard, hesitated for a moment, and then, strictly for curiosity's sake, googled "werewolves."

After surveying the query results for a moment, he clicked a link. A website entitled "Lycan Lessons" opened, and he started scrolling down the page, scanning the information on curses, origins, and reported sightings. His eyes dropped to a cartoon of a werewolf attacking a scantily dressed woman with overly exaggerated curves.

He shook his head and closed the site. What was he doing? Nate wasn't a werewolf. *There were no such things as werewolves.*

Yes, there was some strange stuff going on, but that didn't mean he should let imagination run away with reason. That's what happened when you didn't have enough facts, but there were only two people he was aware of who could provide the facts he needed. One claimed not to remember anything, and the other had gone mute.

Toby decided he would check in on Ashley before school tomorrow to see how she was doing. He had to find a way to get some answers. But he couldn't do that until morning. So what should he do until then?

He sat and stared at the screen for another moment, debating. His fingers then danced across the keyboard as he googled werewolves again.

Bimisi knew the only way he was going to get his sister-in-law to return to the reservation was to convince his niece to come back first. It was going to be a difficult task, especially after his disappearing act a little over a month ago.

Leaving the area had been necessary though, as was his trading in his old pickup for the rough-steering, inferior model he drove now. As he rumbled along through the forest, he turned down the classic rock station he was listening to and tried to determine the source of the rattling that had developed somewhere behind the dashboard. It had started two days ago.

Flashing lights ahead caught Bimisi's attention and prompted him to slow his vehicle. He smiled with malicious delight when he realized the lights were from Walter's police SUV and Deputy Rogers's cruiser. Wanting to get a closer look at what was sure to be more carnage, Bimisi pulled over to the side of the road.

Stepping out of his truck, he peered over at the scene to see Walter, Billy, and the county coroner examining a ravaged Dodge Caravan. When Walter spotted him, Bimisi quickly suppressed his smile.

The sheriff strode over. "I'm going to have to ask you to stay back, Bimisi."

"What happened here?" the Indian asked with false concern.

"A family was attacked," Walter explained. "Looks like we've got some kind of animal out here that's—"

"The whole family?"

Walter responded with a solemn nod. Bimisi took a step back, glancing over toward the vehicle again. He watched as the coroner and his assistant lifted a small body wrapped in a sheet from the Caravan. It was clearly the body of a child.

This was not right. The Shaman was supposed to attack hunters, vandals, and money-hungry manufacturing plant operators—all those who polluted and desecrated the land Bimisi vowed to protect. After a handful of savage attacks, it was his hope that the rest of Silver Falls would view the area as cursed and leave, never to return.

The creature's purpose was to purge the area of the white *man*.

But children grow up to be men. It wasn't illogical that the Shaman would attack them too, and that sudden reality turned Bimisi's mock concern real.

Victims of this struggle shouldn't include those still too young to choose a side.

Walter observed the stress lines forming on the Indian's brow and wondered how many more times he would see that look. How many more people would he have to have this conversation with? How many more victims would there be before he, or somebody else, stopped whatever was out here in these woods?

"Hey, Sheriff," he heard someone call out. Walter glanced back at the nightmarish scene behind him to see Billy anxiously waving him over. "Come take a look at this."

Walter signaled to Billy with a quick wave, then returned his attention to Bimisi. "Probably best if you just head home. You don't want to see what's happened here."

Bimisi nodded and slowly moved back toward his truck. As he watched the Indian get back into his pickup, Walter realized that it looked different than the one he thought he remembered Bimisi owning. It's not like he'd ever kept close tabs on the Umatillas' vehicles though, which had proven to be regrettable after his wife's accident. He made a mental note to ask Bimisi if he'd switched trucks recently, knowing that now wasn't the time to do so, then headed back toward the Caravan.

He walked over to where Billy was shining his flashlight onto the ground. Illuminated in the dirt was a large, extended paw print. The sheriff crouched down to get a closer look. It was a solid imprint, about a quarter inch deep and longer than a loaf of bread, far longer than any animal track he'd seen in these woods before.

"Awfully big print for a cougar," he muttered.

"Bear, maybe?" Billy offered. "Except it's leaner than what I'd expect from a bear. It would have to be a pretty strong animal, though, to break through that windshield like it did."

"Take a couple of pictures," Walter instructed. "Send them down to the Oregon Zoo for ID. We need to figure out what the hell we're dealing with out here."

CHAPTER 14

MORNING VISITS

As Nate stood at his bedroom window watching a pink lemonade dawn breaking through the gray clouds hanging over Silver Falls, he was filled with a galvanic feeling of anticipation. It was a new day in more ways than one. A little over an hour ago, he'd woken up naked on the back patio, instantly realizing why he'd felt so strange since falling into that cavern on the reservation.

The supersensitive hearing, being able to smell cafeteria meatloaf from across school, smashing lockers, and blacking out at night—these weren't symptoms of anything he recognized from biology class or one of his sporadic, hypochondria-induced Internet searches.

He did recognize them though.

Nate was as knowledgeable as anyone, except maybe Willard, when it came to fantasy worlds and the creatures that inhabited them, so he was well aware of the condition his symptoms were pointing to. They weren't even symptoms as much as they were traits—traits he'd always assumed were created by the overactive imaginations of storytellers and game designers. Now he knew better.

The traits were real, and he was a therianthrope.

Using the spare key hidden behind the loose brick in the back-yard garden, he'd been able to sneak into the house and up to his room without waking his parents. He'd spent the last hour reflecting on what he now knew to be true.

Once again, he had very little recollection of the previous night's events. The last thing he remembered with any clarity was stumbling out of Rachel's house, which left him with some very significant questions.

Had she seen anything? Was she okay?

Nate lay down on his bed and began thinking up a strategy for the day. He was going to need to begin researching every aspect he could think of about werewolves. He also needed to come up with some sort of reasonable explanation for why he'd left Rachel's so suddenly and figure out how to collect his clothes and other belongings from underneath that cluster of trees in her backyard.

As he tried to come up with an excuse for his abrupt departure that Rachel might actually believe, he overheard his parents talking in their bedroom. They spoke softly, but Nate was still able to comprehend every word, thanks to the home's thin walls and his supersensitive hearing.

"I'm not finding anything," bemoaned his dad, John Schaffer.

"We'll figure something out," Barbara, his mother, replied in an encouraging tone.

"Like what?" John asked. "There's nothing else for me here. Nothing that I can support a family with."

Nate tuned out the rest of the conversation, not needing to hear any more. Like several others in town, his dad had just been laid off from Mr. Bennett's metals manufacturing plant. And like many others, he was struggling to find a new job.

An hour later, Nate trotted down the steps and made his way to the kitchen. He spotted his father sitting at the breakfast table, hunched over the classifieds section of the newspaper. Barbara stood behind him, her hands resting on his square shoulders.

Nate stood in the doorway and watched them until his mom glanced up and gave him a stern look.

"Where were you last night?" she asked. "I tried your cell for hours. Your father was out looking for you."

His phone. Yet another thing he had to go collect from Rachel's backyard. The sooner he could get over there, the better.

Nate entered the room and opened the fridge. "Sorry, I was over at Willard's studying," he said, pulling out a carton of orange juice. "Accidentally fell asleep."

"This staying out all night is not acceptable, young man," she scolded.

"*I said I'm sorry.* It's not like I meant to pull an all-nighter."

He grabbed a tumbler from the cabinet next to the stove and poured himself a glass of juice. His eyes returned to the classifieds section on the table.

"Why are you reading those ads?" he asked, pretending as if he didn't already know the answer.

John and Barbara disregarded the question. His father returned to the newspaper. His mom went to the stove to check on the two skillets she was using to fry their breakfast.

"How many eggs would you like with your sausage?" she asked.

Nate ignored her and walked over to the kitchen table. He sat down and gestured toward the help-wanted ads with his glass of juice. "Were there more layoffs at the plant? Is that why you're—"

"How many eggs, dear?"

Nate glowered at his mother, not appreciating the interruption. "Everyone knows Mr. Bennett is replacing his workers with—"

"Your mother asked you a question," his dad said gruffly.

"Just tell me what's going on!" Nate shouted, startling his parents.

John slapped the palm of his hand down on the table. "What's going on is you're going to listen to your mother. No more staying out all night, not while there's some animal out there attacking folks. And you don't raise your voice to her like that again in this house—ever."

Nate's stomach dropped. "There were more attacks?"

"An entire family was killed out at the Umatilla campsite," Barbara answered. "Including two young children. It's practically all they've been talking about on the radio this morning."

"I haven't been listening to the radio," was all Nate could think to say.

He quickly reviewed what little he knew. He was a therianthrope because he'd been bitten by one of the creatures. Hopefully the beast from the cavern was also the one responsible for attacking the family. Nate didn't really want to consider the alternative. He *really* needed to begin his research as soon as possible.

John picked up the paper and held it in front of him, signaling the end of their conversation. Not that it had been much of a conversation. Nate furrowed his brow, bothered by the fact that his parents felt the need to keep their troubles from him. He didn't need to be protected like some feeble child. Not anymore.

Maybe he could even help somehow.

Now wasn't the time to make that argument though. He had too much on his plate already. As he stood up to excuse himself, the doorbell rang.

"Could you go see who that is, Nate?" his mother asked. "Please."

Nate hesitated for a moment, then slowly exited the kitchen and crossed the living room to get to the front of the house. He turned the deadbolt and opened the door to find Sheriff Hoffman standing outside.

"Good morning, Nate."

"Hey…Sheriff." He forced himself to smile, then immediately worried if the smile was too much. Christ, just act natural. "What's going on?"

"I was hoping you might have a few minutes to tell me what you remember about being out on the reservation a couple nights ago."

Shit. Toby had said something. Or maybe not. The sheriff already knew Nate had been out on the reservation. That could still be all he knew. There was no reason to assume Toby had broken his promise. Nate would tell the sheriff about being chased by Mike and the others. Then he and Toby would get the rest of the story squared away at school. Yet another thing to add to his growing list of tasks for the day.

The sheriff took off his sunglasses and looked Nate square in the eyes. "My son said that when he picked you up, you had some blood on your shirt. I was wondering if you'd happened to remember how it got there."

Shit.

It was a peaceful morning at Carondelet Holy Cross Hospital. The distant voices of the medical staff paging their coworkers were the only sounds resonating down the white tiled hallways. While he, Rachel, and Peter walked through the recovery ward checking the numbers of each room they passed, Toby felt a dull, empty ache gnawing at his insides. Despite the quiet, he felt deeply disquieted.

He thought back to the last time he'd been at the hospital, the night of the accident, and remembered how he and his father had sat waiting to hear the devastating news they both knew was inevitable. He remembered how desperately, and futilely, he'd hoped the doctors would somehow deliver a different message.

"Here it is," Rachel said as she stopped in front of one of the rooms.

The three of them stared at the entrance for a moment, then at one another, as if they were all suddenly lost. Toby finally took a deep breath and stepped through the doorway, carrying a small vase of flowers he'd purchased from the first-floor gift shop.

The overly clean, antiseptic smell of the room, combined with the scent of countless other flower arrangements, created an almost unbearable aroma of fabricated freshness. In the center of a jungle of flowers and balloon bouquets lay Ashley Schultz, asleep in her hospital bed. Her mother, Sally, sat by her side.

The forlorn woman stared at her daughter as if in some sort of trance. There was no sign of Ashley's father, which didn't really surprise Toby all that much.

"Hello, Mrs. Schultz," he said softly while timidly taking a few more steps into the room.

Sally snapped out of her daze and looked up at him inquisitively. "Toby? What are you doing here? Shouldn't you be in school?"

"Um, I've got late arrival today," he lied.

He walked over to the window and found a tiny space to set down his vase, between a monolithic pot of pink roses and an oversized cookie bouquet. Turning back toward the bed, Toby took a moment to watch Ashley as she slept. She looked pale, but peaceful.

"The medication keeps her pretty tuckered out," Sally said. "She...doesn't do so well when she's awake."

"Has she spoken at all?" Toby asked.

Sally shook her head no, then gave him a weak smile. "It's good of you to come by. You and Ashley don't seem to see each other as much as you used to."

"We sort of run in different circles now."

Sally nodded. "What's high school without its cliques?"

Toby watched Ashley for another moment and suddenly felt very empathetic toward her. Although he had never witnessed anything as horrific as a person getting torn apart, he could relate to being in such close proximity to someone who was dying and not being able to do anything about it. He could relate to the nightmares, anxiety, and grief that had likely plagued Ashley ever since the incident.

Toby once again flashed back to his parents' Equinox, almost able to hear the roar of the frigid river water rushing in through the windows. He saw his mother unconscious in the passenger seat, half her face covered by wet, matted hair.

A sudden surge of panic and fear swelled up from his stomach and spread through his chest. Before the sensation could overwhelm him, Toby shut his eyes, took a deep breath, and shook the memories away.

"My daughter is in some sort of deep shock," Sally continued. "Or, at least that's what the doctors say."

Mrs. Schultz glanced over toward Rachel and Peter, who had both chosen to stay back by the doorway. She gave Peter a smile, which he returned. She then greeted Rachel with a curious look.

"I'm sorry. I don't think I know you, do I?"

"No," Rachel answered. "I'm Rachel Chochopi. I'm friends with Toby and Peter, which I guess is fairly obvious since I showed up here with them."

She rolled her eyes at her own awkward introduction, then took a few more steps into the room. Peter followed behind her.

"I don't really know Ashley all that well," Rachel added, before taking a moment to watch her traumatized classmate sleep. "I can't imagine what she must have gone through to end up like this."

Peter shrugged. "She saw a werewolf butcher her boyfr—"

A swift elbow to the ribs delivered by Rachel stopped Peter from finishing his thought. Toby gave his friend a stern glance to make sure he stayed quiet. That theory didn't need to be shared at this particular moment. Even if Peter had meant it as a joke to lighten the mood, this wasn't the time or the place for it.

With his attention temporarily diverted by his friend's poor judgment, Toby didn't notice Ashley's eyes pop open at the mention of the word "werewolf."

"What was that?" Sally asked. "What were you going to say?"

"It's nothing," Toby answered quickly. "I'm sorry, Mrs. Schultz. It's just a silly rumor going around school."

"That we came here to try to confirm," Peter grumbled, rubbing his sore ribs.

"Clarify," Toby muttered out of the side of his mouth. "Not confirm."

Sally stared blankly at them, confused. "Did you say a *werewolf*?"

Ashley sat up with a shot, her eyes wide as saucers, and let out an ear-piercing shriek. Everyone in the room jumped. Peter took a quick step backward and stumbled over a chair, falling onto the floor.

Ashley's mother leapt to her daughter's side and embraced her, trying in vain to calm her down. Toby took a minute to catch his breath and then turned to check on an equally unnerved Rachel. His eyes moved down to Peter, who remained seated on the floor.

Peter met his gaze. "Now, if you ask me, *that* seemed like a confirmation."

CHAPTER 15

I'LL BE DAMNED

Nate had had a busy morning. First there'd been the interrogation by Toby's dad, then a reaming from his own parents, followed by the retrieval of his smartphone and torn clothes from Rachel's yard. Now he stalked down the hallway at school, awaiting what he figured would be an imminent arrest.

Sheriff Hoffman had taken the shirt. The shirt that, up until this morning, Nate had been able to keep a secret. The shirt that the coroner was going to test and likely find was covered in Mike's blood, which Nate supposed would then make him the top suspect for at least one of the attacks. Possibly all of them.

How could Toby have betrayed him like this after promising not to?

Nate stopped stewing for a moment to notice the other students in the hallway. The attacks had created a seriously somber atmosphere around school. Kids stood huddled in groups, talking in whispers that Nate could still hear from several feet away. Many had the red, puffy eyes that resulted from a recent cry, and he wished he could remember enough to know whether he was responsible for their tears.

He needed to learn more about what was going on inside him. Turning into the computer lab, Nate went straight to the nearest available seat and quickly pulled a notebook from his backpack. He opened it to the page where he'd written a list of websites that he'd chosen to investigate during first period.

Before getting started, he gave the other preoccupied students in the room a paranoid glance. Convinced that nobody was paying any attention to him, as usual, he typed the first web address into the browser window and began reading, occasionally scribbling down notes.

Toby sat in the passenger seat of Rachel's Jeep with his hands shoved deep into the pockets of his faux-leather jacket, its hood pulled up over his head. He stared at the floor mat and mulled over their visit to the hospital. Had Ashley's scream really been a reaction to Peter and Mrs. Schultz saying the word "werewolf," or had she simply woken up from a bad dream?

"So what does everyone think?" he asked the group.

They all looked at one another, but nobody volunteered an answer. There was what each of them thought, and there was what each of them was willing to say they thought, and the two were not the same.

"I can go first," Toby offered.

"Please," Peter responded quickly.

Toby shifted in his seat to face them. "Well, for starters, I'm not ready to start believing in werewolves. Not until I actually see one."

"I'm not either," Rachel agreed.

"I can get on board with that," Peter added.

"That being said, there's definitely something going on with Nate that I don't really have another explanation for."

"Agreed," Rachel replied.

"Still on board," Peter chimed in.

"And I think it's safe to assume that he's noticed all the same changes we have. I'm guessing he's even got a couple of theories on why he can suddenly cave in lockers and run like a track star."

"So, like, how do we figure out what he's thinking?" Peter asked.

Toby pulled down his hood, growing more earnest. "We talk to him. He's probably just as freaked by all of this as we are. Probably *more* freaked. He needs to know that he doesn't have to go through this on his own."

Rachel turned into the school lot and brought her Jeep to a stop in the first available parking spot.

"Peter, you take the library," Toby instructed, as he hopped out. "Rachel, you check the courtyard. I'll see if I can find him in the computer lab."

"Who's got the next class with him?" Peter asked.

"I do," Rachel answered. "Calculus."

"Okay." Toby nodded as strode toward the building. "If none of us have found him before then, we'll meet up after you guys get out of class."

According to the website "How to Recognize if You're a Lycan," blackouts were pretty common among recently turned werewolves. As far as Nate could tell, there was no set schedule for when he'd start experiencing some level of awareness while a therianthrope. It worked differently for everyone.

Outside of that little nugget, however, he'd discovered very few new facts while clicking around the site. Actually, to call any piece of information he'd uncovered a "fact" was stretching things a bit. Nate knew that. He had no real reason to believe anything he'd read, but the website seemed to be at least *somewhat* legitimate. It was certainly the most credible source of information he'd found so far.

He mumbled quietly to himself as his eyes scanned the screen. "A person can be turned by sorcery, a Lycaeonia curse, or by being bitten. If one becomes a werewolf against his will, he's not completely damned until he…tastes human blood."

Nate leaned back and exhaled a deep sigh. The tail end of it came out as more of a growl as he glanced up from the computer screen to spot Willard entering the room.

After telling his parents that he'd fallen asleep at his friend's house studying, Nate had been forced to stick with the story when Sheriff Hoffman had asked him for his whereabouts during the previous night's attacks. That meant he now needed Willard to back up his alibi.

"Hey, I got your text," Willard said as he hustled over. "Why do you want me to tell Sheriff Hoffman you fell asleep at my house last night?"

"Only tell him that if he asks," Nate explained while quickly closing the website.

"But why?"

"Because it's what I need you to do."

Nate stood up and started to collect his things. After suffering through the consequences of Toby's loose lips, which had included his being grounded for a month after the sheriff's visit that morning, he wasn't in the mood to discuss what was happening to him with anyone else. Or, at least what he *believed* was happening.

"Did you hear about Jerry and Andrew?" Willard asked with the hint of a giddy lilt in his voice. "They were killed last night."

Sheriff Hoffman had already informed Nate of how the three people who'd chased him into the cavern were all now dead. There was no arguing the fact that the three deaths were quite coincidental, and therefore, likely not a coincidence at all. *If one becomes a werewolf against his will, he's not completely damned until he...*

"I'll be damned," Nate responded quietly.

He knew it was only a matter of seconds until a flood of theories and questions came spilling out of his chubby friend's mouth, so he slung his backpack over his shoulder and attempted to make a quick getaway.

"So what did it feel like?" Willard asked anxiously, starting in with his inquiry before Nate could escape.

"What did what feel like?"

"I know it was you," Willard pressed. "You weren't at my house last night, and I think you lied about it because you're...Well, you know what you are, right?"

Nate looked around uneasily at the other kids in the lab. Even if he were to change his mind about having this conversation, he sure as hell wasn't going to have it here. He shook his head and started for the door.

Willard quickly stepped in front of him. "Wait. I want in. I've read up on this and all you gotta do is bite me. I mean, you gotta be a therianthrope at the time, but..."

Nate made another move for the door. Willard again blocked his path. Nate grew even more agitated, but to his relief, Willard finally seemed to at least register his unease about discussing were-wolves in such a public place.

Looking around to make sure nobody was eavesdropping, Willard continued. "I was thinking I'd wait outside my house to-night, and you could—"

Nate nudged his friend aside. He had to get away from this.

Willard reached out and grabbed him by the forearm. "Wait! Come on. You can't keep this all for yourself. I mean, why should you get to have all the fun?"

"Fun?" Nate yanked his arm away. "You think I'm having *fun*?"

Deep down inside maybe he was, but Nate still felt a bit con-flicted about admitting to that aloud. And okay, so Willard knew. Willard knew and he actually believed. That shouldn't have come as a surprise. It also wasn't necessarily a cause for panic. Willard would be the *only* one to believe. Who outside of his role-playing friend would give such an out-of-this-world theory any credence?

"Who else knows?" Nate asked, just in case.

"For sure? Nobody," Willard replied. Then a look of realization flashed across his face. "But wait, so I'm right? You're a—"

"I think so." Nate kept his voice at a near whisper. "I mean, I'm pretty sure. I don't actually remember much from when I'm... you know."

Nate felt a slight tightening in the pit of his stomach. The fact that they were discussing this made it official. Like, officially of-ficial. Which meant there was no more ignoring the fact that he might be responsible for multiple, brutal killings.

"But that doesn't mean I'm having *fun*," Nate continued. "You know, this isn't like completing a mission in Demon Destroyer. There's a good chance that...that I've actually killed people."

Willard's face pinched up. "Well, considering three of the victims have been Mike, Jerry, and Andrew..."

"Whatever is happening to me, I barely remember it," Nate quickly reminded him. "And I don't have any control over it yet."

"Right," Willard said, once again registering the gravity of the situation. "Okay, so we'll figure out how to gain control. I mean, what do we do better than anyone? We study all there is to study about a problem, and we find the answers."

"What if there aren't any?"

Willard hesitated, and his inability to quickly volley back a response made Nate immediately wish he hadn't asked the question. Not because his friend's silence scared him. He should be scared. He *should* be terrified. Terrified of what he'd most likely become and of the things he'd quite possibly done that he couldn't remember.

But he wasn't terrified, and that's what bothered him.

However, he wasn't troubled enough to wish things were any different. Nate had never felt more alive, more invigorated. If the cost of this revitalization was the lives of the assholes who'd spent the past two years tormenting him, well...so be it.

If anything, he'd been pleased to hear about Jerry and Andrew. If he'd been busy taking care of them, then hopefully that meant he hadn't been responsible for the family in the woods.

Mike's death was different only due to the irritating fact that the sheriff now had Nate's shirt. There was a good chance that the blood on it was going to turn out to be the departed jock's, and Nate didn't have the first clue what to do about that.

"Fucking Toby," he muttered under his breath. And as if on cue, his snitching friend came striding into the computer lab.

What if there wasn't a way to control yourself while you were a therianthrope? As much as Willard wanted to be turned, he certainly didn't like the idea of waking one morning to discover he'd disemboweled his mom and dad.

But there *had* to be a way to control it. Maybe he and Nate didn't know of one now, but they'd figure something out. After all, they were the two smartest kids in school. As freshmen, they'd been the only first-years ever allowed to travel to Portland with the math and science teams. They were also the driving force behind the school having won back-to-back state Academic Bowl competitions.

There was an answer to this, and they would find it.

"You said you were going to help me," Nate said with a sneer. Willard turned to see Toby standing behind him.

"And I've been trying to," Toby answered defensively.

Nate's eyebrows furrowed sharply downward. "My parents freaked after your dad came by this morning. They grounded me for a month. You call that *help*?"

"I didn't know what else to do."

"You promised not to *do* or *say* anything."

"Something happened to you out on the reservation." Toby's tone was becoming sterner. "You've changed. We've all noticed, and we're worried about you."

"Well don't be." Nate's eyes went to Willard for a moment, then back to Toby. As he spoke, the words came tumbling out tempestuously. "You're right. I've changed. I'm stronger. And I'm not just talking about the stuff with Jerry and the locker yesterday; I mean I'm a stronger person—on the inside. I don't need you, or anyone else, to worry about me. I can take care of myself."

Nate stepped toward Toby, almost getting in his face, and his tone grew even more vicious. "You know, maybe helping people just isn't your thing. You don't seem to be very good at it."

Willard barely managed to hold back a gasp. That was a line that shouldn't have been crossed, regardless of how betrayed Nate felt.

Toby responded with a fiery stare that Nate absorbed unflinchingly. Thankfully, the five-minute bell rang just in time to prevent the heated exchange from escalating any further. Nate blinked first and broke off the short standoff, stalking off without another word.

Willard watched him trudge off, bothered. "That was kind of harsh."

Toby took a deep breath, exhaling it slowly in shaky bursts. "Yeah."

Unsure what else to say, Willard simply nodded goodbye and headed for the door.

"Hold up a second," Toby called after him. "What were you two talking about before I got here?"

"Um, I was just, you know, telling him about Jerry and Andrew."

"He hadn't heard about them?"

"I don't think so. No."

"You guys talk about anything else?"

Willard knew he couldn't answer that question honestly. Toby was in Nate's doghouse for talking too much, and he didn't want to end up there too, especially if he was going to try to convince Nate to turn him.

Also, Nate was right. Toby couldn't help. He didn't know about this kind of stuff, or even believe in it. Willard did. He knew all there was to know, or pretty darn close. If he ultimately thought that filling Toby in was the right thing to do, he could always do so later. He couldn't take back anything he let slip now.

"Nope," Willard replied. "That was pretty much it."

It had been a very long forty-eight hours for Sheriff Walter Hoffman. Between driving to multiple murder scenes, calling every name in the phone book to warn people of the attacks, and trying to figure out what was going on with his son, he had maybe gotten a wink or two of sleep.

Sporting a couple days' worth of stubble and a coffee stain on his typically spotless sheriff's uniform, Walter surveyed the anxious crowd that had assembled outside the station. The calls he and his deputy had made to warn residents had naturally caused quite a stir. Several folks had made their way over on an overcast afternoon, wanting answers he wouldn't be able to provide.

And he wasn't the only one stumped. Two self-satisfied members of Oregon's Wild Animal Control had arrived earlier in the day, letting him know straightaway that they'd seen plenty of these types of cases. Their theory was that the culprits were likely a pair of cougars working together, and that tracking the animals would probably only take the better part of a week.

Then Walter had taken them to the coroner's office, which doubled as the town's morgue, to view the bodies. One of the gentlemen nearly puked on the spot. The other hurriedly explained how, in fact, they'd never seen anything like this before.

As they'd hustled out of the office, they told him that they'd have to call in additional colleagues with greater expertise in dealing with aggressive animals. They assured him that they would get back to him soon with a better idea of what they were dealing with.

Walter wasn't going to hold his breath.

As he stood on the front steps of the station with Maggie Hendricks, Silver Falls's sometimes too maternal mayor, he decided he wasn't going to sugar coat any of this for the town's residents. However, just as he was about to speak, Maggie stepped forward to take first crack at tackling the crowd's concerns.

Dressed in a pair of cargo pants and fisherman's sweater, she raised her arms and attempted to quiet the gathering crowd.

"I want to know what the hell it is!" someone shouted. Many in the crowd stirred, a few echoing the sentiment. Their unrest was palpable.

"We don't know what it is yet," Maggie responded. "We do know there are a lot of rumors floating around."

"I heard it's a giant cougar," exclaimed another voice. "Like eight feet long!"

"I can't confirm that," Maggie said, once again raising her arms toward the crowd in what Walter assumed was supposed to be a calming gesture. "What I can confirm is that we are trucking in plywood from the mill in Eugene so folks can board up their windows."

"What about our jobs? Our kids need to go to school."

Walter stepped forward to help Maggie out. "So far the attacks have all been at night, so we're assuming that this animal is nocturnal."

"Noc-what?"

"That it only comes out after dark," Walter explained. "We're going to be instituting a town-wide curfew and—"

"What if it starts coming out during the day?"

"Either Deputy Rogers or I will be watching the schools. We're also asking for volunteers for watch posts around town. We've got a lot of accomplished hunters here, and we'll need every skilled marksman we can get."

"I'll help," a man's voice called out.

"Great. Please, anyone who wants to volunteer, feel free to come inside and sign up for a shift."

Walter glanced toward the mayor. He appreciated her wanting to keep the crowd calm, but he felt the residents needed to be talked to straight. He might not know what they were dealing with, but he'd seen enough to know that underestimating what was out in the surrounding woods would be a mistake.

"Also, if you own a firearm, I recommend carrying it," he added. "Another assumption I think we can make is that, whatever this thing is, it's clearly not as afraid of us as we are of it."

CHAPTER 16

Some Level of Awareness

It wasn't too bad of an evening crowd at Gary's Bar and Grill, considering the course of recent events. Seven o'clock and the cozy booths and walnut tables were about half full, and Gary was good with that. However, the sooner whatever was attacking folks was caught and killed, the better.

Business had already taken a hit due to the layoffs at the plant. He didn't need another prolonged deterrent to people spending their time and money in his bar.

Looking to get a head count, Gary surveyed his patrons. There was a table of twenty-somethings eating the fried and grilled dinner options his establishment offered, and several older customers at the bar enjoying that night's drink special, any light beer for half price. Everyone was still pretty shaken over the attacks, and so few among the crowd spoke. Those who were talking did so at a dull murmur.

As he stepped behind the bar to wash some glasses, Gary overheard a conversation between Sam Grey and Brett Gibson, two commercial fishermen in their late thirties, who sat at the end of the bar.

"I don't even see why our ancestors gave 'em any reservation," grumbled Sam, coated in the red glow of a neon Budweiser sign that matched his baseball cap. "They wanted this land so bad, they should've fought harder for it."

"They gave 'em the reservation so we wouldn't have to smell their raggedy ass stink in our bar," Brett muttered back.

Gary followed their sullen stares over to the front of the room. The target of their disdain was a disheveled Indian sitting at a table near the door. The man was eerily still, his eyes cast downward on the tabletop in front of him.

"Easy boys," Gary said, returning his attention to the glasses in the sink. "His raggedy ass has as much right to eat here as yours do."

Brett stood and raised his voice, looking right at the Shaman. "Well, I don't see him eating."

Sam slapped his palms on the bar and rose to his feet as well. "And I think it's time Tonto get back to his teepee!"

The Indian slowly raised his head to stare straight back at the stewing and over-served fishermen. Gary thought he saw the man's eyes flash yellow, which unnerved him quite a bit. Sam and Brett went silent, so he assumed they'd seen it too.

Settling into a new town had required a plan, and part of Rachel's was to get out of the house as much as possible. One way she did this was by seizing any opportunity to run errands for her mom and

Alan, like going to the grocery to pick up a missing ingredient for that night's dinner or to the bank to deposit Alan's checks from his hardware store.

These trips allowed her to mingle with the people of the town she now called home. After a couple of months of seeing the same faces and hearing their stories, she felt she would fit right in. Or, at least fit in a little better than she did right now.

This evening at the general store, she'd overheard a couple of interesting tidbits, like how Mrs. Dunbar's patch of strawberries was going to have its best output in five or six years and how Mr. Millar was planning to talk to the mayor about the height of his neighbor's new fence. Rachel couldn't remember the neighbor's name.

However, most of the stories she'd heard centered on the recent attacks. Everyone had a theory about what might be behind them. A straying bear. An oversized cougar. Not surprisingly, Rachel hadn't heard anyone suggest a werewolf.

She rounded the corner onto Wilson Street, heading home with a bag of groceries under each arm. Two burly Silver Falls' residents she had not yet met passed her going in the opposite direction, each holding rifles. Rachel gave them a quick nod and then quickened her pace.

This little errand put her dangerously close to being out past the recently instituted curfew. A curfew most folks appeared to be following. As she hustled down the empty street and past Gary's Bar and Grill, the only sound Rachel heard was the rapid clopping of her own boots.

Then she heard the first scream.

It had come from inside the bar, and several more immediately followed. Rachel stopped and stared at the building, frightened but also curious.

The prickling feeling was back. It was the same sensation she'd felt the night before, only more intense. This time it sank deeper into her, all the way down to her bones.

The commotion inside the restaurant grew louder. Rachel could hear glass shattering, people shouting, and furniture being knocked around and overturned. She looked back for the two men with the rifles, but they'd already rounded the corner and disappeared from view. She was alone, and frozen with indecision. Half of her wanted to see what was happening inside the bar, the other half wanted to run.

Before either side won out, the front door burst open, and a bloodied man in a red baseball cap came staggering down the steps. His torso had been slashed by what appeared to be claw marks, and he wore the same terrified expression that Rachel had seen plastered across Ashley's face on the reservation.

He collapsed onto the street and moaned. "Help me."

What Rachel saw next shocked her so much that it left her too staggered to scream. A werewolf crashed through the bar's doorframe and part of the building's brick wall, lunging after the man. The monster landed on the stranger's back and clawed out his spine, splattering his blood across Rachel's shoes and jeans.

She ignored the blood, her eyes remaining locked on the beast in front of her.

Mangy fur covered the creature in clumps, with the exposed areas showing a black, leathery skin. Its head was massive with a proportionately massive jaw. A wolf was probably the closest animal to compare it to, but the beast also had a distinct demonic quality all its own.

Most incredibly, it was real.

Her uncle hadn't been making up ghost stories to convince Rachel to move back to the reservation. *The wolf was real*, and it was more monstrous than anything she could have fathomed. It was also less than a few feet away.

Rachel dropped her groceries, and a bottle inside one of the bags shattered.

The werewolf's head jerked up at the sound.

Then the beast stalked forward. Rachel stiffened as it approached. The creature got so close that she could feel the wet warmth of its breath on her face.

It would rip out her throat before she'd be able to open her mouth to scream, sink its teeth into her leg before she could take a step to run. Rachel did all she could think to do and simply closed her eyes.

Instinctively, she started to count. It was a coping mechanism from her youth, one she'd used to handle her anticipation on Christmas morning or to wait out one of her parents' arguments as she tried to fall asleep. It had become second nature, and so she counted and kept counting. She could feel every inch of her body shaking.

What was the thing waiting for?

Rachel opened her eyes. The werewolf was gone.

Several blocks over, Willard sat on his parents' picnic table, impatiently surveying the trees at the edge of his backyard. He absent-mindedly flipped a flashlight on and off, shining the beam onto different bushes, a two-story birdhouse, and his neighbor's garage. The sun was down. The moon was up.

Had Nate even bothered to consider his request?

The conversation in the computer lab hadn't gone exactly as Willard had wanted, but it also hadn't included an outright refusal.

So he chose to remain hopeful. Nate *would* come. In one form or another.

Tapping his feet anxiously on the table's cracked plywood bench, Willard fantasized about waking up a newly turned therianthrope. Let's see how many more times he got picked last in gym class once *he* could run like the wind. Let's see who still had the courage to hassle him once *he* could cave in lockers.

Of course, for fantasy to become reality, Nate would have to maintain some level of awareness after his transformation. And Nate claimed to have no awareness of his actions while a therianthrope. What he did while a monster was ostensibly up to the monster. But Willard didn't believe it was pure happenstance that three of the town's first victims had been Mike, Jerry, and Andrew.

Nate must have had some input on that. Somehow he'd gotten the beast to seek out the bastards who'd tormented him, and Willard, daily since they were fourteen. And the fact that he had was proof that controlling your actions while a therianthrope was at least *somewhat* possible—even if only on some subliminal level.

Nate just had to want it badly enough.

Willard's mother opened the back door of their cottage home. "Christ, Willard. Are you *trying* to get eaten by that cougar? Come inside. Dinner is almost ready."

She stepped back into the house with a heavy sigh. Disappointed, Willard followed with a deep groan of his own. Fantasy was going to remain fantasy. At least for him. It just wasn't fair.

A sudden breeze seemed to imitate his moan, rustling the leaves in the trees. Not quite ready to give up hope, he absentmindedly clicked the flashlight on and off three more times. After the third click, he saw something.

Willard sucked in a startled gasp. Just beyond the patio lights, two glowing yellow eyes were looking right at him. He smiled an excited smile. It was going to happen. Nate had come to turn him into a therianthrope!

The werewolf stalked into the dim light cast out over the lawn by a single fluorescent bulb that hung above the back door. First its snout came into view. Then its hair, muscles, and fangs were all unveiled. The beast was much larger than what Willard was expecting, closer to the size of a grizzly bear than a wolf. But it definitely had a wolf's body—long and lean. The creature paused in the center of the yard and released a menacing snarl.

This was a bad idea...an idiotically dangerous—only worth trying if you had some sort of death wish—*bad* idea. Seeing the terrifying creature live in the fur and flesh filled Willard with an intense dread. His smile turned to a look of dismay.

Horrified by the monster standing in front of him, Willard jumped off the table and tried to run. He made it only two steps before he was knocked off his feet by one of the beast's paws.

Feeling as though he'd been struck between the shoulders with a baseball bat, Willard tumbled to the lawn. He rolled over the dry grass twice before coming to rest on his back. Too hurt to move, he just lay stunned by how swiftly the creature had chased him down.

The werewolf stalked over, staring at Willard with its wicked yellow eyes. He was certain they'd be the last things he ever saw.

With another nasty snarl, the beast lurched forward, opening its jaw. Willard felt its teeth slice through his skin. He cried out as his shock yielded to the burning pain of the creature's fangs digging deep into his shoulder and upper chest. Overcome by agony and despair, he fainted.

CHAPTER 17

THE ACCIDENT

Not surprisingly, coming clean about what had happened on the reservation had not been enough for Toby to avoid punishment. Although, even if he weren't already grounded for driving without a license and fighting a now deceased classmate, he'd still be stuck at home. The new town curfew required everyone who wasn't armed and standing guard to be inside by 8:00 p.m. until further notice, no exceptions.

So Toby sat in the living room, ill at ease, trying unsuccessfully to read about the rise of progressivism in America, the main topic of chapter twenty-three in his U.S. history textbook. While he read every word, he comprehended none of them. He was too preoccupied with what had happened at school that day to focus on his studies.

Or, more accurately, too dissatisfied with what hadn't happened. His plan to figure out what was going on inside Nate's head—as well as the rest of his body—had failed miserably. After their confrontation in the computer lab, Nate had avoided him for the rest of the day.

Maybe helping people just isn't your thing. You don't seem to be very good at it.

Toby set down the textbook with a heavy sigh. His eyes went to a picture of his family above the fireplace, and, without thinking about it, he focused in on his smiling mother. And just like that, he once again flashed back to the accident.

His memory of that night, the full version of it, always started just after sunset. He was driving the family's Equinox, and his mom, Mary Hoffman, sat shotgun. She was relaxing comfortably in the passenger seat, kindly showing no concern over his considerable inexperience as a driver.

"Let's turn on the headlights," she suggested as the twilight sky grew darker.

Toby flipped a switch on the right lever of the steering column. The windshield wipers swayed slowly back and forth. "Damn."

He turned off the wipers and switched on the headlights.

"How would you feel about picking up dinner at Wolfy's?" his mother asked, ignoring the simple slip-up. "Your dad's working the late shift tonight, and I was thinking we could surprise him with dinner at the station."

"Light is left, light is left," Toby muttered, tapping the lever. He brought his hand back the wheel and glanced over at her. "Yeah, sure. Sounds good."

She pointed to the road ahead. "Slow down a little bit. This next turn is pretty sharp."

Toby braked, but still took the turn too fast. His upper torso jerked against the seat belt, and he heard the tires emit a soft squeal.

"Shit. I mean...sorry."

"That's okay." His mother encouraged him with a warm smile. "You're doing great."

"Yeah, compared to Grandma, maybe."

Her smile widened. "You'll get the hang of it soon enough."

They approached an unnamed wooden bridge that crossed the east branch of the Chetco River. The rushing waters widened considerably in this area, which made the location a popular spot for catching salmon. The hike from the makeshift parking spots at the east end of the bridge down to the river's edge took only about ten minutes.

Fishing was one of his father's favorite activities, so Toby had been dragged down to the Chetco on more than a few occasions to take part in what his dad often called the perfect contradiction: a relaxing challenge.

Toby had always found it to be more of a frustrating bore. During their outings, he'd daydream about floating down the river, all the way to where it met up with the northwest branch about one hundred and eighty miles south of Silver Falls, near Ashland, Oregon, where it then flowed in a southwest direction for another one hundred and thirty-two miles to its outfall into the Pacific at Chetco Cove. All places Toby knew only by name, having never traveled very far south of his hometown.

The Chevy's tires rumbled over the bridge's wooden planks as they began to cross the river. It was a sound Toby had always found comforting. Well, up until that night anyway. If only he'd come to the bridge a little sooner, or a little later. They were about halfway across it when their casual drive turned catastrophic.

Headlights suddenly appeared through the trees up ahead, and the vehicle they belonged to seemed to be really cruising. Within seconds, an old pickup came roaring around a turn and onto the bridge going way too fast. It bore right down on them.

"Toby! Look out!" his mother shouted.

He yanked the wheel and attempted to swerve around the oncoming truck, but it was moving too fast. There was a brief, ear-piercing screech as the pickup sideswiped the passenger side door. The collision rocked the vehicle, and the steering wheel jerked violently in Toby's hands as his parents' Equinox swerved again, this time on its own.

The vehicle crashed through the bridge's railing, its tires suddenly spinning in nothing but air.

His recollections of this part—the actual accident and the Equinox plummeting into the Chetco—were a rapid mash-up of sounds and sensations, none of which were any help during his father's subsequent search for the other driver.

Toby's clearer memories began again with his face slamming into the driver's side airbag upon the vehicle's impact with the water.

The Chevy bobbed up momentarily, and Toby slid back, pushing the airbag down. The vehicle then began to sink. Water poured in through the vents and the broken passenger side window.

Shaking off shock, Toby unbuckled his seat belt and turned to find his mother unconscious. After undoing her seat belt, he attempted to pull her toward him. He could barely budge her.

The passenger side door was smashed inward from where the pickup had struck, and either her arm or leg—maybe even just her foot—was stuck on something.

The rushing water and spreading darkness made it impossible to tell where she was pinned. Toby took a deep breath as water completely filled the Equinox. He yanked frantically at his mother's sweater, then her shoulder, but he couldn't pry her from the seat. That was when the panic really set in.

Instead of trying to get a closer look at what was holding her in place, Toby just yanked harder and more hysterically, desperately attempting to pull her loose. Bubbles burst forth from his mouth and nose. His lungs started to burn. He had to get air.

After one last unsuccessful tug, he turned and maneuvered his way through the broken window. He then kicked for the surface. Or at least for what he urgently hoped was the surface. He was too turned around to be positive about which direction was up. Just as he thought he might drown, he emerged.

Toby sucked in the brisk evening air. His body shivered violently, gripped by a deep, muscle-seizing cold. That was the point at which he also froze psychologically, wishing he could go back in time twenty minutes to avoid the incident altogether.

He so badly wanted to escape this, to just close his eyes and reopen them to find his mom was somehow safe and sound. His petrified state lasted only a moment or two, but they were a moment or two he'd never get back.

He dove underneath the water again. The river wasn't particularly deep in this area, maybe twelve feet or so, but with no daylight left to illuminate what lay below the Chetco's lazily flowing surface, locating the Chevy took longer than anticipated. When Toby finally did find it, his mother was gone.

Had she managed to climb out? Somehow gotten herself free? If he swam up to the surface and she wasn't there, how was he going to find her? It was then that Toby froze a second time, overcome with fear and dread.

Not knowing what to do next, he just stared blankly into the dark, muddy water around him until his lungs strained for him to take a new breath.

Moments later, Toby inhaled another mouthful of the evening's brisk air, then erupted into a coughing fit. Swiveling himself around with a few choppy paddles, he quickly realized his mother was nowhere to be found.

Toby called out for her between sputtering coughs. "Mom! Mom!"

A pounding at the front door snapped Toby from the memory. He blinked away some newly formed tears and wiped one off his cheek. There was more pounding. Getting up off the living room recliner, he hustled for the door and opened it to find a visibly shaken Rachel standing on the front steps.

She brushed right past him and started pacing around the room while trying to catch her breath. Toby glanced outside uneasily. He checked the street and then looked toward her house next door. All was quiet, with the exception of the frenetic girl treading back and forth across his living room floor.

"Hey." He turned his attention toward her. "I'm kind of grounded, so…" Toby trailed off when he realized just how hysterical

Rachel was. She ran her fingers through her hair as she continued to pace, darting her eyes around the room without looking at anything in particular. She was shaking from head to toe.

"Rachel?"

She locked in on him. "It's real," she said tremulously. "It's fucking real!"

"What is?" Toby knew instantly what she'd meant, but couldn't help himself from asking the question. "The werewolf?"

"I just saw it out front of the bar on Wilson Street."

"Gary's?"

Rachel nodded as she gulped air. She continued to pace, her steps slowing as she began to regain her composure.

"It killed a man," she said finally. "Right in front of me."

"How did you get away?" Toby asked anxiously, taking another look outside.

"I didn't. It just...it just didn't attack me."

"Jesus." Toby let the gravity of the situation sink in. "So Nate's really a...a *werewolf*?"

"No. Or, I don't know, maybe he is, but I don't think the thing I saw was him. I think it was the Shaman."

Toby's train of thought derailed. "Who?"

"Okay." Rachel took another deep breath. "Remember how last night I told you that my uncle had come over and was talking all sorts of strange?"

"Yeah."

"Well...part of that strange included a story about a Shaman from our tribe, who, like, hundreds of years ago got turned into a werewolf somehow so he could protect our tribe from, well, white people. Now he's back, and he's trying to reclaim what used to be our land by killing everyone in this town."

Toby stared at her blankly, looking as if he'd been shot and was waiting to fall. The crazy Indian who'd seemingly been keeping tabs on Nate and him ever since they'd found the cavern had just been identified.

Rachel misread his astounded gape. "And now you think I'm just another freak from the reservation."

"No," he responded quickly. "I mean, to be honest, I don't really know what to think, but I definitely don't think that. I'm pretty sure I've seen this Shaman guy you're talking about. I didn't realize he was what he is, but…I guess it makes sense. As much as any of this makes sense."

"We need to tell someone about him."

Toby knew who they needed to tell, and he knew just how a story about an Indian werewolf was going to go over with his father. It would likely add another several weeks to his house arrest, but he didn't see any other option. His dad had wanted the full story. Now he was going to get it.

CHAPTER 18

BELIEF IN MAKE-BELIEVE CREATURES

What had been concern among the residents of Silver Falls had developed into full-blown panic, thanks in no small part to the news that Barb Snyder had burst into the station only moments earlier to announce.

She'd started in a frenzy, hysterically babbling words and phrases like "blood," "monster," and "they're all dead." Walter had eventually calmed her enough to get further details, but he'd understood the most important fact immediately: It had found the town.

He dispatched Billy to Gary's bar right away, along with some of the townspeople who'd shown up to the impromptu meeting on the front steps earlier with guns in hand. Walter remained at the station to try to calm residents and to continue recruiting volunteers to stand watch.

As he took down the cell phone numbers for two men in their early forties, Don Hutchins and Paul Grant, the bleary-eyed sheriff realized he was forming a posse. Not to hunt down a fugitive, but a bloodthirsty animal.

"I can take a shift Saturday night too," Don offered. "If you need me."

Walter jotted down the nights the hunter was available next to his name and number. "That'd be great, Don. Thanks."

He glanced up from his volunteer sheet to address his next potential volunteer, but paused when he saw Toby entering the station along with the girl who'd just moved in next door. Walter felt his blood start to simmer. This was more stress he didn't need.

While he continued trying to settle panicked residents, the kids squeezed their way through the crowd and up to the front of his desk.

"Thought my orders were pretty clear," he said as he rechecked the town watch schedule for Saturday night.

Toby leaned in and spoke in a near whisper. "We know what's been killing people."

Walter's eyes shot up from his clipboard and he gave Toby his full attention. He wasn't the only one. With all the townspeople within earshot stopping what they were doing to listen to him, Toby grew visibly uneasy.

"Could we go to the back office, or—"

"Tell me what you know," Walter ordered.

Toby glanced back at the crowd behind him, all pushing in like a frenzied mob of shoppers waiting for the doors to open on a big sale. His eyes then moved to the Chochopi girl, who Walter noticed was encouraging his son with a determined nod.

Finally, Toby turned back to his father. "It, um…well, it's… well, we *think* it's…"

"Out with it."

"A werewolf."

A few of the townspeople snickered. Others shook their heads, annoyed by the silly and inappropriate interruption. Walter grabbed his son by the arm and pulled him away from the crowd, back by the rear staircase that led down to the jail cells.

Once he judged that they were out of earshot, he took his son to task. "You think this is the time for games?"

"No. I know how it sounds, but the thing that's been killing people is a—"

"Stop," Walter barked. "I don't want to hear you say it again."

Did their new neighbor have something to do with this nonsense? Or did Toby's new belief in make-believe creatures have more to do with Mary's death? Was this some sort of cry for attention? There was a good chance that the kid's emotional scars from the accident were at least part of the issue here—and still something Walter hadn't figured out how to adequately address.

"Now listen, I know we've been going through a tough time," he said as calmly as he could. "You *know* that I do. But I can't have you acting out like this right now. *Not now.*"

The Chochopi girl took a couple of steps toward them. "He's telling the truth."

Walter was going to have to find a way to keep this strange young woman away from his son. He was also going to have to figure out how to get Toby talking with the school counselor again.

"I'm just trying to help," Toby said.

"Well then stop!" Walter snapped. He waved over Paul Grant. "Paul, can you do me a favor and get these two home?"

"Not a problem, Sheriff."

The hunter grabbed them each by the shoulder, and the Chochopi girl began to struggle immediately.

"You have to believe us," she pleaded. "This thing is real!"

Toby shrugged off Paul's grip and frantically moved closer to his father. "Dad, I know it sounds crazy, but I swear—"

Walter slammed his fist onto a nearby desk. "Toby. Home. Now."

Paul grabbed Toby again and started to lead the kids out of the station. "Now don't make this any harder than it has to be."

Toby looked back as he was being escorted away, his eyes filled with distress. The hurt look was genuine, and it worried Walter. It made him think that the explanation his son had just given him wasn't something he'd concocted for attention.

Toby believed in what he'd said. He sincerely thought his friends and neighbors had been killed by a werewolf.

Walter jotted down a note to call Ms. Parker first thing in the morning.

Willard opened his eyes to find himself staring at the stars and the tops of trees swaying in a gentle night breeze. He had absolutely no recollection of how he'd ended up on the ground or any idea of how long he'd been laying there. Since his mom hadn't come back out to find him, he guessed it couldn't have been for more than a few minutes.

He turned his head and glanced over at the picnic table. The last thing he remembered was sitting on top of it and waiting for Nate—and of course the reason he'd been waiting.

Then he saw the blood.

Almost immediately, he sprang up and grabbed his chest. The top of his shirt was torn and soaked in crimson, but he didn't feel any pain. Willard pulled back the shirt and rubbed his thumb over the skin on his upper chest and shoulder. There was no sign of a wound.

Not wanting to be discovered in a torn and bloody shirt, he leapt to his feet and darted back toward the house. He glanced through the windows for any sign of his parents, then snuck back inside as quietly as he could. Halfway up the stairs, he heard his mom call out.

"Dinner is ready, Willard."

"Okay," he called back. "Be there in a second."

He hustled into his room and went to the closet, opening up a drawer of wool sweaters. He pulled off his shirt and used the bottom half to wipe some of the blood off his body. Then, folding up the shirt as neatly as he could, he hid the evidence beneath a short stack of cable knits.

His lips curled slowly into a smile. Nate had done it!

Willard plopped back and sat on the floor, dizzy with glee. Everything was going to be different now. If it all worked out the way it was supposed to, the way the information he'd found about therianthropes said it would, then he was now one of them. There wouldn't be anything he couldn't do.

Several blocks over, Toby lay on his bed reassessing the situation he found himself in.

Werewolf.

He had told himself he'd have to see such a thing to believe in it, and he still hadn't. Rachel had. He'd seen the Shaman. He'd also seen his friend do things he shouldn't be able to do after finding that same friend covered in blood on the reservation. All those factors had him pretty well convinced about the reality of what was going on.

Then he'd actually said the word aloud to his father. *Werewolf.*

He'd felt doubt creep in at that moment, but he'd spent the last hour convincing himself that he no longer needed to actually see the supernatural animal firsthand to believe in it. He'd also decided he was still going to do whatever it took to help Nate, regardless of whether or not his help was wanted.

"So what was all that about exactly?" Walter asked, nearly shouting.

He'd stormed into Toby's bedroom without so much as a knock. His voice was strained and dark bags had formed under his eyes. This man who'd always known how to play the hero now looked exceptionally haggard.

Toby didn't know of a good way to defend the theory he'd presented earlier, so he decided to dance around doing so until he could offer more proof. "You have to admit, a lot of what's been going on has been pretty strange."

"Yes," Walter agreed. "Including you marching into my sheriff station to say you'd seen a werewolf."

"I didn't actually see it," Toby corrected. "Rachel did."

"I want you to stay away from her."

"Why?"

"Because she's apparently got you believing in make-believe creatures!"

"Dad, I swear it's real. Rachel told me there's, like, this super-old Shaman, who's got this werewolf curse. And I know he's real because Nate and I saw him out by that cavern in the woods, and then again when we were…" Toby trailed off when he saw something he'd never seen before in his life—tears in his father's eyes.

The man who had been a pillar of strength in the community throughout the recent layoffs, brutal attacks, and his even own wife's death finally let his feelings show. But only for a moment. That was as long as he was going to allow his emotions to seep through the internal levee he'd constructed to contain them.

He wiped the tears away and steadied himself with a deep breath. "I need you to help me out a little here."

As brief as the momentary breakdown had been, it floored Toby. His father looked exceptionally disheartened, and it was at least partially his fault.

Toby had given his dad a considerably larger amount of things to worry about, including fights at school, using the car without a license, stumbling across a dead body, and now possibly even his mental state. While he might have plenty of reasons to believe in werewolves, nobody else in that sheriff station did.

His dad had probably gotten all kinds of odd looks and questions after Paul had dragged Rachel and him out of there.

Despite what he might believe, Toby knew what needed to be said at that moment. "Yeah, okay. I'm sorry. No more werewolf talk. I promise."

Walter reached out and gave his son an appreciative pat on the knee. "Thank you. Now I've got to get back, but there's one more thing I stopped by to talk to you about. Are you absolutely certain that Nate didn't have any injuries when you found him out on the reservation the other night?"

"Yeah," Toby answered. "Why?"

"The tests came back on his shirt, and it wasn't Mike's blood. So that makes me a little curious about just whose it might have been."

Thanks to several hours of Internet research, Toby had a pretty good idea of whose blood it might be, but he knew that now was not the time to share his theory.

"Okay," Walter said, turning for the door. "We'll both sleep on what happened earlier, and let's plan to talk about it some more in the morning. Sound good?"

Toby nodded as his father exited the room. He doubted his dad would actually find the time to have that talk, and that was fine by him. As far as Toby was concerned, there was no use in discussing this any further until he could present evidence that werewolves existed, and he could think of only one surefire way to get the proof he needed.

CHAPTER 19

A PROFOUND NEED TO HELP

After a quick shower and breakfast, Willard exited his home to find his father sitting on the front porch reading the morning paper and drinking a beer. This had become routine behavior over the past couple of weeks. The forty-six-year-old man looked as though he hadn't bathed in days, quite possibly because he hadn't.

Distressed by the depressing sight, Willard swiftly moved past his dad without as much as a "good morning." His father's situation left him feeling powerless, angry, embarrassed, and confused. This mix of sentiments usually stayed with him throughout the morning, but today it vanished almost immediately when Willard noticed Nate leaning against a tree in the front lawn.

He skipped down the porch steps and hustled toward his friend, hardly able to contain his excitement. "You did it, didn't you? I'm a—"

"How's your dad doing?" Nate asked.

Willard paused and shrugged, looking back at his father. "Pretty much been a wreck since he got laid off from the plant."

"Yeah, mine too." Nate kept his eyes on the defeated man for another moment, then shifted his attention to Willard. "How do *you* feel?"

"Amazing," Willard said breathlessly. "Like I've got this force inside me. I can't even begin to explain it, but then…I guess I don't really have to. Not to you."

His gleeful expression abruptly turned into a grimace as a Harley-Davidson Wide Glide roared toward them from up the street. Willard doubled over, gritting his teeth in pain, his eardrums feeling as though they were going to explode.

"The heightened senses can be a little irritating at first," Nate said loudly as the motorcycle cruised past them and down the block. "But your body adjusts after a day or so."

"This is so cool," Willard practically squealed, rubbing his palms over his ears. "We've advanced to become something beyond just being human. What we've got inside us now…it basically makes us a whole different species."

"Now we need to figure out how to control it."

"Right. And we will," Willard said confidently. "We've got almost a month until the next full illumination cycle."

"Until the next what?"

"Two nights before a full moon, the night of, and the two nights after," Willard explained. It didn't necessarily surprise him that Nate wasn't aware of the cycles. His friend knew plenty about *what* therianthropes could do, but not so much about the *when*. "Those are the only times we turn. Or, at least that's what all the lore says."

Nate considered this new information and looked hopeful. "You haven't told anyone else about this, right? Not Peter, not—"

"Screw Peter," Willard grumbled.

"Or Toby?"

"I told them what I thought, and they laughed at me."

"Good," said Nate. "I mean, not that they laughed at you, but... This way we can bring them in when we think they're ready. When *we're* ready. Until then, I think we should hide what we are. Deny it. At least until we figure out a lot more about it."

They started off down the sidewalk, Willard still with a bit of a skip in his step. This was going to be so much fun.

Billy did a number of things well as the deputy of Silver Falls. Making coffee was not one of them. However, desperate times called for bitter and stale measures. Both Walter and his deputy had stayed up through the night, fielding calls to the station and doing rounds to check the newly established watch posts around town.

With a new day beginning, Walter choked down his twelfth, maybe thirteenth, acidic cup of sludge as he studied a map of the municipality he'd sworn to protect—even when he wasn't sure how to do so.

Multicolored pushpins marked strategic watch posts that circled Silver Falls, in addition to a few specially designated areas within the town. Walter and his deputy were due at the post by the elementary school in half an hour. He should let Billy catch a quick nap until then. There was no telling when they'd get the chance to sleep next.

Hearing the station's front door open, he glanced up and let a low moan escape his lips when he saw Ms. Parker, the school counselor, tentatively stick her head in.

"I should have called ahead," she said apologetically. "I can certainly understand if this is a bad time. I'll come back when things have settled down."

Walter waved her over to his desk. "No. I'm sorry. Just a little tired."

"More than just a little, I would imagine."

This got him to chuckle briefly, and he gave her a nod. "You're right about that, but I've got some time before I need to be over at the grade school. I know you've juggled your schedule plenty to be able to come over here and see me, so let's just go ahead and do this."

Ms. Parker walked over and took a seat. Walter instinctively turned toward the coffee maker to offer her a cup, then thought better of it. He pulled his chair out from underneath his desk and sat down.

"Since our time is short, we can just get right to it," said Ms. Parker.

"That'd be great."

She shifted her weight in the chair, getting comfortable. "You said over the phone that Toby came here last night claiming that a werewolf was behind the attacks?"

Walter responded with a deep sigh and another nod.

"That is quite concerning—and a bit above my pay grade, to be perfectly honest—but I feel like most of his recent issues can still be traced back to one specific cause."

"His mother's death?"

"Well, yes, but more specifically from an intensely profound need to help people as a result of her death."

THE ONE YOU FEED

Walter was a bit thrown by the diagnosis. "Since when is wanting to help people considered an issue?"

"It's good to want to help people," she clarified. "But with Toby, I think it's become more of a dangerous compulsion, to the point where he's apparently creating imaginary threats. It's an avoidance technique he's using to put off dealing with what's really eating at him."

"He's pretending werewolves exist because he feels guilty about his mom drowning?" Walter asked skeptically.

"We all cope with loss in different ways." Ms. Parker shifted again. Walter couldn't tell if it was the chair or the conversation that was making her uncomfortable. Perhaps it was a bit of both. "And I think Toby is upping the ante to fill a void. He couldn't save the person he cared for most, so now he's trying to save everyone else he perceives to be in danger."

"Leading to fights at school, him hiding things from me to protect his friends, and now...werewolves."

"Exactly. And each time things don't go as planned, that void just gets bigger. Even if he were to succeed, I believe that whatever satisfaction he would derive from that success would just drive him to want to achieve such a feeling again. It would never be enough because he's not coping with the real issue. Then there's the example you're setting. The way you've seemingly moved on and gotten back to your work, returning to a job that is *defined* by your ability to help people."

Walter shot her an incredulous look. Was she telling him to retire as the town's sheriff?

"I'm not suggesting you quit or do anything drastic like that," she said, answering his unasked question. "But maybe just focus a little less on putting up a brave front and a little more on talking with your son about how your wife's death has affected him—and you."

Walter digested her advice and again responded with a nod. He had no idea how he was going to give Toby the time he needed though. His son was obviously the most important thing in his life, but if there were ever a situation where his responsibility to the community needed to come first, this was it.

Again, Ms. Parker seemed to be able to read his thoughts. "I know you have a lot on your plate right now, so I can try to get things started."

She could claim this situation was above her pay grade, but right now she was showing more of a talent for reading people than some of Walter's former fellow detectives back in Portland ever had.

"He starts serving his string of Saturday detentions this weekend," she continued. "I can meet with him then and try to figure out why he's escalated to point he has."

"That would be great."

"Again, I can't make any promises."

"I understand," Walter said as he stood to walk her out. "And I want you to know that I really appreciate all that you've done to help him already."

"It's the least I *can* do," she replied, managing a weak smile. "He needs to understand that trying to help everyone he perceives to be in trouble isn't an effective way to cope with his loss or guilt. If anything, it's just going to get him hurt."

Walter wasn't sure if they were talking *only* about Toby anymore, but he didn't have time to let Ms. Parker assess his own hang-ups at the moment. He needed to go over tonight's watch schedule and then get over to the elementary school.

CHAPTER 20

WHAT *DIDN'T* HAPPEN IN EVERGREEN PARK

Six-thirty in the evening and all was quiet in the upstairs hallway of the Schaffer residence. Nate slipped out of his bedroom and across the textured Saxony carpet to the hall closet. He quickly gathered three pillows from the bottom shelf and then, just as quickly, put them back.

It wouldn't work. Even if he could form an acceptable facsimile of himself sleeping under the covers, neither of his parents was going to believe he'd turned in at such an early hour.

Returning to his room, Nate opened the iTunes player on his laptop, started the playlist he typically used while studying, and turned up the speaker volume. He left the door open just a crack, figuring it would look less suspicious than if he shut it completely. This would have to do. If Willard was right, he should get back before anyone decided to check on him anyway.

Nate trusted Willard more than anyone when it came to understanding the supernatural, and he hoped his friend's information about full illumination cycles was accurate, but just in case it wasn't, he wanted to be alone when the sun went down.

Opening his window, Nate stepped out onto the first-floor roof. He moved cautiously to the edge, not due to a fear of falling, but simply to keep from making too much noise. He then got down flat on his stomach and peeked his head underneath the gutter to see if his parents were in the den. The coast was clear.

Springing onto his hands and knees, he dug his toes into the roof's asphalt shingles and jumped. With feline grace, Nate landed on his feet in the backyard and scampered to the far side of the house. So far, so good. But as he circled around to the front of the home, his plan hit a snag.

Toby stood at the bottom of the front walk. "Going somewhere?"

"Uh, just over to Willard's," Nate responded. "We're going to try to get a game of Middle Earth Conquests started before curfew."

"Okay if I join you?"

"Why? You actually want to play?"

"Well I might, um…no," Toby confessed. "Look, to be totally honest, I came over here to apologize. I wanted to say I'm sorry about telling my dad about the shirt and everything else. Maybe as a peace offering I could let you crush me at this Middle Earth Demon Destroyer thing."

Damn. Nate had hoped mentioning Middle Earth Conquests would send Toby running, but instead it had given his friend an opening to stick around. As they started down the sidewalk, he tried to think up some sort of excuse for why Toby couldn't play. He had to get rid of his friend before sunset.

Then he caught Toby stealing a glimpse of the darkening sky, and suddenly the timing of his friend's apology seemed suspicious. Willard had said that Toby and Peter didn't believe his werewolf theory, but what if Willard was wrong about that?

"You don't have to do this," Nate said, trying to give his friend an out.

"I know, but I *want* to do this. I swear."

"You think I'm a werewolf, don't you?"

Nate surprised himself by asking the question so forthrightly. Even in human form, he sometimes found he was more impulsive than he'd like to be now that he'd been turned.

Toby stopped dead in his tracks. "What?"

Nate continued on for a few more steps. "I know about Willard's theory. And I know he told you about therianthropes. He didn't think you believed him, but I think maybe you do believe." He stopped and looked back at Toby. "You know it's not a full moon tonight, right?"

"Wasn't a full moon last night either, and fourteen people were attacked."

That was true, and it was exactly what had Nate worried. Yes, Willard knew his stuff, but it wasn't really possible to *know* this stuff. Half the information they'd found was likely legend or something a fellow fantasy player made up one night in his basement.

Nate frowned and started to walk again, accelerating his pace. He picked up the scent of salmon cooking and wondered how far away the fish was being grilled. He estimated that on a good day, with the right breeze, he could smell certain foods or an oncoming rain from about a mile away. If illumination cycles were indeed real, would his senses dull during the days in between?

The boys entered Evergreen Park, now both sneaking anxious glances at the sky. There couldn't be more than a couple minutes left until the sun officially disappeared below the horizon.

"The results came back on your shirt," Toby said, starting up the conversation again. "It wasn't Mike's blood."

"Really?" Nate was more than a little surprised—and relieved.

"After Willard showed Peter and me that werewolf card, and after you started acting...differently, I did begin researching them," Toby confessed. "And I know that one of their powers is rapid regeneration. Even near-fatal injuries heal up in just minutes."

"So you're not really coming with me to play Middle Earth Conquests. You're coming with me because you think you have a *real-life* mission right in front of you."

"Do I?" Toby asked with the raise of an eyebrow.

Nate was now realizing that, regardless of his intentions, Toby was going to be a problem. "I guess we're about to find out."

Nate stopped by the spiral slide, praying that Willard was right and that this would all end anti-climactically. He didn't want Toby believing in werewolves just yet, and he couldn't afford to ruin another pair of jeans and sneakers due to the turn. His plan had been to strip down once he reached the park, but that was before he'd known he was going to have company.

Toby seemed equally anxious and kept the conversation going as they waited. "I really do just want to help. It was wrong for me to tell my dad about what happened on the reservation after I promised you I wouldn't, but at least now we know it wasn't Mike's blood."

"And if I am what you think I am, how exactly are you planning to help me?"

Toby pulled his smartphone from his jacket pocket, pointing its camera lens directly at Nate. "First, by convincing more people that you actually need help."

Nate stared at the tiny lens, trying hard to hide his alarm. It was clear that Toby didn't get it. A solution didn't need to be found for what was happening. What was happening *was* the solution. No longer having to wake up *every* morning worried about what Mike, Jerry, and Andrew might have in store was a gift.

This wasn't like the short, sympathetic reprieve they'd received after Mrs. Hoffman's death. That had almost been worse than the bullying itself. It was never a matter of if, but when the tormenting would start again—and the waiting had been torture.

Now Nate knew, with absolute certainty, that Mike, Jerry, and Andrew would never harass him again.

A couple more minutes passed. The sky went dark. There was a buzz as the lights surrounding the park flickered on. Nate didn't turn. He wasn't going to turn, which meant he was going to be able to keep his secret a little bit longer.

"You didn't really think I was going to turn into a werewolf, did you?" Nate asked, trying hard not to sound too excited or relieved. "Something strange did happen to me, and I wish I could remember what it was, but I'm pretty sure it wasn't something supernatural. And…I'm also pretty sure that I could have handled it better. I was a real jerk to you at school yesterday. What I said in the computer lab wasn't okay and I'm sorry too."

He gave Toby a pat on the shoulder and did his best to manage a sincere smile. "Hopefully I'm going to eventually remember what happened on the reservation, remember where that blood came from, and then you'll be the first guy I call."

Nate turned and headed home, his smile curling into a sly grin as he strolled away from his confused friend.

The temperature had dropped steadily over the past hour or so, and now that the sun had set, Rachel felt the chill of the oncoming evening all the way from her head down to her anxiously tapping toes.

She sat on her home's front steps, shifting an uneasy gaze from her smartphone over to Toby's house, then back again. Where the hell was he? How could he just go incommunicado at a time like this? She stared at the dark display of her phone and debated calling him...again. Then she spotted Toby coming down the sidewalk, his hood pulled up over his head.

Springing off the steps, she raced over to him. "Where have you been? I've sent you, like, a million texts."

"Sorry," he responded, barely above a mumble. "I was just...not really figuring anything out."

"What?"

Toby lowered his head until his eyes scarcely peeked out from underneath his hood. "Are you sure the thing you saw last night was what you think it was?"

"Yes," she responded firmly. "Absolutely."

"Because, I mean, I told my dad that a *werewolf* was out there attacking people. And, like, I said it in front of half the town."

"A werewolf *is* out there attacking people."

"But it didn't happen," Toby muttered. "I was just with Nate over at Evergreen Park and...it didn't happen. What if we made a huge mistake last night? I mean, nothing I've done has benefitted anyone. What if helping people…what if it really just isn't my thing?"

"*Your thing?*"

"I keep getting it wrong. I keep *failing*. Pretty much everything I've done to try to make up for what happened, it's all done more harm than good ever since I…"

"Ever since you what?"

"Met you," Toby responded. Or, at least Rachel was pretty sure that's what he'd said. His voice had grown so wooden and distant that she could barely understand him.

"So what does that mean?" she asked, doing her best to ignore the lump forming in her throat. "What are you trying to make up for?"

Toby continued on toward his house. "I've gotta go. It's past curfew."

Watching him walk off, Rachel felt a dull, empty ache gnawing at her belly. For the first time since right before she'd met Toby, she felt as though she didn't have a friend in the world.

As he disappeared inside his home, Rachel murmured the question she wished she'd asked moments earlier. "What didn't happen in Evergreen Park?"

CHAPTER 21

ONE OF TWO OUTCOMES

According to Abundant Wildlife Association of North America's web-site, four deaths had been attributed to bear attacks in Oregon since 1973. In that same time span, there had been a little over a dozen nonfatal attacks.

The only series of incidents that was even close to what was happening in Silver Falls occurred back in 1984, when a black bear attacked three people over the course of a week. Wildlife experts theorized, rather safely in Toby's opinion, that the animal had ac-quired a taste for human blood.

Leaning forward, he rested his elbows on the library table and pressed his forehead against his palms. While plenty scary, three killings in a week was nothing compared to an animal cleaning out an entire bar. Not even close.

Toby stared vacantly out from underneath his jacket's hood at the laptop screen, realizing that he wasn't going to find an alternative explanation for the attack at Gary's. But it wasn't like he even really wanted to.

What he wanted was for Rachel's sighting and Nate's new abilities to somehow tie together, to somehow make sense, but Nate hadn't turned. That left a crazed, nearly two-hundred-year-old Indian as the prime suspect—as the most *reasonable* explanation for the attack.

His eyes moved to the other two students in the school library. Colin Dunbar, a senior, sat at the table in front of Toby, his head down, earbuds in. Two tables over, sophomore Megan Thompson appeared to be studying, her nose buried in a U.S. history textbook. Principal Carter, who was supervising their Saturday detention, sat at a table near the front of the room reading a newspaper.

Toby sighed and returned to his laptop. He was about to google "mountain lion attacks" when Ms. Parker walked into the library. She gave the principal a small nod and then proceeded toward Toby's table. He wouldn't have thought it possible only moments ago, but it looked like his morning was about to get even worse.

Ms. Parker pulled out the chair across from him and took a seat. "Mind if I join you for a couple minutes?"

Toby just shrugged, keeping his eyes on his laptop. Maybe if he limited his responses to non-audible gestures, he could also limit the duration of this unwanted interaction.

"So, werewolves huh?" she asked, innocently enough.

And just like that, she had his full attention. Toby looked up at her, unsure. Seeing that he was ready to acknowledge her presence, Ms. Parker reached over and slowly pushed the laptop screen down until it clicked shut.

"Your father and I are concerned about what might have led you to make up such an explanation for the recent attacks."

"I didn't make it up," Toby said defensively.

"Creating a story like that gave you a reason to get involved, didn't it?" she asked, ignoring his response. "It gave you information you could share with your father."

"It's not a *story*."

"Information that might help him protect the town."

Toby crossed his arms and leaned back, growing frustrated. "So I have to listen to you, but I guess you don't have to listen to me."

"I am listening," she said calmly. "And what I hear is a young man with a singular focus to help people in any way he can. Even if it means he needs to dream up stories about werewolves to give himself something to protect us all from."

"You don't think I know how it sounds?"

"It sounds like an excuse." Ms. Parker leaned forward, fixing Toby with an earnest look. "The longer you keep searching for these opportunities to help others, the longer you get to put off facing what's really troubling you. The longer you get to avoid getting on with your life and thinking about your future."

"So it's wrong to want to help people?"

"It is the way you're doing it," Ms. Parker said frankly. "It's not going to bring your mother back. It's also not going to fill the hole you have in your heart now that she's gone, and it's not going to make it any easier to forgive yourself for something that wasn't your fault."

Ms. Parker went silent to give her last point time to settle in. Toby lowered his eyes, unable to meet her focused gaze.

"What are your plans for the future, Toby?" she finally asked.

There was that damn question again. He really hated that question.

"Going on the way you are is only going to drive you crazy," she continued, not waiting for an answer. "Or, depending on how long it takes you to decide to get on with your life, you may not have many options left for doing so. Certainly not as many as you'll have if you decide to let the healing start today."

"And how would I do that?"

"I think a good place to begin would be for us to start up our sessions again, getting together once a week. We can continue to talk about the incident and discuss what comes next, particularly in the case of your studies. I'd like to take a look at which extracurricular activities and AP courses you might want to sign up for next year. I believe you and your mom had begun putting together a bit of a college prep strategy, if I'm not mistaken."

Toby felt a pins-and-needles sensation wash over his cheeks and forearms. He didn't think the college timeline he'd started on with his mother was any of Ms. Parker's business. His father apparently felt otherwise. And his dad wondered why Toby sometimes kept things from him.

"Maybe we could determine which AP classes might be a good fit for you while you're here serving your next two detentions," she pressed. "You can start taking some positive steps toward the future your mom wanted for you, instead of making up monsters just so you can continue beating yourself up over what happened in the past."

She wasn't holding back now, and Toby was getting upset. Not because he felt Ms. Parker was butting in on something she shouldn't—well, not entirely because of that. It was mostly because what she was saying made sense.

Trying to help Nate hadn't worked out, and Toby knew his dad would certainly approve of Ms. Parker's plan over any that involved him continuing his investigation into werewolves.

He begrudgingly pushed back his hood and met Ms. Parker's gaze. As much as he hated to admit it, his attempts at heroism had been largely unsuccessful, if not detrimental, and refocusing on his studies might just keep him from causing any more harm.

The abilities that came along with being a therianthrope had surprised Nate as much as anyone, and that surprise had led to some failures on his part to conceal what he was now capable of doing. Not turning in front of Toby had been fortuitous, but Nate still felt he needed to do more to convince his friend that what had appeared to be new abilities were actually just passing anomalies.

After a weekend of mulling over his options, he'd decided that to keep things progressing forward, he was going to have to take one giant and very public step back.

Nate walked through the brightly lit school cafeteria holding his food tray and surveying the room. Toby, Willard, and Peter sat at their usual table, which was three tables over from where the majority of the football team's offensive line congregated every day for lunch. Nate veered away from his friends and toward the group of mammoth mouth-breathers.

He addressed them with a smug grin. "So I guess you guys are still keeping to yourselves, huh? It's wonderful to see, really, and I just wanted to congratulate you meatheads for finally wising up."

His comments received a couple of raised eyebrows and one curious look, but none of the boys offered a verbal response. They all just kept eating, more interested in their watery spaghetti and meatballs than in whatever it was he had to say.

But Nate wasn't about to give up. He knew that while this group had never been as cruel as Mike's crew had been, they could still be pricks from time to time. He needed one of those times to be now.

"I wasn't sure if teaching Jerry that lesson in the hallway would be enough for you goons to get the message." He spoke up, desperately wanting to provoke some sort of reaction. "But it looks like you all recognize that your days of bullying us are over."

"Shut up, Schaffer," barked Bart Smit, a senior with cropped hair and compact neck. "Just keep walking."

"Why don't you make me?"

Bart instantly stood up and marched over to him. "Walk away. Now."

"Weren't you listening? You can't tell me what to do anymore."

Without a moment's hesitation, Bart slapped Nate's food tray to the floor. Nate responded by throwing a punch, as gently as he could, squarely into the senior's chest. Just as he'd hoped, the blow had little effect. The cantaloupe-sized fist that then connected with his jaw barely registered either, but Nate fell to the floor, pretending as if it had knocked him silly.

He rolled out a capsule he'd hidden beneath his tongue and chomped down on it, letting the fake blood within ooze down his chin. He then looked up to see the large senior guard towering over him.

"Don't forget your place, Schaffer," Bart grumbled, returning to his lunch.

A second later, Toby and Willard were helping Nate to his feet. "What the hell was that?" Toby asked.

"A mistake," Nate responded, acting as if it were a major undertaking to stand erect. "Enough people start telling you how much you've changed, and I guess you start to believe it."

"But you *have* changed," Willard said, delivering his line along with the quickest of a wink.

"Apparently not as much as I thought," Nate replied.

He was quite pleased with himself. His little performance had gone off without a hitch. Hopefully, it had also had the desired effect on Toby. Only time would tell.

CHAPTER 22

A RETURN TO THE RESERVATION

About three weeks after witnessing his dad nearly break down and Nate nearly get knocked out, Toby had officially switched his focus away from the supernatural and toward his studies. With Ms. Parker's help, he'd narrowed down his AP options for his junior year, selecting English and biology as the two courses he was most interested in taking.

He'd also continued his therapy sessions with Ms. Parker and was starting to feel less and less upset whenever he talked about the accident. He'd even come to accept that the collision wasn't his fault, although he still felt plenty guilty about being unable to save his mother from drowning. Ms. Parker was confident that he'd eventually overcome that remorse too.

Toby wasn't so sure.

He'd made enough progress to satisfy her and his father though, and after talking to a few of his classmates about joining the school newspaper, he even had Principal Carter convinced he was back on the right track. Especially after he'd humbly accepted the principal's offer to speak with his teachers about retaking the exams he'd blown off.

One of the retakes had been scheduled for that day at lunch, and Toby had awakened with a serious case of butterflies. As he rode his bike to school on a breezy May morning, he struggled to remember the last time he'd cared enough about an exam to have pretest jitters.

He coasted onto Main Street, the hood of his faux-leather jacket over his head, and met up with Peter. It looked like Nate would be a no-show this morning.

Toby semi-confronting him about being a werewolf had understandably made things a little awkward between them. However, over the past week, Nate had started joining them again on their rides and walks to school. Toby had decided to take that as a sign that their friendship was getting back to normal. His relationship with his father was progressing nicely in that direction as well, as was the town in general.

Toby and Peter pedaled past a family taking a morning stroll, the young daughter holding hands with each of her parents while skipping along between them. A block later, Mrs. Smith gave a wave as they passed her and her slobbering yellow Lab. They then turned onto Jackson and spotted Mr. Wilmarth taking down the last piece of plywood that he'd used to cover the windows of his sandwich shop.

This return to normalcy had been a process.

First, Oregon's Wild Animal Control officers had returned to Silver Falls with reinforcements to look for the animal that had been attacking people. After a week of searching day and night, they determined it had moved on—a relatively safe assumption, given that no attacks had taken place during that time.

After the search concluded, another week and a half passed without incident, and now the residents were starting to feel safe again. Fear had subsided, and almost everybody had let go of their paranoia. *Almost* everybody.

"So I'm tired of you avoiding me," Toby heard Rachel's voice pronounce, as she pulled up alongside him in her yellow Jeep.

The texts and e-mails he'd exchanged with her recently were enough for him to know that she was still obsessing over whatever she'd seen outside Gary's Bar and Grill. Because of that, Toby had indeed gone into avoidance mode. He hadn't told her the real reason why though. Admitting that his dad had forbidden him to hang out with her was too embarrassing. Instead, he blamed his recent recommitment to his studies, which he felt still made for a fairly legitimate excuse.

"I haven't been avoiding you. I've just been really busy."

"Come out from underneath that hood and talk to me for a minute," she challenged. "I want you to look me in the eye and tell me you honestly don't believe that I saw it."

Toby pushed down his hood. "I believe you saw some…"

He trailed off as he laid eyes on her. The first thing he noticed was the jeans she had on or, more accurately, the way in which they showed off her legs. He then moved his eyes upward to her snug sweater, which did plenty to show off the rest of her figure. She looked incredible.

"…thing," Toby managed to blurt out, finishing his thought.

"I'm not sure what you two are talking about," Peter chimed in, while also admiring Rachel's outfit. "But I want you to know that *I* believe you."

Rachel rolled her eyes at Peter and then returned her attention to Toby. "Come with me to see my uncle."

Toby really didn't want to do that. He knew that neither his dad nor Ms. Parker would approve of such an adventure, as harmless as it might seem. They'd see it as a distraction or, to use one of Ms. Parker's words, a regression.

"Why?" he asked. "I mean, there hasn't been an attack in over two weeks."

"So we should just wait around for another one before we do anything?"

"No, it's just—"

"What else do you have to do today?"

Toby braked, getting Rachel and Peter to do the same. "How about school? Look, as far as I can tell, Nate's fine. Nobody else has died or woken up covered in blood, there hasn't been any sign of the Shaman, and since everyone keeps telling me I need to start focusing more on myself, *that's* what I'm trying to do."

"Shouldn't that include making sure you don't get eaten by a werewolf?" Rachel countered.

There was that determination he'd been so inspired by the first time he'd met her. Toby could feel it rubbing off on him yet again. He suddenly had an urge to climb into her Jeep and join her in her search for supernatural monsters.

It was the type of urge he'd spent the past few weeks suppressing at his father's request. And wasn't he better off for doing so? Wasn't everyone?

"I figured out what you meant," Rachel said, "when you told me that you were trying to save people to make up for what had happened. I knew about the accident, but I didn't know you were the one driving. From what I've heard, you don't have anything to make up for. It wasn't your fault. But while it might be for the wrong reasons, I still think your wanting to help people is the right thing to do."

Those last two statements were a matter of opinion, and Toby wasn't sure he completely agreed with either of Rachel's views. Besides, he *still was* trying to help people, by staying focused on school and staying out of trouble.

"C'mon," she prodded. "I'll have us back by third period, and if my uncle doesn't turn out to be any help, I promise to drop the whole thing. What do you say?"

Peter, still transfixed by how good Rachel looked, leaned closer to Toby and whispered, "You should say yes, dude."

Toby held Rachel's look for a long moment. He did miss hanging out with her, and if the plan was to go only to the reservation, then the chances that his dad would see them together were pretty slim.

"Okay, fine," he relented.

So he'd go see her uncle. Maybe if they once again returned home from the reservation without any answers, Rachel really would let it go.

Toby lifted his bike into the back of her Jeep and hopped in the passenger seat. The second his seat belt clicked into place, she pressed the accelerator and they sped off down Main Street.

Toby hadn't been anywhere near the reservation or the surrounding woods since he and Nate had found Mike's body. Driving out there now brought back memories of that morning, as well as the night before. Memories that rekindled his curiosity.

He glanced over at Rachel to see a tiny smirk on her face. She must have guessed that bringing him out to the reservation would have this effect. He should have anticipated it too.

After cruising about fifteen miles down Crater Lake Highway, Rachel turned down a gravel road with forest on either side. They continued down the winding path until they came upon the yellowing brick-and-mortar facades of the reservation village.

The community was a smaller, slightly more rundown version of Silver Falls. There weren't any touristy knickknack shops, just the necessities. They passed a general store, a small diner, an Indian-crafted furniture shop, a doctor's office, and a clothing boutique.

The furniture shop was easily the most successful of the tribe's businesses. About once a month, the owner and his craftsmen drove into Silver Falls with a selection of well-polished tables, chairs, and dressers to sell, and rarely had Toby ever seen them have to drive anything back.

On this Tuesday, several residents of the Umatilla Reservation were busy stringing lights and other decorations on the fronts of all these shops, as well as over all the homes within view.

"What's all this?" Toby asked, taking in the scene.

"It's for the Mother Earth Ceremony," Rachel answered. "One of the few traditions our tribe still celebrates."

She pulled up in front of the general store where some residents were hanging lights over the entryway and hopped out of the Jeep. After taking another moment to observe the bustling inhabitants of the reservation, Toby followed after her.

"Hello, Uncle." Rachel greeted one of the men as she strode up to the group.

Her uncle turned to see her, then Toby. His face bunched up in a disapproving scowl, and Toby knew the look was intended for him.

"Why did you bring *him* here?" asked the non-intermingler.

"We want to know more about the thing that was attacking people," she responded evenly.

"And why it stopped." Toby added.

The Indian shook his head and returned to decorating. Anything he had to say wouldn't be said with someone from Silver Falls there.

Toby thought about offering to step away, but when he noticed the other tribe members in the vicinity keeping an eye on him, he felt a sudden unease about wandering off on his own.

"Where did it come from?" Rachel pressed.

Her uncle continued to ignore her.

Gravel crunched under several sets of feet as more of the village's residents began to gather around. Toby listened to the approaching steps, but stayed focused on Rachel and her uncle. Just as he started to wonder how much longer they were going to keep the silent standoff going, Rachel played the card Toby doubted her uncle would be able to ignore.

"I saw it," she said plainly. "It killed someone right in front of me. It could have easily attacked me too, but it didn't."

Toby noticed Bimisi's expression go from defiant to deathly alarmed. In that instant, with that quick widening of the man's eyes and opening of his mouth, any thoughts Toby had about the werewolf being something Bimisi had made up to manipulate his niece were gone. Rachel's uncle believed as strongly in the creature's existence as she did.

"It is unlikely that the Shaman would attack his own," Bimisi said tersely. "But that is no guarantee you will be so lucky the next time. If you insist on staying in that town, you will continue to be in danger."

"Shaman?" Toby mouthed the word. Rachel had been right about that too.

Once he'd gotten too old for scary bedtime stories, Toby had asked his mom and dad and then his grandparents where the tales about the monsters living on the reservation came from. As far as any of them knew, the stories had been passed down through the generations, nothing more than make-believe legends created to keep kids from wandering where they weren't wanted.

Perhaps at least one of the stories wasn't make-believe after all.

"What kind of danger?" Toby asked. "Does the Shaman always attack to kill?"

Bimisi shot him an annoyed look, as if to ask why Toby thought he even had the right to speak.

"One of my friends was chased out here by some kids at school," Toby continued. "And ever since, he's been able to do things that—"

"That what?" Bimisi scoffed at him. "You think because your friend was chased by bullies, the Shaman viewed him as some sort of kindred spirit? You think he gave your friend the power to even the score?"

"I don't know. Maybe?"

Low chuckles and whistles rolled through the gathering crowd.

Bimisi sighed and gave Rachel a stern look. "His people have done us no favors. Why do you insist on helping them?"

"Because people are dying."

"*His* people are dying, just as ours once did. And the way they continue to take and destroy what they have no right to claim ownership of...They deserve the reckoning that has come."

Rachel looked stunned by her uncle's words. Toby was officially frightened by them. Glancing around at all the narrowed eyes now focused solely on him, he felt a spreading uneasiness stirring up from his stomach. It was a feeling that wasn't going to be mollified by the fact that he was the sheriff's son or by Rachel being there with him. He wanted off the reservation.

"I think maybe we should go," he suggested.

Rachel finally noticed all the mistrustful eyeballs watching them.

"He didn't put us here!" she screamed out in frustration, pointing in Toby's direction. "Nobody in that town was even alive when the reservation was created. It's not their fault it exists! They're not responsible for the way things are here!"

"Nor have they done anything to help bring about change," Bimisi responded evenly.

Exasperated, Rachel turned away from her uncle and stormed back to her Jeep. Toby followed on her heels, hopping into the vehicle as she started the engine.

"You need to come home," Bimisi called out after her.

"Silver Falls is my home," she shouted back as she pulled out of her parking spot and tore away from the store, the Jeep's tires kicking up gravel.

"I'm sorry," she said as they sped away from the village. "This was a waste of time."

Toby wasn't so sure that it was. Rachel's uncle felt the people of Silver Falls deserved the attacks they'd suffered, and he didn't seem to believe the carnage was over. Knowing this, Toby didn't see how he could just go back to selecting suitable extracurriculars for junior year.

"No, I'm sorry," he said. "I shouldn't have turned my back on what was happening, and I should never have turned my back on you."

Rachel glanced over at him, stunned. Toby couldn't blame her. He'd given her every reason to think he was done with this, mostly because he had been done with it. The setbacks he'd suffered had caused him to lose his nerve to save Silver Falls, but now he was starting to get it back.

"Think we could make one more stop before we head back to town?" he asked.

She realized he was serious, and her stunned look changed into the briefest flicker of a grin. Toby was relieved to see her enthusiasm wasn't completely gone.

CHAPTER 23

AN INTERRUPTED KISS

Rachel's enthusiasm was *far* from gone. She was thrilled Toby still wanted to help her search for the truth, despite the disastrous conversation they'd just had with her uncle.

He'd been distant ever since they'd told his dad about her werewolf sighting, and this unsociable behavior had led Rachel to question the status of their friendship. Her uncertainty had caused her to keep her distance over the past couple of weeks as well, communicating mostly by text message. But after one too many nightmares about that night in front of Gary's Bar and Grill, she'd finally decided to confront Toby in person.

She was glad she had, because now they stood in the clearing where he and Nate had first seen the Shaman and discovered Mike's body, looking down into the cavern that Nate claimed to have fallen into.

"This is allegedly where it all started," Toby murmured. "Maybe there's something down there that can tell us how."

To find out, they would first need to get into the underground cave. Because her uncle had always stressed the importance of being properly equipped in case of an emergency, Rachel had a small collection of necessities packed in the back of her Jeep that would help them do just that. Among the items were a first-aid kit, flashlight, canteen, and a decent length of knotted rope for climbing.

After retrieving the rope, she and Toby tied it around the trunk of a sturdy-looking oak and then dropped the other end into the opening in the forest floor. Soon they both stood at the bottom of the cavern, taking in their dark, dank surroundings.

Toby shined the flashlight around the dungeon-like space, making sure they were alone, before settling the beam onto the cave drawings that covered a large portion of the enclosure's slick, shiny limestone.

Rachel took in the fading symbols and figures. This wasn't the first time she'd seen representations like these. They decorated many of the old tapestries, drums, and tools in Dyami Askuwheteau's relic shop, so she recognized the style as being Umatilla, but that was about all she was able to discern.

When she was younger, her uncle had attempted to educate her on their tribe's drawing techniques. However, like most members of her generation, she hadn't shown much of an appreciation for her ancestors' lost practices and traditions.

Her eyes stopped on what appeared to be a large animal, sketched completely in black. The chalk, or whatever had been used to make the illustration, had been scratched furiously around the beast. Rachel supposed it was meant to represent fur. The way it was scrawled added to the creature's size, making it much more menacing.

Around the beast lay figures drawn mostly in red. Many of them also had red lines drawn downward from their bodies. Blood, Rachel assumed.

"Well, it's pretty obvious which one is the werewolf," she said.

"Any of the rest of it make sense?"

"To be honest, I never really learned how to read these," she confessed. "I'm not even sure where it starts or ends."

Rachel ran her fingers along the drawings, completely befuddled. "What do you see?"

Toby gave no response. Curious as to why he'd gone silent, Rachel turned to catch him staring not at the drawings, but at her rear end.

He glanced away quickly. "Um, yeah…Well, like you said, the werewolf is pretty obvious."

She couldn't help but smile. "Anything else?"

Toby's embarrassed eyes scanned the cavern wall. "These guys kind of look like they're wearing uniforms."

Rachel stepped closer to take a look, brushing up against Toby as she slid in front of him. The figures he was looking at all wore shirts, or coats, with double buttons. They were drawn in consistent rows, like marching soldiers. Rachel took half a step back to glance to either side of them and inadvertently bumped into Toby again.

He didn't move, despite the contact. Neither did she.

With his chest pressed up against her back, Rachel could feel his heart starting to thump a little faster. Hers was doing the same.

She knew they had more important things to worry about, but she felt herself getting caught up in the moment.

"I agree on the uniforms." She hesitated for an instant, then glanced over her shoulder. "Any other thoughts?"

Toby held her gaze, a palpable tension between them. He had nice eyes, holly green with a bit of a sparkle. She'd noticed them the day they'd met, when he'd saved her box of belongings. They stared at her now with an amorous intent.

He leaned forward to kiss her. She leaned back into him. Just before closing her eyes, she saw a shadow cut through the shaft of sunlight that shone into the cavern.

Rachel lifted her head to see her Uncle Bimisi staring down at her. Toby's lips awkwardly found the side of her chin.

Not exactly what she'd had in mind for a first kiss.

As he walked down the hallway toward honors biology, Nate was startled by a howl. He looked anxiously in the direction of the sound to see a couple of boys pointing and laughing at Ashley Schultz. Standing at her locker, she gave them the finger over her shoulder, keeping her back to them as they giggled and scurried past.

This was the first Nate had seen of Ashley since the night he woke up covered in blood on the reservation. He'd been extremely nervous about what she would tell people once she regained the ability to speak. Luckily, the story she told had cleared him of having anything to do with Mike's death. Not so luckily, for Ashley anyway, it had also caused many to believe that she'd lost her marbles.

Around school, the reaction to her story had been similar to when word spread about Toby and Rachel's conversation with Sheriff Hoffman on the final night of the attacks. Kids had given them a hard time as well, but Toby and Rachel were already outcasts, even before suggesting werewolves were killing people. Ashley—Miss Popularity—was a different story.

Anyone who had been envious of her looks, her boyfriend, or her position as head cheerleader now had their opportunity to take her down a peg.

Because most students felt at least a little sorry for her, they kept their comments about her being a complete psycho within their little cliques. However, a handful of kids, apparently without any sort of conscience, were more than happy to mock her openly, either on Facebook or to her face.

Nate watched her for a moment, feeling suddenly very sympathetic. He and Ashley had never been close, but unlike Mike, she'd never given him any trouble. For the most part, she'd always handled her status well, never talking down to the less popular kids or teasing them like all her friends did.

Nate thought that might be why some were savoring the opportunity to pounce on her now. As much as they might have wanted to before, she'd never given them much reason. Up until now, they would have had to justify their dislike by admitting it came from their own insecurities, unhappiness, and jealousy.

Now they could claim it was because she was nuts.

Ashley had stopped gathering the things she needed for her next class, but continued to stand and stare into her locker, likely not wanting to turn and face the day that was waiting behind her. Nate knew exactly how that felt.

He started to walk over, figuring she could use someone to talk to, someone who didn't think she'd gone totally cuckoo. Someone who knew better.

"First day back?" he asked.

Ashley turned, tears in her eyes. She wiped them away and nodded.

Nate hadn't really thought about what to say next. "Um...how's it going?"

"Well, everyone thinks I'm a freak," she replied in a worn-out voice. "My friends are shutting me out. I'm apparently everyone's new favorite joke. Other than that..."

Ashley seemed to catch herself carrying on and looked down, embarrassed by her display of self-pity. Just then, two more kids walked by. One let out a howl, and they collapsed with laughter as they continued down the hall.

Nate sneered, starting after them.

"Don't bother," Ashley sighed. "Everyone's been doing it."

"That doesn't make it okay."

"Now that the attacks have stopped, they need something to talk about," Ashley said with a shrug. "Might as well be the freak who saw a werewolf."

"You're not a freak," Nate snapped, watching the assholes walk down the hallway.

Ashley shut her locker and briskly walked away. "You're the only one who doesn't think so."

THE ONE YOU FEED

Nate watched her go, feeling oddly connected to her all of a sudden. He knew all too well how it felt to be picked on by nearly the entire school. She didn't deserve this. Nobody did. What she deserved was a chance to get even.

Bimisi joined Rachel and the bushy-haired boy from Silver Falls inside the cavern, trying to forget the near kiss he'd just witnessed. The opportunity to interrupt it had provided a slight silver lining to what had otherwise been one very dark cloud of a day.

He'd become increasingly unsettled while considering the boy's theory about the Shaman turning someone from Silver Falls. It would explain the one oddity about the attacks a month ago that Bimisi was still having trouble making sense of.

One of the victims had been a teenager who was Umatilla—Jerry Ituha. Jerry had never lived on the reservation, but both his parents had. Native American blood had flowed through his veins, and so Bimisi had struggled to rationalize the boy's death.

All the stories he'd been told said that the Shaman couldn't kill those he'd sworn to protect, those who had repaid his protection by sealing him inside an underground cavern and leaving him to rot. In spite of their actions, they were still his people, his blood, and as the legend went, the curse that transformed him also prevented him from ever doing them harm—directly.

So then what if the Shaman had turned someone else? Not because he saw that person as some bullied, kindred spirit, but because that person wasn't bound by the rules of a curse. A second werewolf could attack anyone, including the descendants of the Umatilla Tribe members who'd buried the Shaman alive.

What if the Shaman had turned a boy from Silver Falls to get revenge?

"So what do they say?" Rachel asked impatiently.

Bimisi focused intently on the cave drawings. He knew the story by heart. The other living protectors of the cavern had told it to him countless times, but just like them, he'd never actually seen the images firsthand. He felt an odd sense of comfort that this ancient record and warning was consistent with the tales he'd been told.

"The drawings explain how, well over a century ago, the American army's regiments moved through this land, killing thousands of Cherokee and Umatilla." Bimisi turned back to look at Rachel, then the boy. "A holocaust you will not find mentioned in any of your school books."

The boy glanced at Rachel, uneasy. "I know the area's history," he answered defensively, apparently growing tired of being made the bad guy.

There was something familiar about his voice, something that left Bimisi even more ill at ease. He'd noticed it earlier in the village too, but could not put his finger on what it was.

"Our tribe's Shaman vowed to turn back the white man," Bimisi continued, returning his eyes to the drawings. "He went on a vision quest and vanished for seven days. When he returned, the attacks began. Soon the tribe discovered that he had been cursed, and that his curse gave him the power to rid our land of the invaders, along with their guns and their disease, but our people viewed this as an unacceptable resolution. As much as our tribe despised the white

THE ONE YOU FEED

intruders, they also rejected the idea of a demon animal protecting them. They tricked the Shaman into coming down here, and then they buried him."

He glanced back at his now captive audience. Both Rachel and the boy scanned the drawings with their eyes, trying to decipher which sections told the details he'd just shared with them.

"What happened during those seven days?" asked the boy. "How did he become the werewolf to begin with?"

"The stories told to me never included how he became cursed, and those details do not appear to be shown in these drawings either."

Rachel's eyes broke away from the pictures and returned to her uncle. "How did he escape?"

The Shaman hadn't escaped.

The events of the night on which Bimisi had unsealed the cavern were still crystal clear in his mind, and as he recalled them, he realized with a slight dread why the boy's voice was so familiar. It had been too dark, and he'd been too far away to make out his face, but Bimisi had clearly heard, and still remembered, the boy's panicked cries as he thrashed about in the Chetco River.

He was the sheriff's son. He'd been the one driving the vehicle Bimisi collided with on his way to opening the cavern.

CHAPTER 24

UNLEASHING THE SHAMAN

The first thing Bimisi always remembered about that night was how unpleasantly cold it was. He'd watched silently at the end of the bridge as the sheriff's son paddled against the current of the river, frantically calling out for his mother. For a moment, he'd considered scaling his way down to the river to help, but that moment passed quickly. If the boy's mother was going to drown, she'd do so long before Bimisi could reach her.

He returned to his pickup and continued through the darkening forest, eventually coming to a stop on the side of the road. At the time, Bimisi hadn't known that the accident had killed the sheriff's wife, but he knew the crash itself would require an investigation.

He also knew that as long as he finished what he'd set out to do, any investigation would soon take a backseat to coming events.

The accident was just the latest in a long list of reasons for why he couldn't falter in his mission. The people of Silver Falls had taken away his land, his job—even his sister-in-law and niece.

He wasn't going to let them take any more.

Bimisi exited the truck, too focused on the task at hand to register the chirps and hoots of the forest's nighttime creatures playing in a chorus all around him. Snagging a shovel and flashlight from the truck bed, he began his trek through the trees.

After several yards, he stopped and removed a small bundle of leather from his jacket pocket, then carefully unfolded it. On one side was a faded, crudely drawn map that he consulted before glancing up to check his surroundings. Bimisi then moved to his left and continued up a short hill, eventually coming across a small clearing.

This was the place. He rested the flashlight on a log at the edge of the clearing and began to dig. The tales Bimisi had been told said he'd have to shovel three feet down to reach the seal. Sure enough, at just about that exact distance, he heard a deep thunk as the shovel's blade struck a plank of wood.

It took him a little over an hour to dig out the area and uncover the entire seal. The chore left his shoulders aching.

The seal was circular, like a manhole cover, but about five times the size. The wood was Sitka spruce, one of the heavier woods found in Oregon. Carvings were etched in its face to warn those who saw them of what would be found underneath. Just to the left of the carvings a handle had been crafted into the surface of the seal.

The covering would be too heavy for Bimisi to lift on his own. He returned to his pickup and hoisted a large coil of two-inch thick manila rope from the truck bed. He tossed the coil to the ground and tied one end around the pickup's hitch. He then began to unwind the rope as he carried it through the forest, back to the clearing.

When he reached the seal, he tied the other end around the covering's handle, yanking at the knot to make sure it was good and tight.

One more trip. One more walk to his truck and then back to the clearing and he'd know if the stories were really true. He'd know if there actually was a chance for his people to regain all that had been taken.

Anticipation and unease roiled around inside him as he climbed into his pickup. He sat with the keys in the ignition for a long moment, simply staring at them.

This was the right thing to do.

He started the engine and put the vehicle in gear, slowly pressing on the gas. The pickup inched forward and then stopped as the rope ran out of slack. Bimisi pressed the pedal down a little farther. The truck's wheels kicked up dirt, then took hold. The vehicle lurched forward, and he knew he'd just lifted the cavern's seal.

Grabbing a canvas pack that rested on the passenger seat, he quickly exited the pickup. Several thoughts bounced around inside his head as he headed back toward the clearing. Many of those who knew about the Shaman theorized that it would take some time, hopefully no more than a month, for the ancient Indian to regain his strength and restart his mission.

Until then, Bimisi would have to disappear to avoid the imminent investigation into the accident on the bridge. He'd tell Dyami what he'd done. He'd then ask the elder protector to continue this endeavor while he was gone. The seal would need to be buried too, or maybe just hidden deeper in the forest.

Bimisi filed away his mental checklist as he walked into the clearing. The wooden seal lay several feet from the cavern opening, upside down. He pointed his flashlight at it and gasped when he spotted the deep claw marks that had been slashed across its underside.

He shifted the beam of light toward the cavern. Any doubts Bimisi had about a monster being buried under the ground were gone, but they were now replaced by new doubts. Swinging his pack off his shoulder, he tentatively approached the hole in the forest floor.

Another theory among the protectors was that the Shaman would be too weak to climb out of his underground prison after so many years without nourishment. However, at some point, the creature had been able to reach the seal.

As he peered down into darkness, Bimisi opened the canvas pack and removed two bloody dead rabbits he'd hunted earlier that day. "Enjoy," he whispered as he dropped the Shaman's first meal in over a century into the cavern.

CHAPTER 25

THE PARKING LOT PRANK

Bimisi shone his flashlight onto the animal bones that littered the cavern floor. "The Shaman did not escape. He was set free."

"How do you know that?" the sheriff's son pressed.

Bimisi would remember the details of that night for the rest of his life, and he would also take them to his grave. He furrowed his brow at the boy, but then saw the look of horror on his niece's face. Bimisi didn't have to share his story for her to know the truth. With everything he'd already told her about the creature, denying his involvement in its freeing would be futile. He decided to go on the offensive instead.

"It had to be done," Bimisi argued. "Bennett's new machines already spew far more chemicals into the air and rivers than what we had seen before, and he still plans to expand his plant's capabilities. Even more damage will be done with his new road. The people he has laid off illegally poach the forests just to survive, and no one from that town has ever shown this land the respect it deserves."

The boy now wore the same mixed expression of shock and anger as Rachel. To further make his point, Bimisi considered mentioning all the bullet-riddled soda and beer cans he'd collected from around the fence posts that marked the reservation's east boundary, but he decided to save his breath.

The people of Silver Falls, including their sheriff and his son, were mostly ignorant of how their thoughtless actions impacted the land around them. Oftentimes they even seemed proud of that ignorance.

Accepting that he wasn't going to receive any empathy from his audience, Bimisi continued with what he'd come to do in the first place and began exploring the cavern. After a quick search, he was discouraged, but not surprised, that he was unable to find any of the Shaman's personal effects. All that had been left behind were the remains of his meals. Without an item more closely linked to the cursed Indian, Bimisi would be unable to use his unique talents as a mystic to track the Shaman down.

Bimisi and his deadbeat brother were the only *known* mystics among the few elders in their tribe who still recognized and understood such powers. It was presumed his special abilities would come in handy if the Shaman ever escaped and needed to be killed, which is why he assumed the elders had recruited him as a protector.

For now, however, his mystical tracking skills were of no use.

In a way, that was good. Hinting that he had such abilities would only cause more problems with Rachel. Long ago his sister-in-law had made him and his brother promise to keep what they could do a secret from his niece, the tribe's one *unknown* mystic. He'd reluctantly agreed to the request after the girl was born, keeping her unique capabilities a secret from not only her, but the Umatilla elders as well.

Accepting that he'd have to hunt the Shaman another way, Bimisi opened his pack and removed two small, black, disk-shaped devices. He placed the first disk in the far corner of the cavern, then the other at the opposite end of the enclosure.

Rachel's uncle knew so much about the Shaman werewolf because he'd been the one to turn it loose. He actually felt the attacks were warranted and now casually walked around the cavern placing... What the hell was he placing?

"What are those things?" Toby asked, nearly shouting.

"Motion sensors," Bimisi replied. "It's likely the Shaman will come back here before he turns again. Assuming he does, I'll be waiting."

"To do what?" There was no holding back the shouting now. "You let this thing out! Now you expect us to believe you're going to hunt it?"

"Our ancestors were convinced this wasn't the way," Bimisi said evenly.

Toby suddenly sensed something besides a composed righteousness coming from the man. He seemed a bit defeated as well.

"I've come to understand their conviction." Bimisi glanced over at Rachel for a moment. "I will not have the blood of my brother's ex-wife or his daughter on my hands. So yes...I am going to hunt it."

Bimisi helped Toby and Rachel climb out of the cavern and then went on his way without any further explanation of what he'd done or what he planned to do. Not really sure what to do next, Toby and Rachel returned to school. They didn't make it back in time for third period, not even close. It was about halfway through fifth when they pulled into the school parking lot.

Rachel stopped near one of the coiled bike racks to let Toby out. She hadn't said much since the cavern, which was hardly surprising. They'd gotten the answers they were looking for, but none could have been what she'd hoped to hear.

Her uncle had unleashed a werewolf on Silver Falls. A creature that had killed several people. As he jumped out of the Jeep and grabbed his bike from the back, Toby still couldn't think of any words that might help Rachel cope with such a discovery.

He instead settled for a weak smile and slight nod, which she barely returned.

As he watched her drive off to find a parking spot, he wondered just what her mindset was now that she knew about her uncle's role in the attacks. Did she believe Bimisi would hunt down the Shaman? If Rachel decided she was going to trust her uncle, could Toby rely on her?

He considered these questions as he squatted down and slid his carbon lock around the coiled rack and through his bike's front tire. Just as he locked it into place, he spotted Nate and Willard emerging from the field house at the far end of the parking lot.

Toby pushed his concerns about Rachel aside and began to straighten up to get their attention, but when he noticed how his friends were both suspiciously scanning the lot, he went back into his crouch.

Staying as still as possible, he peered at them through a cluster of bike frames and tires. Toby lost sight of his friends a couple times as they wove their way amongst the parked cars, but soon managed to spot Nate through the windows of a Chevy Malibu.

What he saw next caused his jaw to drop.

Nate and Willard stopped next to a midsize, coffee-colored sedan. Nate stepped to the front of the vehicle, while Willard made his way to the trunk. After once again checking for any witnesses, they lifted the car, flipped it over, and placed it back down in exactly the same spot. The whole trick had taken them no more than ten seconds.

Stunned, Toby watched them hustle away from their parking lot prank and scurry back inside the school. He waited until the field house doors had swung shut behind them before coming out of his hiding spot.

The reality of what he'd just seen was almost too much to process. Nate's incident in the cafeteria with Bart Smit had been staged. The powers he'd once demonstrated were clearly still with him. Willard clearly possessed them too.

The Shaman wasn't the only werewolf the town had to worry about.

Rachel pulled into a parking spot behind the field house and took a deep breath. Looking at herself in the rearview mirror, she saw a girl deeply shaken by the events of that morning. She'd always known there were disputes between the area's two towns, but she'd failed to appreciate just how strongly some members of her tribe still loathed Silver Falls.

Her mother's relationship with Alan had given her false hope, turned her into a fool who believed she could find a way to change her people's perceptions of this town or alter how the town's residents perceived her.

She wondered what Toby's perception now was after everything he'd just seen and heard. He'd never made any assumptions about who she was based on where she was from, but who knew what his opinion was of her now?

Rachel felt a sudden stab of anxiety surge through her gut. Their little adventure had given Toby every reason to believe all the negative things he'd ever heard about the crazy Indians on the Umatilla Reservation. And by remaining silent on the drive back to school, she probably hadn't helped alter any of those perceptions.

But what was she supposed to say? What *could* she say?

She should have told him she *absolutely* didn't share their beliefs.

Rachel took another deep breath, then hopped out of her Jeep and headed back toward the bike racks. Cutting across the lawn next to the field house, she quickened her pace.

She had to make sure Toby knew she was ready and willing to do whatever it took to save her new hometown. He had to believe that she was sincere about wanting to figure out a way to stop the attacks together.

Hurrying around a corner, Rachel stopped when she saw the deserted coiled racks. Toby was gone. He'd apparently already decided he was going to figure things out without her.

CHAPTER 26

A New Mission

Later that afternoon, two of the boys Nate had seen harassing Ashley stood in the parking lot, staring with befuddlement at their car. It was in its parking spot, right where they'd left it, but upside down and resting on its roof. Several yards away, Nate and Willard sat on their bicycles and observed the scene with satisfied smiles.

"I am having so much fun with this," Willard said, his smile nearly ear to ear.

Nate was too. While it was troubling to still not know how to control his actions when in werewolf form, being able to exact this kind of justice while human was extremely satisfying. It was also much more enjoyable to have someone to go through these experiences with, especially when that companion had an extensive knowledge of fantastical creatures.

"How's it been going with the research?" he asked, shifting his attention away from their prank.

"I haven't found much," Willard replied, struggling to flatten out his smile. "I think we'll just need to really try to visualize who we want to go after the next time."

"That's hardly a solution."

"It's a start."

"And what if we can't come up with a target?"

Willard shrugged. "You stopped yourself from killing me…"

"But I don't know *how* I did that. I wasn't even planning on turning you."

"Some part of you was," Willard replied, while subconsciously rubbing the shoulder where he'd been bitten.

Nate truly didn't remember the events of that night, and not being able to remember his attacks had made the reality of them slightly more bearable. It also likely meant he had a long way to go before he could prevent them.

Which meant they needed a new target. Someone he wouldn't feel *too* guilty about ending. He looked back over at the upside-down car, racking his brain to think of someone who deserved to have two teenage werewolves seeking him or her out. Then a worthy target popped into his head.

"Okay," he said earnestly. "I can think of at least one more mission for us."

Bimisi exited the rear of his small bungalow home and trudged over to a dilapidated wooden shed in the corner of his backyard. While he walked, he removed a set of keys from the front pocket of his jeans and sorted through them until he got to the one he needed.

He slid the key into the padlock that secured the latch on the shed door, then turned until he heard a click. The padlock fell into his free hand. Bimisi considered how heavy it felt as he slowly pushed the door open.

The shed was dimly lit by what little sun penetrated its lone, dust-covered window. The cramped space housed a grimy lawn-mower, small table, dirt-encrusted shovel, and a few worn tools. All the sort of items you'd expect to find, with the exception of a large steamer trunk with brass fittings that sat against the far wall.

Bimisi knelt down in front of the trunk and quickly opened its combination lock. Its hinges creaked as he lifted back the top and surveyed the items inside.

"I warned you of what would happen." Dyami's voice came suddenly, and his unexpected appearance in the shed's doorway left Bimisi momentarily startled.

"Not strongly enough," he replied, steadying himself.

"What did you expect to happen when you turned the creature loose?"

"It is one thing to hear the stories." Bimisi removed a small metal suitcase and box of bullets from the trunk, placing them on the nearby table. "It is quite another to see them come true."

He stood and opened the box of ammunition to reveal a dozen smooth, shiny silver bullets. Gliding his fingers over them, he glanced back at the trunk. Inside were eleven identical boxes, one for each member of the tribe who had been tasked with watching over the Shaman since he'd been buried.

Each member, as part of his initiation, had to craft four dozen bullets. The box Bimisi had opened, and the first bullets he would load, were from his own lot.

THE ONE YOU FEED

"You feel you have the right to kill something a select number of us have guarded for three generations?" Dyami challenged as he walked into the shed. "Something we've sworn to protect and have placed all our hope in?"

Bimisi considered the question as he opened the small metal case, which held three .44 Magnum revolvers. Did he have the right to make this decision on behalf of all the other protectors? None of them had complained when he'd released the creature, and he'd made that decision on his own.

Since he had been the only one brave enough to set the Shaman free, he felt that *did* give him the right and the responsibility to determine what happened next, even if he didn't necessarily want to.

Dyami continued with his objection. "The Shaman represents our final chance to regain what is rightfully ours."

Bimisi picked up one of the revolvers and began loading the chambers, staring at the weapon with wounded eyes. "I know."

Knowing he needed to make as little noise as possible, Toby hopped off his bike and set it gently against the trunk of a pine tree. He was far enough away from Mr. Bennett's lodge that under normal circumstances he could have tossed the bike down without giving a second thought to someone hearing him. However, normal circumstances didn't include that someone having the supersensitive ears of a wolf.

Toby had been keeping tabs on Nate and Willard ever since seeing them flip a car in the school parking lot that morning. It had been a challenging task at times, especially when it came to following them out to Bennett's lodge. But he'd been able to drop back to a safe trailing distance after they'd reached Crater Lake Highway and headed south.

At that point, this was the only destination that made any sense. But why had they come out here?

Toby surveyed the large, countrified home, which was picturesquely framed by a cluster of Lodgepole pines. Pushing aside a tree branch, he watched as Nate and Willard walked up the front steps of the impressive residence. They stood on the wide wraparound porch for a moment to discuss something, then approached the front door.

Nate knocked on the heavy, wooden door, and moments later, Mr. Bennett answered with a glass of champagne in hand. Living the good life. It must be nice.

"Hi there, Mr. Bennett," Willard greeted him with a sardonic smile. "Celebrating?"

"What do you kids want?" the man grunted back, clearly irritated that they'd interrupted whatever the occasion was that had called for bubbly.

"We want to talk to you about your factory," Nate answered.

"What about it?"

Nate took a step closer to the doorway, eying the cabin's interior for anyone who might be joining Mr. Bennett in his celebration. "You need to rehire the people you've laid off."

Bruce scoffed and started to shut the door. "Get lost, you little punks."

Nate reached out and smacked his palm against the door to stop it from closing. This conversation wasn't over yet, and he didn't appreciate Mr. Bennett assuming that it was. He shoved the door back, easily overpowering Mr. Bennett. He then strode into the plant owner's home as Bruce stumbled backward.

The man's wife and daughter sat in the living room that adjoined the front entryway. Both turned with startled expressions, nearly spilling their champagne, as the door swung back and knocked over a coat rack.

Willard followed Nate in and shot Bruce's wife and daughter a malicious glare. "Stay where you are."

Bruce's daughter was about ten years older than Nate, and he vaguely remembered meeting her at a company picnic his dad had dragged him to once. Maybe he'd see her again at such an occasion if Mr. Bennett could be persuaded into making the right decision.

Not sensing her or her mother to be a threat, Nate turned his attention back to Mr. Bennett. "So what are you celebrating?"

The man had steadied himself and now wore a stern expression. "You boys need to leave."

"Did you fire some more people today?"

"Actually, you little shit, I just got some very good news that should allow me to hire back most of the people I had to let go."

"How many?"

"That hasn't been determined yet," Bruce replied. "Now get out of here, or I'm calling the sheriff."

Despite Mr. Bennett's stout demeanor, Nate thought he picked up on a slight quiver in the man's voice. He likely wasn't accustomed to being challenged so directly. Maybe it frightened him a little. If it did, good. He should be frightened.

"When are you going to hire them back?" Nate pressed.

Mr. Bennett didn't respond, and Nate assumed this was because he was either too startled or too frustrated to formulate what he'd consider to be a strong retort.

He shouted the question again. "When?!"

The man swallowed hard. "If everything goes according to plan, within three to four months."

Nate shook his head. "That's not good enough. People need work now. My dad needs to work now."

"That's not my problem."

Except that it *was* his problem. What Mr. Bennett didn't seem to realize was that he wasn't the most powerful person in Silver Falls anymore. He no longer got to call all the shots. Nate snarled and leapt forward, his eyes smoldering.

His hand shot toward the pompous man's throat.

"Nate!" Toby called out from somewhere behind him.

Nate's fingers froze just prior to wrapping around Mr. Bennett's neck. He glanced back to see Toby standing on the front porch. What was *he* doing here?

He was interrupting. And while his disruption was irritating, it was also perhaps well-timed. Nate slowly drew his hand back, eying the few witnesses around him. Throttling Mr. Bennett at that particular moment wasn't the right way to handle things. The purpose for this visit was to simply talk to the man. If that talk didn't lead to a desirable result, action was to come later.

He leaned closer to Bruce and whispered his first and final warning. "Hire everyone back, or you'll have bigger problems than you can possibly imagine."

He gave Willard a nod, and they headed for the door. They strode right past Toby, marching out of the cabin and trotting down the front steps.

Nate snuck a look back at his friend as he picked up his bike off the ground. "It had to be done."

"What did?" Toby asked, still standing in the doorway with a dumbfounded expression. "What the hell are you guys doing?"

"Your dad may still have his job," Nate said curtly, "but a lot of other people don't."

"So you're going to fix that by threatening Mr. Bennett?"

"For starters."

"Okay, listen, whatever you guys are planning on doing—"

"You won't be able to stop us," Nate snapped. "So please stop trying."

Apparently Nate's efforts at deception hadn't been as effective as he'd thought. Toby clearly knew, or at least still very much suspected, that Willard and he were therianthropes. But that didn't mean Toby was capable of appreciating the responsibility that came along with the powers they now possessed.

Someone needed to stand up to jerks like Mr. Bennett without fearing the consequences and Nate was now that someone.

Maybe he ought to just turn Toby.

No, his heated exchange with Mr. Bennett had him feeling impulsive. This wasn't the time to make that sort of decision. Nate hopped onto his bike and started to peddle down the driveway. Right now he had other important decisions to make.

Unable to think of anything else to say or do to try to reason with his friends, Toby simply watched Nate and Willard ride off until they vanished among the trees. Once again he felt helpless. Maybe he knew what his friends were and how they got that way, but Nate was right about him not knowing how to stop them.

He had to figure out a way to do just that.

But how? As the boy who'd literally cried wolf before the attacks stopped, he wasn't going to be able to convince anyone of what he now knew to be true. Asking his father for help was definitely out of the question. There was Rachel, but Toby wasn't sure how much faith she still had in her uncle. She might want to give him an opportunity to redeem himself, as if that were even possible at this point.

There was really only one person he could think of who might be able to help.

Toby looked up at the early evening sky and grew earnest, then he got on his bike and pedaled like a madman all the way back to Silver Falls. By the time he came up on the Foxes' residence, he was gasping for air and his T-shirt was stuck to his back.

He dropped his bike on the front lawn, unzipped his jacket, and slicked back his sweat-dampened hair.

It was nearing curfew, which was still in effect for anyone under the age of eighteen. Thankfully it was Peter, and not one of his parents, who answered the door when Toby knocked. He waited until he was in Peter's room, with his friend's iPod docking station turned nearly all the way up, before relating the day's events.

He started with the trip to the reservation, trying his best to explain the drawings in the cavern and Bimisi's story about the Shaman. He recapped what he'd seen Nate and Willard do in the school parking lot and finished with what had taken place out at

Bennett's lodge. Peter listened intently, but became far less enthusiastic when Toby finally asked for his help.

"Willard and Nate are, like, on a whole other level when it comes to this stuff," Peter said, as he sat down at a small desk and booted up his laptop. "I'm not going to be able to tell you any kind of, like, secrets or anything they don't already know."

"You can help me get caught up," Toby replied, trying to encourage his friend. "They may know more about all your supernatural hobbies and games than you do, but you're still a hundred levels ahead of me."

"There are only twelve levels in Demon Destroyer," Peter corrected. "Twenty-four in Middle Earth Conquests."

"See? I'm already learning. So what else you got?"

Peter googled Demon Destroyer, then opened the website and clicked on the game's character directory. He selected the therianthrope icon and began scrolling down the page. "Well, for starters, you realize that these descriptions are all made up by the game's designers, right?"

"I was thinking about that on the way over here." Toby leaned in to get a closer look. "Vampires, werewolves, zombies—they all have characteristics that have been around a lot longer than this game, right? Now, these game descriptions may contain some original material, but other elements were probably taken from older descriptions, and those were probably created using a combination of interpretations written before them."

"And so you're thinking that some of this stuff might actually go all the way back to an authentic source," Peter murmured, catching on but not really buying in.

"It's the best shot I've got," Toby argued. "*You're* the best shot I've got. Anyone else I could go to either doesn't trust me or I don't trust them, or both."

"Well, thanks, I think. So, okay…what specifically are you looking for?"

"How do you stop a werewolf, or therianthrope, without killing it?"

"As far as I know, you don't."

Toby was afraid that was going to be his friend's answer. "Okay, so then, how do you reverse the curse?"

"Can't really do that either." Peter shot him a dubious look. "Where did you hear that you could?"

"I didn't."

"Then why'd you ask that?"

"I don't know. I'm just throwing out ideas, trying to find a way to stop them!"

Toby realized he was near shouting and took a breath. He took another look at the screen, and one of the subtitles on the page caught his eye.

"What about that?" he pointed toward the item. "What are Alphas and Betas?"

"They're classifications of werewolves," Peter answered. "Based on the story you just told me, the Shaman, or whatever, would be our Alpha. Nate and Willard would be the Betas."

"What's the relationship between them? Do they, like, protect each other or something?"

"Not that I'm aware of." Peter continued to scroll. "Obviously, you don't have Betas without the Alpha to create them. Other than that, I'm not sure there is much of a relationship. You get bitten by an Alpha, you become a werewolf, and then you...Wait. Here's something. According to this *fictional* character description—"

"Which is as good as anything else we've got to go on..."

They read the sentence together, their eyes widening: "If you are able to kill an Alpha, all the Betas it created will return to one hundred percent human."

"That's it!" Toby exclaimed excitedly, pointing at the sentence. Glancing at the time display in the lower right corner of the screen, he saw it was almost eight o'clock. Perfect.

He hustled out of his friend's room. "Thanks, Peter. You're a lifesaver. Literally."

"Wait. What do you mean? Where are you going?"

"To turn Nate and Willard back."

CHAPTER 27

INJURY ADDED TO INSULT

Toby hustled up the front steps to the sheriff station, counting on his dad and Deputy Rogers to be on their 8:00 p.m. drive through town. Even though the attacks had stopped, his father had still been going out three times a night to make sure Silver Falls was safe. The first sweep was always right around curfew. If that were the case again tonight, Toby would be able to get into the station and collect what he needed without any trouble.

He entered the building cautiously, checking the back office and then the bathroom. As expected, the overhead fluorescents were on, but nobody was home.

He stepped over to his father's desk, found the key his dad kept hidden in the top right drawer, and used it to unlock the drawer on the bottom left. Inside lay his pistol. Or, more accurately, the gun his dad allowed him to use out at Miller's Pass.

Toby stared at the weapon for a moment. He'd obviously never shot anyone before, although he figured it was kind of a stretch to consider the Shaman a someone. More like a *something*.

Kill an Alpha and all Betas go back to one hundred percent human. Toby knew what needed to be done. His father didn't believe in werewolves. Toby didn't believe in Rachel's uncle, and so doing this himself seemed to be his only option. It was time to find out if he could be the hero Nate needed. The hero *the town* needed.

He grabbed the pistol and tucked it into his jeans.

Bimisi eyed the two playing cards laying face up on the middle storage panel of his pickup. A four and a ten.

"Well?" Dyami asked.

The game of Yablon had filled the past hour they'd spent waiting in the woods, allowing their minds to stray from the task at hand. The card game had also taken about twenty bucks from Bimisi's wallet.

He slapped a dollar down next to the cards. "It will fall in between."

Dyami flipped the top card from the deck, and then with a smile, slowly placed the jack of hearts outside the four and ten. Bimisi frowned and snatched the deck away from his mentor. Dyami gladly used his free hands to pick up the dollar bill.

Just as Bimisi started to shuffle the cards, a plastic gadget on the dashboard started to emit a soft beeping tone.

Something had triggered the motion sensors in the cavern.

"Stay here unless I call for you," Bimisi ordered, setting down the cards.

In an instant, he was out of the pickup and weaving through the trees, his feet whisking along through the leaves and twigs that littered the forest floor. The closer he got to the clearing, the more the weight of the mission he was about to carry out sank in.

As Dyami had said, the Shaman represented their final chance to reclaim their land.

But it wasn't right for that reclamation to include the slaughtering of innocent children. Even if they were white children. It also wasn't right for it to include the butchering of Jerry Ituha. Most importantly, it *wasn't going* to include anything happening to Rachel. His niece—that's who he must focus on.

By the time he got to the clearing, Bimisi had steeled himself. He removed his revolver from its shoulder holster and stepped out into the small, pale blue oasis, surrounded on all sides by the high black walls of pines and oaks.

Bimisi approached the cavern and peered inside, leading with his revolver. The moonlight barely penetrated the Shaman's underground lair.

Using his free hand, he quickly unlatched the flashlight hanging from his belt. His body tightened with apprehension as he darted the beam into the cavern.

A possum ambled out into the light. It stopped, looked up at him with a hiss, then continued past one of the motion sensors.

Bimisi's muscles unclenched. His shoulders dropped. He reminded himself to breathe.

Then he heard a twig crack somewhere off to his right. The sound immediately put him back on edge. Bimisi aimed his flashlight toward the trees, catching just a glimpse of the Shaman as the cursed relic of a man darted behind a Douglas fir.

Bark exploded as Bimisi instinctively squeezed off a shot, grazing a tree trunk.

Still a good distance from the clearing, Toby stepped cautiously through two oaks, making his way deeper into the reservation woods. His legs ached with every step, worn out from all the pedaling he'd done in the past several hours.

Meanwhile, everything above his deadened legs shivered uncontrollably due to the adrenaline coursing through his veins, which caused the beam of his flashlight to zigzag in front of him rather wildly.

Then he heard Bimisi's gunshot echo through the woods, and every muscle in his body seized up. The way the sound had reverberated off the trees made it impossible to tell which direction the shot had come from, but it had been close.

Toby shut off the flashlight. He wanted to make sure he saw whoever else was in the area before they saw him. Unfortunately, he could now only see about an arm's length ahead. Anything farther out appeared as nothing but black blobs or shifting shadows.

Then he heard the light rustling of footsteps.

Someone was running, and it sounded as if they were running in his direction. Overcome with panic, Toby ducked down behind a tree. He sat frozen, unsure of what to do next—a familiar feeling. He had wondered how he'd respond when the time came. Now he had his answer.

Holding his breath, he listened intently, attempting to hear even the slightest sound. There was nothing but silence. Had the person run off in another direction?

Toby tightened his grip on the pistol and, after a steadying breath, persuaded himself to move. He slowly peered around the tree trunk, his cheek pressed firmly against the rough bark.

The Shaman stood right on the other side.

"Ah!" Toby shouted as he fell back. He reflexively pulled the trigger—twice. The shots rang out through the woods, and the Shaman buckled to the forest floor.

Several moments passed before Toby managed to move again. He rose to his feet shakily, never taking his eyes off the Shaman. Inching toward the motionless Indian, he nudged the body with the toe of his sneaker.

Nothing. No movement. And just like that, without even having a chance to comprehend what he was doing, Toby had ended the town's nightmare.

The Alpha was dead!

There was suddenly the sound of more footsteps as Bimisi came rushing out of the shadows with his revolver raised.

Toby quickly lifted his arms and cried out. "Wait! It's me!"

Bimisi took in the scene, stunned. "What are you doing here?"

"I didn't believe you'd actually kill him," Toby confessed. "So I did."

Bimisi pointed his revolver at Toby.

"Whoa!" Toby shouted, backing away. "I'm sorry. Really, I am."

"And if I shoot you, so am I."

Toby felt a sudden pressure against his windpipe as a forearm wrapped around his throat. He was yanked backward, and almost simultaneously, there was a sharp sting in his side.

Looking down, he spotted a crudely shaped dagger pressed firmly to his ribs. His eyes then shifted to the ground in front of

THE ONE YOU FEED

him. The body was gone, and Toby quickly deduced that the owner of the dagger was the still very much alive Shaman.

This development didn't coerce so much as a flinch from Bimisi, and Toby realized that his sudden hostage status wasn't about to deter Rachel's uncle from taking a shot.

The Shaman seemed to realize the same. In an instant, Toby felt the ancient Indian's forearm release. Then, before he could even manage a breath, the Shaman's open palm struck him square in the back.

The force of the blow sent Toby flying toward Bimisi, who quickly ducked and stepped aside. Toby sailed right past Rachel's uncle, glancing off a tree and scraping his knee badly before toppling to the ground. Once he'd stopped rolling, he turned over onto his side and looked back to see Bimisi fire at the fleeing Shaman.

The shot missed, and so Rachel's uncle raced after his target, following the Shaman up over a bank of brush. When he reached the top of the small, shrub-covered knoll, he stopped. Toby could just make out Bimisi's head swiveling to scan the area.

He called out. "Where is he?"

Bimisi lowered his revolver and tromped back down the embankment. "Gone."

Toby grimaced as he got to his feet. "But I shot him. Twice. Dead on."

"Not with anything that was going to kill him."

Toby realized his mistake almost immediately. "Silver bullets."

Bimisi shook his head and started to stride away.

"I didn't think I'd need them unless he actually turned into a werewolf," Toby explained. One of the websites he'd been consulting had said as much. He'd be sure to delete it from his list of favorites as soon as he got home.

"He's the Alpha, isn't he?" Toby asked. "If we kill him then all the Betas he's made will go back to being human, right?"

Bimisi glanced back, looking surprised. "How do you know that?"

"A friend and I, well, we basically googled it."

Bimisi shook his head and continued off into the darkness.

"Wait!" Toby called out after him again. "What if he comes back?"

"He will not return now until the next full illumination cycle begins."

"What's an illumination cycle?"

After a couple more steps, Bimisi disappeared into the shadows, but Toby still heard the man grumble, "Google it."

It had only been a minute or two since Toby had stood over the Shaman's body thinking that he'd rescued the town. Now he had to accept the grim reality that the Shaman had just used him to escape.

He pulled his hood up over his head and trudged toward his bike. With his chin sunk dejectedly into chest, he looked down at his ripped jeans and skinned knee. Injury added to insult. No matter what his intentions were, the results always seemed to be the same.

Maybe helping people just isn't your thing. You don't seem to be very good at it.

CHAPTER 28

A CALL FROM THE ZOO

Walter glanced up at a bright gray dome of a sky as he parked his SUV at the driveway entrance gate to Bruce Bennett's extravagant lodge home. He shut off the engine and took another minute to gaze at the soupy mix of clouds before getting out of the vehicle. His exchanges with Bennett always required a moment of mental preparation and a couple of deep, calming breaths.

He exited the truck and walked up the front drive. He was about halfway to the door when he picked up on a scraping sound that seemed to be coming from behind the house. Changing course, he strolled around to the backyard to find Bruce on the lodge's expansive brick patio cleaning off the grate of a gas grill.

"Afternoon, Bruce," he said with a nod.

The plant owner jerked his head up, startled. He then quickly settled when he saw it was only the sheriff. "What are you doing here?"

Walter decided to ignore the anxious reaction and rude welcome. "I heard from my deputy that you had some trouble with a few kids from town yesterday."

"Indeed I did," Bruce replied as he scrubbed away with a steel wool brush. "Including your son."

"Toby was here?"

"Along with Nate Schaffer and that chubby Kraus boy."

"Well then, my apologies." Walter's brow furrowed as he strolled over to the grill. He had no clue why his son would feel the need to come out here. "I'll talk to Toby and find out what compelled his visit. Make sure no such trips happen again."

"See that you do." Bruce set down the steel brush and tested out the grill's side burner.

"I'd like to apologize to Carol and your daughter too, if I could."

"You can't," Bruce said gruffly. "They're headed down to Yachats for a little spa getaway. Celebrating our recent good fortunes. And speaking of good fortune, Sheriff, while I appreciate you coming out here to check on me in person, I can't help but wonder what I did to deserve the complimentary house call."

"I wanted to talk to you about your party," said Walter. "I was a little surprised to hear you'd decided to go ahead with it. Had to reschedule someone to cover Don's post tonight on the east side of town."

"Don Hutchins and Paul Grant are the two best hunters in the county," Bruce replied. "I need them here for my event."

"Town needs them too. It isn't any secret that you're not the most popular guy around these days. Taking folks' protection away isn't going to help that."

"There hasn't been an attack in nearly a month," Bruce said, giving Walter's argument a dismissive wave. "And ensuring everything here goes smoothly tonight can only serve to *help* my popularity."

Walter knew he shouldn't feel the way he did toward Bruce Bennett. He'd dealt with far worse people in Portland, but God help him, he simply loathed the man.

He was already aware that Bruce had obtained, most likely through monetary means, the support of the Oregon Metal Industries Council to begin producing welded steel pipes. While the smug bastard hadn't officially locked up the manufacturing contract, or gotten clearance to build his road, he obviously felt each was enough of a forgone conclusion to pat himself on the back with a celebration.

"As for those not invited, well, I do believe *you're* supposed to be the town's protection, Sheriff," Bruce continued. "Lucky for both of us, looks like whatever was killing folks has moved on. But if it makes the mistake of showing up here, *I'm* gonna make sure it ends up on this grill before the night's over, right alongside the burgers and brats. Now, you don't want to worry about my safety, the safety of my plant, or even the safety of my family, that's fine…"

"Of course I care about the safety of your family, Bruce."

"Just try to protect me from your own son, okay, Sheriff?"

Bruce headed inside, apparently done with their discussion. Walter swallowed the bile bubbling up his throat and glanced at the tree line that ran along the patio and backyard.

It would be easy pickings for anything that felt like leaping out from behind those Lodgepole pines and making a quick meal out of some unsuspecting reveler. While it did appear as though whatever had been attacking folks left the area weeks ago, having a party out here still seemed like one terrible idea.

Back at the station, Deputy Billy Rogers sat at his desk working on the newspaper crossword. This particular diversion had become a daily routine for him, and it had taken a year or so of struggling through the puzzles each morning to finally feel like he was getting good at them. Or at least mediocre.

When he'd started, he hadn't expected them to be all that tricky. He remembered visiting his grandparents while growing up and watching them knock out crosswords in minutes. He'd figured out maybe seven words on his first attempt, and that was after about an hour.

Over time, though, he had gained a better understanding of how to read the clues for puns, learned how some words were used more often than others, and picked up on certain patterns. And now that life in Silver Falls had slowed down again, he found himself with all the uneventful time he needed to keep figuring out these tricks.

He was stuck on the "video game pioneer" whose name occupied thirty-eight across when the phone rang. He reluctantly set the puzzle aside and answered the call.

"Silver Falls Sheriff's Department."

A female voice came back from the other end of the line. "May I speak with Deputy Rogers, please?"

"This is. What can I do for you?"

"My name is Lindsay Turner," said the woman. "I'm with the Oregon Zoo. I'm looking at the pictures you sent us."

Billy sat up straight. He'd nearly forgotten all about the pictures he'd taken on the reservation's campsite. However, even though the attacks had stopped, he was still plenty curious to find out what the heck had been behind them.

"Yeah?" His anticipation raised the tone of his voice an octave or two. "So what do we got?"

There was a short pause. "I...don't really know."

Billy slumped back into his chair. "You've had those photos for weeks."

"I know, and I apologize for the delay. We had a bit of a—"

"Not to mention that you've got just about every animal that walks the earth down at that zoo of yours."

"Well, that's just it," replied the researcher. "We do have just about every animal, and none of them leave a paw print that's anything quite like this."

The previous night's excursion to the reservation had basically been a catastrophe for Toby, but while it had left him discouraged, he refused to be disheartened. At least he now knew that Rachel's uncle was sincere about wanting to take out the Shaman. And he was happy to let Bimisi do just that, especially since Rachel's uncle was the only person Toby knew who was firing silver bullets.

However, there were others, namely his father, who needed to be informed that they weren't properly armed to protect themselves. Which meant Toby still needed to figure out a way to convince his dad that werewolves actually existed. First though, he needed to find out how long he had to accomplish such a task.

Shifting his cell to his left ear, Toby turned on his laptop. "Apparently they won't turn again until the next full illumination cycle."

"Which is what exactly?" Peter asked through the phone.

"Something Rachel's uncle mentioned to me last night. I was kind of hoping maybe you'd have heard of it."

"Sorry," said Peter. "But, so wait. Her uncle actually did try to kill the Shaman? Even after he let it out?"

"I couldn't believe it either, but yeah."

And now the Shaman had escaped again, thanks in no small part to Toby. He shook his head, bothered. Letting his latest failed attempt at heroism bring him down wasn't going to accomplish anything. He had to get over it.

The muffled sound of Peter's dad calling out came through the receiver.

Peter shouted back. "I'll be down in a second."

"You sure you have time to help me with this?" Toby asked.

"Yeah, of course. I'll give you a call back when I find something."

Toby ended the call and did a Google search for full illumination cycles. Frustration came quickly as he started scrolling through the results. Most had to do with the effects of light intensity on the astaxanthin formation in green algae. While Toby had no idea what that was, he was pretty sure it had nothing to do with a werewolf's transformation. After sorting through a few more links, he opened his favorites and began clicking through the handful of werewolf websites he still trusted.

He then heard the muffled voice of his own father calling out from downstairs. "Toby!"

"Yeah," he shouted back.

Stomping footsteps ascended up the stairs and Toby quickly closed the werewolf site he was examining just as his bedroom door flew open.

His dad stormed into the room. "You want to tell me what the hell you were doing out at Bennett's ranch yesterday?"

Damn. Of course he was going to find out about that. Toby had no acceptable explanation for why he'd gone out there. Or, at least, not one his father was going to consider acceptable.

"Um, well…no. Not really," he mumbled.

"All this recent improvement, you refocusing on your studies, was it all just some sort of a con job?"

"No," Toby lied. In all actuality it had been, but in fairness, one he'd used as much to fool himself as his father. He'd gotten serious about his grades because it provided a distraction. A distraction from the fact that he'd lost what little courage and conviction he'd once had to save his friends and the town. It was a distraction his dad had approved of, and one the sheriff clearly wasn't pleased to see coming to an end.

It had to come to an end though. Toby couldn't afford to lose his nerve again.

"Why were you out there?" Walter pressed. Toby needed to provide an answer in the next couple of seconds or there would be real trouble.

"Because I was following Nate and Willard, and that's where they went." The words tumbled from Toby's mouth before he could stop them.

"What did they want with Bennett?"

"They went to warn him."

"Warn him about what?"

At this point, some sort of serious punishment seemed inevitable. Toby figured he might as well just tell the truth.

"I'm pretty sure that..." Toby winced in preparation for the tirade he was sure his answer was going to induce. "That they're the ones attacking people."

Walter just stared back at him, dumbfounded. It wasn't an encouraging reaction or the one Toby had expected, but it did give him an opportunity to try to continue to explain. "And I think the attacks have only stopped because they haven't turned. Which, according to Rachel's uncle, apparently has something to do with illumination cycles. The only problem is, I don't know what those are. So I'm trying to figure out—"

"You need to stop this right now."

"Dad, I know you think I'm losing it, but I swear that this is—"

"I said that's enough!" Walter shouted.

Yeah, it probably was. Toby hadn't mentioned werewolves in weeks. He'd promised not to, and there hadn't been any reason to break that promise. The attacks were over, or at least he had thought they were. Now he knew better. He also knew that, at this moment, the "progress" he'd made by focusing on his studies had been completely undone in his father's mind.

Before Walter could try to make sense of what Toby had just told him, or simply hand out more chastisement, his cell phone rang. The sheriff cursed under his breath as he answered the call.

"What is it, Billy?" he barked.

A short sigh of relief escaped Toby's lips. He was thankful for the brief delay in what he was sure would continue to be a very uncomfortable conversation.

His dad turned away from him slightly. "Okay. So what did she say it is? Uh huh. What do you mean she doesn't know?"

Based on the agitated tone of his father's voice, Toby sensed the conversation he was having with Deputy Rogers wasn't going any better than theirs had. Toby couldn't make out any of the deputy's words, but he could hear his anxiously raised voice coming through the phone. Soon a stupefied expression replaced the look of frustration on his father's face.

Toby felt himself growing anxious now, as Walter ended the call. What had Billy found out?

The answer didn't come right away. Walter stared blankly at the floor for a long moment, then finally turned his attention back to his son.

"So you're saying that Bimisi Chochopi told you that…" He paused and looked down again, rubbing his forehead. The sheriff of Silver Falls was completely confounded.

Toby decided to give the conversation a little nudge. "What did Billy say?"

"Nothing that makes any sense."

Toby hoped that meant that whatever information Billy had just given his father was something that had helped his dad finally realize, as Toby had, that an irrational explanation for all that had happened in town just might be the most reasonable one.

Walter finally figured out what he wanted to say next. "Okay, I'm heading back out to Bennett's ranch, just in case whatever was attacking folks is still out in those woods—or in case your friends decide to do anything else ill-advised."

He hesitated for another moment, then continued with his thought. "This is insane, but…if you find out what the heck an illumination cycle is and when the next one is supposed to be, I want you to call me."

A wave of relief passed over Toby as a feeling of excitement swelled up inside. His dad might not be ready to completely believe in the supernatural, but he was possibly starting to come around. And he was asking Toby for help!

Rather than testing his father's new open-mindedness by bringing up the topic of silver bullets, he decided to focus on the assignment he'd just been given.

"Yes, sir," he replied with the hint of a grin.

Across town, Ashley lay on her bed trying to get through the final chapter of Mrs. Kyle's weekend reading assignment for *Of Mice and Men*. The sounds of her mother and father arguing downstairs made the task difficult. She snapped her book shut and scowled at the hardwood floor, as if the angry voices were emanating from the White Ash instead of the kitchen below.

She jumped off the bed and stormed down the stairs. The drama had become too much. Couldn't they act like normal human beings for just one day?

One day.

That's all it had taken for her father to start drinking again after she'd come home from the hospital. Apparently that was all the time he needed to shrug off everything she'd been through and return to his routine of abusing his wife and the liquor cabinet.

What a miserable existence. The only glimmer of hope Ashley had had to escape it was Mike, but now that hope was lost. She could no longer count on using him to run away from this piddling town. She'd have to make her own way out, and the thought terrified her. In that respect, she was no better than her mother.

Her parents' shouting got louder as she neared the kitchen, and Ashley could now make out the hurtful insults being slung back and forth.

"All you've done for the past month is sit around getting drunk, like some kind of damn bum," her mother screamed.

Ashley rolled her eyes. *No shit, Mom. And what has yelling at him about it accomplished?*

"How the hell else am I supposed to tolerate being around you all the damn time?" her father shouted back.

Exactly. Ashley knew he didn't just mean he needed to drink to tolerate being around her mom though. Truth was, he'd always been a drunk. Now he just had a lot more time and cause for it. Losing his job, being stuck at home with a wife he didn't love, and his freak daughter who claimed to have seen a werewolf...

"You are so fucking worthless!"

Ashley heard her mother get smacked for that one. The sound made her pause just before she reached the kitchen doorway. Her lips curled in disgust. There was no disputing it. Her life had been better when she was lying catatonic in a hospital bed. How sad and pathetic was that? Unable to handle the mix of emotions stewing inside her, she turned and stormed out of the house.

Her mother must have spotted her marching down the sidewalk from one of the kitchen windows, because Ashley soon heard her calling out from the front steps, "Ashley? Where are you going? Make sure you're home before curfew!"

Who cared about curfew? Nobody had been attacked in weeks.

CHAPTER 29

BENNETT'S PARTY

After researching for almost three hours, Toby hadn't made any progress in determining what a full illumination cycle was. He opened the last werewolf site from his list of favorites, this being the third time he'd cycled through them, and began to scan its contents. His index finger flicked over his laptop's scroll pad as he moved down the page. Etymology. Common attributes. Vulnerabilities. Remedies. Norse society. Wolfskin belts. Satanic allegiance. Blah, blah, blah.

His finger came down on the pad once more but didn't move. Toby's entire body went numb as he stared saucer-eyed at the screen or, more specifically, at a tiny blue link in the left navigation pane. How had he missed it before?

Full Illumination Cycles.

He clicked it and started to read. The full illumination cycle consisted of the two nights before a full moon, the night of, and the two nights after. These were the nights when the earth, moon,

THE ONE YOU FEED

and sun were in approximate alignment, with the moon on the opposite side of the earth, so the entire sunlit side of the natural satellite faced the planet. These five nights of "full illumination" took
place once a month and, according to some "experts," were the only
times a werewolf could turn.

Once a month. It had been almost a month since the last attacks.

Toby frantically opened a new browser window and searched for
moon cycles. Several results populated the screen for lunar calendars.
He clicked one and scrolled down the page until he got to May, then
he looked for which night was supposed to have a full moon.

His pulsed quickened. "Oh no."

Ashley had trudged around aimlessly for several blocks after leaving her house, eventually ending up at Evergreen Park. When she'd
arrived, the park had been filled with laughing children and playful
dogs, but now, about an hour later, she was alone.

Sitting on a swing in the center of the park, she swayed in a
circle with tears streaming down her cheeks. The horizon behind
her showed just a glimmer of the recently set sun, and with the oncoming coolness of the evening seeping through her sweater, she
was starting to shiver.

Footsteps crunched across the playground's gravel, growing
louder as someone approached. She kept her head down, hoping
whoever it was would just continue past. The footsteps stopped.
Knowing the stranger was now standing directly behind her, Ashley
anxiously glanced over her shoulder to find Nate.

She brushed away her tears. "Guess you're not obeying the curfew either, huh?"

"No, but you probably should."

"Nobody's been attacked for weeks," she replied with an exasperated laugh. "And even if that creature did come back, so what? My boyfriend is dead, my mom and dad are a nightmare, and all my friends think I'm a freak. So let the thing show up here if it wants to. I wish it would."

Nate didn't deserve to have all this unloaded on him, but he was there and she needed to get it out. All the work she'd done had been undone. Anyone who had viewed her as special now saw her as a spectacle. She was reliving her nightmarish middle school years all over again, only worse. There was no way for her to come back from this and nobody left to help her escape it.

She wouldn't blame Nate if he turned and ran, but she'd vent for as long as he was willing to listen. His reaction wasn't one of shock or awkwardness, however. Instead, he was grinning.

"Being a freak isn't all bad," he replied.

Was he trying to relate? Trying to make it all not seem so awful? It was a sweet gesture, but misguided. He'd certainly taken more than his fair share of abuse from the kids at school, but they saw him as more geek than freak. She'd been branded a whole new breed of psycho.

Ashley started to sway back and forth on the swing again. "People pick on you because they're jealous of your smarts, maybe even a little intimidated. They know you'll get out of here someday and be something special."

"I'm already special."

Now she just wanted him to leave. He wasn't getting it.

Ashley turned away, hoping he'd take the hint, and just missed Nate's eyes flash yellow. She sat unaware as he buckled over, and remained oblivious as his bones and muscles bulged and bent to re-form themselves. His flesh stretched. Fangs emerged. Hair sprouted in clumps. Claws burst forth.

Nate let out a strangled cry as he morphed fully into a werewolf.

All the blood drained from Ashley's face as his cry became a howl. She turned, trembling, to discover what he'd become. Unable to even scream, she managed only a childish whimper just before the werewolf lunged toward her.

Just envision who you want to go after.

Willard repeated the instructions in his head as he stumbled into the kitchen. Focusing on the words helped to distract him from the pain that was surging through every inch of his body. He hadn't expected turning to feel pleasant, but he hadn't thought it would be this bad.

His legs buckled as the bones inside them shifted, pitching him forward. He crashed into the kitchen table, scattering a collection of carefully stacked Tupperware containers and sending a serving dish over the edge. The glass plate shattered into several pieces as it hit the tile floor.

"Willard," his mom called out from the next room. "Are you okay?"

He repressed the urge to scream and managed to grunt back, "Yeah."

He then pushed himself away from the table and toward the door that led to the garage. *Just envision who you want to go after.* He burst through the door and quickly shut it behind him, leaning against it to catch his breath.

A sharp pain shot up his back and he buckled over, slamming his hands onto his mother's Kia Sorento. His fists left baseball-size dents in the hood that were going to be difficult to explain.

He took another deep breath, swung his right arm around, and pressed the button to open the garage door. He was now sweating profusely. Another rush of pain. His hands felt as though they were on fire. Willard looked down to see claws springing forth from his fingers.

As the garage door rumbled open, he steadied himself against the wall, his body starting to shake violently. "Bruce Bennett, Bruce Bennett, Bruce Bennett. Bruce BeneAaahhh!"

Beyond frustrated, Rachel furiously scribbled out what she'd just determined was her latest incorrect answer to that night's calculus assignment. She tore the page she'd been writing on from her notebook, crumpled it into a ball, and tossed it onto the floor of her bedroom where it joined several earlier attempts. Getting caught up in her math and science classes without anyone's help had proven to be a slow, laborious process.

However, her current level of irritation was due to more than just her inability to grasp the concepts of derivatives and arbitrary change.

Her uncle had called and told her about what had happened on the reservation, specifically about how Toby had foolishly shot the Shaman with lead bullets and then allowed him to get away. "Foolishly," of course, being the word he had chosen.

Not that Rachel felt the label was too far off. Toby's decision to go out there alone hadn't been the wisest one in her opinion, plus she was hurt, and more than a little offended, that he hadn't recruited her to go with him.

As she tried to redirect her focus back on her homework, there was a knock on her bedroom window. A bit startled, she drew back the curtain to find her "foolish" neighbor perched on the roof outside.

Rachel quickly opened the window, equally confused and excited to see him. "What are you doing out there?"

"I think you might have your phone turned off," Toby answered.

She nodded. "I shut it off while I was studying."

"Well I needed to get a hold of you, and I saw your light on, and there's that Oregon oak that runs right up alongside your house. It's pretty easy to climb."

"Okay, but *why* are you on *the roof*?"

"Didn't want to risk your parents answering the door," Toby replied. "I didn't think they'd be cool with you going out past curfew."

She gave him a curious look. "I didn't realize I was going out past curfew."

"My dad's not answering his cell, and I've got something I need to tell him, but he's sort of hidden all of our car keys, and so I need to borrow your Jeep. But...I don't really know how to drive stick, so..."

"So after last night you've decided you might actually like to have my help again," she muttered peevishly.

Toby's face bunched up. "Your uncle told you about what happened, huh?"

"We were supposed to figure out how to solve this together!"

"I'm sorry," he said in a regretful tone that convinced Rachel he truly was. "I should have trusted him."

"I'm not upset because you didn't trust my uncle," Rachel said. "I'm upset because you didn't trust *me*. You know that I don't think the way he does, right? I'm not happy about what happened to my tribe, but I don't believe in holding a grudge against people who had nothing to do with it."

"I know, but I was worried that if I told you I was going back out there, then you might try to talk me out of it or, even worse, that…"

"That what?"

"That you'd have wanted to come with me," Toby answered quietly. "If something had happened, and you'd ended up getting hurt, or worse…"

Rachel couldn't help but feel a little flattered. It was sweet of him to be worried about her, but she wanted Toby to know he could count on her. That he could trust her. He also needed to know that she believed in him.

"Nothing would have happened to me," she said as she snatched her keys off her dresser. "I'd have felt totally safe with you there to watch my back."

She lifted the window screen and climbed onto the roof. "But you need someone to watch yours too. I don't want you trying something like that again on your own." She lowered the screen behind her. "So where are we going?"

Bennett's self-congratulatory party was in full swing. Music played and there were a few folks dancing, but the general mood was still somewhat tense. Or at least it was among those who had yet to catch a good buzz from the beer kegs. Bruce had decided to hold off on making any official announcement about the future of his plant until later that night. He was enjoying the groveling and ass kissing of his guests, many of whom were hoping to once again become his employees.

Wishing he could be anywhere but where he was, Walter glanced at his cell as he wove his way through the kids and adults milling about the yard. He'd been trying to get a signal for almost an hour with no success.

The researcher at the zoo had said she'd never seen a paw print like the one in Billy's photo. Walter had called her back to confirm that his deputy had understood her correctly. He had. Billy had gone on to explain how she'd told him she believed they had a new species of animal in these woods. *A new species of animal.*

According to the only surviving witnesses to the attacks, Ashley Schultz and Rachel Chochopi, that new species was a werewolf. When it came to accepting the existence of such a creature, the true believers now totaled four: the two girls, his son, and now Rachel's uncle Bimisi. It was the last member of that group who Walter wanted to talk to next.

It wasn't like Bimisi to waste his breath interacting with anyone in town. The fact that he'd opened up about what was happening, or what he *thought* was happening, likely meant he truly believed Silver Falls to be in danger.

Not something Walter felt the Indian would have cared about a couple of months ago, but perhaps that had changed now that his ex-sister-in-law and her daughter were among the town's residents.

During his drive out to Bennett's cabin, Walter had remembered how Bimisi had shown up at the scene on the night the family had been killed at the reservation's campsite. The Indian had seemed surprised by the killings, but when Walter thought back to their conversation, he remembered that surprise being less about the actual attack and more about how the victims included children. If Bimisi had actually *expected* the attacks, then he must have known, or *thought* he knew, what was behind them.

Walter tried turning his cell phone off, then back on. Still no luck.

Several yards away, an extremely bored Paul Grant stood along the yard's tree line, watching the forest. Occasionally his focus drifted, his eyes wandering over to the beer keg that sat in the center of the lawn. Agreeing to stand guard at this party, instead of simply showing up to enjoy it, was really starting to seem like a mistake.

At least if he were drunk, then maybe Don Hutchins's ceaseless bitching would be easier to endure.

"This is stupid, us being out here," griped his fellow hunter and party protector. "Whatever was attacking folks, it ain't around these parts anymore."

"Easiest two hundred bucks I've ever made," Paul replied in a lazy monotone. "So I'm not complaining."

"You can't tell me you wouldn't rather be at Wolfy's right now, watching the Blazers' game with a pint of—"

Don went silent as a hulking figure darted through the shadows several feet ahead. Paul perked up and peered into the woods, uncertain of what exactly he'd just seen. The thing had looked to be the size of a full-grown grizzly, but the animal had moved far too fluidly to be a bear. Also, Oregon didn't have grizzlies.

Paul watched and listened vigilantly, waiting for any additional signs of movement. There were none.

"Did you see that?" Don asked in a near whisper.

The hunter took his rifle off his shoulder and pointed it toward the trees. "Tell Bruce to get these folks inside."

"You tell him," Don replied, readying his rifle as well. "I saw it first."

CHAPTER 30

THE UNINVITED

Walter glanced up from his signal searching to spot the hunters pointing their rifles into the forest. He quickly recognized that they weren't just watching the trees, but searching them. They'd seen something.

He looked back toward the house, scanning the crowd until he caught sight of the party's host over by the grill. "Bruce, get everyone inside. Now."

"Sorry, but we don't have a curfew at this party, Sher—" Bruce paused when he too noticed Paul and Don studying the woods. He furrowed his brow and clapped his hands together. "Okay, listen up. Everybody needs to get inside."

A bunch of moans and groans came from the crowd until they started to notice the hunters as well. One by one, they gathered together with their spouses and children and started moving toward the lodge.

Walter strode through the dull murmuring of uneasy partygoers until he was standing beside Don and Paul. "What did you guys see?"

"There was something about twenty yards out," Paul replied.

"Something big," Don added.

Walter stared into the trees. He saw nothing except branches dissolving into darkness. Heard nothing except crickets and Don's heavy breathing. Then he heard a shriek.

Startled, the sheriff turned to see Brad and Melanie Levi chasing down their young daughter and instantly started toward them to lend a hand. He had to get all these folks inside before whatever was in those woods came out.

But it was too late. A mammoth animal suddenly sprung from the trees.

It quickly zeroed in on Brad and took him to the ground before anyone could react. The terrified party guest cried out in pain as the creature's jaw clamped down on his upper torso.

Walter looked on in shock as the monster viciously jerked its head back, ripping Brad's arm, shoulder, and part of his chest away from the rest of his body. The sounds of flesh splitting and bones breaking reminded the sheriff of a well-taped package being torn open, only muckier.

Melanie, now holding her child, went rigid, too frightened to scream or move. Walter stood equally frozen. It was as if his brain had shut off, too stunned to process what his eyes had just seen.

Werewolves were real. There was no other way to explain the bulky beast in front of him, which was now stalking toward Melanie.

Shaking off his shock, the sheriff of Silver Falls drew his pistol and opened fire, striking the creature in its shoulder and side. Don and Paul hustled over and unloaded rifle blasts into the beast as well.

Then Walter caught movement out of the corner of his eye. Turning toward the trees, he spotted a second werewolf, much leaner than the first, streaking out of the woods toward the few horror-stricken guests who were still outside.

"There's two of them!" Paul shouted. The hunter spun and tracked the second creature with the barrel of his rifle, then fired. The bullet struck the beast's shoulder with a dull thud, spraying blood, but doing little to slow it. Paul fired again, this time striking the creature in the side. The werewolf snarled and loped back into the brush to take cover, thankfully without claiming any victims.

After taking another blast from Don's rifle, the heftier of the two beasts yelped and leapt lamely back into the trees as well. Both hunters moved in for the kill, hustling after their prey, *but the werewolves were gone.*

Paul stepped a few feet into the trees and stared out into the darkness, stunned. "How in the hell?"

Walter used the brief reprieve to get the rest of the partygoers out of harm's way. He ushered a distraught Melanie and her child toward the large cabin, waving for any remaining people on the lawn to follow them inside.

Bruce stood at the door, his eyes darting maniacally around the yard. "What the hell were those things?"

Walter glanced back at the forest. "I don't know. Just keep everyone inside until I say it's safe to come out."

He helped a few more people through the doorway and then trotted back over to Paul. "Where did they go?"

"No idea." Paul walked out of the woods, dumbfounded. "I hit that thing twice. It ought to be laying at our feet, breathing its final breath."

They all stood perfectly still, looking and listening for any sign of life.

Walter picked up on a dull hum that seemed to be growing louder by the second. "What is that?"

All three men jumped as Rachel's Jeep came tearing out of the woods and down the driveway to Bennett's cabin. It skidded to a halt about halfway down the drive, and Toby and Rachel hopped out.

"Dad!" Toby shouted. "It's tonight! The attacks are going to…" He paused when he saw Brad Levi's slaughtered remains. "…start happening again."

The heftier beast came bounding out of the trees again.

"Look out!" Rachel cried.

The werewolf pounced on Don, digging its claws into the hunter's back. The monster sliced through his flesh and internal organs effortlessly, like a rabid dog ripping into a sofa cushion. Paul raised his rifle to take aim, but didn't fire. Half of Don's insides were already outside of his body. He was gone.

"Go!" Walter called out to the group. "Run!"

They all raced for the cabin. Glancing back, the sheriff saw the werewolf loping after them. He aimed at the beast as best he could and squeezed off several shots. Two of the bullets struck the creature in the head, slowing it down just enough to allow everyone to reach Bennett's lodge. They rushed into the house, stumbling into a group of frightened party guests who stood right inside the doorway.

Manning the entrance, Bruce watched the beast shake off the effects of the gunshots as if they were annoying bee stings and continue in its pursuit.

He attempted to shut the door behind Walter and Toby, but the werewolf leapt and barreled into it, propelling him into the foyer. A sharp pain swelled across the back of Bruce's skull as his head cracked against what he guessed was the banister of the front staircase.

The creature rocketed through the entryway, landing on a large area rug.

As soon as the beast came down on it, the rug gave way and slid across the hardwood floor. Bruce heard the werewolf snarl as its carpet ride continued down the first floor hallway.

Even with his vision blurred due to a likely concussion, he was able to make out several Silver Falls' residents scattering like bowling pins as the monster plowed into them.

Paul chased after the creature, shoving a woman aside as he took aim. Rifle blasts boomed as the hunter unloaded two shots into the werewolf's chest.

Just before blacking out, Bruce saw the beast crumple to the floor.

Panic-stricken party guests scrambled away from the werewolf in every direction. As she sidestepped around two frantic women who appeared to be sisters, Rachel reached for her smartphone only to remember she'd left it in the Jeep. She spotted a cordless phone resting on a nearby table and pushed her way toward it. Squeezing through the hysterical crowd, she only had one thought. They needed her uncle.

The moment she picked up the phone, the second werewolf came crashing through the living room's bay window. It chomped down on the head of one of the sisters Rachel had just avoided, exploding her skull as if it were no firmer than a grapefruit.

"Move!" she heard Sheriff Hoffman shout.

The sound of a rifle blast filled the room, followed by three rounds from the sheriff's pistol. The wiry beast's blood sprayed across the home's enormous ledgestone fireplace as the creature staggered back, attempting to stay on its feet. The echo of another rifle blast reverberated off the walls. The werewolf collapsed.

As she stared at the motionless monster for a moment, her ears ringing, Rachel realized she wasn't breathing. She inhaled deeply and tried to steady her shaking hands enough to dial the phone.

Toby rushed over. "What are you doing?"

"My uncle," was all her fear would allow her to manage in response.

Toby eyes widened with concern. "I don't think either of these things are the Shaman. If your uncle comes here, he'll end up killing—"

A low growl from the werewolf interrupted him. Toby turned his attention back toward the fireplace. The creature stirred, its front legs starting to straighten as it lifted itself off the hardwood.

"He'll know what to do," Rachel said sharply.

They both flinched as Paul fired again. Blood sprayed from the beast's shoulder, and it collapsed back onto the floor.

Toby relented. "Okay. You're right. Call him."

While Rachel dialed, Toby hustled over to his father. "You have to get everyone out of here."

"You all right?" Walter asked, not seeming to have heard him.

"Yeah, Dad." Toby grabbed his father's forearm. "We need to tell people to go back to town."

"We need to figure out how to kill these things."

"You can't," Toby said. "Not without silver bullets."

The Shaman should have struck by now. That was the sole thought echoing in Bimisi's head as he sat in his parked pickup, watching the unsuspecting townspeople of Silver Falls strolling the streets. The cursed Indian had located the town during the last full illumination cycle. He wouldn't regress by going back to attacking isolated campers in the woods.

Of course, the Shaman also knew that he was now being hunted. Maybe he was just being more cautious.

Bimisi felt the urge to do something. Something more than just sitting in his truck and waiting for the Shaman to show. Beyond restless, he decided to get out and continue his watch on foot. As he reached for the door handle, he heard someone call his name.

"Hey, Chochopi," shouted a clearly inebriated Hank Schultz as he swayed across Wilson Street toward Bimisi's pickup. "No invite for you either, huh?"

Bimisi furrowed his brow at the man who used to be one of his fellow drawing machine operators at Bennett's plant. They'd both been let go during consecutive layoffs two months ago. He had no idea what Schultz was grousing about. He didn't really care.

Hank leaned against the driver's side door, temporarily delaying Bimisi's exit. "The bastard's got half of Silver Falls out there kissing his ass right now, but I guess he didn't deem you and me good enough to go pucker up for him."

"What are you talking about?" Bimisi asked, alarmed to hear that such a large number of people were gathered somewhere outside of town.

"Bennett's party." Hank half belched his reply. "Of course, now, the way I hear it, this new contract ain't gonna be enough for him to bring *everyone* back. So I guess it makes sense that he wouldn't be offering any new jobs to an Injun ahead of someone from town. Don't know why *I* was left of the invite list though."

Bimisi sat stunned. He indeed had not heard about the party. If he had, he wouldn't be sitting on a street in Silver Falls. The Shaman didn't need to come into town to find more victims. The town had gone to him.

Just as Hank pushed himself off the truck in an attempt to propel his body toward the liquor store, Bimisi's cell phone started to ring. He checked the display and quickly answered the call.

His eyes widened as he listened to his panicked niece stumble through the details of what was occurring out at Bennett's lodge. She was exactly where he needed to be, and by the sound of things, he needed to get there as soon as possible.

CHAPTER 31

ABILITY TO DISCRIMINATE

The creatures looked much more grotesque than anything he'd imagined. Toby stared at the heap of mangy fur, claws, and fangs that lay motionless in front of the fireplace and struggled to accept the very real possibility that it was one of his friends. His eyes glanced over to what was left of Ms. Kesler. It was all too much for him to process.

Someone's wailing sobs prompted Toby to look over his shoulder. His father was ushering Ms. Kesler's overcome sister, along with several other distraught guests, out the front door and toward their vehicles.

"Get to your homes and lock your doors," Walter instructed. "Anyone who doesn't feel safe at home can go to the station. I'll let Deputy Rogers know the situation and that he should expect people arriving there throughout the night."

Toby heard a groan and turned to see Bruce shaking off the blow to the head he'd taken earlier. The most detested man in Silver

Falls attempted to stagger to his feet, then stumbled backward as if drunk. Toby rushed over to lend him a hand.

"Thanks," Bruce said as Toby propped him up.

The host of the party took a moment to register the hysteria going on around him. Toby did the same. Both beasts lay sprawled on the floor, occasionally growling and continuing to stir. Paul paced the hallway, keeping an eye on the creatures while reloading his rifle. Everyone else spilled out of the cabin, piled into their vehicles, and tore away as quickly as they could, some barely avoiding a collision.

Bruce staggered toward Walter, swaying woozily. Toby followed alongside him, concerned that the man might topple over.

"Why didn't you kill them?" Bruce asked accusingly.

"Not like we haven't been trying," Paul shot back.

Bruce regarded the injured werewolves with dismay. "What can I do?"

Walter glanced over at Toby. "Get my son and his friend out of here. Take them somewhere safe."

"I want to help," Toby protested.

Walter shook his head. "As long as Rachel's uncle shows up here with those silver bullets, he should be all the help we need."

Bruce took a look at Rachel, sizing her up. "There's an Indian that knows how to kill these things?"

"To the best of my understanding, yes," Walter replied.

"We don't want to kill them," Toby objected.

"Like hell we don't," Bruce challenged.

Walter gave his son a disbelieving look. "Don't tell me you still think these things are Nate and Willard."

"I'm pretty sure they are, yeah."

"How much longer until that Indian gets here?" Paul asked uneasily.

The bulkier of the two beasts snarled from down the hallway, getting their attention. He began to crawl toward them, baring his fangs.

Walter and Paul strode down the hall, each man firing a shot into the creature. It flopped down and rolled onto its side, still breathing but staying put.

Bruce shook off the remaining cobwebs from his fall and sprang into action, grabbing Toby and Rachel by their forearms. "You two, come with me."

Rachel barely managed to put down the phone before Bruce yanked her toward the stairs. Without any sort of an explanation, he began pulling them up to the second floor.

Toby heard his father calling after them from the hallway. "Dammit, Bruce, I meant get them out of this house!"

Bruce paid no attention, leading Toby and Rachel to the top of the stairs and then down the second-floor hall. Toby tried to pull away, but immediately felt Mr. Bennett tighten his grip.

Walter called out again from the living room. "Bruce! Get them out of here!"

The stubborn plant owner tugged the two of them into a dark room at the far end of the hallway and shut the door behind them. Toby stood in complete darkness for a second, then Bruce flipped on the lights to his upstairs study and locked the door.

"You think a locked door is going to stop them?" Toby asked incredulously.

"No," Bruce answered as he strode over to an enormous oak armoire. He opened it to reveal several large-caliber weapons hanging on built-in custom racks. Removing a 20-gauge shotgun, he gave them both a wink. "This is."

"No," Toby moaned. "It's not."

Downstairs, Walter and Paul finished reloading their weapons, yet again, as the werewolves wobbled to their feet.

"I'm running out of ammunition here, Sheriff," Paul said as he raised his rifle to fire another round into the heftier of the two creatures. "That girl's uncle better get here soon."

Walter stepped cautiously toward the other beast, getting just close enough to see the werewolf's bullet wounds healing rapidly below its scruffy clumps of fur. Completely flummoxed and frustrated, he fired off three more rounds, but the pistol shots did more to anger the lanky monster than maim it.

The werewolf straightened its front legs and swiped at a coffee table, sending it into the air. It struck the sheriff solidly in the chest and chin, knocking him to the floor and leaving him in a daze. His view now partially obstructed by the table, Walter could no longer see Paul, but he heard the hunter's rifle blast as the creature lunged.

Then both Paul and the werewolf came into view as the beast clamped down on the hunter's arm and, with a twist of its massive head, flung the man clear across the room. Paul crashed into a life-sized portrait of Bruce Bennett that hung on the opposite wall and then fell to the floor in a heap.

The werewolf pounced, clawing out the hunter's throat with one swipe. Too woozy to take action, Walter could only watch as the creature reared back and let loose a victorious howl.

All three of the frightened souls in the upstairs study jumped as the werewolf's howl reverberated through the walls. Toby's heart sank when no sounds followed. Why weren't they hearing more gunfire?

He took a step toward the door, wanting make sure his dad was okay, but then took several steps back when a snarl came from the outside hallway.

Bruce leveled his shotgun at the room's entrance. "You kids, get behind me."

Toby was going to do more than just get behind Mr. Bennett. If a werewolf was coming in, they needed to find another way out. He quickly surveyed the room and hustled over to the nearest window.

Flipping the latch, he slid open the lower pane and punched out the screen. Looking at the hard-packed dirt below, his first thought was that it would be a long fall. They'd get out of the room easily enough, but would be easy prey after twisting a knee or blowing out an ankle.

Then Toby looked up. It was a far more promising option.

"I think I can reach the roof," he said, ducking his head back inside.

Before anyone could respond, the leaner of the two werewolves burst through the door. The sound of Bruce's gun blast immediately filled the room and blood splattered the study wall. The creature collapsed in the doorway, its chest left bloody and ragged from the shotgun's powerful slug.

Toby eyed the wounded beast. If the group could climb over it, they'd be able to get back downstairs, but there was no way to tell how injured the monster really was. Toby had no intentions of getting close enough to find out. He glanced over at Rachel who seemed to be thinking the same thing.

"Roof sounds good," she said.

Toby quickly shrugged off his jacket and dropped it to the floor, then climbed onto the windowsill. He steadied himself, getting a good grip on the outside of the frame. Leaning his body outside the window, he stood up and tried not to look down.

About three feet above his head was a copper gutter that ran the length of the house, a choice Mr. Bennett had possibly made to give his cabin a more rustic, historical appearance. Toby was just glad it looked sturdy.

He reached up with one arm, pushing off his toes, and gave the gutter a good tug. It held. Determined not to let doubt set in, he hurriedly crouched down and took a deep breath.

Leaping up and to his right, Toby grabbed the gutter and pulled. Using his body's momentum, he swung his right leg onto the roof's slate shingles. It landed and stuck, but only for a moment. The shingle below his sneaker then gave way, and the next thing Toby knew, he was swinging back past the window.

"Toby!" he heard Rachel call out from inside.

He held tight as his momentum swung his body to the left. His upper arms burning, he frantically kicked his left foot onto the shingles. Everything stayed put this time. Grunting and panting with the effort, Toby strained to pull himself up over the gutter and rolled onto the roof.

Seeing that Toby had found his way to safety, Rachel turned away from the window to watch Bruce cautiously approach the werewolf and poke it with the barrel of his shotgun.

"Think I killed the bastard," Rachel heard him mumble.

Her eyes moved to the creature. The intense prickling she felt spreading throughout her body, which she'd come to recognize as some sort of werewolf sixth sense, told her something different. Things in this room were about to take a turn for the worse. She wanted out of there before they did.

Rachel spun around and stepped up onto the windowsill.

"Hey," Bruce called out to her. "I said I think I killed the bast—"

The werewolf jerked its head up and chomped down on the plant owner's upper right arm. Then, in the blink of an eye, it tore the limb clear off. Too stunned to scream, Bruce just stared at the shocking amount of blood spilling from his shoulder.

Tossing the appendage aside, the beast knocked its bewildered prey to the floor and completed its assault by splitting open Bruce's chest with its five-inch claws.

Lifting her other foot onto the windowsill, Rachel frantically reached into the air. Not feeling any hands grabbing hers, she looked up for Toby, but he was nowhere to be found.

"Toby!"

His head and shoulders suddenly emerged, and he quickly stretched an arm toward her. "C'mon. Grab my hand."

Rachel reached up again, and Toby grasped her wrist. She wrapped both of her hands around his and held on tight.

Glancing back inside the room, she saw the werewolf gnawing on Bruce's head like it was a chew toy. The creature peered up to notice her hanging outside the window, and they locked eyes. She felt like bait dangling there, and apparently looked like it too. Having polished off its original target, the werewolf released the slaughtered Mr. Bennett and took a step toward her.

"Grab the gutter," Toby grunted. "You need to pull too."

Rachel looked up to see he was starting to slide off the roof. She quickly let go with one of her hands and grasped the copper gutter, straining to lift herself as Toby pulled her up by her other arm. Her torso had just cleared the roof's edge when she heard the werewolf's heavy paws trotting across the study's hardwood floor.

It was coming for her.

A sudden explosion of knotty pine paneling, wood window framing, and Owens Corning showered Rachel as the werewolf broke through the window and part of the second-story wall.

As she was hoisted upward, she caught a glimpse of the creature through all the debris, seeing it snap at her heels and just barely miss. Then she saw the sky as Toby grabbed her by the belt and rolled her over his body and onto the roof.

"It was going to kill me," Rachel said between jagged gasps. "Whoever that thing is, it was definitely going to—"

"I know." Toby's pulse roared in his ears as he lay next to the freshly made crater in the lodge's roof and second-story wall. According to Bimisi Chochopi, the Shaman hadn't attacked Rachel because she wasn't among his sworn enemies. Nate and Willard didn't appear to have the same ability to discriminate. At least Toby hoped that was the case. Otherwise, one of his best friends had just knowingly tried to bite Rachel and him in half.

Toby maneuvered his way around busted timber and plaster, inching towards the roof's edge. In the yard below, he saw what he assumed was one of his friends, glaring up at him with those luminous yellow eyes. The stare down only lasted a few seconds.

With an aggravated snarl, the werewolf turned and loped off into the forest.

Back on the first floor, Walter was regaining his faculties just in time to see the bulky werewolf stalking out the front door, its ample belly swaying from side to side.

Disregarding his aches and pains, the sheriff of Silver Falls shoved aside the coffee table and got to his feet. Walking off the soreness in his legs, he shuffled over to the lodge's entrance and caught a quick glimpse of the creature as it loped down the driveway and into the night.

Walter stepped back from the door and called out. "Toby?"

"Dad!" his son shouted back from somewhere upstairs. A wave of relief washed over the sheriff at the sound of his son's voice.

"Are you okay?"

"Yeah. You?"

Walter rolled his shoulder. Just about every inch of his body felt a little tender, but everything still seemed to work. "Yeah, I'm good. Where's the other wolf?"

"It just crashed through the wall up here and took off," Toby replied.

That was all Walter needed to hear. "Get yourself back to town," he ordered. "Tell Billy what happened here and stay at the station until I get back."

Knowing that his son was safe, the sheriff walked over and picked up Paul's rifle. He then set out after the beast that had killed the hunter, running toward the woods as fast as his body would let him.

Tearing down a narrow forest road, Bimisi found himself preoccupied with one particular question. What was Rachel doing out at Bennett's cabin? He'd been too concerned about her safety at first to realize her being there made no sense, but a few minutes after she'd called him, the question had popped into his mind and stuck.

It evaporated just as quickly when he rounded a tight bend to find the headlights of several vehicles bearing down upon him.

Bimisi veered to avoid the oncoming caravan of terrified guests from Bennett's party, bounding his pickup off the road. The truck shredded a small group of saplings and then glanced off a larger fir tree before one of its tires finally found a yawning ditch.

Bimisi's chest smacked against the steering wheel as the vehicle jerked to a stop.

With no time to waste, he ignored the pain spreading through his torso and exited the pickup. The majority of the vehicles he'd swerved to avoid continued toward town, their drivers not even tapping the brakes to glance back and check if he was okay. Two of the vehicles that had been toward the front had stopped, albeit involuntarily, after spinning out just as he had.

"You idiot!" a middle-aged man shouted as he and his twenty-something-year-old daughter exited their CR-V. "You dumb son of a bitch!"

Bimisi pulled out his revolver and surveyed the forest. The cars' headlights illuminated the woods around them, providing him with a decent view into the trees. Unfortunately, the lights also let anything that might want to find them know exactly where they were.

Bimisi heard the man's shouting, but didn't register a single word. As it turned out, the berating would be short-lived.

A growl from somewhere beyond the reach of the lights made everyone hold their breath. Soon there was the sound of footfalls. The creature was circling them, but it was still too far back in the shadows to be visible.

Bimisi gave the two family members a stern look. "Get back in your vehicle."

Before either of them could move, a werewolf that looked to be carrying some extra weight leapt out from behind the trees. He knocked the daughter down behind the family's SUV, and both she and the creature disappeared from view.

Bimisi swung his revolver around but had no shot.

First he heard the daughter scream, then he heard the crack of a rifle and the dull thud of a bullet striking the monster.

Walter came running up the dirt road and into the headlight beams, rifle in hand. He slowed to a stop and aimed to take another shot. Bimisi saw the beast rear back and snarl at the sheriff, but his view was still too obstructed by the family's sport-utility vehicle to get a clear shot.

The sheriff pulled the trigger, but the rifle was empty. Seizing the opportunity, the werewolf left the sobbing daughter and attacked. Dropping the rifle, Walter reached for his pistol, but the monster was too fast.

The sheriff's cry echoed through the trees as the beast clamped its jaw onto his chest and took him to the ground.

Bimisi now had a clear shot. He stepped up and rained silver bullets into the werewolf. As the bullets pierced the monster's side, dark blood sprayed the trees and ground around it, and its skin sizzled. The creature pitched back away from Walter, howling in agony. It staggered around for a moment, seemingly in shock, and then, unable to stay upright, collapsed to the forest floor.

Fur faded. Claws retracted and disappeared. Muscles morphed and shrank until only a naked, dead boy remained.

Bimisi's jaw dropped when he saw the bloody, bullet-ridden teenager. "There truly *are* others."

As she wound her way down the forest road, Rachel spotted the illuminated trees up ahead and grew uneasy. Both she and Toby had been sitting rigid in her Jeep's seats ever since hearing Walter and Bimisi's gunshots echo through the forest. She knew her uncle wouldn't hesitate to shoot at one of the werewolves if he saw one, no matter *who* the creature might turn out to be in the daytime.

If he hit his mark…

One of the townspeople's vehicles came into view first, then the other. Off to the left she spotted a third vehicle's headlights shining through the woods. Then she saw her uncle standing over what appeared to be a pudgy, naked body.

He'd killed one of them. *Willard.*

"Stop!" Toby shouted suddenly.

She hit the brakes, and he was out of the Jeep in a flash. But where was he going? Toby veered away from her uncle and Willard and ran to the other side of the road. Rachel's eyes moved past the cars until she spotted the sheriff lying motionless on the ground.

"No," she gasped as she too leapt out of the Jeep.

Toby scrambled toward his father, sliding to the ground in front of him. He knelt there in stunned silence, his body starting to tremble. Then he completely broke down.

Rachel stood back and watched, tears springing to her eyes. He was alone now. Both his parents were gone. This devastating truth kept her frozen in place for what seemed like an eternity.

Not knowing what to do, but realizing she had to do something, Rachel shook off her paralytic stupor and walked over to kneel down next to Toby. She placed her hand on his shoulder, wanting desperately to say something, but having no idea what that something should be.

Walter suddenly erupted in a coughing fit, making them both leap back.

Rachel looked on in stunned silence as the sheriff sat up in shock, bringing his hands to the wound on his chest. The three of them stared at the bloody bite mark, mouths agape with astonishment as the gashes began to heal right before their eyes.

A few yards away, back among the trees, werewolf Nate observed everything from the shadows. His body was as still and silent as a statue, but his yellow eyes shifted rapidly from one element of the scene in front of him to the next—Willard's lifeless body, Toby and Rachel sitting awestruck with the sheriff, and finally, Bimisi. The creature locked in on Willard's killer as the troubled Indian paced the forest road.

A new threat. A serious threat.

Not ready to meet this challenge, Nate turned and bounded off into the forest.

CHAPTER 32

EZHNO'S CABIN

Ezhno Poitra had become a well-respected elder on the reservation over his seventy-two years of life. He was a great storyteller, hunter, and craftsman, who, despite having elected to make his home in a secluded cabin in the woods, was always known to be a friendly and regular visitor to the reservation village. He made it a point never to miss important tribal events, like the Mother Earth Ceremony, and usually took charge of manning refreshments or roasting the pig.

He wouldn't be making it back for the ceremony this year.

Ezhno lay dead on the floor of his kitchen, the once beige nylon rug below him drenched a crimson red. The blood the rug hadn't absorbed pooled around the elder, who had countless claw and fang marks covering his torso and upper legs.

At the other end of the small, two-story cabin, Nate exited the den buttoning up a pair of Ezhno's jeans. He studied the home with inquisitive eyes, trying to remember how he'd gotten there.

Tightening the jeans with a belt to keep them from falling down around his ankles, Nate surveyed the damage. Furniture was either upturned or smashed to pieces. There were claw marks in the walls and across a bank of kitchen cabinets.

Then he spotted the deceased Indian. The slaughtered body, splayed out across the blood-soaked rug, triggered a snippet of a memory—the Indian's face stricken with fear. It was a memory of the previous night's attack and lasted no more than a second.

Nate remembered nothing else about killing the man, or how he'd even ended up in the Indian's cabin. He hung his head for a moment, trying unsuccessfully to compose himself. How many more unintentional victims would there be before he learned how to control the therianthrope? *Would* he ever learn to control it?

Blood surged into his fists. Lashing his body around, he drove his right hand straight through a nearby cabinet, smashing it to bits.

He'd awoken with a much clearer memory of Mr. Bennett's death. The details were too crisp to be ignored as a false recollection, so Nate was convinced the attack had actually taken place. More importantly, it was something he'd planned. He and Willard had chosen a target who deserved to be punished for all the suffering he had caused. A target they'd successfully sought out and eliminated.

There was another flash. A brief recollection. This time of Toby. Had he been there? Yes. And not just him, but the sheriff and Rachel too. Little memory fireworks continued to pop in Nate's head. Guns. Blood. Screaming.

He lost his legs for a moment as the vision of Willard's body snapped into focus. Nate stumbled into the kitchen counter and then leaned against it to keep from going to the floor. His insides suddenly felt hollow, but then, just as quickly, a mix of anger and sadness filled the empty space. Willard had been slain.

Nate tried to picture the figure standing over his dead friend, but the man's back had been turned to him. Then he remembered how the killer had glanced over his shoulder for just a moment.

He focused hard, trying to envision the man's profile. Like the body lying in a pool of blood on the floor, Willard's killer had been Native American. Nate bent down to get a closer look at his victim. This wasn't the same Indian, but at least now Nate knew why he'd attacked him.

Toby, his dad, and who knew who else had shown up and gotten between Nate and his mission. That's why things had gone haywire.

Willard had been killed, and he had fled here. He'd needed somewhere to hide and must have massacred this old man out of fear, not anger. Which to Nate meant this wasn't his fault. If anyone were to blame, it was the dark-eyed Indian he'd seen standing over Willard's body.

The one who'd shot his friend with what must have been silver bullets.

Nate hurried out of the cabin, pulling on a denim shirt as he squinted into a bright, peaceful morning. His victim's rustic home sat in the middle of the forest, totally secluded. Indeed a good hiding spot, even for a werewolf.

The man's dog lay on the ground outside, also a mangled, bloody mess. Luckily nobody had been by to notice it. Nate stepped around the animal on his way to Ezhno's truck.

He managed to hold his emotions in check until he got into the pickup. Then he just sat in the driver's seat and cried for several minutes. Willard deserved better.

Unfortunately, there wasn't any more time for Nate to mourn the loss of his friend. There was a newly turned werewolf who he was sure had quite a few questions right about now. Plus, with Willard's death came the realization that they'd overestimated how invincible they actually were.

And there had been witnesses. A lot of witnesses. Which meant more than just a handful of people knew *what* they were.

Resolutely wiping the tears from his eyes, he pulled a set of keys from the stranger's jeans and slid the pickup's key into the ignition. The next few nights were going to be long ones.

No more than fifteen minutes after Nate had left the cabin, Bimisi's pickup rumbled up the dirt path that led to Ezhno's secluded home. He slumped back into his seat when he saw Adahy, Ezhno's Malamute, lying butchered on the ground. There was little doubt in his mind that the animal's owner had met a similar fate.

He brought the pickup to a stop and got out, immediately noticing a set of werewolf tracks in the dirt. Bimisi knelt down to get a closer look. They were the same tracks he'd found earlier that morning when he returned to the spot where he'd killed the first creature. The same tracks he'd followed to get here.

Bimisi drew his pistol. He assumed the second boy werewolf had probably heard his truck approaching from a mile away and fled, but he wasn't going to miss a chance to shoot down another cursed soul if such an opportunity presented itself.

The only person he found inside was Ezhno. The elder had no doubt heard the stories about the Shaman, and Bimisi wondered what must have been running through the poor man's mind during the attack. Not only the horror, but the confusion he must have felt as he was being ripped apart by something he'd been told would never harm him.

Because the legend had said it *couldn't* harm him.

In that instant, Bimisi felt as if a cold fist were closing tightly over his heart. Ezhno's death was his fault, as was Jerry Ituha's. He'd unleashed something he didn't fully understand, and the people he'd meant to protect were now just as likely to become its victims as the people of Silver Falls were.

No matter what actions he took going forward, he'd never be able to make up for what he'd done. But at this point, that didn't really matter. He was still going to kill the hellish beast he was responsible for releasing—or die trying.

CHAPTER 33

ALLIES AND THREATS

The setting sun cast a warm glow over the quiet rooftops of Silver Falls. One would get the impression that it was the type of crisp and serene spring evening that offered the perfect opportunity to take stroll down Main Street, inhale a deep breath of fresh evergreen air, and exhale the stresses of the day—if, for whatever reason, that person were viewing things solely from the rooftops.

It was an entirely different scene down on the street. Frenzied townspeople scurried about, carrying luggage and backpacks, closing up storefronts, and cramming personal belongings into their vehicles. Engines roared as cars and trucks loaded with panic-stricken residents sped away from town. Everyone was frantic to get as far away from Silver Falls as possible before the sun went down.

Aware of but uninvolved in the mass exodus, Toby instead found himself in the windowless bowels of the sheriff station. He'd never liked the building's basement. The dim lighting had always given it a sinister feel, as did the fact that it housed the station's jail cells. He stood in front of one of those cells now, staring through the bars at his father.

"Kind of a strange sight, huh?" asked the sheriff of Silver Falls.

"We still have a couple hours until sunset," Toby replied. "We could keep looking."

"I'm not taking any chances." Walter placed his hand on one of the steel bars. "This is where I stay until morning."

Toby gave his father a look of consternation. "So then what do I do?"

"Lock this place up tight and stay upstairs," Walter said firmly. "I don't want you seeing me after I...you know."

Toby knew all too well. He also knew his father was right. If they continued their search any longer, it could lead to a situation where his dad ended up being somewhere other than safely behind bars when the sun went down.

When he turned, he needed to be secured.

Walter stepped into the doorway of the cell, and they embraced for a long moment. The sheriff then let go and stepped back. Trying not to show how scared he was, Toby placed his hand on the steel door and slowly swung it closed, involuntarily flinching at the clank of metal hitting metal.

The sheriff gave his final order. "Now no matter what you hear up there, do not come down. Not until morning."

Toby gave another slight nod, turned, and tromped up the stairs. He couldn't help thinking that if Rachel's uncle had just told him what a full illumination cycle was, this might have been avoided. Was not telling him supposed to be some sort of punishment for Toby getting in the Indian's way on the reservation? Was Bimisi happy with the results? Was he happy Willard was dead?

With each step he climbed, Toby felt less scared and more and more angry.

When he reached the top of the stairs and walked into the station, he found Billy sitting at his desk and a stone-faced Bimisi stalking back and forth in front of the beleaguered deputy.

"Most folks are happy to do what I ask," said Billy. "But I can't force them from their homes."

"It is for their own good," Bimisi countered.

Billy studied Bimisi for a moment. "Like you shooting and killing a sixteen-year-old boy was for his own good?"

Bimisi stopped pacing and leaned over the deputy's desk. "He was not a sixteen-year-old boy when I shot him."

And whose fault was that? Toby glared at Bimisi's back. How could he stand there and tell Billy what needed to be done for the good of the townspeople? What the hell did he care about the well-being of Silver Falls?

Unable to think up the proper words to adequately express his fury, Toby instead ran and lunged at Bimisi, tackling him into the desk. The larger, stronger Indian quickly got his legs under him and shoved Toby to the floor.

He went down hard, flattening his cheek on the vinyl tiles. There was a significant strength difference between them, and Toby wasn't sure what charging the man again would accomplish, but he didn't care. Willard was dead, and Bimisi was just as responsible for his death as the Shaman was—maybe even more so.

Billy intercepted Toby as he got up to lunge again. "Hold on there, kid! That's enough!"

Toby's frenzied eyes glared at Bimisi. "Willard's dead because of *you*! All of this is because of you!"

Bimisi collected himself and answered in an even tone, "All of *what* is because of me? This battle started long before I became involved. Others' actions caused my suffering and drove me to seek my vengeance. Now my actions have driven you to seek the same."

The Indian stepped forward, looking Toby right in the eyes. "This anger you feel is nothing new. I only pray you never know the regret that now consumes me."

Toby shook himself loose of Billy's grip. He was still furious, but decided another hard charge at Rachel's uncle wasn't the way to deal with his rage.

"I'll never be anything like you," he shouted.

"I will pray for that also." Bimisi turned his attention back to Billy. "Now you said there were three attacks in town last night?"

"Yeah. The Parkers, the Elms, and the Schultzes."

Toby's eyes widened. "Ashley?"

"She wasn't home when it happened," Billy explained. "Sally was, but she escaped. Hank wasn't so lucky."

Jesus, like Ashley hadn't been through enough already. Toby hadn't spoken to her since she'd promised to find out where Mike had taken Nate. Their last actual communication, aside from her disquieting scream at the hospital, had been her text about the "underground cave thingy" Nate had fallen into.

He should go see if she remembered any additional information about that night.

Even if she didn't, Toby still felt like checking in was the right thing to do. If Ashley and her mom hadn't already left, maybe he could help her pack or something. It would be more productive than just standing in the station and staring darts into Rachel's uncle.

"Where are you going?" Billy asked as Toby turned and headed for the door.

"I'm going to go make sure she's okay."

Toby heard boots clicking over the tile floor, following after him. He glanced over his shoulder to find Bimisi right on his heels.

"What?" Toby asked, taking a step away from the determined Indian.

"I will drive us," Bimisi said, brushing past him.

Although he knew time was short, Nate didn't want to rush Ashley toward a realization of what she'd become. He leaned against her bedroom dresser and stayed silent as she packed a suitcase and tried to explain her last twenty-four hours. Not surprisingly, Nate sensed a lot of confusion and apprehension as she spoke.

"I don't remember ever leaving the park," she said as she folded a pair of designer jeans into her suitcase.

Nate shrugged. "You were still there when I left."

"Well, the next thing I know, I'm waking up naked on my neighbors' lawn," she continued. "Who knows how I ended up that way? I mean, I don't even want to think about it. Then I come home to find my dad dead. And as strange and awful as all that sounds, it's not even the worst part. You're going to think I'm insane, or *even more* insane, but…"

She paused with a heavy sigh, and Nate decided to help her finish her thought. "You've never felt more alive?"

She crooked her neck around to give him a curious look, apparently caught off guard by his dead-on guess.

"It took me a couple of days to figure it all out too," he semi-explained.

"Figure out what?"

"You won't remember much until about the third night."

"What are you talking about?"

Nate didn't respond. He'd dropped a few hints, but still really wanted to let her come to the answer on her own. After a moment, the look of realization he'd been waiting for flashed across Ashley's face.

She sat down slowly on the bed. "Oh my god. It was me. I... Am I a...?"

Nate grinned. They were almost there. She seemed to be taking it pretty well, or maybe she was just in shock. No hysterics. That was a good sign.

It had been an impulsive decision to turn her, which Nate had come to realize was the easiest kind of decision to make as a werewolf. The depressed girl he'd seen sitting on that swing needed something to be optimistic about, and he felt as though he'd given it to her.

Hopefully she felt the same.

"Last night, in the park, you...You didn't leave before me. You..."

He nodded, his smile growing wider.

"Holy shit, I feel..."

Nate again attempted to help her finish her thought. "Amazing?"

"Really freaked out." Her eyes widened in fascinated horror. "But, yeah...also pretty fucking amazing."

She glanced down at her hands, then flipped them over and squeezed her thighs. "It's like…I'm more finely tuned or something."

"You are, and honestly, even I'm kinda surprised you turned so fast," Nate said. And he truly was. "It didn't happen for me or Willard until the second night."

He spotted a picture of Ashley and her mother taped to the mirror above her dresser. His grin vanished for a moment. The part of the photo where her father should have been was torn off.

"But then I guess maybe your motivation was a little stronger than ours was."

"I've never been so aware of every inch of my body," she said looking up at him.

"Pretty great, huh?"

"It's incredible. There's like this constant tingling of energy running through me. I feel better than I've ever felt before in my life."

"And it feels like that *all the time.*"

"It's like I'm a whole new person. I feel like I can do anything. I feel…" The corners of her mouth curled into a mischievous smile. "…*special.*"

"That's because you are."

Ashley got up and walked to the door. She slowly shut it and turned to stare at him, her eyes sexually charged. "You're going to have to let me thank you."

She stalked toward him, starting to slowly unbutton her shirt. Her unexpected seduction triggered an equally unexpected and sudden urge in Nate. He felt an uncontrollable burning wave of lust sweep through his insides, and unable to resist it, he lunged in and kissed her.

With their animal instincts taking over, the two teenagers wrestled and clawed at one another, then tumbled onto Ashley's bed. She threw Nate off of her and climbed on top. Now panting, his heart pounding, he flipped her over and ripped away her shirt. They dove into each other, ready to ravage, and then Nate suddenly stopped.

He turned back toward the bedroom door and listened.

Ashley looked up at him with voracious eyes. "What is it?"

"We have to go."

"What? Where?"

"Out your window," replied Nate, jumping off the bed. "We have to go now."

Moments later, Sally Schultz, Toby, and Bimisi entered Ashley's room to find it empty.

"Well, where did she..." Sally checked behind the bedroom door, confused. "She was just here. I told her we needed to be packed and in the car in fifteen minutes. She must have gone somewhere with that Schaffer boy, but I'm sure she'll be back any second."

Toby was certain she wouldn't be—not if Nate had just been there. It wouldn't make sense for him to risk getting caught or killed unless he'd felt Ashley was worth the risk. And there was only one reason Toby could think of for why Nate would suddenly feel that way.

Ashley was a werewolf too.

Not the information he'd come looking for, but definitely something worth knowing. They still had at least three of these monsters to worry about.

"You're welcome to stay and wait if you'd like," Sally offered.

"That's okay," Toby said as he turned and started down the stairs. "I should get back to the station. Also, I don't want to hold you up when she gets back."

"Can I give her a message?"

"I just wanted to make sure she was okay."

Sally gave him a warm smile. "That's so sweet of you. I'll be sure to tell her you stopped by."

Toby gave another slight nod and continued down the stairs. Bimisi did the same. They exited the Schultzes' home and walked briskly toward Bimisi's pickup. Toby's mind was racing. To find out Nate had turned Willard came as no surprise, but Ashley? How had that happened? Whose idea was it? Could Nate have turned anyone else?

Toby ran through the previous night's attacks. The Parkers and Elms had likely been killed by the Shaman. Ashley had done in her drunk and abusive dad. Nate and Willard were responsible for the carnage at Bennett's lodge. Those were all the victims, so there probably weren't any more werewolves to worry about, but Toby would have to ask his best friend to know for sure.

If Nate had willingly come back into town, then Toby had to find him and get him to talk. He needed to know just what Nate was thinking and if there was any hope of convincing him to think a different way.

"You need to let me handle things from here," Bimisi said, interrupting Toby's mental planning. "When we get back to the station, you will need to stay there. This is not your fight."

The words instantly sparked an inner rage within Toby. The man responsible for starting this nightmare had no right to tell him what to do. The only person who did was locked in his own jail cell *because* of the creature Bimisi had released. He didn't care that the Indian wanted to clean up his own mess. That mess had affected too many people Toby cared about, and a lot of them were still in danger.

He whirled around and began shouting in ragged bursts. "Not my fight? My dad is a werewolf! Because he got attacked! By one of my friends! Who's now dead! My best friend tried to attack me! You don't get to tell me this isn't my fight! You *made* this my fight!"

Bimisi held his look for a moment, then conceded with a deep sigh. "Fine. If you must do something, find your friends before the sun sets. Get them to the station and lock them up too."

"Nate's not going to go for that."

"Convince him," Bimisi ordered as he headed toward his truck. "Tell him that soon I will not be the only one hunting him down."

What did that mean? The statement started another cascade of questions within Toby's head. Were there others who knew werewolves existed? Other Umatilla who knew how to hunt them? If so, why weren't they helping?

He hustled into the passenger seat as Bimisi started the truck. "What do you mean it won't just be you hunting him?"

"The Shaman turned your bullied friend to kill the people in this town and in mine." Bimisi pulled away from the curb and checked the rearview mirror. "*That* was what his function was meant to be. It was not to create more werewolves. The more he does so, the more the Shaman will stop considering him an ally and start viewing him as a threat."

"A threat to do what?"

"To take his place."

Toby struggled to make sense of the Indian's answer. "But once an Alpha dies, all Betas turn back."

Bimisi responded with a nod. "True, but there is one exception. *If* a Beta were to decide he did not want his abilities tied to the Alpha's survival."

Toby connected the dots, and his eyes lit up. "Nate can kill him?"

Bimisi nodded again. "He can try. It is unlikely that he would succeed."

Toby had no idea whether that was something Nate was considering, or if his friend even knew it was a possibility, but that didn't matter. By turning Willard and Ashley, Nate had made it appear as though he were trying to build a pack, and in doing so, possibly given the Shaman the impression that he was gunning for him.

CHAPTER 34

BATTLE STRATEGY

"Going somewhere?" Ashley asked as she stood in what was once Ezhno Poitra's bedroom doorway wrapped in a bed sheet and wearing a very satisfied smile.

Nate snagged his jeans off the deceased elder's living room floor and pulled them on. He was indeed going somewhere, but he didn't want to fill her in on the details. Not yet. He didn't want Ashley becoming preoccupied with the same things his mind had been fixated on all day.

Well, maybe not *all* day. He'd spent the last hour living out every dream he'd ever had about her, which had provided a nice diversion. But now Nate once again found himself solely focused on the image of Willard's killer, an obsession he was finding more than a little unsettling.

We just need to envision who we want to go after.

Nate didn't feel prepared to make the man with the silver bullets his next target. He needed to find out more about him first.

"I'm going to go check on things in town," he said as he pulled on his shirt. "See who's decided to stay and who's decided to go."

"What can I do?"

Nate stood and walked over to her. "Stay here and stay safe. I won't be gone long."

Ezhno Poitra's cabin seemed as good a place as any for Ashley to hide out. Not knowing where else to go, Nate had brought her here, and they'd thankfully found the small dwelling empty. That included the dead bodies.

Someone had been there that morning after Nate left and removed the Indian's remains along with the remains of his dog. That same person had surely felt unsafe staying, so Nate felt confident they wouldn't be back—at least not this close to nightfall.

Ashley pulled him in, and they shared a deep, passionate kiss. She was an amazing kisser, or at least Nate thought she was. Admittedly, he didn't have anyone to compare her against. An experience like this would have never been possible for the old Nate Schaffer.

For the new Nate Schaffer it felt as if anything were possible.

It hadn't taken long for stories about what had happened at Bennett's lodge to spread across Silver Falls. Most had the particulars right, but more than a few made-up details were circulating as well, which baffled Rachel. Who would feel the need to exaggerate what was already such an incredible set of circumstances?

Her mom and Alan had heard a few different versions of the previous night's events, and they were beyond disturbed to find out about Rachel's involvement. Like most everyone else in town, they'd spent the majority of the day packing with every intention of leaving Silver Falls as soon as possible.

Rachel managed to convince them to at least let her run over to the station so she could say good-bye to the boy who had saved her life. Unfortunately, Toby was nowhere to be found when she arrived.

She stood on the sidewalk in front of the sheriff station searching the streets for him. All she saw were frightened residents loading up their cars and abandoning their daily lives so as not to lose them forever.

"Is he around?"

Rachel turned in the direction of the voice to see Peter riding up on his bicycle.

She shook her head. "The deputy said they went to check on Ashley."

Peter coasted onto the sidewalk and brought his bike to a stop. "She got attacked too?"

"No. Well, *she* didn't. She and her mom are fine. Her dad's…gone."

Peter exhaled through his teeth, shaking his head. "Is your family leaving town?"

Rachel nodded.

"Mine too." Peter gazed down the street, looking for any sign of their friend. "Are you going with them?"

That was the question she'd been debating for the last hour or so. If she did leave with her parents, she hoped to persuade Toby to come with her. There was no question that it was the safest thing to do. There was also little doubt in her mind that Toby would want to stay.

Bimisi's pickup appeared from down the street—the lone vehicle driving into town, passing several others on their way out. Rachel shielded her eyes from the setting sun and squinted until she was able to make out the two hazy silhouettes sitting in the front seat. A definite odd couple. Leaving Toby alone with her uncle to face the werewolves seemed unthinkable. That would be the shitty thing to do.

Once they pulled up in front of the station, Rachel hustled over. "Is Ashley okay?"

"Not exactly," Toby responded as he hopped out of the truck. "Pretty sure she's one now too."

"Nate turned her?" Peter asked. He looked stunned by the news. "Willard made sense, but why would he do her next? Have they ever even spoken? I mean, it's not like *I* wanted to be turned or anything, but…I don't know whether to be more relieved or offended right now."

"Maybe she's been one all along and we just didn't know it," Toby said. "She was out on the reservation that first night too."

Rachel let this latest development sink in and then reluctantly changed the subject. "My family is leaving town tonight."

"Mine too," Peter added.

"Good." Bimisi thumbed at Toby as he walked by them and headed for the station. "One of you take him with you."

Toby flicked the bird to Bimisi's back as the Indian walked up the front steps.

Rachel grabbed Toby's shoulder to turn him toward her. "I was thinking you *should* come with us. Your dad will be safe as long as—"

"I'm not leaving until this is over."

"Over for who?" Peter asked incredulously.

Toby checked his watch and headed down the sidewalk without another word.

Rachel called out after him. "There's only an hour left until sunset. Where are you going?"

"To see if I can find one of them."

Rachel stood momentarily conflicted. She had told Toby that they'd find a way to stop what was happening together. If he was going to stay, she felt obligated to do the same and follow through on her promise. She exchanged a knowing glance with Peter, and then they both followed after their determined friend.

As she jogged up alongside him, her smartphone started to ring. Rachel pulled the device from her jacket pocket and shut it off.

Silver Falls now resembled a well-manicured ghost town. As Toby stared down yet another street lined with shuttered and abandoned homes, he started filling Rachel in on the details of his trip to Ashley's house. He could tell by the concern in her eyes that she didn't like what she was hearing. He couldn't blame her.

"How is my uncle supposed to take on three of those things?" she asked.

"He might not have to," Toby answered in as reassuring of a tone as he could muster. "He thinks the Shaman is going to turn on Nate and Ashley, and that they're gonna start attacking each other."

They came upon Nate's house. It too was all boarded up except for the front door, which was suspiciously left wide open. It was almost as if someone were inviting them in. Toby decided to accept the invitation.

He marched up the driveway of the white-sided, split-level ranch home he'd been inside countless times. When he reached the door, he hesitated for a moment. Staring in at the empty landing where he'd always kicked off his sneakers, Toby felt a sudden dread.

With Rachel right on his heels, he shook off his apprehension and cautiously entered the Schaffer residence. The house was dimly lit by what little sunlight seeped in through the cracks of shuttered windows. He took a quick look around and then made his way toward the living room, in which he'd spent infinite afternoons watching movies or playing video games.

"Why would they do that?" Rachel asked, attempting to continue their conversation from outside. She lowered her voice to a near whisper. "Why would they attack each other?"

Nate suddenly shouted out from upstairs, startling them both. "That's what *I'd* like to know."

Toby whirled around to look up the empty stairwell.

"Come on up, Toby," Nate called. "Let's have a talk."

He and Rachel tentatively made their way up the stairs and into the empty upstairs hallway. Toby continued down the darkened hall and turned into Nate's room to find his friend sitting on the bed.

Nate was looking down at his hands, which were cupped together to keep Duncan Balfour standing upright between his palms. "We were just going over our battle strategy, which might have to change if the Shaman is really bringing the fight to me. Although, I honestly can't fathom why he'd do such a thing, considering we're already under attack."

"*You're* under attack?" Toby shot back, sounding equal parts cross and confounded.

"Willard's dead, isn't he?"

"He almost killed my dad."

"And you almost killed us," Rachel added sharply.

Nate's lips tightened into a stubborn frown. "You shouldn't have been there."

"We were trying to save lives," Toby reasoned. "Stop you from slaughtering more innocent people."

Nate scoffed at the comment. "Innocent? We were there for Bruce Bennett. You can't really think he was innocent. After all the suffering he's caused? What about Andrew and Jerry? They tormented us for years. Ashley's dad, the abusing drunk…"

"Those aren't the only people who have died," Rachel said bluntly. "And even if they were, you can't honestly think that killing them was the right thing to do."

"Sure I can." Nate shook his head in frustration. He stood up and stepped over to his bookcase where he carefully placed Duncan on one of the shelves. "Look, I'm *truly* sorry about the innocent lives lost. I am. There's no way for me to make up for some of the pain I've caused. I know that. But once I'm able to control what's inside me, I promise you that the only people getting hurt will be those the world is better off without."

Toby had heard enough. "You can't control this!"

"I already have," Nate replied doggedly. "Each night I'm becoming more conscious of what's happening and—"

"And the rest of the time you're a fucking monster," Rachel interrupted.

Nate moved toward her, his eyes narrowing to give his face an almost predatory expression. "*Your* people made me what I am."

"I know," conceded Rachel. "And I'm sorry."

"Don't be," Nate said, taking another step closer to her. "Not about that. As for your uncle..."

Toby got in between them, meeting Nate's intense stare. He wondered if his friend was even in complete control while human anymore, especially now that the illumination cycle had started.

Nate hesitated for a moment, then smiled. "That's cute. As if you could actually stop me from hurting her...or you."

His right hand shot forward with astounding speed and grabbed Toby by the throat, not even allowing him time to flinch. Then, with just the one arm, Nate lifted him into the air.

"Even in human form, I'm ten times faster and stronger than Mike Mulligan."

"Let him go!" Rachel shouted.

"Not until I get some answers."

Even though he'd seen Nate lift a car, Toby was stunned by the strength of his friend's unyielding grip. Coughing and gasping for air, he clawed desperately at the fingers around his throat. Maybe Nate didn't have control of his actions or emotions any longer, but he'd swiftly seized control of this confrontation.

"He can't breathe!" Rachel screamed.

"Why would the Shaman come after me?"

Rachel wouldn't know the answer to that. Toby hadn't explained it to her yet. He took a shallow breath and sputtered out half the explanation. "To stop you…"

"Stop me?" Nate loosened his grasp. "Stop me from what?"

"From taking his place."

Nate shot him a dubious look. "How would that work? He'd have to die for me to take his place, and it's common knowledge that if an Alpha is killed, then all the Betas it created lose their…"

Toby saw Nate's eyes widen and knew the light bulb had just gone on inside his friend's head. The fingers wrapped around his neck released.

Falling to the floor, Toby rolled onto his back and inhaled deeply, going into a coughing fit as he tried to catch his breath. After swallowing a deep gulp of air, he felt Rachel lift his arm over her shoulder. She helped him sit up and then held him steady as he got to his feet.

Nate paced away from them, still working out the puzzle. "Unless…I'm the one to kill him. That's it, isn't it? I do that, and it all goes differently. Then I become the Alpha dog."

Toby had wondered if maybe that had been the plan all along, a strategy Nate and Willard had worked out to make sure they held onto their newfound abilities forever. It was now clear it hadn't been, but equally clear that now it was.

"Nate, please," Toby pleaded. "Let us lock you up at the station. You and Ashley will be safe there until this is all over. And anyone left in town will be safe from you."

"But I've got my target now," Nate responded, a sparkle in his eyes. "And it's the monster who's *intentionally* attacking innocent people. If I can kill him it's a win-win solution. Everyone else will be fine as long as they stay out of my way."

Toby attempted yet again to reason with his friend. "You can't guarantee that. Let us help you."

Nate's face hardened. "I'm tired of having this conversation, Toby. You know you've never *truly* been able to help. You hardly ever have the nerve to do what needs to be done, and then when you do, you don't have the ability to do it the right way."

"That's not true," Rachel protested.

"Sure it is," Nate snapped. "I know it is because that's how it used to be for me too. But not anymore. You have no idea. The stuff I can do. The powers I possess. I don't have to take anybody's shit, and that includes this Shaman. Nothing scares me. I'm with the hottest girl in school. I've reached new levels of capability and transcendence, only in real life. You're not locking me in that station. *I'm not giving this up.*"

He turned and strode for the door.

Toby called after him. "Then we'll have to take it away."

Nate paused and looked back before exiting his bedroom.

"I'm not going to let you hurt any more people," Toby added in as confident a tone as he could muster.

"Well, if that's how it has to be," Nate said. "Then I guess you have your mission, and I have mine. We'll see who actually has the conviction to get theirs done."

A distraught Toby watched his friend disappear through the doorway, then heard him bounding down the stairs. So there it was. Nate didn't think he needed their help. He didn't want it. There was only one way to save him now.

The race was on to see who could kill the Shaman first.

CHAPTER 35

WILD NIGHT AT WOLFY'S

Peter entered Wolfy's Diner with his cell phone to his ear. "Yeah. Mom, I'm on my way. I was just…helping Toby look for someone. I'll be there in ten minutes."

He ended the call, irritated. His search for his half-lupine classmates had not gone well. Since he hadn't heard anything from Toby or Rachel, he assumed they hadn't had any better luck. It shouldn't have come as a surprise. Nate could probably hear or smell them coming from a mile away.

Peter surveyed the comfy hangout's quiet, somber crowd. The establishment's fifty-seven-year-old owner, Jesse "Wolfy" Wolf, stood behind the quartz-topped counter. Doug Mills, now considered the town's best hunter after the deaths of Don Hutchins and Paul Grant, stood guard near the front door, fingers wrapped around his rifle.

The remaining patrons could be counted on one hand. The sparse crowd represented the final few fools still stubborn enough to stay in Silver Falls, and it suddenly occurred to Peter that he was one of those fools. This would be his last stop. He'd ask Wolfy if he'd seen Nate and then he'd head straight home.

Peter hurried over to the counter and took a seat on one of the worn leather stools. Before he could get the proprietor's attention, Chad Burten, the scruffy sixty-five-year-old manager of the Silver Falls Happy Hobby Shop, spoke up from a couple of seats down.

"Let me have a burger plate. Tater tots instead of fries."

"Coming right up," Wolfy replied as he scribbled the order on a pad of paper. He tore off the sheet and hung it up for the cook. He then stepped over to the soda fountain to pour the most syrupy-tasting root beer available anywhere in town.

Chad's variegated eyes scanned the near empty diner, glancing over Peter and then stopping on someone close to the front door. "Now get a load of this fella," he said with a shake of his head.

Wolfy glanced up toward the entrance, then back to the root beer. "With everyone leavin' town, I'll take whoever I can get."

Curious, Peter took a quick peek over his shoulder to see a gout-looking Native American standing in the doorway. The man's noticeably disheveled appearance immediately set off warning bells. First, Peter remembered the stories Toby had told him about the freaky Indian he'd seen on the reservation and later in town. Then he recalled the bit about how that Indian was an old Shaman buried out in the woods by the Umatilla…because he was the original werewolf.

Terrified, Peter fumbled for his cell. He quickly brought up his list of contacts and selected Toby's name. Keeping his head down, he stole another glance at the ageless Indian as the freak of nature walked past him and stood in the center of the restaurant.

"Pick up, Hoffman," Peter muttered, rotating his stool so his back faced the Shaman. "Pick up, dammit. We've got a situation here."

"Shit." Toby brought his hand to his forehead when he saw Peter's name flash on his smartphone's display. With all that had happened, he'd completely forgotten that his friend was also out looking for Nate and Ashley.

"Hold on a second, Peter," Toby said, answering the call as he entered the sheriff station. Bimisi and Billy stood at the deputy's desk, loading the Indian's extra revolvers with silver bullets. Toby would want to make sure he got one of those. He placed the phone against his chest and addressed Rachel's uncle. "Nate knows everything. We found him, and now he knows."

Billy stopped thumbing bullets into his gun. "So then where is he?"

"He's going to try to become the Alpha."

Bimisi looked up at Toby and Rachel and responded with a nod.

"That's it?" Toby asked. "That's your reaction?" He stood confused for a moment, then caught on. "You *wanted* him to know. You told me all that stuff hoping that I would find him and that he'd make the decision he made."

"Having the creatures after each other is a positive development for us," Bimisi replied evenly. "You wanted to help, and now you have."

He'd been set up. And now he'd unintentionally set up Nate to go head-to-head with a Shaman who was well over a hundred years old. A fight his friend couldn't really win, regardless of the outcome. Flustered and furious, Toby marched toward Bimisi.

"Take it easy now." Billy moved in and grabbed him, apparently having noticed the venomous look in Toby's eyes.

Toby removed the cell from his chest and pointed it at Bimisi. "You and me are done!" he shouted at the top of his lungs. "Get out! Get the hell out of here!"

He then heard Peter shouting his name through the cell. He brought the phone back to his ear and spoke hurriedly into it. "Peter, listen, I'm sorry. I forgot that you were still—"

Peter cut him off, speaking in a harsh whisper. "He's here! The Shaman is at Wolfy's!"

Toby's jaw dropped. He quickly stepped over and reached for the revolver in Billy's hand. "I'm on my way. Tell me, what's he doing?"

The deputy pulled the weapon away.

"Give me the gun, Billy," Toby snapped.

"Can't do that," responded the deputy. "I've been downstairs talking with your dad, and he made me promise to protect you. He said he wants you locked up in this station until sunup. So this is where you're going to stay. Now, if Mr. Chochopi here says he knows how to stop this thing, then—"

"He's the one who let it out!" Toby shouted.

"Which will be something your dad and I can deal with once it's dead. Now tell him where you were going."

"No."

Having heard the brief exchange, Peter frantically yelled out his opinion through the phone. "Just tell him, dude! Someone needs to get over here!"

Toby chewed on his lip for a moment, turning back to look at Bimisi. He was going to have to trust this man, whether he wanted to or not.

Bimisi darted out of the station and down the steps, observing that only a sliver of the sun still sat above the horizon. If he could get to the diner before it set, there still might be a chance to end this cleanly. Otherwise, there was no telling how many more victims there would be.

With the restaurant being only a few blocks away, he decided against taking the time to get into his truck and ran right past it, sprinting down the deserted street. The rapid patter of his footsteps against the pavement seemed amplified with the rest of the town so quiet. Everyone who'd elected to stay in Silver Falls had boarded themselves up indoors to wait things out until dawn. Anyone who had decided to leave was already long gone.

Bimisi was so focused on his destination that the usually obser-vant Indian didn't notice Nate and Ashley crouched on the roof of the sandwich shop across the street. The semi-supernatural teens smiled at one another mischievously as he raced past, then began to scamper across the rooftops, following after him.

As he neared the diner, Bimisi slowed his pace and pulled his revolver from its holster. No muffled screaming or shouting could be heard coming from inside the establishment, which was a good sign. Even still, he figured there couldn't be more than a minute or two left before the Shaman turned.

He burst into the diner with his gun raised, and locked in on his target almost immediately. With so few people in the room, the Shaman spotted him straight away too. The cursed Indian upturned a nearby table, sending a handful of patrons scattering away from the airborne furniture and food. It was just enough of a commotion to prevent Bimisi from getting a clean shot.

"He just got here," Bimisi heard Peter shout into his cell as he hustled past the boy, shoving a customer out of his way.

Peter kept his play-by-play going as the Shaman swiftly moved toward the kitchen. "The Shaman's on the run!"

Nate strode into Wolfy's and spotted Bimisi hustling after the Shaman. After quickly assessing the rest of the landscape, he grabbed Doug Mills' rifle and slammed the stock into the hunter's chin, knocking him silly. Doug swayed woozily for a moment and then buckled to the floor, knocking over another table on his way down.

The commotion caused Bimisi to glance back, and Nate seized the moment. "This is for Willard, asshole."

He took aim at Rachel's uncle and fired. However, even with his heightened abilities, Nate was no marksman. The unexpected kickback of the rifle caused him to stagger sideways a step, and he missed his target badly. The apple pie display case on the counter exploded into a firecracker of glass—with several of the shards showering Wolfy.

Stunned, the diner's owner glared over at Nate and Ashley. "What in the hell?"

"What are you doing?" Peter shouted as he jumped for cover. His cell fell from his fingers and dropped to the floor as he scurried behind the counter.

Undeterred, Nate regrouped and raised the rifle again. With equal determination, Wolfy drew a shotgun out from behind the counter. He quickly leveled the weapon and fired before Nate could get off his second shot.

It was a direct hit. Nate felt the force of the buckshot as it struck him square in the chest. He wobbled back against the wall, astonished to experience something that had such a strong physical impact.

Ashley shrieked. "Nate!"

Coughing up blood, he grabbed his chest as he steadied his legs. Glancing up, he saw Wolfy lowering the shotgun and looking beyond amazed, like he'd just seen Santa and the Easter Bunny walk into the diner hand-in-hand. Certainly the man had expected him to drop.

Nate smiled up at him spitefully. "I'll get you for that."

Toby paced across the station floor, shouting into his cell phone. "Peter! Peter!"

He'd heard Nate's voice. He'd heard gunfire. Then the call had cut out.

Had Nate just hurt Peter? Did Bimisi get the Shaman? Had Nate and the Shaman turned and started taking out the entire restaurant?

"You two stay here," Billy ordered, hustling out of the station.

Toby turned and watched the deputy dart out the exit and then stared at the door as it slowly closed and clicked shut. Overwhelmed with frustration, he ended the call and rifled his phone at his father's desk. It ricocheted off the cherry wood and then skidded across the floor until it slammed against the wall.

"Sending my uncle over there was the right thing to do," Rachel said reassuringly.

"Why? Because I didn't want to do it?" Toby snapped. Then, with no clear or immediate way for him to direct or use his anger, Toby felt his fury simply seep away. It was replaced by a feeling of complete hopelessness.

Defeated, he collapsed into his father's chair. "This is all my fault."

"What are you talking about?" Rachel asked, looking confused and concerned.

"Nate's going to get himself killed because of what I told him, and who knows what just happened to Peter."

Rachel marched over to the desk. "None of that is *your* fault."

"Nate was right. Even when I have the courage to try to help, I can't. I just make things worse."

"Stop it," she shouted. "That's not true."

"Nate, Willard, my dad…my mom…"

Walter cried out from the basement, startling them both.

His cry quickly turned into a loud snarl as he transformed into yet another werewolf. Tormented, Toby turned toward the basement doorway.

"I couldn't save any of them."

"You saved me," Rachel said vehemently. "Out at Bennett's cabin, you saved my life."

Toby ignored her, his eyes staying focused on the doorway to the basement. He had had so many opportunities to prevent things from getting to this point. Yet here they were. Utterly despondent, he continued to stare at the dimly lit doorway until he realized Rachel had stopped talking.

Toby glanced over to see her standing at Billy's desk, picking up one of the revolvers from her uncle's case of guns. "What are you doing?"

"My uncle's the one who's really responsible for all this," she said, staring at the pistol. "If something has happened to him, I can't just sit here and do nothing."

"I'm not going to let you go over there by yourself."

"I know." Without another word, Rachel turned and ran out of the station before Toby had a chance to stop her.

He jumped to his feet. She *really was* going over there.

Rushing to the deputy's desk, he snatched the last of Bimisi's revolvers. After quickly checking to make sure it was loaded, Toby chased after her.

Bimisi kicked in the door to the kitchen and continued his pursuit. The first person he spotted was the grill cook, who was staggering to his feet, appearing as though he'd just been laid out by an NFL linebacker. Bimisi snapped his fingers to get the man's attention.

The cook looked over at him with woozy eyes, then pointed toward the rear of the kitchen. Bimisi nodded and signaled for him to go out to the dining area. The cook nodded back and wobbled his way out the door.

With the kitchen cleared, Bimisi moved slowly toward the short hallway that led to the back. As he stepped past the grill where

Chad's burger was still sizzling, he brought a second hand to his revolver to steady his grip. He needed to be prepared to shoot at the first sign of movement.

Rounding the corner, he pointed his gun at sinks, freezers, and finally a bathroom. There was no sign of the Shaman. His eyes went to the exit sign flickering above the back door. Certain that the Shaman had escaped into the back alley, Bimisi lowered his revolver with a deep sigh.

Suddenly he heard screams from the dining area, then loud snarls. Toby's friends were turning. A loud gun blast echoed through the establishment.

Bimisi stepped back into the front of the kitchen to see Wolfy run past the order window, tossing his shotgun aside. Right before the man disappeared from view, he was viciously mauled by one of the creatures.

Bimisi started toward the dining area to help, but paused when he heard a snarl come from somewhere behind him.

The Shaman werewolf burst out from the kitchen bathroom, tearing the door completely off its hinges. It then lunged forward, covering the distance of the hallway in a single bound. With no time to take aim, Bimisi dove to avoid the oncoming attack, but he wasn't quite quick enough. A searing sting spread across his back as the tips of the creature's claws sliced through his skin.

Hitting the floor, he rolled and fired wildly. Bullets ricocheted off the oven and grill. It all happened in a blur, but Bimisi knew at least one of the shots had found its mark when he heard the werewolf bark out an aggravated snarl.

He gathered himself to see the creature hunched down at the opposite end of the room, blood trickling down its left front leg. Bimisi set his sights right between the beast's eyes.

Just as he pulled the trigger, Chad Burten stumbled into the kitchen, and the bullet struck him square in the side. Blood sprayed the door as well as another of the diner's patrons who'd rushed in behind the now wounded manager of the Silver Falls Happy Hobby Shop. The second man froze when he saw all the blood.

"Get out of the way," Bimisi shouted as he tried to stand.

Too focused on Chad, the man never saw the Shaman werewolf. The beast smacked him with its massive paw, and the patron flew into Bimisi, sending them both to the kitchen floor.

Shoving the semiconscious man aside, Bimisi fired again, just missing the werewolf as it darted back down the short hallway. He heard the splintering of wood and crumbling of bricks as the creature broke through the exit and escaped into the alley.

Sitting up slowly, he reached around to feel for where the werewolf had slashed him. Bimisi winced as his fingers found the gashes. Instinctively drawing his hand back, he cringed again when he saw his palm and fingers covered in blood.

The injury already had him starting to feel faint, but more screams from the front of the diner forced him to his feet. He should have known there wasn't really a chance to end this cleanly.

CHAPTER 36

THE TALE OF TWO WOLVES

Peter looked on as the teenage werewolves made quick work of the few foolish souls who'd decided to dine at Wolfy's that night. Ashley pounced on a customer as he ran for the door, ripping into his back. Nate batted a woman to the ground and then split her straight down the middle with a single swipe.

Utterly terrified, Peter crouched behind the counter and closed his eyes. Even though Nate was one of his best friends, he had no faith that the therianthrope now dismembering everyone in the diner would spare him. It didn't seem as if Nate or Ashley had any sort of control over the beasts they'd become.

The screams and slushy sounds of guts spilling onto the diner floor forced Peter to open his eyes again, but he kept them focused on the front exit. With the creatures running out of victims, he knew this would be his best, and likely only, opportunity to make a break for it. But he had to go now. And to do that, he'd have to power through the potent fear that had him petrified in place.

Mustering the will to move, Peter sprang from his crouch and broke for the door, slipping almost immediately on a pool of blood. Pitching forward, he slammed into the hardwood floor shoulder-first and let out a strangled cry.

Now with a clear view of the massacre he'd just been listening to, Peter saw the creature Ashley had become lift its head from one of its victims.

She stared right at him.

He had to keep moving. Grasping at his injured shoulder, he staggered back onto his feet and continued toward the exit—only making it a few more steps before Ashley bounded over and swiped his legs out from under him.

Peter came crashing down to the hardwood again, the pain in his shoulder now dwarfed by a throbbing in his lower right leg. He looked down to see the ankle that had taken the brunt of Ashley's strike, as well as his foot, jutting unnaturally outward from his shin at nearly a ninety-degree angle.

No longer able to run, Peter propped himself up on his elbows and tried to crawl away from Ashley as she stalked toward him. There was nowhere for him to go. He was literally backed into a corner.

Then, over the werewolf's shoulder, he saw Deputy Rogers rush into the diner. The deputy froze, momentarily overwhelmed by the blood-splattered scene.

Peter tried to call out to get his attention, but barely managed a whimper.

It was just loud enough. The deputy saw the predicament he was in and quickly took aim at the creature. Peter felt a glimmer of hope, but it only lasted a moment. Before he could even blink, the

Shaman werewolf leapt into the diner behind Billy and mauled him, ending the deputy's life in half a heartbeat.

Frantically looking around for anyone else who could help him, Peter realized he was now the only person left alive in the room. Terror seized him from head to toe as the three creatures gathered around the front entryway. It would only be a matter of seconds until they were playing tug-of-war with his shredded corpse.

Except now that the three werewolves were all together, they seemed far more interested in each other than they did in him.

Ashley and Nate growled and stalked toward the Shaman. The Indian werewolf stood his ground, arching his back and preparing for a fight. He was about twice the size of Nate and Ashley, yet the teenage werewolves appeared equally resolute not to back down.

Ashley sprang first, baring her fangs. The bigger, far more experienced werewolf countered her attack, swiftly knocking her to the floor with one of its mammoth front paws, then sending her tumbling away with a strike from the other. Ashley regrouped as Nate leapt to her side. They growled at the Shaman, who snarled right back.

The brief faceoff ended there. The Alpha quickly turned and darted out the front door as Bimisi stumbled into the room and fired wildly in its general direction. Nate leapt through a plate-glass window to give chase. Ashley started toward the door, then paused. She turned her head toward Peter, almost seeming to smile.

He closed his eyes and cried out as she lunged.

More shots rang out, sounding as though they came from a different direction this time. Peter felt the bone-crushing weight of the werewolf as it collapsed onto his legs. Then he felt that weight become significantly lighter.

He willed his eyelids to peel back, then popped them all the way open when he saw that the werewolf was rapidly morphing back into a lifeless Ashley.

Behind her, Toby stood in the entryway to the diner, his revolver still aimed at her now bare and bloody back.

There had been no time to think. No time to consider who he was shooting, just what—a creature that was about to tear open his friend. Now that creature no longer existed, and Ashley Schultz was dead.

The room started to spin as Toby felt his head go numb. Taking a couple of choppy steps over to the counter, he braced himself against one of the stools. He'd shot a monster but killed a girl he'd known since he was ten years old.

Peter snapped out of his shock and shoved away Ashley's bloody, naked body. "These things are real," he exclaimed hoarsely. "They're really fucking real!"

Bimisi slowly made his way over to Toby, Rachel, and Peter, his left hand wrapped around his torso and pressed firmly against a wound in his back. He said nothing, but gave an approving nod, and Toby wondered if that was supposed to make him feel better about shooting his high school's head cheerleader. Because it didn't.

Wolfy's had been transformed into a real-life house of horrors with half a dozen disemboweled bodies strewn about the room and walls that resembled a series of Jackson Pollock paintings done in blood. Toby could barely bring himself to look at most of it, but he couldn't stop his eyes from returning to Ashley's body.

He felt Rachel tentatively place a hand on his shoulder. "You had to. There wasn't time for anything else."

"We should go," Bimisi said as he straightened up and stepped toward the door. "Before one of the others comes looking for her."

Toby felt Rachel's grip on his shoulder tighten as she attempted to guide him toward the exit. He closed his eyes for a moment, took a deep breath, and forced his legs to start moving.

"I could use a little help over here," Peter said through clenched teeth, attempting to wrap his hands around his twisted and bruised lower leg.

Looking down, Toby noticed his friend's ankle had swollen to twice its normal size. He stepped over and pulled one of Peter's arms over his shoulders, lifting him up. Rachel ducked under Peter's other arm to do the same. After letting an initial groan escape, Peter did his best to stay quiet as the group headed outside.

Rachel had been running on autopilot since leaving Wolfy's, unable to fully process the ghastly sights she'd seen there. The rest of her bruised and bloodied cohorts all appeared equally scarred, both physically and emotionally. They sat around the sheriff station silently, all starting blankly at nothing in particular.

Toby was slouched at his father's desk, his jacket's hood up over his head. Past him, Peter lay on a bench against the far wall, his hands over his face.

"How much longer?" asked her uncle, who sat directly in front of her on one of the station's desks. Opening his case of ammunition, he picked out a new container of silver bullets and quickly began reloading his revolver.

Rachel refocused on the task at hand. She wiped away the blood from around Bimisi's wounds with an antiseptic cloth, scrutinizing her work. The stitches weren't particularly pretty, certainly nothing her seamstress mother would be proud of, but blood and pus no longer oozed from the claw marks in her uncle's back.

"Almost done," she replied as she peeled the backing off an adhesive bandage and placed it over a section of the stitched-up wounds. Her uncle remained as still as he could while she finished.

Bimisi shifted his focus from his weapon over to Toby. As determined as the boy had been to face down the creatures, it was going to take some time for him to process having actually killed one. Unfortunately, time wasn't something they had.

"You did what had to be done," he offered.

"I killed someone," Toby replied quietly.

"You killed a monster."

"I killed Ashley!" he shouted. "I shot her and now she's gone. She's just...gone."

"And if your friend succeeds in defeating the Shaman, you will need to be prepared to shoot him too," Bimisi countered firmly.

Toby's voice fell all the way to a murmur. "I won't do that."

"Not doing it will not be an option."

"What if Nate actually could learn to control it?" Rachel asked. "Like how the Shaman stopped himself from attacking me?"

"The Shaman is bound by a curse," Bimisi said, dismissing the idea immediately. "He has also been a werewolf for over a century. Many more would die before your friend gained that level of command. And even if he did, as the Shaman has shown us, he could choose to harm even those who have reason to believe they are protected. He could also create more beasts, equally incapable of controlling their inhuman instincts. Friends, family…nobody will ever *truly* be safe."

Toby's eyes shifted downward, and the room went remarkably quiet. As much as he hated to admit it, Bimisi was starting to feel a connection to the sheriff's son—and a begrudging respect. The boy had saved his niece's life after all.

He also felt a compulsion, spawned from an obvious need, to say something to encourage Toby and the others to keep going. There was little doubt in his mind that he'd be unable to hunt down an Alpha on his own, not in his current condition. Bimisi knew he was going to need help.

He began his impromptu pep talk in a low voice. "The Umatilla have a fable, meant for times when we find ourselves facing seemingly insurmountable challenges. It has been passed down through so many generations that its origin is no longer known. In fact, it may even have originated with the Cayuse or Walla Walla. It tells the story of the two wolves we all have living inside us. One is the wolf of fear and doubt; the other brings us courage and strength. And these two wolves quarrel time and again throughout our lives to determine what we are capable of doing, to determine who we are capable of becoming."

He paused for a moment to let the others contemplate the old Indian allegory.

"And does the story say if one ever wins?" Rachel asked.

"Of course," Bimisi answered. "Every battle must have a victor."

"So then who comes out on top?" Peter asked quietly.

"The one you feed."

The room fell silent again, and Bimisi couldn't tell whether the short story had had any sort of effect on the teens. He then thought of another way he could re-instill the group's confidence. He set down his gun and reached for his case of revolvers, only to find it was already empty.

Rachel placed the final bandage over the stitches. Then, noticing her uncle's confused expression, she reached for the gun she had tucked into the back of her jeans and held it up. "Already got one."

Peter stared in disbelief at the weapon in her hand. "So am I the only one here who *doesn't* know how to fire one of those?"

"My uncle gave me shooting lessons growing up," she explained. "Usually against my mother's wishes." She tucked the revolver back into the waistband of her jeans. "So now we go save the town, right?"

"No," Bimisi replied. "Now we wait."

"What?"

"The creatures are hunting each other. We let them finish."

Rachel was completely thrown by her uncle's plan. "What about all that stuff you just said about...feeding the right wolf?"

"That story was meant to inspire you to be brave, not brainless," said Bimisi. "One monster will be much easier to kill than two."

"There are still people out there," Rachel argued. "My mom is still out there! We can't just sit around and wait."

A look of realization flashed across Peter's face. "My parents are still at home too."

"And they were fools for staying," Bimisi responded evenly. "But right now the werewolves are not interested in attacking people."

"And what happens when Nate finds Ashley dead?" Toby pushed his hood down and looked over. "Who do you think he'll be interested in attacking then?"

CHAPTER 37

KILLING AN ALPHA

Two blocks down, werewolf Nate stalked back into the diner. Seeing Ashley's body, he moved toward it, slowly stepping over the ravaged remains of Deputy Rogers. With a whimper, he nudged the lifeless teenager with his snout, turning her over. Her head and limbs flopped onto the bloodstained hardwood as she rolled onto her back.

The werewolf stared despondently at the bloody body of the once most popular girl at Silver Falls High. He whimpered again softly, then reared back and let loose a furious, ear-splitting howl.

The howl echoed through town, causing the group inside the station to look toward the door. A fraction of a second later, Walter answered Nate's howl from the jail cells beneath them, and everyone's necks snapped in unison as their heads swiveled toward the basement's entryway.

Rachel moved for the exit. "We need to go make sure our families are okay."

Bimisi had always admired his niece for her courage, but as brave as she was, he knew she wouldn't walk out into the night without him. As he expected, she paused just before she reached the door.

He also knew that the girl's mother could keep herself safe and that right now the creatures seemed more interested in attacking each other than the people in town. Close to convincing himself that he was making the right decision, Bimisi was startled by a scream from outside.

He stood to intercept Toby, who was now also heading for the front entrance. Reaching out, he flattened his palm against the boy's chest.

After waiting a second to make sure the sheriff's son was going to stay put, Bimisi strode to the door. Opening it just a crack, he peered out into the street. Toby and Rachel crowded behind him, trying to catch a glimpse of what was happening.

They all saw a terrified Betsy Wheeler racing toward the station. An avid runner, the thirty-eight-year-old sprinted down Wilson Street wearing a light blue tank top and jeans that were covered in blood.

"Not interested in attacking people, huh?" Toby challenged as he grabbed at the door handle.

"It could be a trap," Bimisi said, keeping a firm hold on the door. His eyes scanned the buildings behind Betsy. He expected at least one of the beasts to appear at any moment, forcing them to either leave their shelter to save the woman or stay where they were as she met a gruesome end. But as she continued to get closer, there was still no sign of a werewolf.

Bimisi furrowed his brow, puzzled. "Do you recognize her?"

"It's Mrs. Wheeler," Toby answered.

She charged up the front steps, her face stricken. "Help! Please, please help!"

Betsy caught her toe on the top stair and stumbled forward. Bimisi yanked the door back as she came flailing toward them. Reaching out, he and Rachel caught the woman as she fell into their arms.

"She's still in the house!" Betsy shrieked hysterically, as Bimisi and Rachel rushed her over to the nearest desk. "Please!"

The blood on her jeans was at least partially her own, seeping out from three shallow claw marks in her left thigh.

"You have to save her!" Betsy pleaded.

"Save who?" Bimisi asked.

"My daughter!"

Bimisi heard the police SUV start up outside. His mouth quirked in annoyance when he looked toward the door to see Toby was gone. Moments ago, the boy had been solemnly reflecting on his past actions and fearing the future actions he might have to take. Now, he'd apparently decided to just keep acting.

Perhaps telling the story of the two wolves had been a mistake.

Toby skidded the SUV to a stop on the Wheelers' front lawn and leapt from the vehicle, bolting past a tin mailbox that had the family's name stenciled across the side. The front door to the home was wide open, and as he got closer, Toby noticed the deep claw marks running across it. Peeled oak was curled up inside the grooves.

He slowed at the sight of the gashes in the door.

The impulse to save Betsy's daughter had impelled him here, but now his uncertainly stopped him cold on the front steps.

No. He wasn't going to freeze up again. Ever since the accident, he'd been an endless buffet of fear with the fallout of the few brave acts he'd mustered mostly serving to double his doubt. Toby's wolf of strength and courage had to be starving. Now was the time to feed it.

Kill the Alpha and all Betas go back to one hundred percent human.

He stepped through the oak door, leading with the revolver he'd taken from Bimisi's case. A light from the rear kitchen dimly illuminated the living room, casting long shadows across the blood-soaked carpet. John Wheeler, who Toby knew had just celebrated his fortieth birthday last week, lay torn apart on the floor, his shotgun resting only a few feet away from his partially severed right hand.

Toby looked away as he stepped over the body and moved cautiously down the hallway, continuing toward the kitchen.

A thump came from inside the hallway closet as he walked past.

Springing against the opposite wall, Toby took aim at the door. He stayed petrified in the same position for several moments, waiting for another sound. Finally, clothes hangers squeaked as someone, or something, rustled among the jackets and coats hanging inside the closet.

Toby slowly reached for the door handle with one hand, keeping his revolver aimed with the other. Wrapping his fingers around the brass knob, he waited another moment, then twisted his wrist and yanked the door open.

A huddled seven-year-old, Greta Wheeler, stared back at him with wild, terrified eyes. Toby allowed himself a second to exhale.

"It's okay, Greta," he said as he stepped into the closet and knelt down to her eye level. "I'm going to get you out—"

Toby went silent as a guttural growl emanated from behind the opened door. He glanced at the plywood to his right, the round brass knob and the umbrella hanging from a white plastic hook, and imagined the hulking creature, fangs bared, crouched directly on the other side. He quickly stood and tried to close the door to get a shot.

The Shaman werewolf lunged and batted at the door with its paw before Toby could step out of the way. It swung shut with such incredible force that it took Toby along with it, slamming him hard against the doorframe. The impact rattled his ribs and forced the air from his lungs. It also caused the revolver to slip from his fingers, and he heard the weapon clank onto the closet floor.

After quickly nudging the door open just enough to get free, Toby closed himself and Greta inside the closet. Fighting off a fit of coughs while regaining his breath, he began searching frantically for the pistol.

Greta screamed as a claw burst through the door, splintering the plywood. Toby shoved her to the rear of the closet while ducking to avoid the beast's flailing paw.

The werewolf's head came smashing through next, and Toby leapt back farther, grabbing hold of Greta and pressing her as firmly as he could against the rear wall. The creature's fangs snapped shut, no more then half a foot away. Toby could feel droplets of the beast's saliva on his arms, its breath on his cheeks.

Then he spotted the revolver right below its jaw.

It snarled and snapped at them again, missing by inches. Determined to reach its prey, the werewolf briefly backed off, undoubtedly to prepare for one last lunge. That's all it would take to finish off the door.

Toby seized the opportunity and snatched up the pistol. He fired at a blur of mangy fur and serrated fangs through the opening the Shaman had created, squeezing off three shots. The werewolf howled in pain and disappeared from view.

Bimisi strode into the Wheelers' home, fully expecting to find Toby laying dead in a pool of blood. He was struck with utter disbelief when he spotted the injured Shaman werewolf slumped over in the hallway. The boy had shot it, wounded it. Bimisi anxiously stepped toward the werewolf to finish the job, taking aim at the creature's head.

But before he could pull the trigger, he was struck by something extraordinarily powerful. The sudden blow sent him crashing into the wall with such force that plaster crumbled inward where his shoulder and hip impacted. Bimisi buckled to his knees, and his revolver fell from his hand, tumbling into the center of the hallway.

Half in a daze, he watched as Nate stalked past. Snarling at the weapon that had been used to kill his friend, the werewolf raised the same paw it had just used to strike Bimisi, then drove it downward to not only crush the revolver, but smash the hardwood around the gun to smithereens. Without pause, Nate then leapt onto the injured Shaman werewolf and tore out the beast's throat.

Once again, the stories Bimisi had been told were proven to be true. Within moments, the dead werewolf morphed back into the once immortal Indian. While that transformation took place, Nate appeared to double in size.

The Beta had taken its creator's place.

Just as Nate finished growing, Toby stumbled from the hall closet and onto the floor. Now face-to-face with his friend, the boy looked horrified to see Nate crouched over the departed Shaman.

"Shoot him," Bimisi yelled out hoarsely.

Toby took aim, looking right into Nate's eyes, but faltered. Taking advantage of the boy's hesitation, the werewolf leapt down the hallway toward the kitchen. A moment later, Bimisi heard it break through the home's back door.

His eyes went back to the body lying in the hallway, smudged with dirt and grime where it wasn't covered in blood. This night-mare wasn't going to end with the Shaman's death. The hunt would have to continue.

"But I did it right this time," Toby said as he looked at the dead Indian. He spun around to face Bimisi, holding up the revolver. "These *are* all silver bullets, aren't they?"

"To kill an Alpha, the bullet has to pass through the head or the heart," Bimisi responded through a groan.

"Why didn't you tell me that before?!" Toby shouted.

"Because you were not supposed to be the one to kill him." Bimisi let out another grunt as he got his feet underneath him and stood up. The shock was wearing off, and he was becoming more conscious of the extraordinary aching in his shoulder and ribs. "It was not your place. Now...I need you to take me to your friend's home. And we need to hurry."

Toby stood silent, staring at him. Bimisi couldn't tell if the boy's silence was driven by simple frustration or full-blown fury. Not that it really mattered.

"Take me to your friend's house," he said a little more emphatically.

"Why?"

Walking was a struggle. He lifted his shirt to see a massive bruise forming that practically covered the whole left side of his torso. The werewolf's swipe hadn't broken skin, but it had done plenty of internal damage. Bimisi figured at least three or four of his ribs were cracked.

He used his free hand to brace himself against the wall and managed to straighten up as he headed for the door. "I will explain on the way. We have to go. Now."

CHAPTER 38

MYSTIC MEASURES

Bimisi's explanation for why they were going to Nate's did more to confuse Toby than it did to clear things up for him. It started with the revelation that the Shaman was a mystic. Approximately one in every forty members of the dwindling Umatilla Tribe was on some level, and most used their abilities for things like creating healing potions or casting spells that allegedly allowed them to better communicate with the worlds around them—both natural and supernatural.

Using their powers to take such altruistic measures had once earned these gifted individuals the nickname of Medicine Men. But then there was the Shaman. Unlike most mystics, he'd used his powers to communicate with, and become cursed by, something more ominous. Something *far* more ominous.

"How do you know so much about all this stuff?" Toby asked, his head spinning as he turned onto Nate's street.

Bimisi winced as the vehicle's momentum caused his ribs to press against the SUV's seatbelt. "Because I share the same basic abilities."

Toby was dumbstruck. Rachel's uncle had never bothered to mention to him, or possibly even his own niece, that he too was a mystic.

"Now I need you to find me one of your friend's possessions," Bimisi ordered as they pulled into Nate's driveway. "Something he had a lot of contact with."

"What for?"

"A location spell." Bimisi undid his seatbelt and opened the passenger side door. "If we can do it quickly, hopefully we can find him before more lives are lost."

"A location spell?" Toby was furious. This was yet another thing that the Indian shouldn't have kept a secret. If Bimisi had the ability to track a werewolf using some sort of Native American hex, what possible justification could there have been for waiting so long to do so? "Why didn't you use this trick to track down the Shaman?"

"Because it requires a personal possession. You were in the cavern. Did you see anything there we could use? The Shaman knew our abilities better than most mystics. Certainly better than I do. Remember that our people buried him there. He was not going to leave us anything we could use to trap him again."

Bimisi exited the vehicle and started up the driveway without any further explanation. Toby watched him for a moment, then glanced at the rearview mirror to see a still very shaken Greta Wheeler huddled in the backseat.

"We're going to get you back to your mom really soon," he said as reassuringly as he could. "I promise."

He helped her get out of the SUV and then, with the frightened girl grasping his hand tightly, he once again approached his former best friend's shuttered home. Feeling a dull dread spreading through his chest, Toby pulled his jacket's hood up over his head as he stepped through the front door. Bimisi was already in the kitchen, rifling through drawers and cupboards.

"Find me something we can use to find our new Alpha," he directed once more before moving on to the Schaffers' lower kitchen cabinets.

Toby picked up Greta and moved for the stairs, taking them two at a time until he was in the upstairs hallway. He strode into Nate's bedroom and surveyed it for one of his friend's more prized possessions.

Setting Greta down, he stepped over to the bookshelf that held all of Nate's meticulously hand-painted toy warriors. Out front and center from the rest stood Duncan Balfour.

Toby eyed the Middle Earth Conquest combatant for a long moment. Blinking away tears, he snatched up the two-inch tall pewter dwarf and slid the figure into his jacket pocket.

Working his way through the Schaffers' downstairs pantry, Bimisi gathered a collection of herbs and spices from the family's accumulation of seasonings. He hadn't done a location spell in years, not since his brother had run away from his wife, daughter, and other responsibilities, all the way to South Dakota. Tracking down a teenage werewolf within a ten- to twenty-mile radius should be easy by comparison, as long as Toby found a significant personal effect Bimisi could use.

Thankfully, the home's pantry and a medicine cabinet in the first-floor bathroom had all of the other ingredients he needed. He used a cloth placemat to wrap up containers of jasmine oil, basil, flax seed, and a couple of candles. He then snatched a bottle of ibuprofen and made his way toward the front door.

"We need to go," he shouted up the stairs as he staggered past them.

Walking was really becoming a chore. Bimisi grimaced with almost every step he took down the front walk. Opening one of the SUV's rear doors induced a grunt. When he set the placemat on the backseat, he heard a growl.

But that utterance hadn't come from him.

Bimisi straightened up to see the new Alpha werewolf standing on the neighbor's lawn. The beast stared him down, a malicious sparkle in its luminous yellow eyes. He instinctively reached for his revolver, only to remember that the creature had destroyed it just as his hand found the empty holster.

The werewolf snarled and charged toward him.

Toby stood in the center of Nate's room lost in thought. He worked his thumb and forefinger over the pewter figure in his pocket, knowing that it would be the item they'd use to hunt down his friend.

Maybe helping people just isn't your thing. You don't seem to be very good at it.

The SUV's horn startled Toby and propelled him toward the bedroom door. "Come on, let's go," he said as he took Greta's wrist.

As they reached the stairs, the truck's horn went silent. The ensuing sounds of glass shattering and metal crumpling stopped Toby dead in his tracks. His father's vehicle was being attacked.

He let go of Greta and gently pushed her back toward Nate's room. "Actually, I need you to stay here until I come back for you."

Barely waiting for the girl to nod her understanding, Toby turned and raced down the steps. He heard a loud snarl, then the screeching of the SUV's buckling frame as the werewolf continued to strike at the vehicle. He reached the bottom of the staircase and moved toward the open front door. Glancing outside, he caught a glimpse of the dismantled SUV and gasped.

The windshield was gone, the front right panel looked as though it had hit a tree, and the driver's side door was torn completely off. There was no sign of Bimisi or the werewolf.

Toby took a deep breath, yanked down his hood, and readied his revolver. He scoured the yard and the street as he stepped onto the front lawn. Then he returned his attention to the clawed and crumpled SUV.

As he made his way down to it, he kept his eyes on the surrounding homes as much as he did his father's truck. Once he was close enough, he ducked his head inside the vehicle and was relieved to find Bimisi laying on the floor, crammed halfway under the rear seats.

"Took you long enough," Bimisi sputtered out with a cough.

"I'm sorry, I—"

"Did you find an item?"

Toby nodded.

"Then we should get to the station."

Toby climbed into the driver's seat and started the SUV. The engine stuttered for a moment, and then came to life.

After another sigh of relief, he called back to Bimisi. "I'll be right back."

He rushed back toward the house to retrieve Greta as Bimisi protested with a loud groan.

Fretfully tapping his uninjured left foot on the wooden bench he was resting on, Peter eyed the station's front door. Rachel watched him from behind a desk a few feet over, bothered. His fidgeting and tapping were only increasing her own anxiety and she had had enough.

"Could you just...stay still for a minute?" she asked tersely.

"How much longer are we supposed to sit here and wait?"

"Until they come back."

"And what if they don't come back? What if they're dead?"

"Don't say that."

"What if one of those things shows up here before they do?" Peter continued as if he hadn't even heard her. "A damn werewolf could come crashing through that door any second."

Rachel held up her revolver. "We have protection."

"And what if Toby's dad gets out of his jail cell?" he asked. "Are you going to shoot him too? Let's use that gun to get out of here. You said your parents are still at your house. Mine are still at home too. Let's go get them and get as far away from here as possible."

"You can barely move," Rachel said as she looked over at the front door, unconsciously twirling her hair with her free hand. "And they're coming back."

As if on cue, Toby and Bimisi came bursting into the sheriff station with Greta Wheeler in tow. Bimisi leaned heavily on Toby, holding a bundled placemat under one arm. Betsy Wheeler let out a grateful gasp and ran over to scoop up her daughter, hugging her tightly. Rachel rushed over to her uncle and helped Toby get him settled into the deputy's desk chair.

"What happened to him?" she asked.

"Nate happened." Toby moved toward the doorway to the basement, finishing his answer over his shoulder. "The Shaman is dead. We didn't kill him."

"I need something to light these candles," Bimisi said as he unwrapped the items inside the placemat.

Toby pointed toward the sheriff's desk. "Top drawer on the right side."

He then trotted down the stairs to the basement without another word. Not knowing what else to do, Rachel retrieved the book of matches from the drawer Toby had pointed to and brought them over to her uncle, overwhelmed by all the questions accumulating in her head.

She chose one to ask first. "What's all this stuff for?"

"A location spell."

"A what?"

Bimisi glanced past his astonished niece and spotted a couple of thermoses next to the coffee maker. He pointed to them. "Empty one of those, then fill it with water and bring it to me."

Rachel was too stunned to move. "You're a mystic?"

Upon first laying his eyes on the jail cell that held his father, Toby froze. Several of the cell's bars had been smashed and jutted outward, but thankfully the steel had held strong. Through the bent and twisted bars, he could see his dad laying flat on his stomach, sprawled out on the cold, concrete floor. The man was naked, his shredded sheriff's uniform scattered everywhere. But more importantly, he was human.

Toby descended the remaining steps and went to the cell's door, quickly realizing that it was too damaged for him to open. Examining the bars, he found a spot where they'd been bent far enough apart for him to slip through. He squeezed his way into the cell and knelt down beside his father.

Unsure of what to do next, Toby shook the sheriff's shoulder gently, then again with more urgency. He momentarily panicked when his jostling got no response, but quickly calmed when he noticed his dad's ribs rising and falling with each breath the man took. His father was alive, but apparently out cold, his body completely exhausted from all it had been through.

Toby reluctantly stood and backed out of the jail cell. Trudging up the stairs, he felt his stomach knot as he fully realized the situation he was in. Silver Falls had actually faced down its own supernatural challenges, just like the ones he'd read about in *The Hero with a Thousand Faces*. But there was still one challenge left, and neither his father nor Rachel's uncle were in any condition to combat it.

Toby would have to confront this threat on his own. And this final challenge, the one *he'd* have to conquer to become a hero, was Nate.

It was the opportunity he'd wanted all along, ever since finding his friend covered in blood in the reservation woods, but this wasn't at all how he'd wanted it.

Walking back up to the first floor of the station, he found Betsy and Greta Wheeler huddled together in the back office. Peter was still on the bench, and Bimisi was busy mixing spell ingredients together in one of the deputy's old thermoses.

Rachel stood alongside her uncle, practically shouting at him. "How come you never told me about this?"

"There was never any reason," Bimisi replied evenly. "The gift was not passed along to you."

"How do you know?"

"There's a spell that's done for all newborns, to determine if they are one of the chosen." Bimisi glanced up from his concoction to look his niece square in the eye. "You are not one of us."

"Then how come I can feel the werewolves when they're nearby?" she challenged.

Bimisi appeared surprised by her revelation, as was Toby, but he gave no verbal response. Instead, he simply returned to his spell preparations.

Toby couldn't let the comment go that easily. "You can feel *what*?"

"I don't know how, or why, so I didn't say anything about it before now, but I always get, like, this super pins-and-needles sensation anytime there's a werewolf around."

"That's messed up," Peter commented.

"And probably just something you're imagining," Bimisi mumbled.

"No, it's not!" Rachel shouted. "What if that spell you did was wrong?"

Bimisi barked right back at her. "Now is not the time to discuss this!"

And that ended the conversation. His head spinning, Toby stepped over next to Rachel and watched as her uncle sprinkled flax seed into the thermos. It apparently was the final ingredient to his spell because the Indian then screwed the lid on tightly and gave the container a good shake. He set the thermos down next to Duncan Balfour, removed the lid, and slid both the items between three lit candles that he'd arranged in a triangle on the deputy's desk.

Shutting his eyes and bowing his head, Bimisi began murmuring something under his breath. Keeping his eyes closed, he picked up the thermos and took several gulps. Toby watched anxiously as the Indian then set the thermos down and, with his eyes still closed, covered Duncan Balfour with his left hand.

Bimisi leaned back in the chair, murmuring another chant, or at least something that sounded like a chant, before stopping abruptly. He then caused Toby and Rachel to stumble backwards as he shot up straight in his chair with wide-open eyes.

After taking a long, deep breath, Bimisi finally spoke, although his voice was still barely above a murmur. "I know where it is headed."

His dispirited tone worried Toby, and apparently Rachel too.

"Where?" she asked apprehensively.

CHAPTER 39

The Final Confrontation

The Mother Earth Ceremony had begun. Most residents of the Umatilla Reservation village were gathered in the main square, surrounding a small stage constructed of bleached plywood. Dyami Askuwheteau stood among them, admiring the thousands of tiny white lights that hung from the stage and nearby storefronts. They were the only lights allowed to be lit during the ceremony, which made the village appear as if it had been sprinkled with stars from the sky.

An elder, well into his eighties, stood on the center of the stage. He wore a buckskin ceremonial shirt with four strips of quill and beadwork that extended over his shoulders and hung midway down his back. With his eyes aimed up at the vast night sky, the elder raised his arms and began leading the ceremony's first chant.

"Behold! Our Mother Earth is lying here. Behold! She giveth of her fruitfulness. Truly, her power she giveth to us. Give thanks to Mother Earth who lieth here!"

The crowd also raised their arms, many dressed in equally authentic tunics with beaded belts, and responded, "We think of Mother Earth who lieth here. We know she giveth of her fruitfulness. Truly, her power she giveth to us. Our thanks to Mother Earth who lieth here!"

"Behold on Mother Earth the growing fields!" the elder continued. "Behold the promise of her fruitfulness! Truly, her power she giveth to us. Give thanks to Mother Earth who lieth here!"

Dyami chanted along with the others, feeling especially invigorated after hearing of the mass exodus of residents from Silver Falls. "We see on Mother Earth the growing fields. We see the promise of her fruitfulness. Truly, her power she—"

He paused when he spotted a dark, hulking silhouette dart through the alley that ran between two nearby buildings. The figure disappeared from view in an instant, but Dyami continued to stare at the alleyway. He was certain of what he'd seen, despite only getting a brief glimpse.

His lips parted and a frightened whisper escaped. "No."

Bimisi lifted himself out of the deputy's chair and headed for the door. He made it all of about three steps before stumbling and falling into the wall. With a loud groan, he grabbed at his side and slid down to the floor.

Toby and Rachel rushed over to him.

"Just give me a moment," Bimisi grunted.

"You're not in any condition to do this on your own," Rachel protested.

Toby wondered if her uncle was in any condition to even move. The man's body had taken an immense amount of punishment and couldn't be capable of handling much more.

"You are right," agreed Bimisi reluctantly. "I am not, but I will not be staying here. Help me up."

Toby and Rachel each took an arm and assisted Bimisi back to his feet. With Toby leading the way, the group moved slowly toward the front exit. Once they reached the door, Toby glanced over at Peter.

"You okay staying here and keeping an eye on the Wheelers?"

"Your dad is human again now, right?" Peter asked.

"Yeah."

"Then yeah, I'm good."

Toby gave him a slight nod. "We'll be back soon."

"You better be."

Toby tore down the highway in his father's banged-up SUV, praying that it wouldn't start falling apart beneath them. Rachel sat perched on the edge of the passenger seat, the worn leather behind her covered in a puddle of laminated safety glass pebbles from the shattered windshield. Bimisi lay across the bench seat behind them, sporadically grunting each time they hit a bump in the road.

In less than five minutes, they'd be pulling into the reservation village to save its people from Toby's best friend. And to think that just three days ago Toby had been concerned about escaping the village in one piece. The irony of the situation was not lost on him, nor was the undesirableness of it, but he knew he had no other choice.

With the windshield gone, the night air whistled loudly through the vehicle as it sped along. Toby glanced over at Rachel to see her staring into the blackness in front of them, looking beyond distraught. He shifted his eyes back to the beam of light shining from the sole working headlight that led their way.

More than a little distraught himself, he shouted a question over the wind. "Why would he go to the reservation?"

"He is scared and he is angry," Bimisi shouted back. "His emotions are taking over, which means the creature is taking over. And now that he is the Alpha, the beast side of him is much more dominant. It has driven him to the nearest place it can do the most damage."

Toby pressed down on the gas, and everyone jerked back in their seats as the SUV accelerated. Nate hadn't wanted anyone to save him. Now, according to Bimisi, nobody could. Toby wasn't ready to accept that. Nate had claimed to have garnered some level of control over the beast and Toby was willing to let him prove it.

A sharp turn off Crater Lake Highway was followed by a bumpy ride down the winding path that led to the reservation village. They found mass hysteria when they arrived. People were shouting and scattering everywhere.

Toby swerved to avoid an old Lincoln that tore away from the scene, barely managing to steer clear of a collision. He skidded the SUV to a stop and then, without a moment's hesitation, jumped out, followed quickly by Rachel.

"Stay close," he shouted to her as they bobbed and weaved against the flow of fleeing reservation residents.

Bimisi called out from the vehicle. "Look up ahead, to the left."

As he sidestepped a few more Umatilla, Toby tripped over the mangled corpse of one of Nate's latest victims. He went to the ground hard, losing sight of Rachel.

The retreating tribe members continued to bump and knock him about, making it impossible for Toby to get back on his feet. He had no choice but to wait out the stampede.

Eventually the street cleared, revealing several more slaughtered bodies. Then Toby saw the werewolf. It looked directly at him, letting out a bloodcurdling howl before darting toward an empty lot between two buildings.

Toby raised his revolver and took aim at the creature. His finger twitched over the trigger, but he couldn't bring himself to pull it.

The crack of Rachel's revolver firing caused him to flinch slightly as the sudden sound filled the empty street.

The bullet struck the corner of the building the monster dashed behind, crumbling the brick. It was impressive that she'd managed such a close miss. At this distance, it would take total luck to hit a moving target, even one as big as the werewolf, never mind actually striking its head or heart.

But that wasn't why Toby hadn't fired.

Hearing rapid footsteps off to his right, he shifted his gaze to see Rachel sprinting toward the lot. Leaping to his feet, he hustled after her. He was already a good distance behind after getting trapped among the fleeing Umatilla. If she didn't slow down, she'd reach the lot before Toby could catch her.

He called out. "Rachel! Wait!"

Rachel trotted into the empty lot with her revolver raised. She knew she should have waited for Toby, but common sense had momentarily left her when she saw the people she'd grown up with butchered in the street.

The sight had sparked a blaze inside her, and that blaze had motivated her to pursue the werewolf without giving it a second thought. Now that she was standing alone in the dark, deserted lot, the blaze quickly subsided. It was replaced by concentrated fear.

A familiar prickling sensation suddenly spread throughout her entire body. Panicked, she looked up to see the werewolf crouched on the rooftop above, a woman's body clenched between its jaws. The creature flung the corpse at Rachel, and she barely managed to take a step before the body knocked her to the dirt.

The werewolf leapt down from the roof, landing only a few feet away.

Rachel shoved aside the body, trying to breathe through her panic. She got to her hands and knees, then froze as the werewolf lunged directly in front of her. The beast growled, drool running down its chin, its snout mere inches from her face.

She tried raising her revolver, but scarcely managed to lift the weapon off the dirt before she felt the powerful impact of the werewolf's right front paw.

The beast's swipe sent her sailing.

Rachel slammed into the side of Takoda Chayton's furniture shop, the collision with the wall knocking the gun from her hand, and then fell to ground in a heap. She closed her eyes as the creature moved in for the kill.

A shot rang out.

Almost simultaneously, Rachel felt the sickening sensation of the beast's blood spraying across her face. She opened her eyes to see the monster staggering to one side. There was a fresh, ragged bullet wound in its left shoulder.

No longer interested in her, the beast snarled, regained its balance, and loped angrily toward Toby, who stood near the entrance to the lot.

Toby kept his revolver trained on the beast, but didn't fire. Rachel opened her mouth to scream at him to shoot, but there wasn't time. With the werewolf almost upon him, Toby dove out of the monster's path.

Nate bounded right past him, continuing out into the street.

The instant the werewolf hit the gravel road, Rachel heard the roar of an engine. Then she saw Bimisi slam into the creature with the SUV. The werewolf flew into the nearby general store, its massive body smashing through the building's wall. The SUV followed, plowing into a display window.

Within seconds, both monster and vehicle disappeared from view, leaving crumbling brick and broken glass in their wake.

Toby rushed to Rachel's side, praying desperately that she hadn't been too severely wounded. He helped her sit up and saw that the left side of her shirt was soaked in blood. He carefully lifted it up to find four gashes across her ribs.

"Can you move?" he asked her.

She nodded. "I think so."

As he slid his shoulder under her arm and lifted her up, Toby noticed both of her hands were empty. "Where's your gun?"

Rachel glanced around their dimly lit surroundings. "I dropped it."

Knowing there was no time to look for the revolver, Toby tightened his grip on his own weapon as he dragged Rachel toward the gaping hole in the side of the building. With each step, he heard her grunt through clenched teeth, doing her best to hold in more agonizing utterances.

They cautiously stepped into the general store, maneuvering around toppled display cases and scattered home goods, until they were alongside the SUV. Toby leaned Rachel against it, then stepped toward the front of the vehicle. He glanced in through the passenger side window to find Bimisi still alive.

Alive but in really bad shape. Seeing the battered and bloodied Indian inside the trashed SUV triggered Toby's memories of the accident—the impact with the river, his unconscious mother, the water rushing in. Just as he had that night, he wanted to close his eyes and make this all go away.

"He is hurt," Bimisi groaned, bringing Toby back. "But now you *must* finish him."

Toby glanced at the revolver in his hand, the only one they had left. He then glanced back at Rachel. She was gripping her side, blood now covering her hands. Finally, he looked over to a large crater in the main interior wall. The SUV's headlight lit up the white paint around the smashed timber and plaster, but the area on the other side of the opening was enveloped in black.

The blood splattered around the hole made it clear it had been created by the injured werewolf, and Toby knew Nate was watching him from somewhere in those shadows.

He raised his weapon and took a step toward what was left of the wall. Before he could take a second step, he felt Rachel grab his shoulder and pull him back.

As he turned around to face her, she kissed him on the lips.

Just as quickly, she pulled away, seemingly as surprised as he was by her own impulsive action.

"You can do this," she whispered. "I know you can. Just…be careful."

Toby held her look for a moment and nodded. After gently leaning her back against the SUV, he started to once again move slowly toward the hole in the wall. It wasn't until he was within a few feet of the opening that he began to see the stocking shelves of the backroom. Then he saw the werewolf's yellow eyes.

Just stay there.

If Nate was in fact inside the beast somewhere, maybe he could resist the urge to attack now that they were face to face. Toby was convinced that once his friend turned human again, and saw the carnage that he'd caused, he'd be willing to listen to reason. There was still a chance to save him, as long as he stayed put until morning.

The creature sprang.

Toby fired on reflex, but the bullet only grazed the beast's side. Nate howled in pain as he butted Toby with the top of his head.

Sent airborne by the blow, Toby landed violently on the hood of the SUV, smacking the back of his head against the vehicle's steel exterior. Vision blurred and ears ringing, he felt a numbing pain reverberate through each and every one of his bones.

While still distantly aware of the position he was in, Toby lay too concussed to get his body to do anything about it.

He then felt himself being pulled through the broken windshield and heard Bimisi groan as the man strained to drag him inside the vehicle. Toby tumbled into the passenger seat, briefly feeling the dull pebbles of the laminated safety glass underneath him. The vehicle then bobbed violently, almost jostling him out of the seat, as the werewolf leapt onto the hood.

Toby blinked the beast into focus to see its yellow eyes fixed directly upon him. Woozily coming out of his stupor, he registered another hard jostling as Bimisi shook him frantically.

"Shoot!" Rachel's uncle shouted. "Shoot him!"

Bimisi reached for the pistol in Toby's hand, but before he could grab the gun, the werewolf plunged its fangs into the Indian's shoulder.

"Aaaaahhhhh!"

Seeing the creature was about to rip off her uncle's arm, Rachel grabbed the nearest weapon she could find—a large, splintered shard from one of the store's smashed shelves. She mustered what little strength she had left and plunged the makeshift dagger into the sizzling bullet wound in the werewolf's shoulder.

The creature released Bimisi right away and reared back with an angry snarl.

Quickly locating its assailant, the beast struck Rachel hard with the back of its paw, sending her tumbling along the store's cluttered tile floor. She came to rest against the checkout counter and dizzily looked back toward the SUV to see the werewolf gather itself and let out a victorious howl.

Watching helplessly, she saw it turn its attention back to Toby and Bimisi, ready to finish them.

Then the creature hesitated.

Rachel's diversion had given Toby just the time he needed to recover his faculties. He steadied his nerves, and his grip on Bimisi's revolver, as he pointed the firearm directly at the werewolf. Before it could lunge again, he fired and struck the beast square in the chest. Nate staggered back, leaving paw-sized imprints in the vehicle's hood as he toppled off the SUV.

Stumbling out the passenger side door, Toby spotted Rachel lying several feet away among the store debris. He started toward her, but stopped when he spotted Nate sprawled in front of the vehicle, wounded and laboring to breathe, but still in werewolf form.

The bullet must have just missed the beast's heart. The creature bared its fangs as they locked eyes, barking out an indignant snarl. It was as if somewhere inside the hulking monster, Nate was actually challenging Toby to do what needed to be done.

He held the werewolf's look and wondered if the creature was actually capable of attacking again.

It was.

The werewolf lurched toward him, opening its jaw. Startled by its sudden movement, Toby stumbled. Every muscle in his body tensed. His finger squeezed the pistol's trigger as he fell back.

He shot the creature right between the eyes.

The werewolf fell dead.

Toby collapsed to the floor and dropped the revolver. With a distant look, he watched as the massive beast morphed back into a very bloody, very dead Nate Schaffer.

CHAPTER 40

A GREATER PURPOSE

Sleeping soundly in her hospital bed, Rachel looked incredibly peaceful and, despite being quite battered and bruised, beautiful. As he sat watching her rest, Toby found himself envying her a little. At least she could sleep.

After killing his best friend two nights ago, he'd barely been able to catch a wink. Physically he was exhausted, but for the past thirty-eight hours, his emotions had been an unrelenting cyclone, denying him any sort of respite.

He'd failed Nate, but succeeded in saving the town. That success brought with it an undeniable sense of fulfillment. He'd finally mustered the courage and conviction to do what needed to be done.

Next time he'd just have to do it better.

And he did believe there would be a next time. All the supernatural circumstances Silver Falls had endured couldn't just be a random series of tragically life-altering, and life-ending, events. There had to be something more—a greater purpose to all the loss and tribulation. He just didn't know what it was yet.

Rachel stirred and slowly opened her eyes. Toby greeted her with a warm smile. It was the first time he'd seen her conscious since she'd kissed him.

"Hey," she said as she looked around the room. "Is it over?"

Toby responded with a simple nod. "How do you feel?"

Rachel sat up a little in the bed, wincing. "Guess."

"Well, the official damage was three cracked ribs, thirty-eight stitches, and a grade-two concussion, so…I'm gonna guess, not great."

She smiled and shook her head. They held each other's look for a long moment.

"Thanks for saving me…again," she said finally.

"Yeah, I'm getting pretty good at that, huh?"

Rachel snorted a laugh, then grimaced and held her ribs.

"How's my uncle?" she asked, straightening up as much as she could.

"He got about forty more stitches than you did. Then he left before officially being released. I don't think anyone has seen him since."

Rachel furrowed her brow, and Toby did his best to alleviate her concern. "I figure if he felt good enough to see himself out, then he's probably fine. Anyway, your mom and Mr. Franks are downstairs talking to the doctors about it."

"What about Peter?"

"He's a couple of rooms over. Broken ankle. I was just about to go see him."

"I'll go with you."

"You sure?"

Rachel nodded and reached out for Toby to give her a hand. As he helped her out of the bed, she stumbled and nudged the bedside table, sending a small vase of flowers over the edge. Toby reached out and caught the vase before it hit the floor, while experiencing a slight twinge of déjà vu.

Rachel apparently felt it too. "My hero."

He smirked and started to return the vase to its spot on the table when they both noticed the small slip of paper that had been hidden underneath it. Rachel picked up the scrap and read the note scrawled across it.

"What does it say?" Toby asked.

"For when you have questions," Rachel replied, showing him the note. "And then there's a phone number."

"For when you have questions about what?"

Rachel shrugged. "No idea. I'm guessing my uncle left it."

Toby set the vase down as Rachel wrapped an arm around his torso and leaned into him. She stepped gingerly as they walked out into the hallway.

"You know, for the record, you kind of saved my ass too," Toby said, leading her gently toward Peter's room.

"I know."

Toby doubted either of them would still be alive without the other. They'd agreed to end the terror that had besieged Silver Falls together, and they had. She'd been amazing. She *was* amazing. And then there had been that kiss.

It had been pretty amazing too.

Toby couldn't quantify how incredibly thankful he was that Rachel was alive. The same was true for his father, Peter, and even Bimisi in a way. The act of saving them brought with it a real satisfaction, but it wasn't enough. He hadn't done nearly enough. After all that he'd lost, after all those he'd failed to help, he needed to do more.

He desperately needed to feel the satisfaction of saving people again.

As they headed toward Peter's hospital room, neither Toby nor Rachel noticed a man in his early forties with a sturdy build and grizzled, washed-out appearance watching them from down the hallway. Jack Steele had arrived at the hospital only minutes earlier, coming directly off a seventeen-hour flight from Germany. He'd made this his first stop because the hospital records his employer had been able to access showed that the Chochopi girl and Peter Fox were still here. He figured that meant the Hoffman kid would be too.

And he'd figured right. The teenagers showed plenty of bumps and bruises from their werewolf encounters, but considering how young they were, Jack found it remarkable that they'd even survived. After watching and waiting for a minute or two, he walked over and stood outside the doorway to Peter's room.

"How much longer you stuck here?" he heard Toby ask.

"Another week," answered Peter, who appeared to be in pretty good spirits despite having one of his legs elevated and in a cast. "But on the plus side, no school for at least a week, which means I've got loads of time to find a new Demon Destroyer guild. Plus my nurse is super-hot."

"Anything we can pick up for you?" Rachel asked with a grin. "A book? Maybe some—"

"Toby Hoffman?" Jack interrupted her, feeling edgy and impatient after his long flight. He was ready to get things moving.

Toby and Rachel turned to face him, both looking uncertain.

"Um, yeah," Toby answered.

Jack took another moment to size up the group. Even though he'd been about the same age when he'd started hunting, they seemed far too young for what he'd come to enlist them to do. "Jesus. You really *are* just a bunch of kids."

"And who are you?" Peter asked, bothered by the disruption.

"Jack Steele. You Peter Fox?"

Peter nodded.

"You've written some fascinating blog posts recently."

The kid's two friends both shot Peter irritated glances. Apparently their run-ins with supernatural creatures, and resulting near deaths, had hit the blogosphere without their knowledge.

He shrugged apologetically. "It gets boring in here."

"How many of the stories are true?" Jack asked.

"I'm sure they're all true," Rachel responded defensively. "It's not like he'd need to exaggerate any of the details."

Jack regarded the three unintentional heroes for a moment. His boss had said they didn't need Peter Fox and that it would actually be preferable if he didn't join them. Rachel Chochopi was desirable, but not yet a must. Whatever that meant. It was the third kid, Toby Hoffman, who he was supposed to give the hard sell to.

Toby had shot and killed two of the creatures and suffered more than his fair share of loss and tragedy, even prior to the attacks. He was a perfect recruit, and therefore the one Jack's employer was the most interested in.

"Then it was a very brave thing you all did," Jack said. "But... why'd you feel the need to do it?"

He glanced over at Rachel. "Was it because of your uncle?"

Then he returned his gaze to Toby. "Or maybe you were stepping up for your father. Or...maybe working through some things in regards to your mother?"

It didn't feel right to be manipulating the boy by pushing these particular buttons, but Jack needed help, and these were the prospective new recruits his employer had presented him with. If he messed up this opportunity to expand the network, there was no telling when the next chance would come.

"Mister, who are you?" Toby asked, clearly agitated. "And what do you want?"

"That all depends," Jack replied. "Tell me. What are your plans for the future, Toby?"

Dear Reader,

I hope you enjoyed *The One You Feed*, the first book in the Shadow Tales series. It was a blast to write and even more of a blast to publish and share. I want to quickly thank Vicki, who edited the book, and Wojtek, my cover designer, as well as everyone else who supported me in this effort. Many thanks to you as well for reading this book and supporting an indie writer.

The feedback I've received on *The One You Feed* has been gratifying and enlightening. Readers seem to really like the characters of Toby and Rachel, and how they both had to overcome not just the supernatural but also their own insecurities as they fought to save their hometowns.

I've also learned that telling parts of the story from an adult perspective helped to hook some of my readers, how several others liked the fact that bad things happened to both good and bad people in this book, and how my lack of understanding of the different parts of different guns took a couple folks out of the story (thankfully, they left specific examples that I was able to correct). Overall, it was exciting to see readers react to the characters who I very much enjoyed creating.

I read and truly value all the reviews I receive. As an author, I love feedback. Please feel free to tell me what you liked, what you loved, even what you hated. You can write me at james@jamesdrummondwrites.com, follow me on Twitter at @jdrummond1273, or leave a review on Amazon.

Thank you so much for reading *The One You Feed*.

In gratitude,

James Drummond

Made in the USA
Lexington, KY
02 July 2016